"My lady, your hands work a comforting magic." When she put the bowl down he caught her hands, kissing them.

"Please, you must not." She pulled her hands from his grasp, but she knew she could not force herself to move away from him as she knew she ought to do. As if she were the one held by a magical charm, her fluttering fingers touched his lips, his cheeks, his brow. She brushed aside an errant lock of his brown hair.

"Sweet lady," he murmured, "I fear I can no longer resist your spell." His arms encircled her, drawing her close, and this time he did not stop short. This time he took her lips with firm assurance.

Flora Speer

Heart's Magic

LOVE SPELL NEW YORK CITY

LOVE SPELL®

June 1997

Published by

Dorchester Publishing Co., Inc.
276 Fifth Avenue
New York, NY 10001

Copyright © 1997 by Flora Speer

Printed in the United States of America.

To Gail Link, the only person I know who remembers more old romantic movies, more plays, and more love songs than I do. Thanks for sharing your enthusiasm and your affection for all things theatrical. Your letters make me laugh out loud and the beautiful love stories you write always touch my heart.

To Lynda Varner, thank you for your down-to-earth common sense (a quality all too rare in today's world), for practical suggestions when I am at my wit's end, for writing wonderfully romantic books, and for letting me see Scotland through your eyes.

Heart's Magic

Prologue

In early March of the year of our Lord 1122, two men rode northeastward along a forest path from Nottingham into Lincolnshire. Both were identically cloaked and hooded against the damp chill and their black stallions might have been twins, yet there were differences between the men. The taller, more muscular of the two rode with a certain boldness, as if he knew he had every right to be where he was and even more right to be at his destination when he finally reached it. The second man, shorter and more slender than his companion, rode surrounded by an aura of silence and a peculiar reserve.

The pair traveled without guards in a part of England not notable for its safety. The rest of their company had been left behind at Nottingham with the order to wait there. That order had generated a remarkably vigorous discussion around the table of the tavern where they had all spent the previous night. A nobleman's retainers did not often dare to dispute their master's decisions. This nobleman's companions were more his friends than his servants and so they had felt themselves free to object to the daring scheme he proposed to follow.

"I wish you would reconsider, my lord," the older squire, Hidern, had cried. "If you are found out, you will be consigned to the lowest dungeon in the castle."

"Or killed outright," added the younger squire, Bevis, who harboured a tendency toward lurid notions.

"And then conveniently forgotten, should anyone ask after you," Hidern finished.

"It is best that I travel alone and unrecognized during this first excursion," the tall nobleman insisted. "The rumors you two and Hugh heard while we were at court only confirm what King Henry told me during my audience with him. All is not well at Wroxley Castle."

The nobleman did not think it appropriate to add that the king blamed himself for whatever problems had arisen at Wroxley. Devastated by the death of his two sons in a shipwreck in the autumn of 1120, a still grieving Henry had agreed to the current arrangements for Wroxley without much thought on the matter—a hasty decision he repented now, more than a year later.

"A certain feeling of insecurity at Wroxley would be quite natural," said the fourth man at the tavern table. Of medium height and slender build, with straight black hair and dark eyes, his features were so bland that they were always immediately forgotten after he had left a scene. His accent was an odd one, unfamiliar even to men who had in recent years mixed with the men—and the women—of distant countries. The squires and the nobleman's men-at-arms knew him as Hugh and, trusting their leader, they assumed Hugh would not have been granted the nobleman's friendship were he not worthy of it. Furthermore, during their travels together they had found Hugh to be honest and dependable. Thus, they gave him their full attention as he continued. "When the baron of a castle dies, there must be concern for the future amongst the folk who live in that castle or on the nearby lands. In this case, with the heir absent in the Holy Land, the people of Wroxley will no doubt be wondering when—or if—that heir will come home, and what will happen to them until he does."

"And if the newly confirmed baron of Wroxley arrives in full panoply, with banners flying and men-at-arms behind him, do any of you think the truth of the old baron's death will ever be told?" asked the leader of this group. "If only half the rumors are true, the inhabitants of Wroxley will not dare to reveal the events of the past year and a half. If the stories we have heard are fact and not imaginary, then for the new baron to ride in as if he expected to be welcomed home would only result in death to many of those same folk who are still loyal to the old baron's son. We do not want a battle. The use of force is acceptable only after all other methods have failed."

"Well spoken," said Hugh with a faint smile. "You always were a good student."

"For myself, I would prefer more straightforward means. I see nothing wrong with a good battle." The squire, Hidern, paused as if wrestling with an alien concept before he continued. "You have never failed us before, my lord. Bevis and I will not quarrel with you over your plans. But know that if you and Hugh do not return from Wroxley or send us word within the time you have allotted, then we will investigate. If we discover that you are in trouble, we will at once send word to King Henry."

"Who will not be able to raise troops and move them to Wroxley in time to be of any help to me," his master told him. "The king warned me of the problems I could expect to encounter. Indeed, I have been well and truly warned by him, by both of you, and by the friends I have at court. I do not undertake this campaign unaware of the risks."

"But you are undermanned," Bevis persisted, voicing the chief concern of both squires. "Please, my lord, let us go with you. We can leave the men-at-arms behind if you want, but for you and Hugh to enter that castle alone is folly."

"No." The single word was gentle enough, yet it was spoken in so firm and commanding a tone that all protest ceased from that moment on.

Later, while the squires were occupied with the preparations their master had ordered for his journey, a more private conversation occurred.

"The others don't know all of it, Hugh."

"I never imagined they did." Away from public gaze, Hugh's features had assumed a more definite cast. His dark, almond-shaped eyes shone with intelligence. Hugh's low voice still held the foreign inflections he seldom bothered to disguise. "Since you have raised the subject, my friend, I assume the time has come for us to speak of magic and of unnatural events."

"Magic," Hugh's companion repeated. "I have a premonition that I am going to need your art, and your strength, if I am to succeed. It's why I have asked you to go to Wroxley with me. I want a man by my side whom I can trust completely, who will not lose heart at the touch of magic."

"You will also need a name other than your own," said Hugh.

When morning came Hidern and Bevis armed their lord, though not as completely as they would have liked, and packed a bit of food into the saddle-bags. Then they stood outside the inn watching while their master and his friend rode away through the twisting streets of Nottingham.

The early morning sunshine vanished by afternoon behind ominous gray clouds. As the hours wore on the clouds thickened and lowered into fog. A light drizzle began to fall. With every mile that shortened the distance between the travelers and Wroxley Castle the dampness seeped a little deeper into the very bones of the two men. Still, they pressed on, determined to reach their destination before nightfall.

"Not at all like Jerusalem, is it?" the nobleman said with a rueful laugh. "Until today I had all but forgotten the weather of my youth, when I was so accustomed to fog and rain that I scarcely noticed either."

"This climate is certainly different from others I have encountered," Hugh responded. "Fog and rain are conducive to fantastic tales of ghosts and magic and wicked deeds."

"Do you think the stories we heard while at court were fabulous?" his companion asked. "Or do you believe them?"

"I have not enough evidence to allow me to form a reasonable opinion on the subject," Hugh said. "We are yet too far from Wroxley, and I am unfamiliar with the castle. Still, from what we have heard, I do believe the prospects of furthering my education there are favorable."

"I have no doubt," said the other man with a chuckle that contained little true mirth, "that before long, we will both learn more than we expect or care to know about wicked deeds."

Chapter One

It was a small thing and perfectly round, its gleaming surface smoothly polished. Made of crystal so clear that it appeared to be a raindrop, the sphere fit snugly into the palm of Mirielle's left hand. It had been a present from her nurse, Cerra, on Mirielle's tenth birthday, given to her because Cerra said that Mirielle had the gift of inborn magic.

Most of the time when Mirielle looked into the globe she saw nothing but the clear crystal. However, there was an almost invisible inclusion at the exact center of the sphere, one tiny point at which the crystal was not perfect. Occasionally, when Mirielle turned the sphere in just the right way, light would strike off the inclusion. At such times she would see a swirl of clouds in the crystal. On very rare occasions, she could discern the figure of a man in a dark cloak. The man's face was always hidden from her, but whenever his image appeared, an important change occurred in Mirielle's life.

She had seen the mysterious image before the deaths of her parents and Cerra, and had seen it again on the night before her cousin, Brice, had knocked on the door of her parent's manor house to rescue her from her cold-hearted uncle's plan to consign her to a convent rather than provide a dowry for her. Brice had demanded that Mirielle be made his ward and her uncle had been glad enough to hand over guardianship of the orphaned niece who was of no use to him.

Some years later Mirielle had seen the man in the crystal once more, just before she and Brice had left North Wales to move to Wroxley Castle, where Brice was to become the new seneschal. And she had seen the vision in the crystal shortly before Brice had announced that he was making her the chatelaine of Wroxley.

Now, on this late winter morning, compelled by a desire she did not understand, Mirielle had taken the crystal globe in her hand—in her *left* hand, as Cerra had instructed. The crystal was cool against Mirielle's palm. She sent her thoughts into the sphere, finding and then concentrating on the imperfection she could just barely see. Without thinking, she moved, turning toward the window until the fog outside appeared to enter the room and fill the globe with gray light . . . and the man appeared, muffled as usual in his dark cloak.

A tremor passed through Mirielle's body. Her hand shook a little, the motion disturbing the scene within the crystal so that, for a moment, Mirielle thought she saw not one, but two men, and she thought they were on horseback.

"It cannot be! The vision never changes." Mirielle's surprised exclamation wakened her companion. Snuggled into the bed in a fold of the quilt, a small gray cat stirred, stretching. In the shadowy room Mirielle sensed rather than saw the movement. It was enough. Her concentration was broken and the image in the crystal globe vanished.

Damp morning air filtered in through the window. The room was cold; the fuel in the charcoal brazier that warmed it had burned away during the night. Shivering, Mirielle knelt at the foot of the bed to wrap the sphere in the piece of silk she used to prevent the crystal from being scratched. She put the treasured object away in the clothes chest and shut the lid. Deep in thought, she stayed where she was until the cat walked across the coverlet to rub its face against her shoulder. Mirielle gathered the cat into her arms.

"Minn, who is that man I see?" she whispered to her pet. "Why did the scene change just then, when it has never changed before?

" 'In danger lies the seed of change; in change lies the seed of opportunity.' Now, who put that saying into my thoughts? Certainly Cerra never did. She believed in holding to the ancient ways and did not like change."

Mirielle sat on the edge of her bed, her hand gone still on Minn's back while she thought about her old nurse, Cerra, who had taught her young charge all she knew of herbs and healing, and of certain other skills that must never be revealed save to another who was also a practitioner. Or a pupil, as Mirielle had been, eager to learn, eager to practice the Ancient Art.

Aged and frail, Cerra had died in a winter epidemic that had also claimed Mirielle's parents and her infant brother. Mirielle herself had been too ill to do anything to help them. Remembering her loved ones, she fought back a sob.

"At least I have Brice. Were it not for him, I should have been forced into a convent, where I do not belong. And Brice is right when he says the time for mourning my dead is long over. Whatever the vision I saw in the crystal may foretell, I will continue to practice what Cerra taught me, and I will face whatever changes the future may bring with all the courage I can find in my heart." Mirielle's next words, softspoken though they were, rang with the power of a solemn invocation. "In gratitude to Brice, let me on this day do all I can to help him, let me fulfill my duties with a cheerful heart and a smile on my lips—and please, *please*, on this day let me not lose my temper with Alda!"

"Lady Mirielle, I did not expect to find you on the battlements on such a damp afternoon. Dressed all in gray as you are, a man might miss you standing there in the corner. Is anything wrong?" The captain of the guard paused in his steady pacing. His rather plain face was made attractive by a pleasant expression and by his warm, intelligent eyes.

"Good day to you, Captain Oliver." Mirielle wished she could confide to this honest man the worry that had made recent days uneasy for her, but it would not be fair to burden anyone else, so all she said was, "I came here because it is a quiet place."

"Ah." Captain Oliver inclined his head as if to say he understood what, out of loyalty, Mirielle would not reveal. "Well, then, my lady, I will leave you to the peace you seek." After a polite little bow in her direction Captain Oliver continued on his late-day rounds of the castle's defenses.

Mirielle resumed gazing through the crenel, the opening created in the stonework for defenders to use during warfare, through which arrows could be shot or vats of hot oil or boiling pitch dumped upon attackers below. The merlons on either side of the crenel were so high that she could not see over them. Nor could she see much through the thick fog. It was almost always foggy or rainy here at Wroxley. She was used to it by now. The weather did not matter. Her thoughts were inward looking.

She had been at the castle for slightly more than a year, having arrived the previous February with her cousin Brice after he was appointed seneschal. When it quickly became evident to Brice that Alda, the lady of Wroxley, was at best an indifferent chatelaine, he had given that position to Mirielle. Alda had accepted the change, saying only that it was right for Mirielle to earn her keep by honest work. Alda then proceeded to treat the new chatelaine as if she were a personal servant.

Mirielle was twenty-three years old and she had been well trained by her late mother to be competent in all housekeeping tasks. Despite the gloom that hung around it like a pall, she had grown to love the castle and, with a few exceptions, she liked its quiet, remarkably serious people. Considering the path her life might have taken, she should have been content. Instead, she worried constantly and her worry had much to do with the relations between Brice and the lady of the castle. In Mirielle's opinion, there was something very wrong with Alda and Alda's influence on Brice was not a positive one.

"Or perhaps I am only imagining it. I am not always correct in my evaluations of other people," Mirielle mused, her eyes on the enclosing fog. "Donada may be right when she says I need a man to love, children, a family of my own to distract me from my concerns over Alda's behavior. I wish there were a man who would love me as my father loved my mother, but who would ask for me when I have no dowry? By the time Brice is able to provide one for me, I may well be too old for marriage. More important, what man would not fear the magical art I cannot lay aside? No, I will not destroy what happiness I may find here at Wroxley by wishing for a life I cannot hope to have. Nor will I criticize Brice and Alda again, not even in my thoughts."

She bent over to pick up a basket of herbs she had set down on the stone walkway of the castle wall. Minn, who had been sheltered from the damp in the folds of Mirielle's skirt, rubbed against her hand.

"Oh, Minn," Mirielle said, scratching the cat's ears, "I wish I knew why I felt compelled to come out here and stand for so long in the cold when I have duties inside. Alda will be angry if she doesn't have her bath herbs when she wants them and I promised Donada a new supply of dried woodruff to keep the moths away from all that woolen material she is working on."

With a last caress along the cat's back Mirielle straightened, the chatelaine's keys swinging on their chain at her waist, their weight familiar and reassuring. She was well aware that she was fortunate. She had honest work to do that benefitted every person in the castle, and when each day's labor was done she had her secret studies, which were also of benefit to others. Her life was useful. That knowledge ought to be enough for her.

"Come along, Minn. I have finished daydreaming for this afternoon. Come." With the cat trotting just behind her Mirielle started toward the gatehouse and the spiral stairs that would take her down to the bailey. She cast a final glance into the mist, thinking it would soon be too dark to see anything.

A movement in the fog caught her eye. Two men on black horses rode out of the mist and onto the drawbridge, which had not yet been raised for the night. They wore black cloaks with the hoods drawn up to conceal their faces.

Mirielle halted there on the battlements, watching those two figures and fighting the impulse to go below and meet them. There were good reasons why she should not obey that inner urging. She had no idea who the men were, she could not even see them clearly, and Brice had warned her often that it was best to be cautious when dealing with strangers.

The larger of the two men lifted his head, as if he were scanning the gatehouse walls for men-at-arms who might be preparing to fire their arrows at him and his companion. Mirielle still could not see his face, yet something about that cloaked figure was as familiar to her as her own heart's longing.

The light from the torches set at either side of the main gate flickered over the riders, making their shapes appear to waver, just as similar forms had wavered when Mirielle beheld them in her crystal globe. Comprehension flooded over her as that earlier vision merged with reality. This was why she had been unable to resist the urge to climb to the battlements and why she had stayed there for so long. She had been waiting for *him*.

And then she was running for the steps, racing down and around the narrow, spiral stairway, almost tripping in her haste to reach the bailey and meet her fate.

Chapter Two

"Do not confuse fact with reality."
                        —Old Welsh saying

"Who goes there?"

The routine challenge from the gatehouse was anything but polite to weary travelers. Nor did the facade of Wroxley Castle offer much of a welcome. On each side of the main gate towers bulged outward into the moat, their solid stone bulk broken only by a few arrow slits. The torches lighting the portculis hissed like angry snakes when drops of rain fell on them. In the fog and gathering darkness this forbidding entrance was all that could be seen of the castle.

"We are two pilgrims, returning from the shrine of Saint James at Compostela and traveling north to Durham," came the reply to the watchman's shouted demand. "I am Master Hugh, a scholar. My friend is Sir Giles, a simple knight."

"There's an abbey not far away, where pilgrims are welcomed," the watchman said. "Go there."

"Bardney Abbey is a full day's journey from here in good weather. My friend is weak from an old battle wound made painful by the dampness," Hugh countered. "He can go no farther. We ask lodging for a night or two, until he can regain his strength."

"Is it truly a battle wound, or sickness?" the watchman asked. "How can I be sure you won't be bringing some pestilence in with you?"

"In the name of Saint James, in the name of God, I entreat you to allow us to enter," insisted Hugh.

There came another voice from within, where someone demanded to know what the problem was. This second voice was a woman's. She sounded slightly breathless, as if she had been running.

"Open the wicket gate and let them in."

"Not so fast," the watchman protested. "For all we know, these two innocent-looking fellows have come here with an army at their backs."

"If that is so, they will have a great deal of trouble passing all their men and horses through the wicket gate." The woman's voice was now tinged with deprecating humor, to which the watchman responded with truculence.

"I won't be responsible to Sir Brice," he proclaimed. "Or to Lady Alda."

"I will be responsible," the woman said, repeating even more firmly than before, "Tell your man to open the gate."

There followed a short pause before the wicket gate, which was set into the main castle door, slowly creaked open. It was designed to be too small for a mounted man to pass through, so the two travelers were forced to dismount. In case they were being closely scrutinized, the one called Giles pretended to need the aid of his companion in order to reach the ground without falling. On foot they led their horses across the drawbridge and into the gatehouse. Aware that they were being observed through ceiling holes and that the archers posted just above the entrance would kill them without question if they appeared to be dangerous in any way, Giles affected a sagging stance and let Hugh deal with the horses.

"Come in, good sirs, and welcome," said the woman's voice. "I will see you safely to the great hall, where you will find food and warmth."

She stood in the misty circle of light cast by the torches on the bailey side of the gatehouse. Giles saw to his surprise that she was trembling and he had a quick impression of tall, slender loveliness. The woman made a gesture with one hand and the light appeared to dim.

Giles blinked, not sure if his eyes were playing tricks on him. The woman he now saw before him was no taller than Hugh and her shape was a sturdy one. In her plain gray woolen gown and darker gray shawl, with a basket slung over one arm, he would have taken her for a servant were it not for her dignified bearing and her cultivated voice. He took a step toward her and then stopped, his eyes now on the gray cat who had just appeared from behind her to curve close about her ankles.

"It is only Minn," the woman said. "She likes the herbs." She indicated the basket she carried, from which pleasant odors made their way across the few feet separating them. Giles could smell mint and lavender along with a faint hint of rosemary.

The woman's eyes were gray. Everything about her was gray except for the faint flush on her high cheekbones and the black hair just showing at the edge of the gray scarf that covered her head. She was a remarkably plain creature. Ordinarily, Giles would have paid little attention to her, save to render the politeness owed to one who had lived for many years. But he sensed there was more to her than met the eye. It was as if the woman was deliberately trying to make herself unnoticeable, as if she wanted to blend into the mist and the shadows. How old could she be? Giles was unable to decide, for when he tried to see her more clearly, her features became even more blurred.

While Giles stared, straining his eyes to produce a sharper image of the woman, the watchman came swaggering down the stairs from his post. He was a big, burly fellow, untidy and far from clean. But he did know his duty. Brushing aside the young man-at-arms who had pulled the wicket gate open, the watchman looked the two travelers over with a decidedly unfriendly eye.

"You must swear to me that you take full responsibility for admitting these two," the watchman said to the woman, using a tone that made Giles want to knock him down for the lack of respect he displayed toward a lady.

But was she a lady? Or was she just a lady's servant who had learned to copy the dulcet accents of her betters? The woman made another gesture with her free hand before addressing the watchman.

"Mauger, I have said that I will see to their care and I do promise to report to Sir Brice that these guests were admitted at my word," the woman told the watchman. "Now, come, good sirs. It is cold here in the entrance, and the chill cannot be the best thing for any wounds, old or new."

"They do not enter until I pass them." Mauger thrust out a stubborn lower lip. "And I will not pass them until I have seen their faces and examined the staff that's bound to this one's horse. I want to see their shells, too. Everyone knows that folk who have been to Compostela wear real scallop shells."

"How very wise of you," Hugh said. "No lord could ask for a more responsible watchman to guard his castle. Here is a shell sewn to my cloak, and another on my tunic. My face I show you gladly, and that staff your sharp eyes noticed is but the pilgrim's staff I used on my long journey, for you surely know that pilgrims approach the shrine of Saint James on foot. The wood fits my hand so well that I brought the staff home with me, hoping to use it again on some other pilgrimage."

As he spoke Hugh lifted his right hand to push back the hood that covered his head. At the same time, with his left hand he made a gesture similar to the one the woman had made. Giles, aware of the movement, having seen it countless times in the past, kept his eyes on the woman, awaiting her reaction. He saw her expression of surprise, saw the way in which she hid her shock, and he knew that Hugh had also seen.

"You, too," Mauger said to Giles. "Remove that hood."

For Giles there was no need for concealment. He

did not think the watchman would recognize him or find anything unusual in his visage. Like Hugh, Giles had sewn scallop shells to his clothing as proof of his visit to the famous shrine at Compostela, for both men had in fact stopped there on their way to England.

Giles lowered his hood, aware that the watchman would see light brown hair, mustache, and beard, all of which were in sore need of trimming as befitted a weary pilgrim who had been on the road for weeks, and blue eyes surrounded by lines, the result of many years spent squinting against the glare of a desert sun. While the watchman stared at him and then looked once more at Hugh, Giles was conscious of the woman's gaze on his face. Her rather blank expression did not change, but Giles thought he saw a flicker of anxiety in her eyes.

"All right," Mauger said. "You look harmless enough. If there's any trouble later, it's on your head," he added to the woman.

"If you will come with me, good sirs." The woman turned and began walking across the lower bailey, her cat like a gray shadow at her heels.

It was a crowded, busy place, reeking with the odors of horses and dogs and unwashed men. Stables, kennels, and storehouses were all built with their backs against the inner walls. Late in the day though it was, the castle blacksmith was hard at work, the heat and light from his forge and the ringing sound of his hammer reaching the bailey through the open door of his workshop. Hugh paused to look inside for a moment before hurrying after Giles and the woman. For his part, Giles tried to remember to move as if he were in pain from the wound in his side, while at the same time he took careful note of sights once familiar to him but half forgotten in the passage of years.

"Your horses will need stabling," the woman said, stopping at the stable entrance. "Robin, I have need of your aid," she called to a youth inside.

"My lady Mirielle." The boy came running and went down on one knee as if he were a page at the royal court and the plain, middle-aged woman were a princess. "Whatever you ask, I will do."

"It is but a small favor, Robin." The woman's smile was sweet, lighting her face with warm affection, making her look much younger. "These two pilgrims have just arrived and their horses need care and food."

"It shall be done, my lady." Robin took the reins to lead the horses into the stable.

"A moment, lad." Hugh reached to take the saddlebags and to unfasten the long staff that had drawn the watchman's attention. "We will need these. Be kind to the horses, boy. They have carried us far today."

"Gentle sir, you need not worry," Robin answered. "I will personally see to them as my lady has bidden me."

"For that we thank you." Giles looked from the earnest face of the boy to the woman in gray, wondering why the watchman had treated her as if she were a common servant while young Robin knelt to her and called her "my lady."

"All questions will be answered at the proper time," Hugh murmured beside him, as if he had read Giles's thoughts.

"So you have often told me," Giles responded.

Lady Mirielle did not appear to hear this exchange. She guided them to the inner gate where, in contrast to their reception at the main gate, half a dozen men-at-arms gave them scarcely a glance. Then they were inside the second ring of stone walls and crossing the inner bailey toward the very heart of the castle. Here there were not so many people as in the outer bailey and more of them were women and children. At one side a wooden palisade blocked casual entrance to the herb garden and to the formal garden that were the domain of the lady of the castle.

The lady of the castle. Giles wondered where she could be. It had been so very long since he had looked upon her perfect face and golden hair. He had not taken a woman for months, since before his visit to Compostela, yet he felt no quickening in his loins at the thought of beautiful Alda.

Up the narrow steps of the tower keep they went behind Mirielle. Two-thirds of the way up there was a landing and the stairs angled to the right. Some years earlier Lord Udo had ordered the stairs rebuilt in this way, jesting to the stonemasons that he relished the thought of sending invaders plummeting off the landing to break their necks or skulls on the hard-packed earth below. Once Udo had been renowned for his warrior's skills and his courage. Now his remains lay in the crypt below the chapel. Giles's lips tightened at that thought.

"Here we are, good sirs." Mirielle led them through the entrance and into the great hall.

Giles looked around, fascinated. Bright tapestries hung on the walls. Twin fireplaces built into the walls on opposite sides of the room sent out a pleasant warmth that could not quite banish the day's dampness. The great hall was filled with bustling servants, children, men-at-arms, and barking dogs. One particularly unpleasant looking cur ran toward the newcomers with its teeth bared, snarling. Suddenly the dog stopped short, whimpered, put its tail between its legs, and headed in another direction, and the gray cat, Minn, sat down beside Mirielle and calmly began to wash its paws.

"Sir Brice, our seneschal, is not here," Mirielle said. "Perhaps he is in the mews. One of the falcons was ailing this morning."

"I am not so well myself." Giles made a sound and clutched at his side as if in pain. Mirielle regarded him in silence for a moment. The idea came into Giles's mind that she knew, or at least harbored a strong suspicion, that he was only pretending to weakness.

"We have no other guests at present," Mirielle said. "I see no reason why you should not be given one of the small rooms for your own use. It will be more comfortable for you, and certainly quieter than sleeping in the great hall."

And easier to guard us and to lock us in if need be, Giles thought. He must take care not to underestimate this intelligent woman.

Leaving the great hall, Mirielle took them up a curving staircase to a room built into the thickness of the castle wall. A single arrow slit provided light and air. A wide wooden bench along one wall and a three-legged stool were the only pieces of furniture.

"Had I known you were coming, I would have ordered the room properly prepared for you," Mirielle told them. "I will send a mattress and quilts." She left before either Giles or Hugh could ask any questions of her.

"Well," said Hugh, tossing the saddlebags onto the bench that would serve as both seating and bed space, "at least we are inside Wroxley. I can make this room warmer if you wish." He lifted his wooden staff.

"Not just yet." Before he continued Giles stuck his head out the door to make certain no one was near enough to hear what he said. "There have been changes made."

"Would you expect otherwise in eleven years?" Hugh shrugged. "I would be concerned if there were no changes at all."

"That woman, Mirielle." Giles paused, waiting for Hugh's comment.

"So you did notice. I thought you would." Hugh's quick smile came and went. "She is most adept. Her true form is quite different from the illusion she wished us to see."

"She is younger than she appears to be," Giles said. "I saw it when she smiled at the stableboy. Nor does she move like a middle-aged woman. And her voice is youthful."

"An ordinary observer, one not expecting to see beyond the surface appearance, would not notice such details."

"I wonder," Giles mused, "what her true appearance is, and if she will ever allow us to see it."

"Where have you been? Keep that cat out of my room!" Lady Alda, mistress of Wroxley Castle, rushed to her chamber door before it was fully open. She aimed a kick at Minn, who leapt out of range before Alda's bare foot could connect with her nose. "Come in, Mirielle, and be quick about it. My bath-water will grow cold before the herbs can scent it."

"Surely not, my lady. The water is still steaming." Mirielle crossed the room to the wooden tub. She said nothing about Alda's treatment of her cat. Both Mirielle and Minn were used to Alda's ways.

"What are you waiting for?" Alda exclaimed. "Hurry. I want my bath now!"

Mirielle set down the basket of herbs she was carrying. After testing the temperature of the water with a finger she began to strew lavender and mint across the surface, crumbling the dried leaves and flowers as she did so. A sweet fragrance began to rise, filling her nostrils. Mirielle wished the soothing qualities of the herbs could calm Alda's ever-restless spirit.

After the death of her father-in-law, Lord Udo, Alda had refused to move into the lord's chamber at the top of the tower keep. She had ordered the lord's chamber closed and locked. Only Mirielle went there from time to time with a maidservant, to clean and air the room in case Udo's son, Gavin, should return unexpectedly.

Alda remained in the room where she had slept since first coming to Wroxley as a young bride. At first Mirielle, as a newcomer to the castle, had taken Alda's refusal to occupy the lord's bedchamber as a sign of respect for the old baron. Now that Mirielle knew Alda better, she was not sure what the real reason was.

"Mirielle, stop daydreaming!" Alda commanded. "I am waiting."

"Do you want me to add the rosemary also?" Mirielle asked.

"No. No, he—I—prefer the lavender to predominate. Take the rosemary to the kitchen." Dropping the shawl that was her only covering, Alda stepped into the tub, sinking downward with a sensuous wriggle until she was sitting in the steamy, fragrant water. "Give me the cloth. And check the braziers. I am not sure there is enough charcoal to keep me warm until I am dressed again."

"We have guests for the night, possibly for several nights." As she spoke Mirielle handed a linen cloth to Alda, then added more charcoal to one of the braziers. The room was already too warm for her taste, but Alda preferred to wear as little clothing as possible. Mirielle did not like to think why that was so, for it disturbed her to know that people to whom she owed respect and allegiance were behaving in dishonorable ways. Still, were she a passionate woman left alone for the years of her youth by an uninterested husband, perhaps Mirielle would think in a different way. Perhaps, in the cold and dark of a lonely winter night she, too, would be capable of forgetting honor in favor of human warmth and tenderness. And desire. Perhaps.

Or perhaps not. It might depend upon her feelings toward that absent husband. In truth, Mirielle did not believe Alda had ever loved anyone, not even her two children. Alda did not appear to be capable of thinking about anyone but herself, which would seem to preclude the ability to love her husband, or to uphold his honor. But then, Mirielle had no experience of husbands, nor was she ever likely to acquire it.

"Don't stand there staring at me, you silly girl," Alda snapped at her. "What is the matter with you today? Give me the towel." Having finished bathing while Mirielle was distracted by her thoughts, Alda was again standing up in the tub. She preened a bit, as if she imagined Mirielle might be admiring her perfect figure.

"I am sorry, Alda. I was not paying proper attention to you." Hanging on to her temper, Mirielle wrapped the towel around Alda and helped her to step out of the tub. "I was thinking about the guests."

"What guests?"

"The ones I just told you about."

"Did you? Oh. Are they important?"

"Not to you, Alda, I am sure. They are only two simple pilgrims, returning from Compostela. One of them is troubled by an old wound. They may have to stay for a day or two, until he is well enough to travel again."

"You are right, they cannot be important. Pilgrims are always boring, with their tedious talk of miracles and salvation." Alda shrugged off the guests and her duties toward them. "You see to their needs. Do whatever you like for them. Talk to Brice if you have any questions. Where is Brice?" Alda broke off when a knock sounded on the chamber door.

"I believe Brice himself has just answered your question." Mirielle stood facing the door and breathing deeply before she opened it, so she could compose herself enough to hide her true feelings. "Good evening, cousin."

"Good evening to you, Mirielle." The darkly handsome Brice entered Alda's bedchamber with a predatory step, his gaze sweeping past Mirielle to rest on Alda. She, still flushed and slightly damp from her bath, smiled a wicked, knowing smile and lowered her eyes. She also lowered the towel until the rosy tips of her breasts were all but uncovered.

"If you have no further need of me, Alda," Mirielle said, "I will excuse myself to see to my duties in the kitchen and great hall."

"I have no further need of *you*." Alda's meaning was unmistakable.

Mirielle picked up the herb basket and left the room. She heard Brice slide the bolt home behind her. She did not doubt what would now occur in Alda's room.

She must not think of it. She had tried to talk to Brice when she first became aware of the true nature of his relationship to Alda. Out of gratitude and family affection she had tried to warn him, but he would not listen to her. He had assured her that he knew exactly what he was doing. With a sigh, Mirielle headed for the great hall, Minn once more trotting silently beside her.

"You are late, Brice." Scarcely bothering to wait until Mirielle was gone and the door closed, Alda let the towel fall to the floor. "I expected you to join me in my bath."

"I do have other occupations." Brice stood calmly looking Alda over as if he were contemplating the purchase of a horse. She posed for him seductively, but he made no move to embrace her.

"This is your most important occupation at Wroxley."

Alda flung her arms around his neck and, when Brice did not readily lower his mouth to hers, she pulled on his neck, forcing his head downward. "You are to keep me happy."

"An impossible task."

"If you are too weary after fulfilling your duties to Wroxley to spend time with me, perhaps I will find a younger, more vigorous lover and make him seneschal in your place."

"I am seneschal here by King Henry's appointment," Brice reminded her. "You cannot alter the king's command."

"Then I shall have to encourage you to greater efforts on my behalf." Taking her hands from around his neck, Alda applied them to a different part of his body.

Brice stood quietly, letting her fondle him, knowing his flesh would respond to what she was doing. It always did. He had loved Alda once. He still admired her strangely unchanged beauty. He might even marry her if it could be proven that her long-absent husband was dead. But only if marrying Alda meant that Wroxley Castle would be his, at least for a time, and that the rich estate she had brought as a dowry to her marriage to Gavin of Wroxley would become her second husband's permanent property.

Alda had a son, Warrick, who was Lord Udo's grandson and therefore the next heir to Wroxley if Gavin was dead. Warrick was much too young to hold an important castle in a dangerous area of England. However, a seneschal who had proven himself reliable and loyal to King Henry, a seneschal who was also the boy's stepfather—surely that man would not be removed from his post. And in the years before Warrick reached an age to take control of Wroxley there would be ample opportunity for a clever seneschal to amass a fortune. Brice already had a small, secret hoard of silver plate and jewels.

Alda lifted his tunic and loosened his lower garments. Her fingers worked skillfully on his exposed manhood. She was an avid lover. She knew how to drain him like a sponge squeezed dry. For the sake of the physical pleasure she gave him and for control of Wroxley, he could afford to ignore her uncertain temper and the black emptiness that lurked behind Alda's lovely, golden brown eyes.

"Easy," he said, removing her hand. "My beautiful lady, if you want me to give you pleasure and not just take my own, then you must leave me some control of my body."

"Brice," she panted, wrapping herself around him, pushing her hot, moist womanhood against the hardness she had created, "hold me. Kiss me and touch me all over. Make me forget."

"If adultery troubles you so much," Brice said coolly, "perhaps you ought not to commit it."

"Not that. What does Gavin matter? He has been gone so long that I scarcely remember how it felt to have him inside me. I am sure I was bored by his lovemaking. But you are so strong, Brice, so vigorous." Alda writhed against him, moaning.

Her contortions were having their effect. Brice could feel his blood rising. He caught her by her long, golden hair, bending her head backward. Quickly he kissed her slender throat, taking care not to leave marks on it. The necklines of Alda's gowns were always cut low. There was no point in embarassing either of them with flagrant evidence of their affair. But Alda's breasts would not be seen in public.

Alda cried out in pleasure, arching back against his arm, her hips thrusting forward to meet his rigid manhood. Brice began to work his way toward the bed. He fell onto it with Alda beneath him. Thanks to her wriggling he was perfectly positioned so, as he landed, Brice drove hard into her.

"Don't stop," she cried, eagerly meeting his cruel thrusts. "Oh, Brice, help me, make me forget—yes! Yes!"

Alda's eyes closed. Only in the throes of passion, when she was totally caught up in what was happening within her own body as she was now, only then was the petulant expression absent from her face. At such times she looked once more like the innocent girl Brice had first known, long ago, before she had married Gavin of Wroxley. For the sake of that young Alda he would have been more gentle with her, but she screamed, bucking beneath him, crying out to him to pound harder into her, and harder still, until his ears rang and his sight blurred and his seed poured forth in a hot stream of passionate release that left him exhausted.

"I do not know why, in more than a year, I have not got you with child," Brice said later.

"There are ways to prevent conception." Alda moved restlessly on the bed beside him.

"Mirielle would never give you herbs for such a purpose. I hope you have not upset her by asking her for them."

"You love Mirielle more than you love me," she accused.

"There is no reason for you to be jealous. Mirielle is my blood kin and like a daughter to me." *Yes, I love her, in an innocent way that you would never understand.*

"So am I your kin," Alda said, pouting.

"On your mother's side, by marriage and not by blood, and a distant connection at that," Brice reminded her. He swung his legs over the side of the bed. "It is time to dress for the evening meal. I understand we have guests. They can entertain you with their stories."

"Mirielle reports that they are only pilgrims. Their stories will be dull ones. Brice, you cannot be leaving me so soon?" she whined, seeing him begin to straighten his clothes.

"I want to wash and put on fresh clothing before I present myself in the great hall," he said. "It is only courtesy to our guests."

"You will change your clothing for strangers, but you come to me with the sweat and stench of the stables still on you."

"You love it when I smell like a stallion. You have told me so many times." He bent to tweek one of her nipples, the touch eliciting a whimper of renewed sensual interest from her. "Shall I send your maidservant to help you dress?"

"She knows when to come to me."

"Then she knows I am here. Alda, you really should be more discreet."

"Why?" Alda reached toward him, to caress and cajole him into returning to the bed. "Everyone in this castle knows we lie together."

"Still, it would be better if you did not flaunt the fact. The same folk who might overlook a quietly conducted liaison often voice loud objections to an affair whose participants flaunt it in public." Brice pulled away from Alda's searching fingers. Finished straightening his clothing, he smoothed his hair with his hand. Without a backward glance he let himself out of the room.

Left alone, still sprawled naked on the bed, Alda shuddered. There were shadows in the corners of the room. If she were alone for very long, they would begin to encroach upon her and she would not be able to breathe. For some reason on this evening the shadows were darker and more threatening than usual. She could see their shapes and their movements.

Alda knew of only one way to keep the shadows at bay. After an hour in his arms she smelled of Brice, of the stables and the horses, just as he did. She wished he were still with her, still hard inside her. She would order him to come to her again later after the evening meal was over and she would see to it that he pleasured her again and again. She would keep him with her all night long.

In the meantime . . . She let her hands slide down to the place where Brice had been, her fingers rubbing and pressing, and for a little while the menacing shadows retreated into the corners once more.

Chapter Three

"Gentle sirs," said Robin, appearing at the guest room door, "I am sent to conduct you to the great hall for the evening meal."

"I am surprised to see you here," Giles responded. "I thought you were a stableboy."

"No, sir." Robin's face was freshly scrubbed, and beneath a tangle of damp, reddish-brown curls his gray-green eyes were bright. "My father was the seneschal here at Wroxley before Sir Brice. My mother is seamstress now to Lady Alda and I should have been a page, but Lady Alda took a dislike to me and told me to get myself off to the stables and occupy myself there. I am good with horses. I cared for yours very well."

"I am sure you did, lad," said Hugh. "Tell me, why is your father no longer seneschal here?"

"He died soon after Lord Udo. They had the same

disease." The cheerfulness faded from Robin's face, but he seemed to be a boy who held a positive outlook on life and he soon brightened again. "Then Sir Brice came to Wroxley and brought Lady Mirielle with him. She is teaching me to read and she begged Lady Alda not to send my mother away." Robin's face glowed as he spoke of Lady Mirielle.

Giles thought of the scene in the stable with Robin on his knees to the plain, middle-aged woman. Once again he wondered about Mirielle's true appearance. Perhaps when Robin looked at her he saw something Giles and Hugh were not permitted to see.

"Sirs," Robin asked, looking from one man to the other, "will you come with me now?"

"Of course we will," Giles said. "Lead on, Robin. I am hungry."

"At evening we usually eat the cold meat left from the midday meal, with cheese and bread," Robin informed them as he showed them the way along a narrow stone corridor, the walls of which were pierced at intervals by arrow slits. The boy continued down a stone staircase with the two men following him. "For tonight Lady Mirielle has ordered special dishes prepared in your honor, so we will feast on roasted fowl. There is a pigeon pie freshly made, and an almond custard. I do like almond custard."

"I take it you are allowed to roam the castle at will," Hugh said. "You range from the stables to the kitchen to the great hall."

"My favorite place is Lady Mirielle's workroom," Robin said. "Mother tells me to stay out of Lady Alda's way and *she* never goes to the workroom, so it is quiet there. Sir Giles, is it true that you are suffering from an old battle wound? Would you tell me the story of how you got it?"

"Warfare is not as exciting as it is made out to be," Giles said. "But if there is time while I'm here, I will tell you of my adventures."

"Sir," Robin asked Hugh, "are you a knight, too?"

"Only when I cannot avoid it," Hugh said. "I prefer more scholarly pursuits."

"Then you must talk with Lady Mirielle," Robin told him. "She knows *everything*. She is a most learned lady.

"Here we are," Robin continued, leading them into the hall and toward the dais. "Lady Mirielle said you are to sit at the high table. Now, if you will excuse me, gentle sirs, my place is below, with my mother." With a bow Robin left the two men standing beside the benches set at the high table.

"He has fine manners for a boy who spends his days in the stables," Giles noted. "Is it the result of Lady Mirielle's training? It would seem she has informally made him her page after he was denied that position by the mistress of the castle."

"I rather think his mother has had something to do with Robin's manners." Hugh indicated one of the lower tables, where Robin had joined a woman of graceful bearing, who wore a plain, brown woolen dress. From under the woman's neat wimple a few curls escaped that were identical to Robin's in color and texture. "She looks to be a gentlewoman and the folk near her treat her with respect. Her son is a credit to her."

"I believe our host is coming now," Giles said. "And the ladies with him."

A man and two women were just entering the hall.
Lady Alda came first, her well-buffed fingertips resting lightly on the wrist of a dark-haired man of im-
pressive build. Alda's golden hair was bound into a
net of gold threads no brighter than the strands they
enclosed. A wide gold circlet topped the net. The
deep green of her gown was calculated to show the
glory of her hair to best advantage and the low-cut
neckline revealed most of her white bosom. Con-
trary to custom she wore no underdress.

Behind this pair a second woman walked, and the
dark-haired man's head was turned toward her as
he said something. The woman was listening to him
and was not concerned as yet with the guests awaiting them on the dais where the high table was set.
Thus, Giles saw Mirielle with his eyes unbeclouded
by the illusion she had cast at their first meeting.

"Now there," said Hugh in a reverent whisper, "is
a woman worthy of young Robin's devotion."

"And of any grown man's admiration," Giles
added.

She was gowned in unadorned blue wool, high-
necked and long-sleeved over a cream-colored underdress. The loose robe ought to have concealed
her figure but in fact it offered hints of delicious
curves with every graceful step Mirielle took. Her
hair was a gleaming blue-black, bound into two
braids that fell almost to her knees. The circlet on
her brow was of thin gold, set with a single, glowing
garnet. The smooth, rounded surface of the red
stone caught and seemed to hold within itself every
flicker of light from each torch in the hall and every
candle on the high table, surrounding Mirielle's face
and form with a rosy aura.

Mirielle saw Giles and Hugh and lifted one slender hand as if to trace the former veil of illusion over herself once more. Then her hand dropped to her side again and a faint smile curved her lips as she realized there was no point in trying to hide her true appearance from those who had already glimpsed it.

"Welcome to Wroxley Castle." The dark man bowed courteously to the guests. "I am Sir Brice, seneschal here and in charge of the castle in the absence of the late baron's heir."

"We thank you for your generous hospitality." Giles studied Brice, detecting in the man's manner a strong sense of his own importance, as if Brice thought of himself as more than a mere seneschal who had been temporarily appointed by King Henry.

"My lady," Brice said to Alda, "may I present our visitors? You have already heard their names from Mirielle."

Alda inclined her head when Giles and Hugh bowed to her. Not the least sign of interest showed on her lovely face, a fact for which both men could be grateful. In a world in which any interruption to daily routine was regarded as an excuse for celebration and, in the case of visitors, a chance to hear entertaining news of life outside the castle confines, Alda appeared to be singularly unconcerned with her guests.

"It is cold in the hall," Alda said, taking her seat in a high-backed chair. "I want my green shawl."

"Is this it, my lady?" Hugh reached behind Alda to take up the shawl that was laid over the chair arm. He draped the wool around Alda's shoulders.

Treating him as if he were merely one of her servants, she did not trouble herself to thank him.

Giles watched the scene with a growing chill in his heart. This was the lady of Wroxley, wife to the absent Gavin, mother of the young heir. The boy was not present. He was old enough to be a page by now, so he was most likely fostering at another castle. Nor had Giles seen any sign of Lady Alda's second child. For there had been a second child who, if it had survived infancy and early childhood, would be almost eleven years old.

"You have already met my ward, the lady Mirielle," said Sir Brice.

"We have, indeed. She made us most welcome." Giles wished the lady Mirielle would put out her hand so he might have an excuse to touch her, but she only smiled a little and nodded at him and Hugh.

She was a rare beauty, slender and graceful of figure but not fragile. There was a strength to Mirielle that went well with the kindness of heart she had displayed toward Robin, and toward two unexpected guests. There was intelligence in her sweet face and her silvery gray eyes. Looking into her eyes, Giles thought he could find peace with such a woman, and rest from the worldly problems besetting him. He put the thought aside with some difficulty, telling himself he could not afford to lose himself in a woman. He had important work to do.

With Brice organizing the seating at the high table to his own taste, Giles was placed next to Mirielle and Hugh sat beside Alda. Making a remark about the shortage of chairs and benches that was intended to be humorous, Brice took the chair usually reserved for the baron of Wroxley, seating himself between the two women.

From Mirielle's point of view this arrangement was both awkward and unseemly. She wished Brice would not act as if he were the lord of Wroxley. Too often when guests were present he took the baron's chair. Sooner or later a guest offended by this usurpation of rank would carry word of it to King Henry, and if Henry in turn were sufficiently annoyed, he might well remove Brice from his post as seneschal.

On this particular evening Mirielle had an even more personal interest in the arrangement at the high table. She had planned to take the place beside Hugh for herself. She had sensed upon first confronting him in the gatehouse that Hugh was a brother soul, for by his indistinct features she had recognized another who was cloaking himself in disguise as she was then doing. And she had known, with a natural instinct well honed by Cerra's teaching, that Hugh was honest. Eager to improve her understanding of the Ancient Art to which she was devoted, Mirielle wanted to speak privately with Hugh, to ask him many questions. Since he was so well traveled, she was sure there was much she could learn from him.

Sitting beside Hugh would also resolve Mirielle's most immediate personal concern, for it would put her at a safer distance from Sir Giles. This second guest frightened her and excited her at the same time. She did not think he was handsome. It was difficult to tell for certain, with his face covered by that thick beard and mustache, but his nose was straight, if a bit long, and his brow was high and wide. Unlike Hugh, Gavin was not a mage, of that

Mirielle was sure. Yet his blue eyes burned into hers as if he could read all the secrets of her soul, all the hopes and wishes she kept so carefully hidden. Giles was big—much taller than Brice—and muscular and healthy looking. Much too healthy for a man who claimed to be troubled by chronic pain from an old wound.

Mirielle suspected that Giles's supposed wound was an excuse formulated to allow him to remain at Wroxley Castle beyond the single night that Christian charity allotted to wayfarers. If he had some ulterior purpose for wanting to stay at Wroxley for several days, then Mirielle believed it was her duty to discover what that purpose was. She also admitted to herself a deep curiosity about him. This was why she had arranged for the two guests to sit at the high table. She knew Brice would question the men about their recent travels. Their responses might provide some useful information. While she considered how best to go about learning what she wanted to know the servants began offering food and Giles started his own polite interrogation.

"Have you always lived at Wroxley?" he asked.

"No." Mirielle sensed that he intended to direct their table conversation into the areas where he wanted it to go. Very well, let him lead. She would follow with apparent docility, while not giving away any information that might compromise Brice, or Wroxley Castle and its inhabitants. "I was born in Wales. Sir Brice is my cousin. When my parents died, I became his ward."

"Then Sir Brice is also Welsh?" Giles glanced at his host as if he were trying to recognize him but could not recall a previous encounter.

How odd. Mirielle did not think the two men had ever met before. Or had they?

"Like me, Brice is half Norman, part Welsh, and part Saxon," Mirielle said. "A very mixed heritage."

"You appear to have inherited the best qualities of all three races." Giles smiled at her. The effect on her ability to think was devastating, making her forget the questions she had been planning to ask him.

"I have never heard it said that Normans thought well of either Welsh or Saxon." Irritated by her own reaction to the man, Mirielle responded rather too sharply. Oh, why could she not turn her eyes from his?

She had a piece of meat in her fingers. She was holding it over the trencher she and Giles were sharing, letting the gravy drip from the meat back into the trencher so it would not stain the tablecloth. Giles reached for a succulent morsel for himself and the back of his hand brushed across hers. Mirielle shook with an emotion she could not identify. A tiny spot of fatty brown gravy soiled the white linen. She stared at it, appalled by this evidence of a lack of self-control on her part.

"Tell me how you came to Wroxley," Giles urged, apparently oblivious to her discomfort.

"It is an ordinary tale." What was wrong with her? She had been properly schooled in manners and she had acted as Brice's hostess on many previous occasions. She knew how to make light conversation with passing guests who would be on their way within a day or two, never to be seen again. Why should this evening be different? Why should this one man affect her so strongly? She knew why it was so. Sir Giles was connected to the image she had seen in her crystal globe. Something about this stranger tugged at her heart—and something about him started a warning bell ringing in her mind.

"Ordinary or not, I would like to hear your story." Again he flashed her that smile, revealing remarkably even, unbroken white teeth, accompanied by a glint of humor in his blue eyes. His deep, mellow voice was so persuasive that Mirielle had no desire to resist what he asked of her. "How old were you when you were orphaned, Lady Mirielle?"

"I was thirteen."

"And you became Sir Brice's ward immediately?"

"It was his wish. Brice has been kind to me."

"He has not found you a husband." The words were disparaging, the slightly raised brow that accompanied them even more so.

"I have no desire to marry," Mirielle said, annoyed. "Being the daughter of a poor nobleman, I have no dowry, so no one is likely to ask for me. At age twenty-three, I am too old to think of marriage any longer. I am grateful to Brice for bringing me to Wroxley with him. It is charitable of Lady Alda to allow me to stay."

She stopped, asking herself why she was talking so freely to a man she did not know. She had sounded like the fox in the old fable, who declared he did not want the grapes he could not have, because they must be sour. She did not feel that way about marriage. She wished she could have a good husband, but since she could not, she would make her spinster's life as useful as possible.

"Forgive me if I speak improperly, my lady, but I have noticed how the servants follow your bidding as if you were in charge of all domestic arrangements. I do believe you earn your keep here."

"I simply help as best I can. Lady Alda has other interests."

"Which do not include fulfilling her duties as chatelaine." His quiet voice suggested a low opinion of the beautiful lady of the castle.

"I have no complaint to make of Lady Alda." That was not entirely true, but Mirielle did not intend to divulge her opinion of Alda to Sir Giles. "Nor will I hear a word against her from anyone else."

"Admirable discretion. Perhaps we should speak of another subject. Tell me, my lady, did you learn your conjuring skills in Wales?" Giles lifted their winecup. He sipped from it, then passed it to her. Again their fingers touched, and a new tremor rocked her.

"You cannot deny your skill," he said. "When first we met you convinced me with a single gesture that you were aged and homely. Which is plainly not the case."

"Your friend was not similarly convinced," she told him, trying to deflect a compliment she was afraid to acknowledge.

"Hugh is not easily tricked."

"Why are you here?" She abandoned all pretense. "I do not believe you are merely pilgrims traveling homeward. I sense some other reason for your presence at Wroxley." At her words he went very still, watching her while Mirielle stared boldly back at him.

"Why, my lady," he said at last, "what reason could two strangers have for entering such a strong fortress under false pretenses? Outnumbered as Hugh and I are, what could we hope to gain?"

"I know not." Mirielle ran her tongue across lips suddenly made dry by fear. "My every instinct tells me you are an honest man at heart, yet I fear your coming means danger. Sir Giles, I beg you, do no harm to my cousin Brice."

"You love him." It sounded like an accusation.

"Brice is the only true kin I have left since a terrible sickness took the rest of my family from me. Yes, I love him—and I owe him all my loyalty."

"Lady Mirielle, I give you my word. As I am the honest man you think me, I will never do harm to another man who is honest."

"That is only half an answer." She was made even more fearful by his words, for she knew things about Brice that might give another man cause to wish her cousin harm. "Please, do not hurt Brice." Her hand touched Giles's forearm. She felt the solid strength in him, and she wished she could put her head on his shoulder and pour out all the fears and the concerns that too often kept her awake with worry far into the night.

Then Brice, turning from Hugh and Alda, with whom he had been talking all this time, asked Giles a question about his journey from Compostela to England. Mirielle took her hand off Giles's arm, telling herself she owed her loyalty to Brice, not to Giles. She spent the rest of the evening in a state of confusion, trying to convince herself that she could not be feeling what her heart and her body warned her she was feeling.

"I cannot bear this cold hall any longer." Lady Alda stood, pulling her shawl close about her shoulders. "There are too many drafts here and there is

53

nothing interesting to do, no one worth talking with. I will seek my own room, where it is warmer. Sir Brice, you will attend me."

Hearing this speech, Mirielle glanced at Brice. If Alda was unaware or did not care that she had just insulted their guests, at least Brice was not completely immune to social niceties.

"Good sirs, I apologize for leaving you so precipitously." Brice rose from his chair. "I would gladly remain here to talk with you, but my lady Alda is in fragile health. It is my duty to see her safely to her room."

Alda tapped her foot in impatience, heaved an exaggerated sigh, rearranged her voluminous shawl to better display her bosom and, as if to give the lie to Brice, managed to look as if she were in the very best of health.

"Since you will remain at Wroxley for a second night," Brice went on to Giles and Hugh, "I hope we will have time to talk longer on the morrow."

"Brice!" Alda's full lips pouted, her golden brown eyes signalling her annoyance. "You will escort me at once!"

"Of course, my lady. I am ever at your service." Brice extended his arm, Alda laid her fingertips on his wrist and together they stepped down from the dais and left the great hall.

This kind of scene on Alda's part was so commonplace that no one in the household paid any attention. But the guests did. Giles and Hugh had risen as soon as Alda stood. Mirielle noticed that Giles's teeth were clenched and his hands were balled into fists. A moment or two after Brice and Alda disappeared from view, Giles moved with purposeful strides to the door they had used.

"Stop him before he does great harm." Hugh's voice was little more than a whisper but Mirielle heard it clearly, for Hugh echoed the warning in her own thoughts. She looked at him with a question in her eyes.

"Do it now," Hugh said. "I cannot. He would not listen to me and I cannot blame him for that. But you can stop him."

"Yes." She hurried after Giles, into the darkness of an anteroom from which stairs wound upward. Above her she heard Brice and Alda climbing toward Alda's chamber at an upper level of the keep. Alda was complaining about a cold draft. Mirielle ran up the stairs, knowing she dared not call out to the man pursuing the couple for if she did, Brice would hear her.

She caught up to Giles just before he reached the landing where the steps opened onto the musicians' gallery built above one end of the great hall. The woolen curtain over the entrance to the gallery had been drawn back so light from the hall could illuminate this portion of the stairs, thus saving the use of a torch. Above, Alda and Brice continued their climb.

"Sir Giles, wait, please."

He heard her whisper and stopped, turning. The bleak expression in his eyes reminded Mirielle of the mountains of her native North Wales in wintertime, all bare and cold, hard as the flint that was their chief component. She had seen men look that way when they were about to erupt into violence. She did not know why Giles was so angry, but she did know she had to deflect his fury.

"Sir, I believe you are lost." It was the only thing Mirielle could think of to say that, in his present mood, he would not dispute. "Your chamber lies on the other side of the keep."

"I was not seeking my chamber." Giles drew a deep breath. "Surely you know that your cousin Brice is acting dishonorably. So is Lady Alda."

It was exactly what Mirielle thought, but she knew that she was unawakened to the sensual desires that could drive men—and women—to foolish deeds. Perhaps, once aroused, those desires were uncontrollable. In any case, she must forestall the threat of violence against Brice.

"You do not understand," she said.

"Would you care to explain it to me?" Giles ground out the words from between clenched teeth.

He stepped onto the narrow balcony that was the musicians' gallery and Mirielle, with a sigh of relief, followed him. Below, in the great hall, the servants were clearing the tables, snuffing the candles, dousing the extra torches that had been lit during the meal. The men-at-arms who slept in the hall were finding their places. Even the dogs were settling down for the night. Hugh had disappeared. As more and more torches were put out the gallery grew shadowed.

"Well?" Giles's eyes gleamed in the half light. "Your explanation of your cousin's behavior, if you please, Lady Mirielle."

"Brice and Lady Alda are very distant cousins by marriage," she began.

"And clearly also more than friends," Giles snapped.

"This is not your affair," Mirielle said.

"No, it is theirs. A shameful affair. Tell me about it."

Ordinarily, Mirielle would not have made any explanation for Brice's actions to someone who was a stranger. But Hugh had bidden her to stop Giles before he caused trouble. If she kept talking Giles would stay with her, rather than rushing up the stairs to a confrontation with Brice that could only result in violence and, probably, bloodshed.

"Lady Alda was only thirteen years old when she was married to Gavin of Wroxley," Mirielle said. "She bore a son when she was but fourteen and she was with child again the next year when her husband went off to the Holy Land on crusade. Alda was left here at Wroxley with no companion save for servants and her father-in-law, who by all reports was a fierce old warrior, not a person inclined to humor a frightened young girl."

"Say rather, a foolish girl, who cared only for her own comforts." Giles's voice was harsh. "Other wives have remained at home, directing the welfare of their castles or manor houses, recalling always their duties to husband and children. Other wives, however young and frightened, have been faithful."

"Sir Giles, I tell you again, this is not your concern. Alda does not know if her husband is alive or dead. She has had no word of him for five years. In January a year ago, when old Lord Udo and his seneschal died within a week of each other, Alda begged Brice to come to Wroxley to act as seneschal because she could not hold the castle by herself and she wanted someone she could trust in that post. Brice went to court and formally applied to King Henry for approval. That approval was granted, to the great benefit of Wroxley, which now has a firm, manly hand in control of its lands and people.

"The castle's defenses have been strengthened until no one would dare to attack us. Once there were robbers in the forest who preyed on villeins and travelers alike; now they are gone, captured and punished, or fled far away. When Brice and I first came here, the houses in the village were in a sad state. Under Brice they have been rebuilt. New fields have been brought under cultivation. The castle itself is better managed. Stores of extra food have been laid by in case of famine. The people are remarkably healthy. In the winter just past, there were not even any serious illnesses."

"These are matters usually attended to by the lady of the castle, including the defenses, the robbers, and the clearing of the fields, all of which a woman can order in the absence of her husband." Giles interrupted her list of improvements. "Left to herself, Lady Alda would have done none of what you describe."

"You do not know Alda. Therefore, you cannot say what she would or would not have done."

"I am not a fool, Mirielle. I think much of the good done here at Wroxley in the last year has been done by your instigation. Nor, from what I have seen of her, do I imagine that Lady Alda has ever thanked you for your efforts."

This was too much. Giles's words hit too close to home. While she valued his recognition of all she had done, still she could not allow him to speak so slightingly of Alda. Mirielle drew herself up, gathering her courage, concentrating her will. She looked directly into Giles's eyes and lifted her left hand to make a gesture.

Giles caught her wrist, twisting her arm behind her and pulling her against him. His eyes were blue as the sky, and as boundless. She could not take her gaze from Giles's eyes.

"Stop it!" he commanded. "Play none of your conjurer's tricks on me, lady. I recognize them, so they can have no effect on me."

"You are not ill," she whispered, too deeply shaken by his hard embrace to pretend that she did not understand what he meant. "You have suffered wounds in the past, but they are well healed. Why do you pretend to be weak and unable to travel any farther? Who are you? Why have you come to Wroxley?"

"A man whose wounds have healed may still bear scars that ache," he said. "Perhaps it is my scars that bring me here."

"You would do well to leave in the morning," she told him, "for if you stay, I will tell my cousin Brice that you have come for some nefarious purpose."

"You have no proof to back such an accusation." His arms tightened around her, making her even more aware of his masculine strength.

"I need only tell Brice that you have laid hands on me. My word will be all the proof he needs." She could not bear to think what Brice would do if she carried out her threat, but Giles could not know that. She expected him to let her go at once. He did not.

"Ah, well," he said, "if I am to be tortured and

hanged at your accusation, then, my lady, let it be for good cause." The pressure of his arms shifted subtly, so that Mirielle was held in a gentler manner, though still securely.

"What are you doing?" Both of her hands were now free. She could have fought him, could have pushed against his shoulders or his chest. She could have called for help from the men-at-arms below in the hall. She did none of those things. Instead, she stood quietly while Giles, a stranger to her and perhaps a villain, lowered his mouth toward hers.

Mirielle trembled, wanting the kiss she knew was coming, aching for it. Untouched and innocent though she was, still she desired Giles's kiss. He had a beautiful mouth, the lips firmly molded and tempting. Those lips parted a little, and moved closer.

And then, unexpectedly, he released her, holding her at arm's length, steadying her, for without his support surely she would have crumpled to the floor in shock at the abrupt change that had come over him.

"On the other hand," he said, "you may be right. Perhaps I should go. Will you stand on the battlements and wave your scarf in farewell to me, Lady Mirielle? Will you give me a ribbon to wear on my sleeve in memory of you?"

She could not answer him for fear she would burst into tears. She turned from him and fled the musicians' gallery, running down the stairs toward the one place where she knew she would be safe and undisturbed.

* * *

Though she did not know it, Mirielle left behind a man who was every bit as confused as she. He had come to Wroxley prepared to meet danger and dark magic and in the knowledge that his true mission at the castle might be discovered. He was ready to face imprisonment and even death if required in order for him to uncover the truth he sought.

Prepared for deceit and violence, he had not expected to lose his heart in an instant, nor to be perfectly certain that the loss was not due to any magic other than that of the heart. Clothed in dignity and innocence Mirielle had walked into the great hall and looked at him with a rueful smile, accepting that disguise was no longer possible, and he had seen in her eyes all the honesty and goodness he had always wanted in his mate.

He could only marvel at the ironic turn his life had just taken. Scornfully rejected in his youth, when all he had wanted was the chance to prove his love and to woo his beloved, in the last dozen years since that rejection he had sternly refused to allow himself to love again. Yet here, in the most unlikely and treacherous of places, love had found him despite his firm intentions against it and he knew in his innermost soul that this new love would would never release him from its tender and all-encompassing embrace.

He dared not tell Mirielle of his feelings. It would be too dangerous for her and he would not expose her to the chance of harm if he could avoid doing so. He wished he could send her to some safe place and keep her there until he was finished with what he had come to do. At the same time, he knew Mirielle must remain at the castle. He also knew that, when she was aware of the full truth of his presence there, she might hate him for using her, for lying to her and perhaps destroying her cousin, Brice.

But he was bound to continue what he had begun. It was his duty to see the task through to the end, for lives other than his and Mirielle's depended on his actions. The very existence of Wroxley depended on him.

Chapter Four

"The essence of all art is to conceal art."
—Gerald of Wales
The Description of Wales

Mirielle's workroom, the place that was her private sanctuary, was located in a quiet part of the keep. The walls were lined with wooden shelves to hold the supplies and the vessels necessary to her work. Herbs hung from the rafters to dry above the oak worktable. A single, shuttered window opened onto the inner bailey to provide light during the daytime hours.

With Brice's permission, Ewain the blacksmith had seen to the building of the low, square furnace that was tucked into one corner. Though untutored in Mirielle's skills, Ewain understood her requirements and Mirielle was well pleased with the furnace, which served several purposes. It kept the room warm, so the herbs dried quickly and evenly. The flat, waist-high top of the furnace provided a hot surface when Mirielle was making certain herbal preparations requiring heat. And there was space on the top surface for the athanor she used when she undertook other, more esoteric work.

There were only two books and one scroll in the room, which Mirielle kept in a box for safety when she was not using them. Having studied those written materials frequently, she knew them almost by heart. With the scroll and the books as her guides Mirielle had gone on to create her own experiments with herbs and with the few metals she was able to acquire with the blacksmith's help. She had become expert in making herbal medicines, though her other projects were not always so successful.

The castle folk valued Mirielle's abilities as chatelaine and healer and they were grateful for her influence over Brice, which she used to encourage him to improve living conditions on Wroxley lands. Those same folk were more than a bit wary of the arts Mirielle practiced in her workroom and so they kept away from it. Being well aware that some of her preparations could do more harm than good if they should fall into careless hands, Mirielle used a special latch she had devised to keep the workroom door securely closed when she was not there.

Reaching the door after her flight from Giles, Mirielle found the latch untouched since she had secured it earlier in the day. Minn sat beside the door, waiting for her. There was no one about to see Mirielle and her cat enter the unlit workroom and thus no one to hear her exclamation of surprise when she realized she was not the only person present.

"There's naught to fear," said a voice from some-where near the furnace. "I mean no harm and I have disturbed nothing of yours."

"Master Hugh?" Mirielle stood perfectly still, try-ing to locate him. Beside her Minn began to purr. The sound convinced Mirielle that Hugh had spo-ken a simple truth. She need not fear her visitor. "How did you come inside without unfastening the latch? And why have you neglected to light one of the lamps?"

"It seemed to me likely that you would seek respite in your own special place," Hugh replied.

"But the latch—"

"Perhaps I flew in the window."

"You could not. The shutter has a similar latch on it." Mirielle responded to the humor in Hugh's voice, and then she caught her breath. "When you spoke just then, you sounded like my dear Cerra."

"Your teacher?"

"Yes. Master Hugh, you may be able to see in the dark, but I have never learned that skill. Let me strike the flint." She knew where it was. She knew where everything in her room was, for she kept the place neat and clean, as Cerra had explained was necessary for the practice of healing—or for al-chemical experiments or the study of magic.

Mirielle's fingers found the pieces of flint where they lay on the table, but before she could strike a spark every oil lamp in the room burst into light and the fuel piled inside the furnace flared with joyful, dancing flames. A kettle filled with water that Mir-ielle had left atop the furnace began to bubble and boil. Hugh stood beside the furnace, clad in the same plain, dark robe he had worn to the meal in the great hall.

In Hugh's hand was the staff that had caused concern to the watchman, Mauger, at the outer castle gate. Mirielle remembered how Hugh had made a point of unfastening the staff along with the saddlebags. The staff was at least five feet long. It was crooked in places, as if it had been made from a sapling that had branches growing out of it. The branches had been cut off, the bark had been stripped, and the wood cured by a process that made it hard as metal and turned it to a dark reddish-brown. The staff was highly polished, but it was undecorated.

"I knew you at once for a mage," Mirielle said.

"As I knew you, Mirielle. I believe we have much to teach each other."

"Will you show me your true face, Master Hugh?"

"I will, if you will tell me why you greeted my friend and me with a face not your own."

"You are very like Cerra. She always required an equal exchange for everything she taught me."

"In nature a balance must always be maintained." Hugh paused, awaiting her explanation.

"Isn't it obvious?" Mirielle said. "These are dangerous times. I hide my face from strangers because it is the safest course. The disguise prevents problems from arising."

"Great beauty can be a curse." Hugh nodded his understanding.

"Those who know me here at Wroxley see me as I am," Mirielle said. She raised her left hand in the gesture so familiar to her. "This affects only strangers.

"Now, Master Hugh, I have fulfilled my part. Show me your face."

"See it, Mirielle." Hugh stood very still, his left hand wrapped around his staff.

His face changed as though a veil was slowly being drawn aside, allowing Mirielle to see skin of a hue similar to vellum that had become slightly yellowed with age. Hugh's cheekbones were high and wide, his eyes almond shaped and dark. His hair remained black and straight. His chin was round and his mouth bore a humorous quirk to which Mirielle responded with a lifting of the corners of her own lips. She could not tell his age. Hugh was both old and young at the same time.

"It is a pleasant face," she said, "but I perceive that you come from some distant land, for it is a face unlike any I have ever seen before."

"It is the face of a friend."

"I know that. Hugh, I saw a vision of you and Sir Giles before you reached our gates." She explained about the crystal globe and the scene in it. "All of my previous visions have foretold important changes in my life. Thus, I believe that you and Sir Giles will be the agents of the next change. What have you come here to do?"

"You will want to know something about my homeland."

"I am curious about it," Mirielle admitted, willing for the moment to let him avoid a direct answer to her question. She would learn what she could from him and then ask again.

"If you will draw some of that boiling water from the kettle on the furnace," Hugh said, "I will prepare a beverage which we can drink while we talk."

67

Using her long-handled dipper Mirielle filled two wooden cups with the hot water and set the cups on the table. Hugh reached inside his robe to pull out a metal box engraved with a winged dragon. He opened the hinged lid, revealing a supply of dried leaves. A scent she did not know wafted toward Mirielle's nose. Hugh put a few of the leaves into each cup and instructed Mirielle to stir the water for a moment.

"To be certain the *tcha* is moistened," he said. "Now, let it steep for a while. In my land, we drink *tcha* after a large meal, to aid the digestive process."

They sat together on the bench beside the worktable, with Minn curled up at Mirielle's feet. When Hugh told her the brew was ready Mirielle sipped the hot *tcha*.

"An unusual taste," she said, taking a second sip. "Not like any herb I know, but clean and fresh. Master Hugh, I believe this *tcha* must be a stimulant."

"So it is. But it is never harmful." He regarded her in silence for a while. Mirielle found she did not mind his gaze. There was nothing lascivious in it. Hugh wanted only to know her as Cerra had once known her. She drank the *tcha* and felt herself relaxing, her previous concerns about Hugh's purpose at Wroxley fading. Minn purred contentedly, the room was warm, and when Hugh began to speak Mirielle could see in her own mind the scenes he described.

"My homeland lies far to the east," Hugh began. "You in the western world call it Cathay. It is a beautiful land and large enough to contain within its borders every aspect of nature. There are mountains and wide rivers, lush green gardens and barren deserts, steaming jungles and places where snow piles high in winter and lasts well into the following spring. And we have built great cities. In all my travels I have never seen a palace to equal the one in which the emperor of my land lives. We employ the use of many wonderful machines and inventions unimagined by those who live outside the Middle Kingdom.

"I was born into a family of scholars. My education was extensive in many subjects but my greatest interest has always lain in the Ancient Wisdom, which concerns the methods by which objects can be transmuted from baseness into perfection."

"Then you are an alchemist as well as a mage," Mirielle exclaimed, fascinated by these revelations.

"The study of the one art leads inevitably to the other and both together are but a small portion of the Ancient Wisdom," Hugh said. "From the contents of this room I think you already know it is so."

"How did you come to England from a land so far away?" Mirielle asked.

"Let us prepare another cup of *tcha* and I will tell you." Hugh paused, waiting until Mirielle emptied their cups of the damp leaves, rinsed them, and refilled them with hot water. Again he sprinkled the dried *tcha* leaves onto the water. When the brew was ready to drink, Hugh resumed his story.

"Most men of the Middle Kingdom believe that all knowledge is contained there, in that blessed land," Hugh said. "Thus, there is no need to look outside our borders, for nothing of any importance exists in the world beyond. In my youth, before I learned the value of silence, I was often in trouble, for I could not accept the limitations of that belief and I did not hesitate to say so. If there is no purpose to the lands outside the Middle Kingdom, I asked, and nothing worthwhile there, then why were those lands created at all? Since they were created, I reasoned, then the man seeking knowledge will want to explore foreign lands and to learn what he can from the people who live in them.

"And so," Hugh went on, "I persistently begged my father for permission to travel, that I might seek new truths and new knowledge. It took many years of persuasion before he agreed to let me go. We parted with sadness, for he was aged by then and we knew we would never see each other again. Still, he understood my compelling need to learn all I could and in his heart I think he envied me the experiences I would have."

"I, too, have sometimes yearned to travel to distant lands," Mirielle told him. "In which direction did you go, Master Hugh?"

"Southwestward on a trader's ship," Hugh said. "Though the scholars of the Middle Kingdom do not concern themselves with other lands, our merchants do. I voyaged first to a place called Hind, where I dwelt for a dozen years. Then I traveled farther west to Baghdad and lived there for another dozen years."

"Baghdad is a place I have heard of," Mirielle interrupted. "The Saracens rule there."

"So they do, and they have many wise and learned men in their schools. When I had learned all I could from their physicians and mathematicians, and from their astrologers and alchemists, I joined a caravan bound for what you English call the Holy Land. Though your Christian crusaders have taken that land from the Saracens, still, neither side balks at trade with avowed enemies. The goods carried by the caravan I was with were welcomed in Jerusalem and it was easy for me to enter the city with my traveling companions. It was in Jerusalem that I first met Sir Giles. We became friends and when he decided to return to England, he invited me to travel with him.

"I have acquired more learning than I ever dreamed existed before I left my homeland," Hugh said, finishing his story, "but with knowledge came the realization of how little I know, of how much I have still to learn. A wise man in Jerusalem told me it is always so, that there is no end to learning. I hope to discover yet more knowledge here, in this damp and cold northern land."

"Master Hugh," Mirielle asked, "with all your studies and your remarkable travels, have you learned the secret yet? Are you able to change base metal into gold?" The question was a trick, and if Hugh was all he claimed to be, he would recognize the trick and give her the correct answer. Mirielle did not really doubt Hugh's honesty, but Cerra had repeatedly emphasized the need for caution where her art was concerned. She was impressed by the solemnity with which Hugh now looked into her eyes.

"As you profess to be a student of the art," he said slowly, "surely you know that the tale of making gold is but a parable for the true end of alchemy, which is the perfection of the human soul. All efforts, all experiments, and all true knowledge lead to that goal, which is more valuable than the purest gold."

"I do know it." Mirielle let out the breath she had been holding. "It is among the earliest lessons Cerra taught me. She died too soon, leaving me half-taught, and I have been forced to experiment on my own. I have had some slight success, along with too many failures."

"For a woman to engage in this effort is unheard of in my land." Hugh frowned.

"But not altogether unknown in other lands," Mirielle said. "In Wales, where I was born, there are many women who know more than just the simple herbal healing they are careful to practice while others are watching. Some people call those women sorceresses, but disapproval does not stop them. Cerra believed I was born with a talent for the art."

"I would like to learn what you know of the local herbal lore," Hugh said, his eyes on the bunches of lavender and rosemary and other herbs hanging above the worktable. He turned his attention to the mortar and pestle on the table, then to the retorts and the alembic on the shelves.

"Master Hugh, I propose an exchange of information." So enchanted was she by his story and by the possibility of acquiring valuable new knowledge that Mirielle had all but forgotten that he would be leaving within a day or two at most. She knew only that she had found a friend, a possible teacher, one who understood how she craved learning. As she was beginning to understand was Hugh's custom, he did not give her a direct answer but instead made a remark that at first hearing seemed to have no relevance to her request.

"My true name," Hugh said, "is Hua Te. In this

land it would be best if you continue to address me as Hugh."

"Thank you, Hua Te." She tried to say it in the same way that he did and when he smiled at the sound she smiled in return. Then she did remember that he would not stay long at Wroxley Castle, and she thought about Giles, and her smile disappeared. "Master Hugh, what is your purpose here?"

"I cannot tell you all of it, for it is not my story," he said. "I know that in the beginning many questions will beguile your thoughts. As events unfold those questions will be answered."

"Is it Sir Giles who has some particular reason for coming to Wroxley?" For a little while, intrigued by the tale Hugh was recounting, Mirielle had been able to push Giles to the back of her mind. Now the image of the tall, bearded man with the seductive voice returned to disturb her.

"My friend's intent is the restoration of the proper balance," Hugh said. "From what I know of you I cannot think you will have any objection to that goal."

Mirielle looked down at her empty cup, trying to formulate a response that would not implicate Brice in wrongdoing. She wanted to explain to Hua Te that, while she did not fear for her personal safety, if Brice were turned out of Wroxley, or if he were imprisoned or worse, then she would have no place to go save to a convent, a prospect she dreaded. Nor did Mirielle want to see Brice harmed, not when he had been so consistently good to her.

When Mirielle finally looked up, Hugh had disappeared. His cup still sat on the table, she had not heard him move from the bench, and the door to the workroom was closed, but he was gone.

"Truly, he is a great mage," she said to Minn. "And though he tried to reassure me, I am more afraid than ever."

In the guest room Giles was feeding the brazier with charcoal. Two maidservants had brought the brazier and the fuel for it, along with the mattress and quilts that Mirielle had promised, a pitcher of water, a basin for washing, and a small oil lamp, which did no more to chase away the dark than the brazier did to send the damp cold of the stone-walled room into retreat. Giles glanced up as Hugh entered, but he did not speak until Hugh had closed the door.

"Were you able to learn anything useful?" Giles asked.

"I spoke with Lady Mirielle."

"Did you?" Giles found his friend's look a bit too sharp. To avoid Hugh's eyes, he turned back to the brazier. "I had forgotten how uncomfortable an English castle can be. I have grown soft in foreign lands."

"We need not shiver. I think it is too late for anyone to disturb us. All but the sentries seem to be abed."

"Including Sir Brice and Lady Alda." Giles's voice was bitter.

"You knew the stories before we came here," Hugh said. "I thought you had made your peace with them—and made your decision."

"It is quite another matter to have the evidence before my eyes," Giles said.

"Would warmth improve your mood?" Hugh

stretched out his arms, holding his long staff as always in his left hand. A slight breeze swirled about the room, stirring the sleeves and the hem of Hugh's dark robe. The air in the room turned noticeably warmer. Hugh tilted the staff in the direction of the brazier and flames leapt upward from the charcoal, providing a smokeless torch to light the tiny chamber. Another motion of Hugh's wrist banished the smell of mildew in favor of the tang of fresh-cut cedarwood.

"Thank you." Giles sat down on the bench. Hugh joined him, still holding his staff.

"Mirielle knows we are not mere pilgrims as we claim," Hugh said. "More than that, the girl is a healer with a talent for my own art, and she is far better trained than she realizes."

"Then she may prove to be a hindrance to us," Giles said. "Her loyalty to Sir Brice is obvious. She will protect him if she can."

"Were we to remain at Wroxley for a few days—" Hugh spoke slowly, considering all possibilities—"I might bring her to the point that I could confide our true purpose to her. She possesses a strong conscience. She will see the justice in what we do."

"We dare not forget that Mirielle lives every day in Alda's company," Giles said. "Do not imagine that Alda has no influence on her—or her cousin, Brice. Whether she has a conscience or no, we cannot rely on her, Hugh. Be careful what you teach her."

"I am always careful."

"I apologize, my friend. That was not meant as a reproach. You know I trust your judgment. But we tread a dangerous path here. We cannot depend on anyone at Wroxley."

"Of that I am not certain," Hugh responded. "The situation is more complicated than we realized. After you quit the great hall in such haste this evening, I spoke with several men-at-arms and then I betook myself to the kitchen. In any household the servants always know more of what is transpiring than their masters do. This axiom holds true in every land."

"And?" Ordinarily, Giles would have chuckled at Hugh's last remarks. Not tonight. He understood the gentle censure in Hugh's words. The plan had been for the two of them to ask questions but he had allowed himself to be overcome by anger and by a more primitive emotion. He and Hugh had become close friends because Giles had seen the damage uncontrolled rage could do. Sickened by battle and by the religious intolerance of both sides in the war in the Holy Land, Giles had known he must mend his soul or go mad. Too much blood had been spilled in the various names of God, too many bodies had been dismembered, too many women raped. . . . In desperation he had asked Hugh how it was possible to find peace within himself, only to learn that Hugh was also seeking inner peace.

"The people of Wroxley are divided," Hugh said. "One camp consists of those who are still loyal to the memory of Lord Udo and who await the return of his son and heir, Gavin. A small contingent favors Lady Alda and will do whatever she commands. The largest group has been won over by the improvements in their lives during the year since Sir Brice came here as seneschal."

"From what I learned from Mirielle," Giles said, "I suspect much of the improvement is her doing.

76

Certainly, Lady Alda is not of a character disposed to care for common folk."

"I think Lady Mirielle is careful to give all the credit to Sir Brice."

Giles nodded his agreement with this statement. Rising, he began to prowl around the room as if it were a cage.

"Sir Brice has been captured by the charms of a certain woman," Hugh remarked.

"We already knew that. I do not need to hear it again." Giles paused to send his friend a frowning look before he resumed his pacing.

"Lady Alda is not Brice's only interest," Hugh said. "There is another woman."

"What?" Giles swung around to stare, disbelief written on his face.

"Obviously, Lady Alda does not guess at the affair, else the woman would be dead or, at the very least, turned out of Wroxley wearing only her shift." Hugh's tone was dry.

"I do not doubt your information, Hugh, but how did you come by it?"

"As I told you, the kitchen servants know exactly what goes on in any household and, invariably, they love an excuse to gossip. A soft word, a cup of wine containing just a pinch of the right powder, and an understanding companion who listens well can work wonders in loosening a tongue already more than willing." Hugh's smile came and went.

"This mission grows more complicated by the hour," Giles exclaimed. "Now there are three women involved."

"One of these women is honest, though not on our

77

side," Hugh said. "Of the other two, one is false, as we know."

"Even if the third woman should prove honest," Giles added, "*especially* if she is honest, then she, too, will be opposed to what we do."

"As I am your advisor in this," Hugh said, his quick smile appearing again, "I would suggest that you befriend the honest women, while perhaps you ought to make love to the dishonest ones."

"The problem," Giles mused, "lies in discovering which woman is which."

Chapter Five

"We have followed too much the devices and desires of our own hearts . . . we have done those things which we ought not to have done. . . ."

—General confession
Book of Common Prayer

There are certain herbal medicines that require frequent attention during preparation. On the morning following her conversation with Hugh, Mirielle was once again in her private room working on a distillation when a knock came at the door. Without waiting for her response the door swung open.

"Come in, Robin," Mirielle said, recognizing the boy. With great care she set down the bottle she had just finished filling and stoppered it. After wiping both the bottle and her hands on a cloth she gave

Robin her full attention. "I trust you have not come to me with an injury or an illness. You look well enough."

"No, my lady. I mean, yes, my lady." Robin would have gone to his knees before her had Mirielle not caught his shoulders to keep him on his feet. The boy's cheeks turned bright pink at her touch and he stammered as he spoke. "It's not me, my—my lady. It—it's the blacksmith."

"He has not burnt his hand again?"

"No, Lady Mirielle. It's his forearm, and Ewain says 'tis not serious. He would think nothing of it save that you have warned him about burns festering. He asks if you could send a bit of the same ointment you gave him to use last time?"

"It is one of the preparations I am making this morning, but the fresh batch is not quite ready. You may tell Ewain I will send a pot of ointment shortly, or I'll carry it to him myself. Assure him he will not have long to wait. In the meantime, he can put clear, cold water on the burn."

"I will tell him. Thank you, my lady." With a wide-eyed look around at the bunches and jars of herbs and the glass vessels, Robin left.

Minn, who had opened one languid golden eye when the door opened and had lifted her head at Robin's familiar voice, snuggled down again in her favorite warm spot near the furnace and went back to sleep.

Mirielle also went back to what she had been doing before Robin's interruption. It was not often that the superstitious castle folk knocked on the door of her workroom. Most preferred to stop her while she went about her daily chores elsewhere to ask for the herbal medicines she provided. Only Robin, his mother Donada, Ewain the blacksmith, and one or two others were brave enough to come directly to the workroom when they needed help. Therefore, when a new knock sounded at the door Mirielle at first assumed that Robin had forgotten part of the message for the blacksmith and had returned to ask her to repeat it. With her back to the door while she stirred the bowl of burn ointment, she called out to the boy.

"Come in again, Robin. What have you forgotten? No matter; if you can delay a few minutes longer, I will give you the ointment to take with you. It is almost ready."

"If you mean the lad from the stable, the one who has it in him to be far more than a stableboy, he has run off to the bailey. We passed him on our way."

"Master Hugh." Mirielle turned to greet him. She nearly dropped the bowl she was holding when she saw that Giles was with him. Her heart began to pound. Giles's eyes were on her face with a look that said he was recalling how close he had been to kissing her on the previous evening. It took some effort to remember her manners. "Good day to you both."

"We have interrupted you." Hugh crossed the room to see what she was doing. Mirielle explained about the blacksmith's injury.

"If you like, I will take the ointment to him," Hugh offered. "It will serve as an introduction, since wherever I go I try to converse with others who also work with metals."

"I imagined you were here to tell me more about the wonderful things you have learned on your travels," Mirielle said, to hide her dismay at the thought of being left alone with Giles.

"I only came to guide my friend to your door," Hugh replied. "Thanks to this cold and rainy day, the wound that forced us to stop here at Wroxley is even more painful this morning and it will require treatment. But it is not necessary for me to stay if there is an errand I can do for you. We two can talk later, after you are free of your duties." Hugh put out his hand.

With a sense of inevitability Mirielle set into it the small jar into which she had scooped a supply of the ointment. The workroom was quiet after Hugh had left. Giles's gaze was still fixed on Mirielle's face, while she tried to look anywhere but at him.

"What is this wound that so troubles you, Sir Giles?" she asked when she could bear the silence no longer.

"Must you see it?" He looked unhappy at the prospect.

"I cannot relieve your pain if I do not know what causes it," Mirielle said with an inward sigh. If only he would go away, she could breathe properly again and her heart might resume its normal rhythm. She would be as quick as she possibly could about treating his wound and hope he would leave as soon as she was done.

"Very well. Hugh promised that you would be able to help me." Giles unbuckled his belt and tossed it onto the table. He pulled off his woolen tunic and then his linen undershirt to reveal on his right side a thick ridge of scar tissue across his lower ribcage.

"This is an old wound and a well-healed one." Mirielle pursed her lips, studying the scar, trying to keep her eyes on the problem rather than allowing them to stray to the strong muscles of Giles's arms and shoulders or the taut line of his manly torso. With a single finger she poked at the scar. "From your complaints, I expected to find an open, sup-purating sore."

"Lady, I think you expected to find nothing," Giles said. "I think you believed my wound did not exist."

"It is not my habit to disbelieve a holy pilgrim," she snapped, irritated because he was right.

"I am in truth a pilgrim, my lady." He sounded amused. "All my sins were expiated at Compostela, save for those I have committed since I left that shrine—or those I may commit in the future."

"Sir, you are close to speaking blasphemy." Mirielle refused to look into Giles's eyes to discover if he was laughing at her as she suspected he was. She considered the possibility that Hugh had used his art to conjure up the appearance of a wound on Giles's side, and then dismissed the idea as unworthy of that honest mage. The injury was real and it might have cost Giles his life.

"How did you come by this wound?" she asked in a gentler voice.

"In battle against the Saracens," he answered. "I had raised my sword arm to strike an opponent, when a second man ran against me, slashing with his scimitar."

"Yes, I can see just how the blade cut through your flesh. It was a painful wound, Sir Giles, and it might have been fatal."

"At the time it happened, I was too busy to notice whether it was painful or not."

"What you mean by that is, you killed both Saracens," she said.

"It was kill them or die myself." A simple enough statement spoken in a calm voice, but when Mirielle at last lifted her eyes to his she saw in his face and his tormented look all the anguish of that old battle, and she knew that for Giles, killing would never be as easy as it was for some men. She found the realization comforting.

"Tell me exactly where it hurts and I will try to ease your discomfort, Sir Giles."

"Here." He touched the midpoint of the scar. "It pulls most painfully when I move too quickly, and it aches in damp weather."

"The scar tissue has attached itself to the flesh below." She pressed her own fingers next to his. "It is the rigid connection that restricts your movement. The wound was not well sewn."

"There were so many wounded that day," he said. "The barbers had no time to work with care."

"I have a liniment that may help." She took a jar off a shelf. "I keep a good supply of this at all times and use it often. The men-at-arms suffer frequent aches after too-vigorous weapons practice. Some of them have scars similar to yours and as you say, old wounds are worsened by the cold, damp weather of which we presently have a plentiful supply."

She expected him to put his tunic on at once but, without seeming to notice his own half-naked state, he began to walk about the workroom, peering at the contents of the shelves, sniffing the hanging herbs.

"Hugh said it was a pleasant room." He glanced at the jar of liniment. "Will you rub some of that into my side now, my lady? Since I am right-handed, it will be difficult to do it for myself, and if I know Hugh, he will be an hour or more talking with the blacksmith. Like most men, I desire relief from any discomfort as soon as possible." His sparkling blue eyes challenged her.

"I will warm it first. Heat makes it more effective." She poured a little of the liniment into a clay bowl and set it on top of the furnace. Giles came to stand beside her. Unlike the men-at-arms or the servants whose aches and pains and stomach upsets she regularly treated, Giles's body odor was fresh and clean and, with her senses heightened by his nearness, deeply disturbing.

"Sir Giles, you must step back. I need room in which to move."

"I beg your pardon, my lady." But he did not move by a single step. Mirielle was trapped in the angle formed by the furnace and the wall. Giles put a hand on either side of her head, bracing himself against the wall.

"You could help me if you would," he murmured.

"I am attempting to do so. Step aside, Sir Giles." Her voice trembled.

"Mirielle, you need not fear me," he said.

"I think I would do well to fear you greatly," she responded.

"Perhaps it is I who should fear you."

"I believe the liniment is warm enough now. Please, Sir Giles, let me apply it before it becomes too hot."

"I could scarcely tell if it were." But he dropped his arms, letting her reach the bowl of liniment.

"May I stand here?" he asked. "It is warm by the furnace."

Mirielle did not answer him. She was trying to convince herself that she could apply the liniment to his side without giving way to the emotions that threated to overcome her. She wanted to put her arms around Giles, and she wanted to feel his arms around her. She wanted to rest her cheek on his hard chest, to feel safe and cherished. . . .

Telling herself she ought to have more pride than to give way to unseemly desires, especially with a man she barely knew, whose motives were suspect, Mirielle took up the bowl of warm liniment, dipped her fingers into it, and began to work the thick liquid into Giles's scar. There was mint in the mixture, and finely ground nettles, and a special oil that Cerra had taught her to make from thyme leaves.

"It tingles on my skin," Giles said, "and the warmth is soothing, but I think the greatest efficacy comes from your skillful fingers."

"Hold still." Save for the scar itself, his skin was smooth and firm, the veins beneath pulsing with life.

"Ah, there," he breathed. "That's the sore spot."

Mirielle rubbed steadily, massaging the liniment into the scar, paying special attention to the place he indicated.

"My lady, your hands work a comforting magic." When she put the bowl down he caught her hands, kissing them.

"Please, you must not." She pulled her hands from his grasp, but she could not force herself to move away from him as she knew she ought to do. As if she were the one held by a magical charm, her fluttering fingers touched his lips, his cheeks, his brow. She brushed aside an errant lock of his brown hair.

"Sweet lady," he murmured, "I fear I can no longer resist your spell." His arms encircled her, drawing her close, and this time he did not stop short. This time he took her lips with firm assurance.

It was a bliss Mirielle had never anticipated, had not known could exist. If Giles claimed to be caught in a spell she had woven, then she was equally caught in his. She could not help herself. Her mouth welcomed Giles's, her hands crept around his shoulders. He pressed harder, deepening the kiss, and she opened her lips. She uttered one soft little gasp at the flood of new sensations, and then she was clinging to him, returning his kiss, suspended outside time, aching for an eternity of Giles's kisses.

It ended too soon.

"Dear heaven." He released her and stepped back. The shock of leaving his embrace sobered her at once.

"What have we done?" she cried.

"We?" Giles shook his head. "Lady Mirielle, I thank you for that kind *we*, when the fault is so clearly mine. Still, it is an error in judgement that I find I cannot regret." His fingers lightly brushed across her cheek.

"It is my fault, too," she whispered. "I do not know you, I fear your presence at Wroxley, yet I have allowed this to happen." How could she not feel shame for what she had just done? But she knew no shame, only a wild, singing joy that coursed through her body in a tumultuous flood.

"Wroxley," he repeated, as though he had just remembered something important. "Mirielle, were you here while the old baron was still alive?"

It was the last thing Mirielle expected him to say. She stared at him until, unable to bear the cool assessment of eyes that had burned passionately into hers only a few moments before, she let her own gaze stray downward to his firm mouth surrounded by a thick brown beard and mustache. How sweet that mouth could be, how tender in a kiss. His lips moved but she was too bemused by him to comprehend the words he spoke until he repeated them.

"Lord Udo. Did you know him?"

"We never met." Mirielle made herself pay close attention to what he was saying because she was beginning to understand that the questions he was asking were the real reason for his presence in her workroom. And for his kiss, which probably had meant little to him. To him, the kiss would have been no more than a way to soften her resistance to the questions he planned to ask. He could not know how much it had meant to her or how hurt she was to learn he did not share the emotions she had felt—was feeling still.

He was Hugh's friend; therefore, she told herself, he could not be a villain. Behind the deceit of Giles's kiss there must be some honest purpose. She had to believe it was so.

"Brice and I did not come to Wroxley until after Lord Udo was dead," she told him.

"Brice did not know Udo, either? Are you sure of that?"

There was a note in his voice that made Mirielle wonder why the answer to that question was so important and why he should ask it of her and not of Brice.

"I am not entirely sure," she admitted. "Lord Udo did take Alda with him to court several times when he went to fulfill his yearly forty days of service to King Henry. Alda told me about it. She loves to talk about her visits to court. Brice could have been there at the same time. Since Alda and Brice are distantly related, it is possible that the three of them might have come together then."

"Perhaps they did. I never considered that possibility."

"Why are you asking these questions?"

"I cannot tell you why."

"Then you will understand that I can supply you with no more answers." Hurt made her angry, made her speak coldly to him when all she really wanted was to go back into his arms, to be kissed again. But she had her own loyalties to consider. She had already given Sir Giles too much.

"If you will leave tomorrow," she said, "if you will go from Wroxley without touching me again or seeking me out in private, if you will not attempt to speak with me beyond the polite formalities required in public places, then I will say nothing to Brice about the questions you have asked of me."

"The questions were innocent enough," he said in a smooth voice she had not heard from him before. "They might have been asked during the midday meal, while I sat at the high table."

"But you did not ask them there," she said. "You sought me out in my workroom and waited until we were alone. You kissed me first, to make me more amenable to providing the answers you wanted."

"Perhaps I was only making polite conversation."

"You and I both know that is not the case." She met his eyes squarely, unmoved now by the sensual temptation he presented. He had used her. Why, or to exactly what purpose she did not know, but she did not like the feeling.

"I have not lied to you." When she did not respond to his statement, Giles sighed. "Perhaps you are right. Perhaps Sir Giles the pilgrim should be gone from here."

"Then I wish you Godspeed." She made her voice as hard and cold as she could. "Do not return to Wroxley, for if you do, I will certainly tell Brice about this last hour."

"My lady, I do swear to you that after I have left Wroxley Castle, you will never again see Sir Giles the pilgrim." He took up his undershirt and drew it on, then grabbed his tunic.

"Sir Giles! Wait!"

He was already at the door and he turned with his eyebrows raised in surprise that she should call him back after such a dismissal. Mirielle picked up the belt he had left forgotten on the table. Coiling it quickly into a roll of hard leather, she threw it at him. He caught it in midair before it had time to unroll.

"My thanks, Lady Mirielle. For everything." His rich voice was filled with humor and his sparkling blue eyes laughed at her. And then he was gone.

Mirielle sank down onto the bench, shaking with unpleasant and barely repressed emotion. Her right hand came up to her mouth, the fingers tracing her lips as she recalled Giles's kiss.

"False and yet honest," she whispered. "No liar

and yet untruthful. Innocent questions and important answers. What a fool I am, for all my learning! Have I unknowingly betrayed Brice? Should I report to him the things that Giles asked? And what of Hugh? I believed everything he said, but he is a powerful mage. Did he lie to me while making me believe each word he spoke was true? Am I entirely mistaken in Hugh?"

Her head was aching. Because of all the questions tumbling through her mind she could not fix her thoughts on any one matter and thus she could not come to a decision about what she ought to do. Folding her arms on the table, she put her head down on them, closed her eyes, and tried to think of nothing at all. It was a method she had employed all too often in recent months, usually after Alda's demands had driven Mirielle to near distraction.

She took deep breaths, concentrating on the scents of the herbs and oils and on the warmth emanating from the furnace. Minn jumped up on the bench to sit beside her. Gradually, the sound of the cat's purring combined with the quiet of the workroom to soothe Mirielle until she was able to sort out the events of the last two days. Half an hour later she lifted her head and straightened her back, her decision made.

"I will not tell Brice that Sir Giles embraced me twice and kissed me," she said to Minn, "but I do owe it to him to report those questions Giles asked of me. Brice needs to know, in case the threat I sense is aimed at him or at Wroxley. At the very least, I owe it to Brice to explain that Giles and Hugh are not the simple pilgrims they pretend to be. I must find Brice. He is most likely in the mews again with that sick falcon of his."

Brice was indeed in the mews, but there was no sick falcon. The birds sat upon their perches restlessly, as if responding to the unsettling presence of humans. The mews were in shadow, with the shutters fastened tight against the lashing rain. The falconer lavished great care upon the birds and Brice was equally fussy about his beloved falcons. Not wanting to disturb the birds, Mirielle opened the door only as much as was needed to allow her to slip inside, and she moved as quietly as she could.

The falconer was absent, but a couple stood in the center of the mews, wrapped in a close embrace. Mirielle stopped short.

"Brice?" Mirielle whispered, not believing her eyes. Then, louder, "Brice!"

To his credit, he did not jump away from the woman. Brice gave no sign that he was doing anything wrong. In fact, there was no wrongdoing, as Mirielle quickly realized. But there was danger in what she beheld, danger to Brice and to the woman in his arms.

"Donada?" Mirielle knew the woman well. She was Robin's widowed mother, whose late husband had been the seneschal before Brice, and Mirielle was on excellent terms with her. Donada's good looks and her demure manner had brought her several offers of marriage, all of which she had steadfastly refused, preferring instead to make for herself a not-very-secure place as a skilled seamstress to the demanding Alda.

"Yes, Lady Mirielle." Donada stood quietly, hands

clasped at her waist, betraying neither anxiety nor confusion. "If you wish to speak with Sir Brice in private, I will leave."

"That would be best, my dear." Tenderly Brice touched Donada's hands. "I promise that Mirielle will not betray us. We will talk again soon." He saw her to the door and closed it after her.

"Brice, have you gone mad?" Mirielle cried, trying to keep her voice low so as not to disturb the birds. "Have you considered what Alda will do when she discovers this affair? She will discover it, make no mistake. Alda may be selfish and completely dedicated to her own interests, but she knows what happens within this castle. She will make your life miserable. Brice, can you not see how you are set upon a self-destructive path?"

"Listen to me, cousin." Brice stood with fists planted on his hips, legs astride, a physically powerful, determined figure. His hair and eyes were dark and the bones of his clean-shaven face were harsh. "You and I were given little in this world save gentle birth. I have undertaken to protect you because you are my nearest kin and because your father was kinder to me than my own father ever was. I have promised you that we will rise in the world, that I will find a way to grasp the power and the land I desire, and I will always share whatever I have with you."

"Brice, this is not the way," Mirielle protested. "You regularly commit adultery with Alda, and now you are lying with Donada—"

"There are few opportunities for people like you and me, who have no high connections," Brice interrupted her. "I have no lands and, thanks to your miserly uncle, you were left without even a small dowry."

"If I had a dowry, would you have sold me to some lord for your own benefit?" Mirille cried, almost beside herself with worry for him.

"I would never force you to marry against your will." Brice was almost shouting and the birds began to move about on their perches, making irritated sounds. Brice lowered his voice but he could not keep the intensity out of his next words. "I have no more calling to the Church than you have, Mirielle, and so the only other way for me to earn reknown, wealth, or a title is by selling my services as a knight. I have no fear for myself; I would gladly risk wounds or death in hope of gaining what I want so badly, but if I should be wounded or killed, what would happen to you then? And where would you live while I was away fighting? I will not have you become a servant to some great lady nor will I send you to a convent, not even temporarily, when I know how unhappy you would be.

"When Alda sent to me after Lord Udo's death, asking me to come to Wroxley and hold it as her seneschal, the invitation seemed like a benediction from heaven," Brice said. "The only condition I made to Alda was that you should accompany me. Mirielle, I do know how hard you work here and how devoted you are to the welfare of Wroxley and its people. I am grateful to you, if Alda is not."

"Sooner or later, Udo's son will return to claim his inheritance," Mirielle said. "Do you imagine he will allow you to remain as seneschal after he learns of your affair with his wife? He will turn you out of Wroxley. More likely, he will kill you."

"After so many years with no word of him, Gavin may well be dead. His only son is still a child. Wroxley will need a seneschal for some while yet. By the time young Warrick is of an age to be knighted, I will be ready to move on to greater titles."

"You cannot be sure these dreams will come to pass."

"Do not trouble yourself, Mirielle. I swore to your father and mother on their graves that I would take care of you, and I will. I know exactly what I am doing and I know how to deal with Alda. When I am a great nobleman you will wear silks and jewels and have servants to prepare those herbal medicines of yours for you. I will search the world for ancient scrolls and books and you may sit all day and read them."

"Brice, your foolish ambition will destroy you." *If your lust does not destroy you first,* Mirielle thought, but she did not say it. Though she loved Brice, it was clear to her that he had not thought his ambitious plans through to their inevitable end.

"Don't worry. All will be well." Brice enfolded her in his arms for a quick hug. Then he patted her on the shoulder and told her to run along, to leave the mews because it was time to feed his favorite falcon and he knew she hated to watch the bird feasting on the living mice or smaller birds that were its diet.

Mirielle was so upset that she neglected to tell Brice about Giles's peculiar questions.

That midday Mirielle sat at the high table in the great hall, looking around at the people gathered there for the main meal of the day. How false their faces were, how many improper motives were hidden behind their banal conversations.

Seated beside her for this meal was Hugh, whom she had so quickly—perhaps too quickly?—begun to think of as a friend, but whose every word she now doubted, not because of anything Hugh had done but because of Giles's questions and actions. Next at the high table she, herself, was doing her best to conceal her fears for Brice and her unruly emotions toward Giles. Brice, at the center of the table, was once again sitting in the baron's chair. On the surface Brice was the good seneschal, the firm commander of the castle and its forces, while beneath that surface he lusted for wealth and power and for two women, either of whom could destroy him.

On Brice's right hand Alda sat, gowned this day in deep blue with her golden hair in an elaborate arrangement of braids wrapped about her head. Alda spoke peevishly to Brice, complained of the drafts in the hall and, with breathtaking rudeness, ignored Giles completely. Yet Mirielle knew that Alda saw everything that happened in the hall and if aught was amiss, Mirielle would soon be blamed for it. Mirielle was amazed that Alda, always attuned to anything that concerned her in a personal way, did not know of Brice's liaison with Donada.

On Alda's right, Giles looked grim. He picked at his food and drank a bit too heavily. His glance constantly ranged over the hall. Mirielle wondered if he was counting the number of men-at-arms.

At one of the low tables Donada sat with her son, Robin. Mirielle could see her instructing the boy in table manners. Donada appeared to be serenely unaware of the conflicting emotional currents in the great hall.

"Have you nothing to say, Mirielle?" Hugh asked, smiling at her in a friendly way. "I regret that we have so far today been unable to discuss our mutual work. Perhaps this afternoon we can find the time."

"I do not think so. I have my duties to keep me busy for the rest of the day. Since you and Sir Giles are to leave Wroxley tomorrow morning, there will be no opportunity for the exchange we discussed." She was sorry for it, but she dared not trust herself alone with Hugh. She did not doubt that if he wished to do so, he could draw out of her everything she knew about the castle's defenses or, worse, all she knew about the desires and misdeeds of its inhabitants.

"Cousin, you are mistaken." Brice had overheard her cool words to Hugh. "Did no one tell you? Well, no matter. You are always so well prepared that two extra mouths to feed can mean no more work for you than a few commands to the servants. Don't look so surprised, Mirielle. You know Giles's wound is causing him great pain. The man can barely eat because of it. It would be most inhospitable of us to send him out into the rain and cold in such a state. Our guests will stay with us until the weather improves."

Chapter Six

Mirielle did not see either Giles or Hugh for the next day and a half. They did not appear for meals in the great hall. The servants told her that severe discomfort from his old wound was keeping Giles in his room, with Hugh serving as his nurse. Since neither man sent to her for medicine, Mirielle did not believe the story, but she did not go to the guest room to investigate. Fear of her emotional reaction to Giles, and of what she might be induced to reveal while there, kept her away.

She was not sure whether Giles or Hugh frightened her more. She knew that Hugh had the capacity to use real magic upon her. She guessed that the strong core of morality she had recognized in him had prevented his doing so thus far. But if he had not learned by now whatever it was that he wanted to know, Hugh might be desperate enough to try to trick her. Giles's effect upon her senses was even more unsettling than Hugh's magic and therefore even more threatening to her—and to Brice's well-being.

Mirielle was more certain than ever that there was some secret purpose to their continued presence at Wroxley. What that purpose was she could not discern, no matter how often she considered the possibilities. She knew of no envious baron with a desire to take and hold Wroxley for himself. If King Henry had decided to end Brice's tenure as seneschal he would simply have sent to the castle his new choice for the post with an order dismissing Brice, though Mirielle could think of no reason why the king should be displeased with her cousin. Conditions at Wroxley had improved during Brice's service, with a corresponding increase in the taxes sent to the king. It did not seem likely that Henry would want to alter an arrangement that was profitable to him. No, there had to be some other reason than a royal change of mind or a jealous neighbor that had brought Giles and Hugh to Wroxley and that now made them extend their stay.

Mirielle tried several times to talk to Brice about her worries but, since her intrusion on his rendezvous with Donada, her cousin had been avoiding her. To make matters worse, Brice and Alda had quarreled and Alda was in a nasty mood.

The rain continued unabated, turning both inner and outer baileys into seas of mud that men-at-arms, servants, and roaming dogs all tracked into the great hall. Tempers grew short. Everyone longed for a glimpse of sunshine or at least a temporary reprieve from the neverending rain.

"I wanted to hunt today." Alda slammed the shutter over her bedchamber window, closing off the dismal view of rain-drenched fields and low clouds. "I am bored. There is no pleasure to be had here at Wroxley, no entertainment."

"My lady," Donada said, "if you will stand still for just a moment or two more, I will be able to take the length on this new gown, so I can finish it in time for you to wear it at tomorrow's midday meal."

"Why should I bother?" Heedless of the damage her action might do to the unfinished dress, Alda threw herself onto the bed. "What difference does it make if I am well dressed or not? There is no one important to see me or to appreciate the pains I take with my appearance."

"My lady, everyone who beholds you knows that yours is a rare beauty," Donada said with careful patience. The glance she sent toward Mirielle spoke of her frustration with the irritable lady of Wroxley.

"If I continue to be so bored," Alda fretted, "I will soon develop wrinkles and gray hair."

"Nonsense," said Mirielle in a tone of fond teasing that did not convey what she was actually thinking. "Everyone who sees you remarks on your beauty and how fresh and young you look. This dreary weather has put you out of sorts. Alda, perhaps if you were to take over supervision of the meals, you might find the work would distract you from your boredom."

"Certainly not. That is your task, Mirielle. You must earn your keep if you are to remain here at Wroxley." With a long sigh Alda rolled off the bed and approached Donada. "Take the length and then

100

get out. You annoy me, Donada. You are always too serious."

Sighing repeatedly, Alda stood still while Donada marked the bottom of the dress with a round piece of chalk. Then she pulled off the garment and tossed it into Donada's arms.

"Go away and do not bother me again until the gown is finished. Oh, how I wish it were time to go to court!"

As was often the case, Mirielle did not know whether to dislike Alda for her selfishness or pity her for the character flaw that kept her always and only concerned with her personal comfort and her own needs. And as always in her dealings with Alda, Mirielle was aware of an undercurrent of aversion between them. Mirielle put it down to jealousy on Alda's part over the warmth that existed between Brice and his cousin.

"Where is Brice?" Alda demanded, making Mirielle wonder if the woman could read her thoughts.

"I believe he is with the captain of the guard," Mirielle replied.

"Find him. Tell him I want him to attend on me at once."

"I am sure Brice will come to you as soon as he can." The words were meant to calm Alda. Instead, they aggravated her already testy mood.

"I did not say, as soon as he can!" she shouted at Mirielle. "I want to see him now! Immediately! Do you hear me?"

"I heard you, Alda. I will find Brice and give him your message." Having witnessed Alda's tantrums in the past, Mirielle knew the time had come to get out of the room as fast as she could.

As Mirielle pulled the chamber door shut behind her, Alda shrieked in rage and something hit the door. By the cracking sound the object made and the seductive odor of roses that began to drift upward through the narrow space between the bottom of the door and the floor, Mirielle was sure the broken object was the bottle of rosewater she had brought to Alda only that morning. Undoubtedly, Alda would demand a new bottle once she had calmed herself.

"Let her wait," Brice said, after Mirielle found him in the great hall and told him of Alda's insistent command.

"She is in a high temper," Mirielle warned.

"What do I care?" And off Brice went with Captain Oliver by his side.

"If you are determined to play this dangerous game with Alda, then you ought to care when she is angry," Mirielle muttered to his retreating back.

The tensions of the last few days were wearing upon her spirit. Needing half an hour or so of quiet reflection, Mirielle was about to flee to the privacy of her workroom when she saw Hugh entering the hall. If he was looking for her, he might well search her workroom. She would have to find another place in which to be alone, for Hugh was one of the people whom she wanted to avoid. She was in no mood to fend off his subtle questions.

There was only one place in the entire castle where a mage was not likely to go. Since Wroxley lacked a resident priest, few people bothered to visit the chapel. To Mirielle it seemed the ideal spot for solitude. Hugh had apparently not seen her. Quickly she left the great hall, hurried across the entrance hall, and descended the inside staircase to a narrow anteroom. From this room one could enter the chapel or continue down the stairs to the crypt below. Alda's late father-in-law, Lord Udo, was buried in the crypt, along with his wife, his parents and grandparents, and a number of children from the family that held Wroxley for three generations.

The heavy chapel door squeaked a bit on its hinges as Mirielle pushed it open, but otherwise all was silence. Tall, narrow stained-glass windows set into the plain stone walls were the only decoration in the little chapel. On rare sunny days shafts of multicolored light coming through the windows made the chapel glow. Not so today. Lacking sunlight to bring it to life the stained glass was dark and muted. Nor was the rest of the chapel much more cheerful. The unused altar was a bare stone slab. The floor was made of polished stone. There were no cushions to kneel upon, no benches or chairs, not even candlesticks or a crucifix.

Yet here was the comforting peace that Mirielle sought. She felt it at once and the knots at her heart and in her stomach began to unwind. She went to her knees on the stone altar step and bowed her head.

How long she remained there she did not know. Nor was she able to formulate a suitable prayer. She was not aware of any prayers applicable to her immediate circumstances. All she could do was send a plea for help to the Presence she knew was with her in that place.

"Please, give me the patience to deal with Alda's jealousy and with Brice's stubbornness where Alda is concerned. Show me what I ought to do about those two men, Giles and Hugh, whom I am certain should not be here at all. Give me the courage to do what is right."

When she had entered the chapel she had not shut the door tightly after her. Through the slight opening she heard the soft scrape of footsteps on stone. Mirielle lifted her head. Someone was descending the stairs to the anteroom. At the level of the anteroom the footsteps paused before continuing down the next flight toward the crypt.

Mirielle got to her feet, her prayerful mood gone. On tiptoe she sped to the doorway to look out through the opening between the door and its frame. As she'd expected, the anteroom was empty. The footsteps stopped below, at the bottom of the stairs. Then a deliberate pacing sound reached her ears. Someone was in the crypt, walking among the marble tombs.

Her curiosity aroused, Mirielle slipped out of the chapel and went to the steps that led downward. She could see a flicker of candlelight below. There were tall, three-branched candelabra in the crypt, made by the blacksmith in Lord Udo's time because Udo went daily to the crypt to pray at his wife's tomb. As part of her duties as acting chatelaine Mirielle saw to it that fresh candles were always in place on the candelabra, with the flint and the wool lint necessary to light them close at hand, but seldom in these days did anyone pray in the crypt.

Mirielle went down the stairs as quietly as she could. At the bottom she drew into the shadow cast by the tomb of Gavin, the first baron of Wroxley. She knew his story, in part because Udo had named his only son after the man. Everyone in the castle knew the tale. The first Gavin had come to England with William the Conqueror and, like many other Norman warriors in that band of invaders, had won a title for his loyalty and courage. He had been given Wroxley because it lay in a rebellious area and William trusted him to bring it under control. Lord Gavin had held his lands with brutal justice. His tomb was a massive, shoulder-high oblong of stone with a harsh face carved onto the supine figure atop it, a fitting tribute to a man of iron and blood who had died in battle against rebels. Lord Udo had made his son the first baron's namesake in hope that the second Gavin would be as strong and valiant as his ancestor.

Mirielle peered around the corner of the first Gavin's tomb. On one of the candelabra all three candles had been lit. The flames sent a ghostly light across the stone walls and the low, arched roof. The other person in the crypt was standing beside the tomb of Lord Udo, a lower, less bulky place of interment than the block of stone behind which Mirielle was hiding. Seeing who it was, Mirielle pressed one hand to her lips to stifle her cry of surprise.

Giles put both of his hands on the tomb of Lord Udo in a motion that was almost a caress.

"Justice," he said in a low, passionate voice. "I will see to it. I swear by your own bones that I will not rest until all is put right and justice is done."

Giles lowered his head, standing in silence for a long time. Mirielle watched him, not moving, scarcely daring to breathe until, finally, Giles stirred and took a deep breath. Mirielle heard him walking away from Udo's tomb, but she could not see where he was going. Risking discovery, she looked around the corner of her hiding place. Giles now stood next to the tomb of Udo's wife. A sweet, sad smile curved his lips as he gazed upon the polished marble features of that former lady of Wroxley. His fingers lightly traced the contour of her cheek.

"I promise." Giles's whisper echoed against the stone vaulting. "I will not fail you."

A few moments later he snuffed the candles. By the dim light filtering down from the anteroom he made his way to the stairs and started up them. With one foot on the third step he stopped. Within the space of half a heartbeat he whirled, came back down the steps, and caught Mirielle, dragging her out of hiding and pulling her into the faint light. Mirielle had thought he was unarmed, but suddenly there was a dagger at her throat.

"God's holy teeth!" he swore. Recognizing her, he lowered the dagger. "What are you doing here?"

"I was in the chapel and heard a noise," she said, her voice shaking. "I—I thought perhaps one of the men-at-arms was meeting a lover in the crypt, which would be most inappropriate, and so I—" Seeing his grin and the way he was shaking his head, she cut off her hastily improvised excuses.

"Lady Mirielle, you are a bad liar. Nor are you much better as a spy."

"I was not spying! I did not know it was you, for you are reported to be sick in bed. I can see that you are not sick. I think you are the spy here."

"Why? Because, thanks to your excellent liniment, I have regained my health? Or because I have chosen to pay my respects to the last baron?" He spoke lightly, as if he were making a joke, but Mirielle saw no humor in his visit to the crypt.

"I wish you would tell me the truth," she said.

Giles had replaced the dagger wherever he kept it hidden, but he had not let go of Mirielle. She was still pulled tight against him, an arrangement that made her most acutely aware of his strength and his tough masculinity. Mirielle's hands rested on his chest, her fingers grasping the wool of his tunic. This position brought to her mind the scene in her workroom, when it had been his naked torso she touched. A wave of yearning swept over her. She forced it back, refusing to give way to her emotions.

"When you stood by Lord Udo's tomb, I heard you speak of justice," she said, hoping to prod Giles into revealing what she wanted to know.

" 'Tis only what all men desire," he responded.

"Please, just once, speak truth to me."

"Truth?" His blue eyes caught what little light there was. They glowed with passion and conviction. "In truth, I mean no harm to you, or to Wroxley and the honest folk who live here. You, and they, have nothing to fear from me."

"How I wish I could believe you." With an effort that cost her more than he could know, Mirielle wrenched herself free from Giles's embrace. "Whether you actually are a pilgrim as you claim, or whether you gained admittance to Wroxley by a lie, I cannot tell, but I am certain that you have remained here so long by deceitful means."

"If you think so, why haven't you warned your cousin Brice about me? Or if he will not listen to you, why not tell the captain of the guard?" His words were a soft taunt, echoing the question Mirielle asked herself each day.

"Is a warning needed?" A new voice intruded upon

the two in the crypt. Alda stood just above them on the steps. She was perfectly still, with not the slightest motion noticeable in her full skirts, which told Mirielle she had been there, listening, for at least several minutes. In the shadowy light Alda's face was also still, as if her features were carved out of cold, hard stone. Only her eyes were alive, blazing with a golden flame.

But there was no light in the crypt to reflect itself in Alda's eyes. With the candles extinguished, the only light was filtered down the stairway from the anteroom above. Seeing Alda standing like a statue, with her eyes aglow, Mirielle felt a chill. Then Alda lowered her eyelids and took a step downward toward the crypt and the illusion of her strange eyes was gone.

"What has Sir Giles done to make you mistrust him, Mirielle?" Alda asked.

"You misunderstood, my lady," Giles said at once, before Mirielle could respond. "Any fault here is entirely mine, but there is nothing in my mistake to cause distrust. Seldom have I been in so large and fine a castle. I was wandering about, which I confess I should not have been doing without a guide, and I lost my way. Lady Mirielle has just scolded me for intruding where I should not be. I believe she was about to lead me back to the great hall."

"You could have found the great hall yourself," Alda said, not troubling to hide her disbelief of this explanation. "It is at the top of these stairs, on the level above the chapel and just across the entrance hall."

"I thank you for the directions, my lady." Giles bowed to Alda. He held out his hand to Mirielle.

"May I offer you my arm to help you ascend the stairs, Lady Mirielle?"

"Mirielle will remain with me." Alda turned her blazing eyes upon him and spoke in a low, hissing voice. "Get you gone, Sir Giles."

For a moment the two stared at each other, Giles's blue eyes locked with Alda's golden brown ones in a tense battle of wills. Alda was still a few steps above him, looking down upon him with all the arrogance at her command. Never taking his eyes from hers, Giles slowly mounted the steps until he stood on the same step as Alda. Now he glared down at her from his superior height. Alda tilted her head so she could continue to look into Giles's eyes, but her steady gaze did not falter for an instant. It was Giles who broke off that fierce contest by moving his head to look at Mirielle.

"My lady Mirielle," he asked, "do you wish to come with me?"

"I believe Lady Alda wishes to converse with me in private," Mirielle said.

"You are certain you wish to remain?" Giles said.

"Of course." Mirielle summoned up a smile.

Giles looked hard at her. Then, with a nod, he went up the steps and disappeared from view. Alda ignored his going. When Giles's footsteps died away Mirielle was still standing on the floor of the crypt, looking upward at Alda. But Alda was not looking at her. Alda was staring at Udo's tomb, her face set in hard lines of either anger or disgust, Mirielle could not tell which. The silence grew ever deeper.

"You wished to speak with me?" Mirielle prodded, wanting to be done with the tongue-lashing she was sure would come. All the same, she was startled by the vicious tone of Alda's voice.

"Are you so desperate to have a man that you will lie down in a crypt with a stranger?" Alda demanded. "What will your cousin say when I tell him of this?"

"There is nothing to tell," Mirielle said stoutly. "I have done no wrong and neither has Sir Giles. You heard him. He lost his way—"

"I do not believe that and neither do you," Alda interrupted. Her eyes narrowed in speculation and a slow, crafty smile curved her lips. "Or is it Sir Giles's friend who intrigues you? I understand you spent an hour or two alone with him in your workroom the other night. A wooden table makes a hard bed, but then, if one is eager enough . . ."

"Stop it!" Mirielle cried. "I have lain with no man, and if you try to convince Brice that I have, he will believe me, not you."

"Do not be too certain of that, Mirielle. I saw you in Sir Giles's arms. If Brice were to learn of that, he might well kill the man." Suddenly, inexplicably, Alda shrugged. "Get back to your work. And do not let me—or any of my servants—see you loitering again with either of those worthless pilgrims."

"They are our guests." Mirielle stood her ground. "I have done nothing wrong, and you cannot prove that they have, either."

"I have dismissed you, Mirielle." Now Alda sounded bored.

Thankful that the scolding had not been worse, Mirielle hastened up the stairs, past Alda and out of the crypt.

When Mirielle was gone Alda descended the steps

to stand before Udo's tomb. Again she was perfectly still, as if she were listening for a sound that did not come. Finally, she spoke.

"What was that man doing here?" Alda whispered. "What could he hope to discover? There is nothing in this crypt but darkness and cold stone. So cold. So dark and empty. Why did Sir Giles challenge me that way? And the other, Hugh, I can *feel* him, searching, seeking. I am certain he has wrapped himself in a disguise I cannot penetrate. Who are these men?" She fell silent again, listening to the quiet crypt.

"Well, then," she said after a while, "I must discover if both are mages, or only the one. Only then can I understand what they have come to do. The best way to draw them out will be to bring down Mirielle. If I handle the matter carefully, I will destroy all three at once, which will leave Brice for me, alone.

"Poor, poor Brice," Alda said with a little, trilling laugh, "at my mercy without Mirielle's innocence to protect him from my hunger. What a delightful thought."

Chapter Seven

*"Evil people . . . deep down inside . . . believe
that they are without fault . . . As a result, the
people of the lie are continually running away
from their own consciences."*

—M. Scott Peck
The People of the Lie

"My lady." Giles seemed to materialize out of the
shadows. He put a hand on the door to Mirielle's
bedchamber, preventing her from closing it.

"You are indeed lost, Sir Giles, to find yourself in
this part of the castle." Mirielle pushed on the door,
trying to force it closed. Giles pushed harder, keeping it open. He was the stronger. Within a heartbeat
he was inside Mirielle's room with his back against
the door, blocking her escape.

"I wanted to be sure you were safe," Giles said. "I

112

was afraid of what Alda might do to you."

He must have seen the tears she was trying to blink away. He left the door to move to her side, to gather her into his arms and hold her against his chest.

"My dearest, what is wrong? What did Alda say?"

"She accused me of lying with you in the crypt. And also of lying with Hugh in my workroom." Mirielle had not meant to tell him, but she had been keeping too many conflicting emotions bottled up for much too long. It seemed altogether right to her that she should reveal her feelings to the man whose presence most disturbed her.

"No one who knows you would believe such slander," he said. "Everyone at Wroxley loves and respects you. Alda is not loved. Nor is she much respected."

"How can you know that?" she asked, her cheek still pressed hard against his chest. "You have spent only a few days in this castle."

"I do know it," he murmured. "I have eyes and ears, Mirielle. And I have a heart."

"I know. I can hear it." Mirielle was beginning to think that, though he was no mage like his friend, Giles was capable of working his own particular kind of magic on her. When he was present she found him irresistible and in his absence she thought of him far too often. She knew nothing could come of it. He would leave Wroxley in a day or two and very likely she would never see him again. It made no sense for her to be so strongly attracted to him.

She lifted her head so she could look into his eyes. If she was caught in a spell, it was a lovely one, fragile, tender, sweet . . . Giles's mouth found hers. Mirielle did not resist. Women who had spells cast upon them seldom could resist, perhaps because they knew it was useless to struggle against the inevitable.

Reality and imagination began to merge. Giles's arms tightened, his kiss deepened. Mirielle responded with her entire heart. Her blood singing, her thoughts spinning, she opened herself to him.

Giles began to caress her, his hands skimming over her shoulders and back and hips, up her spine and around, ending with one palm resting over her left breast. She was standing close enough to him to understand that his need was growing, and that he was trying to restrain it. She was not sure she wanted restraint from him, or from herself. He was the only man who had ever touched her so intimately, the only man ever to stir her heart and her hopes. She lifted parted lips to him, offering yet another kiss. His response was softer than she wanted, tender when she was just beginning to be aware of her own passion. It was almost as if Giles was saying good-bye.

"If my life were ordered in another way," he whispered, "I would not hesitate to make you my own in this hour, or to claim you before the world when I am . . ." He broke off, holding her a little apart from him.

"I will not do anything to harm you," he said. "You are dearer to me than honor itself. For your sake, I could forget all I am meant to do. When I look into your eyes, even a sacred trust seems unimportant."

"Giles," she asked, "have you taken a holy vow binding you to chastity? If so, you must leave me at once. I am not certain I can stand here with you, after the kisses we have shared, after the way you have touched me, and respect your vow."

"The only sacred vow I have taken," he said, "is a promise to uncover the truth no matter what the cost to me, in order that justice may be done. But there are other reasons, which I cannot tell you, that make it unsafe for me to involve you in my life. I wish it could be otherwise."

"I think I am begining to understand. You have undertaken a quest," she said. "A sacred quest."

"You could call it that."

"You should have told me so at once. If you had, I would not have asked so many impertinent questions or made false assumptions about your actions." She paused, searching his face, wishing she could see the features beneath his thick beard. "Hugh is acting with you, isn't he? He implied as much, but I did not hear the truth behind his words. I thought he was talking about the Ancient Art. Giles, tell me if there is anything I can do to help you?"

"It is possible that you are too trusting, Mirielle," he cautioned. "You may again be making false assumptions about me."

"I do not think so." She expected him to smile or provide some other sign of pleasure at her trust in him. Instead, he looked deeply troubled.

"There will come a day," he said, "when you may hate me for this moment."

"Giles, no." She touched his face, her hands lightly stroking his beard. "I could not hate you. Not ever."

"And when you do," he went on as if she had not spoken, "remember that I valued your virtue and your honesty. And remember this." His mouth brushed hers for the briefest of moments.

"If I do not leave now," he said, "I will forget all my good intentions where you are concerned. But before I go, a warning. Walk carefully here. Trust no one of whom you are not absolutely certain."

"I will take care. I beg you to do the same."

He touched her cheek with a quick, light caress, and then he was gone, leaving Mirielle to deal with an entirely new point of view regarding him—and with new fears.

As the hour for the evening meal approached, Alda arrived in the great hall asking the question so often on her lips.

"Where is Brice?" she demanded of Mirielle. "I gave you a message for him."

"Which I delivered promptly," Mirielle replied. "Brice has many duties and is not always free to stop when he might like."

"I am mistress here! I will tell Brice when to stop."

Alda turned away from Mirielle, her skirts swirling at the abrupt motion. With quick, determined steps she crossed the hall to where a group of men-at-arms stood talking together. They stopped their conversation as Alda approached.

"Where is Sir Brice?" Alda asked the men.

"When last I saw him, my lady," said one of them, "he and Captain Oliver were headed for the stables."

"Indeed?" Alda thrust out her lower lip. "What business can he have at the stables that is more important than my summons?"

"I do not know, my lady," the man-at-arms replied, but Alda was already headed for the door, leaving the men grinning and shaking their heads at the vagaries of their lady.

Thinking to calm the angry woman before she could reach the stables and take her ire out on Robin, Mirielle was about to follow Alda. She paused when she caught sight of Donada and Robin, who had just come into the hall through the screens' passage and the kitchen. At least they were both out of range of Alda's tongue. As for Brice, Mirielle decided that when his lover found him, he would have to take care of himself.

"Lady Mirielle," said Robin, coming up to her, "did I hear aright? Has Lady Alda gone to the stables looking for Sir Brice?"

"I believe so." Over Robin's curly head Mirielle met Donada's eyes.

"She won't find him there."

"What do you mean, Robin?" asked his mother.

"Sir Brice rode out early this afternoon with his squire," Robin answered.

"What, in this rain?" Donada cried. "He will take a chill and be sick for it."

"He said he needed exercise," the boy said. "Why shouldn't he ride, Mother?"

"Ah, well, who can blame him?" Donada sent another look toward Mirielle. "We are all weary and irritable after being indoors so much."

They separated then, going about their own chores. In the hall there was relative quiet for half an hour or so. Mirielle was giving last-minute instructions to a maidservant about the evening meal when a commotion at the entrance to the keep drew her attention. Above the calm tones of the captain of the guard, Alda's voice could be heard, issuing a

117

series of commands. Mirielle hurried to the entrance hall.

"He is to stay in the dungeon," Alda said to Captain Oliver. "Am I the only one at Wroxley with the wits to see that the man is dangerous?"

"Alda, surely, you are not talking about Brice?" Mirielle cried.

"I have not been able to locate your cousin, but I await with eagerness his reaction to what has happened, since the fault lies with you." Alda spoke to Mirielle in the same vicious tone she had used earlier that day while in the crypt. "You ordered those thieves admitted to the castle on your responsibility. This good watchman, who was on duty at the time, told me so." She waved a hand toward Mauger, who was standing just inside the keep door.

"My lady Alda means our two guests," Captain Oliver explained to Mirielle.

"Those men are up to no good," Alda declared, speaking loudly enough for everyone in the entry and the great hall to hear her. "I misliked their looks from the first moment I saw them. Earlier today I found Mirielle in secret conversation with the one who calls himself Sir Giles. Now, not half an hour ago, I found that same false knight, Giles, prowling around the tower of the inner gatehouse, where he had no excuse to be, and asking questions of the men-at-arms. When I accosted him and required him to tell me why he was there, he dared to laugh at me and claim that he had lost his way—for the second time in one day, mind you. I have ordered him imprisoned," Alda finished with a malicious look in Mirielle's direction.

From what she knew of Giles, Mirielle was sure

he had not been lost at all. Whatever he had been doing in the gatehouse, it was part of his reason for being at Wroxley. She could not help wondering why Alda had been at the main gate. It was not a location likely to appeal to the lady of the castle. Perhaps Alda had been following Giles. Perhaps she knew about Giles's visit to Mirielle's bedchamber that afternoon. Convinced that Alda had a purpose of her own for ordering Giles confined, and feeling as if she was caught in a net that kept tightening around her, Mirielle made the decision to trust her instincts and defend Giles.

"For no more than being lost and asking questions, you ordered a guest cast into the dungeon?" she cried. "Alda, that was not well done of you."

"I intend to have his friend, Hugh, incarcerated with him," Alda threatened. "Consider yourself fortunate, Mirielle, if you do not join them. More likely, I'll have you sent from Wroxley to walk barefoot to the nearest convent wearing only your shift, if I discover you have been in league with those two!"

" 'Twould be a great loss to Wroxley," Captain Oliver said beneath his breath.

"Alda, this is a most inhospitable way to treat guests," Mirielle insisted. "Nothing you have said offers any proof of a crime. There is nothing missing in the great hall. All of the silver is in place. See for yourself."

"Nor have I any report of weapons or armor lost," Captain Oliver added. "Not even a tunic is reported gone. I finished checking the castle's defenses less than an hour ago and all is well. My lady Alda, there has been no theft, and there is no sign of treachery from within or imminent attack from without our

119

walls. There is no reason to hold Sir Giles."

Alda dismissed these protests with a shrug of her shoulders. Stepping to the doorway into the great hall she looked around.

"I do not see Hugh in the hall," Alda said. "Mirielle, have you hidden him?"

"Certainly not," Mirielle declared firmly. "I have not spoken to Hugh for more than a day. And until I met Sir Giles by accident earlier this afternoon, it was my understanding that he was ill of the old wound that has kept him here and that his friend was entirely occupied in nursing him."

"Ill?" Alda's voice dripped scorn. "Ill, and yet well enough to wander about the castle, prying into corners and counting the men-at-arms we have to defend us? Ill, but neither one of them sending to you for any of your marvellous herbal medicines? Did you not wonder at that, Mirielle, when you are so famous at Wroxley for healing the sick?"

"They did come to me on the second day they were here, asking for my help," Mirielle said. "I provided some liniment then, but no medicines since."

"They came to you?" Alda took a menacing step toward Mirielle. "Where? To that secret room of yours? The one you keep so carefully locked? Those strangers to the castle knew the way to your workroom?"

"I believe one of the servants told them where to find it," Mirielle said. "Alda, I keep my workroom locked because certain of my medicines could be harmful if they are used by someone who does not know the proper dosage. And some of the preparations I make are meant to be used outside the body, rather than ingested. It is for safety's sake I keep that room locked."

"For *his* safety's sake, perhaps you have concealed Hugh there," Alda suggested.

"I told you," Mirielle repeated, "I have not spoken to Master Hugh for more than a day."

"My lady Alda," said one of the men-at-arms, coming up the steps and into the entrance hall from the bailey, "we have searched as you told us to do, but we can discover no trace of the man Hugh."

"Captain Oliver," Alda ordered, "call out all your men and find Hugh. Don't just stand there gaping at me. Do it now!"

"Yes, my lady." Beckoning the men-at-arms in the great hall to follow him, a frowning, openly disapproving Captain Oliver departed for the bailey.

"Not you, Mauger," Alda said when the watchman started to leave, too. "I have a special asignment for you. Choose four or five of your most reliable men and assemble them here. I will have orders for them."

"Aye, my lady." Mauger stuck his head out the door and yelled a few names to men in the bailey, calling them to the keep.

"Perhaps this search ought to wait for Brice's return," Mirielle said. She was growing steadily more and more uneasy, and she did not like the look on Alda's face. This hunt was prompted by more than mere suspicion on Alda's part.

"Do you think so?" With withering scorn Alda looked her up and down as if Mirielle were an ugly blot on the immediate landscape. "I rule here, not you. And not your cousin Brice, either, though he thinks he can rule me—or neglect me—as he pleases."

"Do not let your irritation with Brice make you mistreat and imprison innocent guests," Mirielle begged. "Alda, this is a serious breach of the customs of hospitality."

"It was not innocence that took Sir Giles to the crypt or to the gatehouse when he was supposed to be too sick to leave his bed," Alda said in a cold, tight voice. "Nor are you innocent in what is happening in this place. Mauger, where are your men?"

"Here, my lady." Mauger had assembled half a dozen of the biggest, most surly, and unpleasant of the men-at-arms.

"Come with me," Alda commanded. "Bring Mirielle along, too, whether she wishes to join us or not. Let us discover what secrets she is keeping."

"Alda, what are you going to do?" Mirielle asked.

"You will soon discover what I intend."

"Do as Lady Alda says." Mauger took Mirielle's arm in a tight grip.

"Unhand me!" Mirielle twisted and pulled against Mauger's greater strength.

"Better let her go, Mauger," advised one of his men, grinning. "I've heard she can cast spells. If you make her angry, she'll cast one over you."

"My cousin Brice will have you flogged when I tell him what you are doing to me," Mirielle said.

"More likely, Lady Alda will have Sir Brice flogged." But, whether from the threat of flogging or from his friend's hint of magical spells, Mauger did let Mirielle go. He gave her a shove between her shoulder blades to send her on ahead of him.

Alda paid no attention to this mistreatment of a

gentlewoman. She led the men-at-arms through the keep and down a flight of stairs until the group drew up before Mirielle's workroom. Mirielle was not at all surprised that Alda knew where it was.

"Open the door, Mirielle," Alda commanded. "I want proof that Hugh is not hiding in your room."

"The lock has not been tampered with," Mirielle pointed out. "Therefore, no one can be inside."

"Do you take us for fools?" asked Mauger. "Mayhap you let Hugh in, and then you fastened the lock again from the outside, to make us think he's not in there."

"Mirielle, if you do not open the door at once," Alda said, "I will send one of Mauger's friends for an axe and have the door chopped down. Much good your special lock will do then."

Mirielle was certain that, in her present mood, Alda would carry out her threat. With much trepidation, she began to unfasten the complicated lock. Fearing that Hugh might in fact have taken refuge in her workroom just as Alda suspected, and might then have used his skills as a mage to make the lock appear to be untouched, Mirielle worked as slowly and made as much noise as she could. She hoped thus to give Hugh ample time to make his escape. He was not a very large man. If he was inside, he could probably flee through the window into the inner bailey, where he would have to take his chances with the men-at-arms who were searching for him. Hugh might escape, but if he did not she would trust Captain Oliver to keep both of the prisoners safe until Brice returned. Unless, of course, Alda interferred—or Mauger, at her order.

"Will you hurry?" Alda exclaimed. "Mauger, you

open the door, if Mirielle will not do it."

"There is no need to damage either lock or door," Mirielle said, hiding her fear behind a mask of calm assurance. "It is open now."

Mauger's friends pushed her aside and rushed into the workroom. After a quick glance around Mauger flung open the shutter to look out of the window.

"There's no sign of Master Hugh in the inner bailey," the watchman reported. "He's not in here, either."

"What do you mean, he's not here? Of course he's here! Mirielle has hidden him somewhere. There must be a hiding place behind the shelves. Perhaps there is a secret room." With her lovely face contorted into a grimace of anger and distaste, Alda entered the workroom. She walked into it as if the floor were a bed of hot coals.

"Alda, don't be ridiculous," Mirielle said. "You know these walls are solid stone and rubble. There are no secret rooms—no, don't!" This last exclamation was directed at one of Mauger's men, who had just swept the contents of a shelf lined with pottery jars onto the floor so that he could pound on the wall at the back of the shelf. The man trod carelessly upon the fallen jars, their lids, and the spilled contents, leaving an assortment of broken pottery, dried herbs, and oils in his wake when he moved on to destroy the contents of the next shelf.

"Alda, make them stop," Mirielle pleaded.

"First, tell me where Hugh is hiding," Alda said. "I want that man found. I want to know his reason for coming to Wroxley."

"I have told you, I don't know where he is!" Mirielle wrung her hands at the destruction being wrought upon her workroom. Mauger's men were throwing every jar of herbal preparation they could find onto the floor. Taking open pleasure in what they were doing, they then went on to smash all of the glass vessels, and her wooden work table. Using the tongs Mirielle kept handy for her work with hot materials, they tore at the metal door of the furnace, breaking the hinges. Mauger himself pulled down the bunches of dried herbs from the rafters and threw them on top of the furnace where, after a moment or two, they burst into flames from the residual heat. One of the men grabbed the wooden box and dumped out the books and the scroll that Mirielle so treasured. Picking up the books, the man tore apart several pages before he let the scroll unroll onto the floor. The parchment was soon torn beneath the boots of Mauger's uncaring friends.

"Get that cursed cat out of here!" Alda ordered as the frightened Minn ran into the room to seek shelter under Mirielle's skirts.

"Leave Minn alone!" Goaded beyond endurance, Mirielle launched herself at Alda.

"No, you don't." Mauger caught Mirielle around the waist, preventing her from reaching Alda. "She gives the orders here, not you."

"Let me go!" Mirielle fought him but Mauger held her tight and Alda advanced upon her with hand upraised.

"You dare to defy me?" Alda's cold, controlled rage was more terrifying to Mirielle than her usual wild tantrums. Alda slapped her so hard that Mirielle was forced back against Mauger's chest.

"I'll have you whipped for disobedience." Again

Alda's hand connected with Mirielle's cheek. "I'll have your cat skinned alive and make you watch." Another slap followed.

"Stop this, Alda!" Before Alda could hit Mirielle yet again, Brice appeared in the doorway. He caught Alda's upraised arm, restraining her.

"Release my cousin!" Brice's dark eyes blazed at Mauger.

"Lady Alda gives the orders here," Mauger said again, still holding Mirielle tight.

"Have you forgotten that you answer directly to me, Mauger?" Captain Oliver stood to one side just within the doorway to let a dozen of his men-at-arms file into the room. "Neither you nor your friends have my permission to manhandle a noble-woman. If you value your lives, do as Sir Brice commands. Let Lady Mirielle go."

"Not till my lady Alda says so." Mauger remained defiant.

"Alda," Brice warned, "give him the order." His fingers tightened noticeably on Alda's arm. Alda winced. Not one man in that room, not even Mauger, objected to what Brice was doing.

"Let her go," Alda said to Mauger, speaking between gritted teeth. "I will deal with her later, in my own way."

With a show of reluctance, Mauger released his hold on Mirielle.

"You," Captain Oliver said to Mauger and his accomplices, "take yourselves to the gatehouse and wait for me there.

"Lady Mirielle," the captain of the guard said when Mauger and his men were gone, "I am sorry for the mistreatment you have suffered, and for the damage done here. I know how much good you do with your herbal preparations and now it looks to me as if we will all have to do without medicines until you can restore this room so you can make more of them. Shall I have my men sweep out the debris? Or would you rather have the maidservants to help you?"

"She will have no help," Alda declared. "Let the wench clean up her own mess. She defied me, Brice. I want her punished."

"Leave us, Captain Oliver." Brice was still holding Alda to keep her from attacking Mirielle again. "This is obviously a woman's quarrel. I will see it settled."

"As you wish, my lord." Oliver gave Mirielle a sympathetic look before he obeyed Brice's order.

"Now, Alda," Brice said, "what is the cause of this disturbance?"

"Your cousin," said Alda, still struggling against Brice's restraining hands, "your sweet Mirielle, has been scheming with those two strangers to hand over Wroxley to them. Hugh visits her here at night. I, myself, discovered her in the crypt with Giles. What could two people be doing in such a place but plotting?"

"Actually," Mirielle broke in, "at first Alda suggested a romantic reason for my accidental encounter with Sir Giles. Brice, you must know these accusations are not true. Please, order our guest released."

Over Alda's golden head Mirielle's eyes met those of her cousin. She saw that Brice did believe her rather than Alda. But in the next moment Mirielle also saw that Brice was not going to free Giles. Brice was so convinced that his hopes for future advance-

ment lay with Alda and Wroxley Castle that he
would ignore justice in order to keep Alda's favor.

Mirielle watched Alda wriggling and squirming in
Brice's tight hold. Alda's hair began to work loose
from its pins and fall about her face and shoulders.
Alda was panting, her breasts heaving as she twisted
and turned. Finally, Alda kicked backward, striking
Brice on the shin.

Shifting his hold on her, Brice caught a thick lock
of hair and used it to pull Alda's face around to his.

"Calm yourself," he ordered, "and then I will let
you go. You cannot walk through the keep in this
state. You will only embarass yourself."

Alda went limp in his arms, as if all the anger had
gone out of her. She leaned against Brice.

"That's better," he said, his hand against her
cheek. "Alda, my dear, you must learn to control
your temper."

Alda turned her face into Brice's hand. Opening
her mouth she bit him hard. Brice's howl of pain
filled the workroom, making Mirielle clap her hands
over her ears.

With his free hand, Brice grabbed Alda by the hair
again, forcing her to open her teeth and release the
hand on which they were clenched. In the next instant Brice picked Alda up and slung her over his
shoulder. She hung face down, kicking and yelling.
He gave her a hard smack on the buttocks.

"Oh, Brice, stop!" Mirielle cried.

"I will handle this." Brice looked angry, but in
control of himself. "You know nothing about such
things, Mirielle. Alda is often beside herself with
strong emotion. I know how best to calm her." Brice
surveyed the destruction in the workroom. "Call as

many servants as you need to help you here."

"She shall have no help at all!" Alda shouted from her head-down position over Brice's shoulder. "Let her get onto her knees and scrub the floor herself."

"Be quiet, Alda!" Another sharp smack on her buttocks sent Alda into renewed kicking and complaining. Brice only laughed, as if he were enjoying himself. "Don't worry, Mirielle, I will see to Alda." He disappeared out the door, still carrying Alda over one shoulder.

For the first few minutes after he'd left, the benumbed Mirielle could not move. After a while she groped for the overturned bench, found it, and set it upright. By then she was shaking so badly that she was forced to sit down on the bench. There she remained, with her hands folded in her lap.

"Brice," she whispered, "what is wrong with you? Can't you see that Alda is mad? What else can explain her rages, her disregard for anyone else, or her petty cruelties? The extravagant emotion she displays is not passion, it is madness, and it is destructive. Here lies the evidence, in this room, yet you imagine you can use her to gain your heart's desire."

Bending down, Mirielle picked up one end of the scroll that was lying at her feet. Her thought was to roll it up while smoothing out the creases and brushing off the dirt. But the parchment was so badly spotted that cleaning it was going to be difficult if not impossible, and some of the tears would require much time and patient gluing. Giving up her efforts, Mirielle sat still once more, the partially rerolled scroll dangling from her fingers, with one end of it falling off her lap and onto the floor.

* * *

In the room to which he had carried Alda, Brice was reaching much the same conclusion about Alda's mental state as Mirielle had done. He knew he would not be able to carry the yelling, struggling mistress of the castle through the corridors and rooms and then up several flights of steps to her bedchamber. It would be too undignified to try. Someone might decide to come to Alda's assistance. And it was growing more and more difficult to keep her slung over his shoulder when she persisted in fighting him. Sooner or later she was going to land on the floor and if she was hurt in the fall, the fault would be laid at Brice's door.

Over the past few weeks Brice had grown weary of his mistress's constant hysterics, though he did like the way she needed him so desperately when she was in one of her tantrums. His ability to dominate her was remarkably satisfying, but if she behaved like this once she was his wife, he would have to keep her locked in her room. At the present moment, he did the first sensible thing that came to his mind. He carried his scratching, kicking burden into a storeroom and tossed her onto a sack of grain. Kneeling over her, he caught her wrists, holding her down.

"Now," Brice grated, "explain to me why you attacked my cousin and let her workroom be destroyed."

"Because she is helping those cursed pilgrims." Alda spat out the words. "They are all three involved in a plot against Wroxley."

"Have you gone completely mad? Those men are harmless," Brice told her. "Where our security is concerned I am not as lax as you seem to think. I have had them watched since I first learned they had entered the castle. Captain Oliver agrees with me that their curiosity is perfectly natural. Sir Giles was once a fighting man before he was so badly wounded, and thus he is interested in talking to the men-at-arms. Master Hugh, on the other hand, is a scholar and has shown no interest at all in matters of defense. He is more absorbed with Mirielle's herbal healing. I tell you, Alda, your fears are groundless."

"And I tell you, those men are dangerous! And so is Mirielle." Alda could not reveal to Brice why she was so certain in her suspicions. Brice would not understand, and if he knew all that she was capable of and all that she had done, he would send her to the king for judgement. Alda shivered at the thought. Whether she was hanged or beheaded or only confined in a cell for the rest of her life, she would in the end be cold. And alone. In the dark. Forever.

"Hold me, Brice. Warm me. I am cold. And so afraid." The ploy worked. It always did. Brice could not resist the pleasure her body would give him. He released her wrists so he could work at his clothes, freeing himself for her. Alda grasped her skirts, pulling them upward to her waist. Moving around on the grain sack, she let him see what awaited him.

She knew he was greatly annoyed with her and so she expected—and hoped for—fierceness from him. Instead, Brice kissed her in a gentle way that told Alda he was trying to calm her fears.

The memory of another man drifted into her mind, of Gavin, her husband, kissing her in a similar gentle way and tenderly doing his youthful best to overcome the concerns of a girl who he believed was lying with a man for the first time. Gavin, himself still innocent about women if not actually a virgin at his marriage, had been unaware of how far short he had fallen in his attempts to please his new wife on their wedding night. Alda needed not gentleness or kindness to reach her fulfillment, but unrestrained passion teetering on the brink of violence.

Feeling Brice's hard masculinity pressing into her, Alda dismissed the memory of Gavin from her mind and concentrated all of her thoughts on her present lover, who was moving deeper in a bold thrust. Brice stroked her yearning center, warming her, allowing her to forget everything but the overheated joining of their bodies. Alda pretended to fight him, knowing her apparent resistance would force Brice to be rougher in his efforts to reach his own release. She cried out and struggled when Brice gripped her more tightly. Brice's insistent passion and his rough handling—yes, that was what she required. From Brice's hot desire she would draw the strength she needed. Alda moaned with the approach of her pleasure. She was no longer cold, and she no longer remembered her absent husband.

Chapter Eight

Mirielle was still sitting on the bench in her workroom when Donada found her. After a quick look at the room, Donada sat down and put both arms around Mirielle.

"Captain Oliver told me what happened," Donada said. "I will help you put this room to rights again. So will the others."

"Others?" Mirielle repeated with a bitter laugh. "Who will defy Alda? Even Brice gives in to her rages."

Mirielle fought the urge to rest her head on Donada's shoulder and weep. Crying would solve nothing. Having spent the last half hour trying to accept what had been done to her and to her workroom, she was convinced that there were unspoken reasons behind Alda's cruel actions.

When Mirielle considered the events of that day

she saw again the peculiar emptiness that lay at the core of Alda's character. On the surface Alda displayed a formidable selfishness. Beneath the selfishness lay an icy coldness and then . . . nothing. Try as she might to understand Alda and to make friends with her, Mirielle had never been able to reach Alda's heart. Now she thought that, while Alda might indeed be mad, madness was not the whole of it. Something far more terrifying than madness had caused Alda's outburst against her.

But far worse than any flaw in Alda's character was the change that had come over Brice since their arrival at Wroxley. Once warm and affectionate in the way a protective older brother might be, Brice was growing ever more distant with Mirielle. Knowing Alda was at fault in the destruction of Mirielle's workroom, still Brice had taken Alda's part. As a result, Mirielle felt abandoned by her nearest blood kin.

"Mirielle, you are shivering." Donada rubbed her hands. "Here, take my shawl."

"Blessed saints in heaven!" Ewain the blacksmith came through the door, followed by his wife. "Lady Mirielle, I heard the tale from an angry man-at-arms whose injury you once cured. He said you would need help, but I never expected to see this kind of damage. You would think an invading army had destroyed this room."

Close behind Ewain came Robin, accompanied by a few maidservants with brooms in hand. To Mirielle's surprise, three men-at-arms also appeared.

"Captain Oliver sent us," one of these men said to Mirielle. "We have his orders to do what we can to help you, my lady, and when we are finished we are ordered to stand guard at the door and not to let anyone enter whom you do not want in this room."

"Just tell us what you want us to do," Ewain said.

Mirielle looked around at them, seeing the friendship on their faces, seeing how willing they were to make up to her for what Alda had done, and for Brice's defection. They gave her hope. They needed her, not only for her healing skills, but for the balance she could provide against the violent swings of Alda's moods. From the trust and affection offered by these honest folk she would draw the strength to continue her work. They would succor and sustain each other.

"I can fix this with little trouble." Ewain picked up the furnace door to examine its hinges. His wife began to give directions to the maidservants, setting them to work with their brooms.

"We can have the carpenter in here tomorrow to repair those shelves," said one of the men-at-arms. "And while he's here, he can hammer this table together again. The planks are solid enough; they have only been knocked apart a bit. Most of the nails are still holding."

"Look," Robin cried, stooping down, "here's a jar that wasn't broken, and here is a lid that fits on it. There are still some dried herbs inside, too."

"I think there is much we can salvage," Donada added.

"Yes." Pulling Donada's shawl closer about her shoulders, Mirielle stood on somewhat shaky legs. She looked from face to eager face. "We have a lot of work to do. Let us begin at once."

It was late evening before all of the broken materials had been swept together and carried away by the maidservants. Every one of Mirielle's costly glass vessels was gone, but Robin had retrived several more whole jars from the debris, some of them containing usable herbs. Donada had carefully cleaned the remnants of the books and had made a start at repairing the pages torn out of them.

"Mirielle, I can finish the last of the work here, and these good men-at-arms will stand guard to keep everything safe," Donada said. "You must be weary after such a distressing experience. Why don't you go to your room now, and rest? In the morning you will be better able to think how best to go about restocking your preparations."

"Until this night, I never appreciated how kind you are, Donada." Mirielle did not say what else she was thinking, that Donada's calm and practical temperament must be a great relief to Brice after Alda's unrestrained emotions.

In her bedchamber, which was on an upper level of the tower keep, Mirielle lit an oil lamp, then poured water into a basin and washed her face and hands. She was tired, but she did not think she would be able to sleep. She had too much to think about, from Alda's accusations and vicious actions, to Brice's inability—or unwillingness—to defend the cousin he claimed to love, to Giles's incarceration.

She knew she would have to do something to help Giles. She could not leave him to Alda's mercy, or to Mauger's brutality. She trusted Captain Oliver to keep Giles safe through the night and that was the reason why she had not rushed to him as soon as Alda had left her workroom. She would walk carefully as Giles had warned her to do, and she would take no steps that might make his situation worse or cause Alda to prevent her from helping Giles, but in the morning Mirielle intended to speak to Brice about the prisoner. If her cousin was not amenable to releasing him and sending him on his way, then Mirielle would try to enlist Captain Oliver's aid. The captain of the guard was a decent man and he had not been pleased by Alda's mistreatment of a guest. Surely he would know of a way in which Mirielle could help Giles.

"Mirielle, please do not cry out." A soft voice interrupted her thoughts. From behind the bed hangings, a shape with a staff in its hand moved into the light.

"Master Hugh!" She kept her voice as low as his. "What a relief it is to see you. I am glad Mauger and his men did not find you in my workroom, but how did you reach my bedchamber without being captured?"

"By a method I intend to teach to you," Hugh said.

"Do you know Giles has been arrested on Alda's orders?"

"I do." Hugh drew nearer. "Mirielle, your assistance is vital to us."

"You shall have it, with one condition," she said. "I want to see you and Giles safely out of Wroxley, but I will not betray my cousin or cause trouble for him with the king. Brice has hopes of one day being rewarded for his fine administration of Wroxley Castle. Though he was not willing to stand by me this evening, I will not abandon him."

"Whether the recipient is worthy or not, your loyalty is admirable," Hugh said. "Giles and I have done nothing here that has not been approved by King

Henry. If your cousin has been an honest seneschal, then he will have his just reward."

"The king?" Mirielle repeated, surprised by this claim. "I did not know."

"Having heard rumors that all was not well at Wroxley, King Henry sent us here to restore the proper balance and order," Hugh responded.

"Considering today's events, it would seem you have failed," Mirielle said with a sigh.

"I am more inclined to consider what has happened as a useful delay," Hugh said. "I have learned that someone who is able to cloak himself from my discerning is working against Giles and me. His power is great, for I did not detect his presence until a few hours ago."

"Another mage? Here at Wroxley? But who is it? You cannot think I am that person," Mirielle cried.

"No." Hugh offered one of his quick smiles, comforting but too soon gone. "When I look at you, Mirielle, I see brightness surrounding you. There is no evil in your character. But there is another within the walls of this castle who walks away from the light. Unfortunately, I cannot tell who he is. The shadows with which he has surrounded himself are too dense. I only know that he is an implacable enemy to Giles and me, and he is working to prevent Giles's escape. That is why we need your help."

"You must leave Wroxley," Mirielle said. "I am sorry to say it, Hugh, but to save your lives, both of you must go."

Giles's leaving would rend her heart in two. In less than a week he had taken command of her hopes and all the sweet longings that had lain unexpressed in her heart until his coming. She was not sure she could survive without the sight of him each day, without the sound of his voice or the intense warmth of his embrace.

Still, Mirielle knew with an instinct she did not question that if Hugh and Giles remained at Wroxley, the shadowy force Hugh perceived and yet could not identify would destroy both men. In the process, it might also destroy Wroxley and all of the people there, including Brice, to whom Mirielle was still bound by family loyalty, whatever she might think of his personal decisions.

"Of course, I will help you," she said to Hugh. "Only show me what to do."

"I have seen the gesture you use to veil your identity," Hugh said.

"As I have told you, that gesture and the use of my crystal globe were all the magic Cerra had time to teach me before she died."

"Let me demonstrate the next step in your education." Spreading his arms wide, Hugh pointed his staff at Mirielle. Suddenly, where Hugh had been standing there was only a blur. A quick movement of the air and Hugh was back again.

"You can make yourself invisible!" Mirielle cried. "Master Hugh, what a remarkable achievement. Wherever did you learn it?"

"From one of my Saracen teachers," Hugh said. "I must caution you. Because the illusion requires so much of a practitioner's vital energy it lasts for only a short time and it can affect only a few people at once. You will have to concentrate all of your thoughts if you are to copy what I have just done."

"You expect me to . . . no Master Hugh, I am sure I cannot! I am only an herbal healer, with but one magical gesture in my learning. Besides, I have no staff."

"My child," Hugh told her, "you require no instrument to work your magic. It was born in you. I can see it, as I think your beloved Cerra must have seen it. That is why she planned to teach you all she knew of the Ancient Art."

"But I have never before tried to work such strong magic," Mirielle objected.

"Do as I have done. Spread your arms," Hugh instructed. "Make the gesture. And *believe.* You must be absolutely certain in your own heart that no one will be able to see you."

Mirielle told herself that if Cerra believed she could learn the Ancient Art, and if so great a mage as Hugh had faith in her, then she could do what Hugh was asking of her. The ability to make herself appear to vanish might be Giles's only hope of escape. She had to try. She had to believe that she would succeed.

Willing herself to disappear from Hugh's vision, she spread her arms as he had done and used her left hand to make a gesture similar to the one he had made with his staff. At once she felt a tingling in her fingertips and a sensation in her hair similar to the crackling that happened when she brushed it vigorously on a cold, dry winter's morning. She was aware of no other change, but when she lowered her arms a few moments later, Hugh smiled at her.

"Excellent," he said. "Together, we can rescue Giles."

"And then you must leave. Forever." Mirielle thought of all she would be denied by their going, of the love that might have been and of the learning

Hugh might have imparted to her. Her voice broke. "I will not see you again."

"Dear child," Hugh said, "you are still too young to know that even the saddest farewells are not final."

"You must not return!" she cried. "It will mean your lives if you do. And, Master Hugh, I know enough of magic to believe it will mean your soul if that creature of the shadows should win over you."

"When Giles and I have gone," Hugh said, "the dark mage may withdraw, thinking he has won. For your sake, I hope it will be so. I wish you could leave with us, Mirielle, but you are meant to remain here, at Wroxley. It is your destiny."

At least Mauger was not on duty. There was another watchman at the main gate, up on the battlements. With the drawbridge up for the night, the gate closed and barred, and sentries posted on the walls, the men stationed in the gatehouse felt themselves free to relax. They were playing a game with dice. No one looked up as Mirielle, using the disguise Hugh had taught her, slipped among the men and started down the stairs to the dungeon.

She was frightened and still somewhat unsure of the magic Hugh claimed she possessed. But she was not going to leave Giles to Alda's whims or to the merciless shadows that Hugh had recognized. Whether it cost her life, her newly stirring magical abilities, or even her soul, she was determined to set Giles free.

The dungeon was located directly below the main entrance to the castle. Because of their closeness to the deep moat, the gatehouse walls at this level glistened with dampness. A single torch burned outside the bolted dungeon door. Mirielle went to the door and slid back the bolt. She had to pull hard to make the heavy door open. Giles was chained against the wall, his wrists and ankles in shackles.

"Who is it?" he whispered. "Mauger? No, not Mauger. Hugh? Let me see you."

"It is not Hugh. It is Mirielle." She let her disguise slip then, being still too inexperienced to hold the illusion of invisibility in place while she proceeded to the next part of her mission.

"You should not be here," Giles protested, straining against the shackles.

"Hugh sent me to you. We have a plan." Mirielle drew nearer to him. She saw by the torchlight beaming through the doorway that someone had hit him several times. There were bruises around his mouth and beneath one eye.

"Captain Oliver never allowed you to be beaten," she muttered.

"He did not. It was Mauger who did it."

"Mauger? I thought he would be confined to his own quarters. Captain Oliver is angry with him."

"I know nothing about that," Giles said, "but Mauger must have a key to the dungeon, because he came into this cell to see me. He seemed to enjoy our visit rather more than I did, which is why, when you first opened the door, I thought he had come back to beat me again. Then I saw the light and realized it was you.

"Mirielle, I cannot think why Hugh let you come here. I wish you would go. If you are discovered with me there is no telling what might happen to you before Captain Oliver could come to your aid."

"Nothing will happen to me. I have Hugh's promise on that. Just hold still and let me work." Mirielle took from the ring on her belt the oblong metal object that Hugh had given to her. Following Hugh's directions she inserted it into the locks on the bands at Giles's wrists and twisted it.

"Now I begin to understand. Hugh has given you his wonderful key that will open any lock." Giles chuckled. "I have seen it before, on several occasions. Was it your idea or Hugh's to hide it in plain sight among all the ordinary keys you carry with you every day?"

"The idea was mine. There, your hands are free." She rubbed his wrists. "Those shackles were so tight."

"They are not meant for comfort. Wait, it will save time if I do that." Brushing aside her hands, Giles massaged his own arms and flexed his fingers. "If you will unlock these fetters so I can move my feet, then I will be able to defend you—and myself—if we are discovered."

Kneeling in the damp, moldy straw covering the dungeon floor, Mirielle unfastened the metal bands, releasing his feet. With his hands usable again, Giles massaged one ankle and foot, while Mirielle worked on the other until he could walk across the cell and back without discomfort.

"Where is Hugh?" Giles asked.

"He is attending to your horses." Mirielle straightened, ready to move on to the next task. She was puzzled when she first saw Giles closing the shackles. Then she smiled, understanding his purpose. "The guards will think you have escaped by magic."

143

"So I hope." He answered her smile with his own. "What next, Mirielle?"

"I am to let you out the postern gate," she said. "You will have to swim the moat, but Hugh wanted me to tell you that he will have dry clothes awaiting you. He will be in the forest, just beyond the village." '

"I suggest we leave this dungeon at once," Giles said. "You can give me the rest of Hugh's directions as we make our way to the postern gate."

"The directions I give you are mine," she informed him. "I know the landscape around the castle well, because I often roam over it looking for herbs. However, you are right about leaving the dungeon as soon as possible.

"Giles, you must stay directly behind or beside me," Mirielle went on as they looked out the door to be sure no one was about before they left the cell. Giles closed and bolted the door on the cell to give the appearance that he was still inside.

"That ought to confuse the guards and delay the search for me," he said. "Now, Mirielle, it is time for you to work your magic."

"Hugh showed me several times how to do this," she said, "but I warn you, I lack his great experience."

"Hugh once told me that you have powers of which you are unaware," Giles murmured. "If he instructed you, then I am certain of your ability, Mirielle."

"According to Hugh, that is the most important aspect of using any kind of magic," Mirielle said. "You must believe in it. There can be no doubt at all, or the magic will not work."

"I do believe in you. And I trust you completely."

She had not realized how close he was, but they had been whispering and their heads had gradually moved nearer so they could hear each other. Giles's lips were at her ear. His warm breath stirred a lock of her hair that had worked loose from its braid. She turned her head a little and his mouth was almost on hers. Giles drew a sharp breath.

"My lady," he whispered, "your sweet presence makes this rank dungeon seem like a bower filled with roses, but if we are caught here, it will become our tomb. I would far rather live without you than have you die with me. Show me to the gate I am to use and then I'll take my leave of you. I would not keep you in danger any longer than I must."

Mirielle raised her arms and made the gesture Hugh had taught her. To her surprise Giles put an arm around her waist so she was close against his side.

"Once, during our journey to England, Hugh and I escaped from a similarly difficult situation by leaving arm-in-arm," he said in explanation.

She was glad of his touch. It steadied her and gave her the courage she needed. They moved as one out of the dungeon and up the stairs, taking the same route by which Mirielle had come. The men-at-arms were still playing at dice. One of them looked up as Mirielle and Giles passed among them. The man squinted as if he thought he saw something but could not make out what it was. With a shake of his head the man picked up a wine cup and drained it, then went back to the game.

"Hugh has told me," Giles whispered, "that the disguise is not perfect, that the air seems to vibrate and to blur where the unseen person is."

"I noticed that effect when Hugh demonstrated his skill to me," Mirielle replied. "Giles, the wicket gate is the closest one but we cannot use it, because these men would hear it opening and know some mischief is afoot. Since we are not under siege there will be only a single guard who passes the postern gate each hour as he makes his rounds. That is the way you will leave, when the guard is far from the gate."

In fact, there were two postern gates at Wroxley. One had been built into the wall near the tower keep in case the lord of the castle and his family should have to flee during an attack. The other gate was located in the outer bailey and was intended for defending forces to use for secret, armed sallies against a besieging army. It was to this postern gate that Mirielle led Giles.

Leaving the gatehouse they hastened across the bailey. At this late hour there were few people about but all the same, Mirielle kept the cloak of disguise around them. It took all of her strength and concentration to do so and by the time they reached the door she sought, her step was faltering and her hands were shaking. It was Giles who took the key from her girdle and opened the door to a room set in an outward projection of the main castle wall. In this room the men-at-arms gathered for their final orders before leaving the castle to strike at besiegers. Here, lengths of boards nailed together in sections were kept, ready to be dragged out and linked together to span the moat so the men-at-arms did not have to swim as Giles would have to.

With a sense of relief, Mirielle let her disguise slip

away as soon as she was inside the room. Quickly she took yet another key and used it to unlock the outer door. At the same time, Giles pulled the door to the bailey shut. Now they were alone, visible only to someone standing in a direct line of sight across the moat.

Mirielle stood looking out at the water. The light of a full moon flooded into the room, so she could see Giles clearly when he came to stand beside her while they exchanged keys, Mirielle returning the one Hugh had entrusted to her.

"I wish you did not have to take your leave on such a bright night," she said. "You must use extra caution not to be seen."

"I wish I did not have to leave at all." His arm was about her waist again. Mirielle leaned against him, her heart beating slowly and painfully. Only a few more moments and he would be gone.

"You are rightfully an enchantress," Giles murmured. "Since first I saw you, I have not ceased to think of you, and now I cannot bear to part from you." Pulling her closer, he lowered his head.

His mouth was as Mirielle remembered, a rich, warm delight on hers. Opening her lips she drank him in, the warmth, the taste, and the manly scent of him. She reveled in the length of his strong body against hers. His hair was thick and soft when she wound her fingers through it. His mouth on her eyes, her cheeks and throat, and then on her lips again brought her to the trembling brink of total abandon. She had never known desire for a man before Giles had come into her life, but she had recognized it at once and she understood now how it could make an ordinary life beautiful—or entice and destroy those who gave way to it at the wrong time.

"We must stop. Please, Giles." Tears of regret filled her eyes. She did not want to stop. She wanted the most intimate embrace of all. She felt the languid heat flowing through her veins, urging her to hold him more closely, to keep him with her.

"You are right," he said. "We are not likely to be discovered where we are and that is a great temptation. But every moment that I linger only puts you in more danger. And Hugh will risk his life to wait for me until I join him, when it would be safer for him to be away from here at once."

He held her face between his hands. She clutched at him to keep herself from falling to her knees and begging him never to let her go, to stay with her, to take her with him.

"Giles." She saw in his moonlit eyes a longing that matched her own. If she cared for him, she must not cause him greater pain. She nodded her acceptance of this ending, the motion scattering her unshed tears across her cheeks. "Only kiss me once more and then go."

His warm lips brushed across hers for a moment too brief and too sweet to ease the ache in her heart.

"Do not forget me," he said.

"Never." She broke away from him, turning from the light in his eyes that offered all she wanted as a woman, knowing she could not have what he offered. For her, there would be nothing more than these few moments, already gone, already in the past.

"Farewell." He went through the door. It was only a few steps to the edge of the moat. Giles lowered himself into the black and silver water. Praying that no guard patrolling on the wall would notice him, Mirielle watched the shadow of his head moving across the moat. She could not see him pull himself onto the opposite bank, but as she stared into the night she thought she saw a motion, as though a hand were waving to her. Only then did she close the postern door and lock it.

She paused just long enough to cloak herself in disguise once more before hurrying across the bailey toward the inner gatehouse and then on to the tower keep and the safety of her lonely bedchamber.

Chapter Nine

"I will send to Lincoln or Nottingham—even to London if need be—to find new glass vessels for you, Mirielle. I have ordered the castle potter to make clay jars in the sizes you require. I promise, this room will be restored to its former state."

Brice stood in the workroom looking as if he had just returned from battle. Mirielle suspected that Alda had allowed him little sleep the night before. To add to Brice's weariness he, Captain Oliver, and two dozen men-at-arms had spent most of the day scouring the territory around Wroxley Castle in a fruitless search for Giles and Hugh.

Giles's daring escape had caused a sensation because no one could guess how it had been done. Neither the guards in the gatehouse nor the sentries on the walls had seen or heard anything unusual. Both the bolt on the dungeon door and the shackles that had secured Giles's wrists and ankles were still in place and locked when his absence was discovered shortly after dawn.

As for Hugh, no one could recall seeing him since noontime on the previous day. A tale was circulating that Hugh had somehow left the castle unseen during the daylight hours and had gone to a safe place, from where he had whisked his companion out of the dungeon by magic.

"I am sorry for the damage done here." Brice ran a hand through his hair.

"In the future," Mirielle told him, "I expect you to keep Alda away from me and out of my workroom. She is not to interfere with my duties as chatelaine, nor will I allow myself to be treated as her servant any longer."

"You need have no concern about Alda," Brice assured her.

"If she will not agree to these terms," Mirielle went on as if her cousin had not spoken, "then let her assume her rightful place as chatelaine with all the duties that position entails. I will then leave Wroxley and take myself to a convent to live."

"We have always agreed that you would be unhappy in such a life," Brice said. "With no dowry to donate to the Church, you would be looked upon as nothing more than a servant there."

"Better to be merely unhappy and a servant to the Church than tormented as I have been for the last few days," Mirielle snapped. When Brice still looked doubtful, Mirielle continued, "If your claim that you know how to control Alda is true, then you can do this for me, Brice."

"I need you here, Mirielle. We all need you."

"Alda does not think so."

"I will speak to her." With a final, pleading look in Mirielle's direction, Brice left her.

It was amazing, Mirielle thought, the changes that had been wrought in her in one week's time. She was no longer naive. She saw Brice much more clearly and understood him better, she had made a dear friend in Donada, and her knowledge of the magical arts had been greatly increased.

Most important of all, she had met Giles. In him she had found the love for which she had always longed and together they had tasted passion. Parting from Giles had been the most painful farewell she had endured since the deaths of her family and Cerra, but in his leaving she had the comfort of knowing he still lived and that she had contributed to his safety. Though they might never meet again, her love for Giles would burn forever in her heart, sustaining her through the lonely years ahead.

"I am glad those two men have gone," Alda said to Mauger. She paced restlessly across the formal garden, trailing her long skirts through the March mud. "I do not care if Captain Oliver finds them. Let us hope they never return."

"Do you imagine they will not?" Mauger's attitude was anything but respectful toward his liege lady. "You are more foolish than I thought. What, I ask you, is to become of Mauger the watchman? Captain Oliver does not love me. Not that he ever did, but now he cannot bear the sight of me."

"He will not dismiss you, Mauger. I will see he does not. Now, go away. I want to think."

"We would be better off if you had stopped to

think during the past week," Mauger said. "Those two strangers frightened you until you lost your wits and took foolish action."

"I said, go away!"

"Aren't you cold?" Mauger paused at the gate in the palisade around the garden to send a malicious glance at Alda. "Since you are always complaining about the cold, I would not expect you to stand here so long in a freezing March wind, arguing with me, especially when you know I am in the right." When Alda did not answer him and gave no indication that she was aware of his continued presence, Mauger gave a contemptuous laugh and strolled off in the direction of the outer bailey.

"Yes, I am cold," Alda muttered, "but I will be warm soon enough. Brice will warm me and give me some of his strength. But later. First I must think."

Through the gate that Mauger had left open Alda glimpsed the hem of a brown skirt as its wearer hurried into the mews directly across the bailey. The sight distracted her from the problem she ought to be considering.

"Now, who was that?" Alda asked herself. "Is the falconer holding an assignation in the mews? If he is, it will disturb the falcons, which will annoy Brice."

She was about to leave the garden to investigate when Brice came out of the keep and made for the mews. Alda drew back, hiding behind the fence. Brice disappeared into the mews. Immediately, Alda decided that whatever was going on over there was intensely interesting. She made her way across the bailey. She did not have to go inside the mews.

One of the shutters had carelessly been left open. Alda had only to stand outside it to hear what was said within. At first what she heard made her angry, but as she continued to listen she began to smile.

"Well, Brice," she said in a low, deadly voice, "now I learn that you have withheld some part of your affection from me and given it to Donada. No, no, that will not do. I require your complete devotion.

"But how convenient," Alda went on. Knowing if she stood too long where she was, someone in the inner bailey would surely notice and remember her presence by the mews, she began to walk toward the keep, still speaking to herself. "Just when I was trying to devise a way to punish Mirielle for defying me, Brice himself has put the means of punishment into my hands. Mirielle and Donada have become such good friends of late that Mirielle would be heartbroken were anything to happen to Donada. Mirielle would do everything she could to help her friend. And then there is that brat, Robin. Harm done to him would hurt both Mirielle and Robin's loving mother. Now, where shall I begin? The mother or the son first? The mother or the son?"

Chapter Ten

"Tell us everything." In the only private chamber in the inn at Nottingham, Hidern and the other squire, Bevis, attended their lord and his friend, Hugh. Bathing facilities were nonexistant at the inn, but the squires had managed to commandeer two jugs of hot water from the inn's owner and, from one of the kitchen wenches, two large mixing bowls to be used for basins. The squires carried with them at all times their lord's supply of cedarwood-scented soap and clean towels. Two sets of fresh clothing were laid out on the bed.

"Aye, my lords, do tell us about your adventures." Bevis handed a towel to Hugh. "Was your spying successful?"

"We learned all that two men could be expected to learn before the time arrived when it was wise for us to leave," Hugh responded.

"Which means they found you out," said Hidern, grinning. "Was there a fight? How I wish I could have been there."

"I am sorry to disappoint you," the nobleman said, his words muffled by the clean shirt he was pulling over his head. "There was no battle."

"Will there be one when we go back?" Bevis wanted to know. "You are going to return, aren't you, my lord?"

"With all my men behind me," came the response. "Hugh and I will rest from our recent travels for a few days, during which time we will make our preparations. Find a barber, Hidern, and bring him here in the morning. I will need to be shaved and to have my hair cut. Bevis, order a good meal for us tonight. Roast beef, if you can get it." At his nod of dismissal, the squires went off to carry out their respective orders.

"While they are gone," said Hugh, "I will walk about the streets of this fair town, to hear what conversations are being held."

"You did that for two days before we rode to Wroxley," came the response.

"It may be that a word heard here, or another there, will make more sense to me now that I have been to the castle." Hugh looked at his companion with serious eyes. "We had to leave her there, my friend. We could not jeopardize the task we were given. As you have seen, two men can melt into the forests and reappear elsewhere. If they are not found, eventually the search for them will end. Add a woman to the group and the men must travel more slowly and stop more often. Thus, they are more likely to be overtaken. Nor will the search ever end when a lady is concerned."

"I know. It was the only thing to do." The nobleman's expression was as bleak as his words. Hugh watched him for a while longer and then left him in peace, for which the nobleman was grateful.

He freely admitted to himself that he had overstepped the boundaries of his own plan by all but seducing Mirielle. He regretted what he had done only because he knew she would be hurt when the next step was taken.

In all his scheming and thinking on how to accomplish his task while causing the least amount of harm to innocent people, he had given no thought to the effect his efforts would have upon his own emotions. Try as he might to convince himself that deceiving Mirielle had been necessary to get the information he needed, he knew that he had taken entirely too much pleasure in his brief moments with her. Now, he found her lingering in his thoughts.

He wanted her. And he wanted no one else. He had seen below in the common room of the inn the tavern wenches who were available should he choose to crook a finger to any one of them, and those women disgusted him. After touching Mirielle, with her gentle heart, her sweet face, and clear, pure eyes that mirrored her every emotion—after kissing Mirielle—how could he take a tavern wench to his bed? For the rest of his life it would be Mirielle, or no one.

He prayed he would be able to keep that silent vow. For there was a chance that, in order to learn the full truth he had been sent to discover, he was going to have to take physical possession of a woman he did not desire. If he did so, the act would destroy any hope he might have of earning Mirielle's love.

"I stand balanced on the edge of a sword blade," he sighed. "To fulfill what she has chosen to call my *guest*, I may have to lose Mirielle. But if I do not do what I came from King Henry's court to do, I may lose her anyway, and justice will lose, too. Evil will win."

When he closed his eyes he could see her face again, drenched in moonlight as they made their farewells. His heart sat heavy within his breast, his soul cried out to the one woman whose love could save him from a lonely life. But his body was prepared for battle, his face grim, his mouth tight, his hands flexing on the pommel of his sword.

"Oh, Mirielle, Mirielle. . . ."

Chapter Eleven

More than two weeks had passed since the false pilgrims, Giles and Hugh, had overstayed their welcome at Wroxley Castle and then left most unceremoniously. Several days' search had revealed no sign of either man. The servants and many of the men-at-arms still spoke with lowered voices about the amazing manner in which Giles had disappeared from the dungeon and they were convinced that the two men were wizards, who had used their magical abilities to fly far away to some distant land. If the seneschal of Wroxley, or Captain Oliver, or either of the two ladies living in the castle thought differently, they did not say so. In fact, they did not speak of the departed strangers at all. While Mirielle continued her duties as chatelaine, Alda withdrew into her private chamber, appearing only for the middday and evening meals, during which she did her best to ignore Mirielle's presence.

By the end of March, spring began to touch the land around the castle. The pastures turned pale green, while in the cultivated fields pease, wheat, and barley were sprouting. Buds were swelling on trees and badgers were stirring. The birds had begun to return from warmer climes. During the few days when there was no rain and the clouds lightened a bit, butterflies and bees also took wing, dining on nectar from the earliest primroses or the flowers of coltsfoot and ground ivy.

Knowing how the weather could change with little warning and, in the area around Wroxley, usually change for the worse, humans were more wary of venturing out than the other creatures. It was still too early to begin the traditional spring cleaning of the keep and muddy baileys, and in both the castle and the village just down the road from the castle, winter sicknesses lingered.

Donada was not feeling well. Her appetite was poor and she had grown pale and listless, not at all like her usual energetic self. Mirielle insisted her friend must take an herbal preparation which, so far, had done little to alleviate the ailment. There were several other castle folk with similar complaints. Putting the illness down to weariness at the end of a long, damp winter and the effects of a steady diet of salted or dried foods, Mirielle dispensed tonics with a free hand and assured the patients they would feel better when summer weather came to stay and fresh food was once more available.

Busy though she was in these weeks, still Mirielle could not stop thinking about Giles or wondering where he and Hugh might be. She missed him with all the sadness of a woman who knew she would never again see the man she loved. The knowledge that she was responsible for his safe escape was poor comfort when her heart was aching. Struggling with her pain, telling herself she must go on, Mirielle threw herself into her daily work. But that work only filled the daylight hours. Each night she retired to her room, where no one but Minn could see her, and there she wept from loneliness and from a pervasive fear for Giles.

There came a night when the need to know if he was safe overcame her and she took out the crystal globe. Holding it up before the single oil lamp that lit her bedchamber, Mirielle sat down on her bed, steadying her elbow on her knee.

"I understand Cerra's warnings about not using my power for my own benefit," Mirielle whispered. "But please, just this once, let me see Giles, or at least something to show me he still lives. I promise, I will not ask again."

The crystal glowed in the lamplight. Mirielle held her breath, staring into the sphere in her palm, concentrating. Slowly the crystal clouded with swirls of thick gray. Through that drifting mist a man stepped. As always, he wore a hooded black cloak. But this time, for the first time in all her visions of him, the hood was pulled back just enough for Mirielle to see his face.

In the gray dimness of the crystal sphere, wherein everything else constantly shifted and changed shape with the movement of the fog, the man's features were curiously distinct. His brow was wide and high, his nose long and straight, his jaw square.

Seldom had Mirielle seen a jaw so determined. The man's mouth was a hard slash to match the firmness of his jaw. She could not see the color of his hair or his eyes.

In a mysterious way that Mirielle could not explain even to herself, those features were familiar to her. She frowned, concentrating still harder, certain that in a moment or two the memory would return to her and she would recognize and understand. . . .

"Meow?" Minn jumped onto Mirielle's lap, purring.

Mirielle jerked in surprise. With the shifting of her concentration from the crystal sphere to the cat, the vision in the sphere vanished.

"Oh, Minn, how could you? Now I'll never know what might have happened. There was something in that vision I needed to learn and, thanks to you, it's gone." Still purring, Minn pushed her head against Mirielle's arm. "Go to sleep, you silly cat," Mirielle said, choking back tears of disappointment.

Knowing the vision would not return and feeling oddly tired from her efforts, Mirielle put the now-empty orb away and got into bed. Minn settled down at her side, curling herself into a furry ball. Mirielle scarcely noticed. She dropped into a deep, dreamless sleep from which she did not awaken until well past her usual hour the next morning.

That day the weather turned unseasonably warm, though the constantly threatening clouds still lingered. In midafternoon Mirielle set out for Wroxley village. She went on horseback, taking Robin with her. No men-at-arms were necessary for so short a trip in the heart of Wroxley lands.

Mirielle knew Robin was worried about his

mother's illness. Having lost his father to sickness only a little more than a year before, the boy quite naturally feared the loss of his remaining parent. Mirielle hoped an hour or two outside the castle might cheer him up.

As it happened, the diversion did not take as long as Mirielle had planned. After visiting all of her patients, she and her youthful companion turned homeward through the forest rather sooner than Mirielle had anticipated. She sought for an excuse to keep Robin distracted awhile longer.

"Let us stop by the stream," she suggested. "It is pleasant to be outside the castle walls after being enclosed for so many days. I was beginning to feel like a falcon confined in the mews. I yearn to fly free before returning to my perch."

They dismounted to drink from the stream and while Robin watered the horses, Mirielle sat upon a dry rock. She lifted her face into the warm, damp breeze. Without warning she discovered it was all she could do to keep from crying. Her aborted effort to learn Giles's whereabouts from the crystal sphere had saddened her greatly.

With a sigh she told herself it was unlikely that she would ever know what had become of Giles. She would be wise to accept that fact and make her peace with the life heaven had allotted to her. The love of a man, children, her own household to manage were all blessings denied to her, but still she could make a useful place for herself. She did have a few treasured friends at Wroxley, on whom she knew she could rely. When Robin started whistling a funny little tune, her spirits began to rise and she tried to turn her thoughts to more cheerful matters than the sad absence of the man who held her heart.

The castle had been peaceful for weeks. Alda had been in a remarkably mild temper of late, perhaps in anticipation of the journey to court that she and Brice would make in another month, when they would leave the castle in the care of Mirielle and Captain Oliver. And, thought Mirielle, if Brice and Donada were continuing their liaison, they were being remarkably discreet about it. Clearly, Alda did not know of it, or she would have created a screaming scene with Brice, and Donada would have been turned out of Wroxley with her son. Mirielle thought about the busy spring to come and hoped there would be no new disturbances.

"My lady." Robin stopped his whistling to break into Mirielle's daydreaming. "I can hear horsemen coming this way. We should return to the castle at once."

"Horsemen?" Mirielle repeated, at first unwilling to give up the pleasant thoughts she was determined to keep in mind. Then, noting Robin's serious face, she returned to reality. She listened for a moment until she, too, could hear the steady drumming of horses' hooves along the castle road. "It sounds like a large group of men. I fear they are coming too fast for us to reach the castle before they do."

"Then we must hide. I do not think these can be friends." Robin's gray-green eyes were round in his pale face. "If a large group of visitors was expected, you would know about it so you could have food and beds prepared for them. It is my duty to keep you safe, my lady, but I am sorry to say I have no sword."

"You needn't worry, Robin. We are a good twenty

feet off the castle road and if you stand here beside me, next to this rock—"

"My lady, the rock might hide us if we crouch down behind it, but those men will certainly see our horses!"

"They will not. Come here." Mirielle took the reins from the boy's hands, pulling the animals toward the rock. "Stand close beside me, Robin, and keep still. Now, you must be absolutely certain in your mind that we will not be seen."

"What are you going to do?" Robin whispered, as if the oncoming horsemen were close enough to hear.

"Do you trust me, Robin?"

"Oh, yes, my lady. With my life."

"Then do as I tell you and we will be safe."

Mirielle waited until the troop of horsemen was in sight before she spread her arms. Reminding herself that this was something she could do so long as she *believed* she could do it, she concentrated as Hugh had shown her how to do on the night when she had released Giles from the dungeon. She moved her left hand and the two horses went perfectly still, as if they were frozen where they stood. Mirielle gestured again, including Robin and herself in the spell. All that was left was for her to believe, and wait, and maintain her concentration when the horsemen drew nearer.

There were at least two dozen riders. The first man, a squire who rode a little ahead of the others, bore an upright lance from which fluttered a blue-and-green pennant with an identifying device sewn onto it in golden threads. The squire went by too quickly for Mirielle to see the device clearly. The other men in the troop were mostly knights, with a few squires included. They looked ready for battle, with mailed coifs raised and rounded metal helmets on. Every man had a sword belted at his side. There were maces attached to their saddles, several men carried battle axes, and one or two even had dangerous looking metal stars on chains, but this band of warriors brought with them no siege machines. On they came, riding hard, their cloaks billowing, the horses sweating and throwing up chunks of mud from the wet road.

The troop swept right past the spot where Mirielle and Robin were standing. With one exception, none of the riders gave any indication that either woman or boy, or their statuelike horses, had been seen. The exception was a man riding half a horse's length behind the leader of the troop. This companion to the leader turned his head suddenly as he went by, as if he perceived that he and his fellow riders were being watched. For an instant the man looked directly at Mirielle.

Hugh!

Mirielle almost lost her concentration, almost allowed Robin and the horses and herself to be seen. Unlike the others in that troop of fighting men, Hugh did not wear armor. He was richly dressed and the face he wore was a visage Mirielle had never seen before. Still, she knew him, and she knew that, despite the aura of invisibility she had pulled around herself and Robin, Hugh had seen the two of them standing there, beside the rock.

Who were the men with whom he rode? Was Giles among them, hidden behind one of those metal helmets? If so, why were the fugitives risking a return to Wroxley?

Breaking the spell, Mirielle stood with one hand at her throat, staring after the horsemen as they pounded down the narrow road. She did not know whether to be terrified or wildly happy at the possibility of seeing Giles again. She feared she would be drawn into whatever he and Hugh meant to do at Wroxley. There might be danger to Brice, danger to herself. She did not care. All she could think about was Giles, his kisses, his strength.

"My lady?" Robin dared to touch her arm, a sure sign that he was frightened. "Do they mean to attack the castle?"

"There are too few of them for that," Mirielle responded. "I see no sign of more men coming after that first group, or of war machines, either. I think they expect to gain easy admittance to Wroxley."

"We should return at once," Robin said. "We may be needed. My mother—"

Mirielle understood the thought Robin did not finish. If there was going to be trouble at Wroxley, he wanted to be at his ailing mother's side. For her part, Mirielle wanted to find Hugh and demand of him an explanation for his sudden reappearance in a new guise. Most of all, she wanted to find Giles, if he was in fact among that troop of knights. At the very least, if Giles was not present, Hugh could give her news of him.

Quickly Mirielle and Robin mounted and rode to the castle gate. There, above each tower of the gatehouse, new blue-and-green pennants were being raised. The light breeze caught the fabric, making it billow so that Mirielle could make out the golden device embroidered at the center of each pennant: a single scallop shell.

The main gate stood wide open. Through it Mirielle could see signs of extra bustle in the outer bailey, with a dozen lathered horses being walked by squires and stableboys. The mounted troop had gained ready entrance.

Mauger was the watchman on duty at the gatehouse and he was more surly than ever.

"You shouldn't have been out," he said to Mirielle in a rude voice. "You'll be needed inside, to see to food and beds for the new men-at-arms."

"Who are they?" Mirielle asked.

"The squire who rode first shouted the news to one and all," Mauger told her, in a sour way that vividly conveyed his opinion of these unexpected events. "The leader of the troop is Gavin of Wroxley, our new baron, returned from the Holy Land after eleven years' absence."

"I am so glad you are here." Donada met Mirielle at the entrance to the tower keep. "I have told the cook to prepare the finest feast she can on such short notice, but I am certain you will want to give additional orders. The water is being heated now for baths. We ought to air the lord's chamber and have fresh sheets put on the bed. If you will give me the keys to the linen press and the lord's chamber, I will see to it." Donada pressed a hand to her pale forehead.

"What you will do," Mirielle told her, "is lie down for a while. If Lord Gavin wishes to arrive unannounced, then he cannot expect us to be waiting for him, can he?"

Mirielle sent Donada off to her room, then began to issue orders to nearby maidservants. She tried not to show her impatience with the duties requiring her attention, when all she wanted to do was rush into the great hall to find Hugh, so she could ask where Giles was. Her instructions to the servants completed, she stepped through the arch into a group of unfamiliar men-at-arms, who at once moved aside to allow her to pass into the great hall.

Brice stood before one of the huge fireplaces, talking to two men. One of them was Hugh. While Brice spoke to the second man, whose back was toward Mirielle, Hugh fixed her with a warning gaze. A slight motion of his head, a movement of one hand, and she understood that he wanted her to pretend she did not know him.

Questions crowded her mind. Who was that second man, still with his back to her, engrossed in conversation with Brice? Where was Giles? Had he returned with Hugh, or not?

And then, by the shape of the unknown man's broad shoulders, by his height, and by the expression on Hugh's face as he looked from her to the tall newcomer, Mirielle knew the answers to all of her questions.

Before Mirielle could say or do anything, Alda came into the room. She was still gowned as she had been for the midday meal, in bright blue silk, with her hair bound up beneath a sheer white veil and the wide gold circlet of her station sitting upon her smooth brow.

"Brice, what is happening here?" Alda demanded, marching toward him with arrogance in her every step. "The servant who gave me your message said

169

only that I was commanded to present myself in the hall at once. I warn you, Brice, I will not accept such a summons from you. *You* are to come to me when *I* call."

"Sir Brice did not send for you." The man standing with Brice and Hugh turned around, allowing both women a full view of his features. "The summons was mine."

Mirielle stood frozen as if caught in a trance. The stranger's brilliant blue eyes were fixed on Alda, a diversion that gave Mirielle a chance to study the man. His hair was cut short so it just reached his earlobes and he was clean-shaven. With the thick beard gone, Mirielle could see his features in all their chiseled strength.

A strangled sound from Alda made Mirielle tear her gaze from the man's face. Alda's face was chalk-white. She struggled for breath.

"Gavin!" Alda gasped. "But . . . but . . . you are dead!"

"As you can see," the man said, his face and his voice both strangely hard and cold at this reunion of husband and wife, "I am not dead. I have returned at King Henry's behest, to take my rightful place as baron of Wroxley."

Alda fainted.

Mirielle wished that she could faint, too, that she could sink to the floor of the great hall as Alda had done, and thus blot out all questions, all doubts and fears, at least for a few moments. For Giles—*her* Giles—was not Giles at all. He was Gavin of Wroxley, son of a line of fierce warriors, and he had won her heart with lies.

She could not imagine what he would do next.

She expected no mercy from this cold, self-contained man who was truly a stranger to her. One thought nudged at her mind, terrifying her. While secretly at Wroxley to spy, Gavin had learned of Alda's adulterous affair with Brice. Surely, now he would have Brice cast into the dungeon to be tortured and executed, or would challenge Brice to combat, or, at the very least, would expel his wife's lover from Wroxley Castle in disgrace. Mirielle could tell that Brice had no inkling of his fast-approaching fate. Fear for her cousin was a fist clenched in the pit of her stomach. Her worst nightmare was coming true.

The most recent scene from the depths of her crystal globe was becoming real, too. For the man she had seen only in mysterious visions, whose hauntingly familiar but unrecognized face she had clearly glimpsed for the first time on the previous night in her crystal globe, was Giles without his heavy beard—and Giles was Lord Gavin of Wroxley.

"There is no need for a welcoming feast this night," Gavin said to Mirielle. "Save it until tomorrow at midday. Merely be certain my men have what food they want and make the best guest chamber ready for my friend, Hugh. See that he has whatever he needs to make him comfortable. All I will require for myself is bread, a piece of cold meat or a wedge of cheese, and a pitcher of wine. And a hot bath."

"Yes, my lord." Mirielle looked directly at him, not ashamed to let him see how frightened and angry she was. Gavin looked back at her with the same hard expression he had shown to everyone else in the great hall.

She was not surprised that she was the only one who recognized him. Gavin of Wroxley stood straighter and, therefore, appeared to be taller than Giles the pilgrim had been and there was about him an air of stern command. The beard, of course, had been an excellent way to cover his face, but his hair was a darker shade of brown than she remembered. Thinking about the difference in color, she concluded that his hair had been bleached by the burning sun of the Holy Land in much the same way in which linens could be bleached by sunlight. When the barber had shorn his hair, the bleached strands had been removed, revealing the darker layer of hair beneath.

Nor did anyone appear to recognize Hugh. He maintained the altered face that Mirielle had noticed at her first sight of him on horseback, and his bright green tunic and hose were very different from the dark robes he had worn on his previous visit. As for the name he continued to use, it was a common one. There were at least three Hughs among the servants and men-at-arms living at the castle.

"I will be in my chamber," Gavin said to Mirielle in a voice that carried across the hall. "Your cousin tells me you are serving as chatelaine, so I expect you to bathe me."

"I?" Mirielle was on the verge of declaring that he could bathe himself, when he spoke again.

"I also expect Lady Alda to attend me. See that she does. I am certain she has recovered promptly from her swoon, so I will accept no excuses from her." With those words, Gavin stalked out of the great hall.

"I hate this room," Alda said. She stayed near the door, as if she would leave on the slightest pretext.

"I am surprised to hear it." Stripped to the waist, Gavin prowled about the lord's chamber, lifting the lid on a clothing chest to look inside, testing the softness of the newly made bed, peering into corners. Idly, he slid the bedcurtains closed, then opened them again. "I should have thought, Alda, that the moment my father died, or as soon as he was buried at the latest, you would have moved yourself and all your belongings in here. It is much the best room in the castle. With two pairs of windows there is plenty of light, and these braziers make it warm enough even for someone like myself, who is accustomed to the heat of the Holy Land. And there is privacy here.

"Why didn't you take this room, Alda?" Gavin paused to watch her reaction to the question.

So did Mirielle. She was directing the servants who were preparing Gavin's bath. A large wooden tub had been dragged up the steps and into the room, a sheet had been draped over the tub to prevent splinters from causing damage to the baron's most private parts, and now buckets of hot water were being poured into the tub.

"This was your father's room," Alda said to Gavin. "He always despised me."

"If that is true, why did he arrange our marriage?"

Alda looked startled at this question. She shook her head, sending furtive glances around the room as if she expected to discover the ghost of Lord Udo waiting to confront her.

"Udo died in this room, in that very bed," Alda said, pointing.

"Alda," Mirelle spoke up, "only the wooden frame is the same as in Lord Udo's time. The mattress, the hangings, and the linens are all new. I saw to the changes myself."

"I will not sleep here," Alda repeated. "Not ever. Nor will I stay in this room any longer." She reached for the latch to open the door.

"Then you will force me to join you in whatever lesser bedchamber you presently occupy." Gavin's palm slammed flat against the wood just above Alda's head, keeping the door closed.

"No!" Alda cried. "You are a stranger to me. I have not seen you for eleven years."

"After sleeping alone for so long a time you ought to be eager for my embrace."

Mirelle wondered if she and Gavin were the only ones who appreciated the full irony of his statement. Alda's wild words and Gavin's cool response to them aroused open interest in the servants who had by now dumped all of the buckets of hot water into the tub.

"My lord," said Mirelle, "I think these servants should leave your room. And so should I go." She could not look at him. She could not bear to think that he would lie with Alda and assert his rights as Alda's husband. Gavin knew that Alda and Brice were lovers. Did he hope to reclaim his wife's devotion? His treatment of Alda so far did not suggest that this was his plan. Or was he going to punish Alda in an intimate way that Mirelle could not guess at? She could not be certain what this new version of Giles, this Lord Gavin, would do.

"The servants may go," Gavin said. "You are to stay here, Mirelle." The instant he removed his hand from the door, Alda jerked it open and ran out of the room. Seeing the fierce look on Gavin's face, the servants quickly followed their mistress. Gavin closed the door again after them.

"Which leaves only you to help me bathe," he said to Mirielle. When she did not answer him, he resumed his wandering about the room.

"I assume that this chamber has been thoroughly cleaned since my father died." Gavin paused, brows raised, awaiting her response.

"Lady Alda ordered the room locked after Lord Udo was buried." Mirielle spoke through stiff lips, wondering what he really wanted of her and determined to provide as little information as possible. "Since my coming to Wroxley, it has been scrubbed and new bedding brought in, as you heard me tell Alda. I have ordered it aired and dusted at regular intervals. In case you should finally decide to return home," she ended sarcastically.

"I did not really expect to find anything useful here." Gavin stopped his pacing to stand close to Mirielle. "I can guess at your feelings," he said.

"Can you, my lord?"

"You are angry. You believe your trust in me was betrayed. You wonder if I kissed you only to gain information from you."

"That is a fair description of my present emotions, my lord. With one minor omission."

"And what is that?" He dared to touch her cheek in a soft caress. Mirielle drew in her breath, shocked at her warm reaction to him when she was so angry.

"I regret helping you to escape," she said.

"If you knew everything—"

"But I do not," she interrupted. "I know only that

175

you deceived me and everyone else at Wroxley. You abused my trust in you to gather information for your own purposes. Oh, I wish you had not returned! Before this day I was able to think of you with kindness, and with sorrow that we would not meet again. Now I know what a liar you are."

"This is my castle," he said in a soft, dangerous voice. "I hold it in fief from King Henry. I have Henry's prior consent to everything I have done here, and everything I intend to do in the future."

"After the way you have treated me, how can you expect me to believe you again?" she cried, her thoughts in painful turmoil.

"Believe this." He caught her by the elbows and when she tried to pull away, he only drew her closer. His hands slid down her arms to grab her wrists, to force them around his waist until she was embracing him. Then he kissed her.

Mirielle knew she ought to fight him, but she could not. She had ached for his kisses since their moonlit parting at the postern gate. She had fallen asleep each night thinking of him, wishing he was with her. The touch of his mouth was as necessary to her as the air she breathed. When he released her wrists, her hands slipped upward along his spine, tightening their embrace. The pressure of his lips on hers increased and Mirielle opened her mouth, accepting him. Gavin groaned softly and fitted himself even more closely to her. They stood thus, straining against each other for a long, breath-stopping time, until Gavin loosened his hold on her enough to enable him to speak.

"I have not deceived you about my feelings for you," he whispered, his lips still against hers. "I have wanted you since that first evening, when you stopped me from chasing after Alda and Brice. I want you still, Mirielle, though my desire for you could endanger all I mean to accomplish."

"I will not forgive your deception so easily, my lord. Nor will I believe what you say to me now." Though she was aching to remain in his arms, she pulled away, stepping out of his embrace. Her next words broke her heart, but she had to say them, if only to remind herself of the truth he had apparently forgotten. "This night you must go to your wife and lie with her. Perhaps you will give her another child."

"Or, perhaps not." The tenderness was gone from his face. "I do not give you permission to leave me. Come, Lady Mirielle, it is your duty to help me bathe." In one swift movement he pulled off his lower garments to stand naked before her.

Mirielle had seen unclothed men before. She had often attended guests in their baths. It was a polite custom of hospitality. Guests were almost always wise enough not to take advantage of the opportunity, and there was usually a servant or two close at hand to act as chaperone against improper advances.

Never had Mirielle seen a man as well made as Gavin—or one so obviously aroused. She did not know where to look. Wishing there were half a dozen servants in the room with them, she ran her tongue across her dry lips. Frantic for some action to take her thoughts away from forbidden desires, she snatched up the jar of bath herbs and began to sprinkle them into the water.

With lordly indifference Gavin did not appear to notice either his condition or Mirielle's quickened breath. He waited until she had finished with the herbs and stirred the water before he stepped into the tub.

"Ah, this is wonderful." He grinned at her as if he had no worries at all, no faithless wife, no deceitful seneschal who had made a cuckold of him, no castle chatelaine toward whom he had admitted lustful desires—and no lies he ought to explain to the woman who had trusted him. Gavin sat back in the tub, basking in the hot water and the fragrance of the herbs. "You may wash my hair first, Mirielle."

The man was maddening. He must know what he was doing to her. Mirielle was sorely tempted to dump the bowl of gelatinous soap over his head and tell him to wash his own hair. Then she thought of a better idea. On several occasions she had watched Donada scrub a wriggling, unwilling, and very dirty Robin after a boyish escapade. Repressing a mischievous smile, Mirielle knelt beside the tub, rolled up the loose sleeves of her gray woolen dress, pushed the tighter sleeves of her linen underdress above her elbows, and went to work on Gavin in the same energetic way in which Donada washed her son.

"Yeow! There's soap in my eyes." Gavin wiped at his face with a soapy hand. "Ow!"

"Keep your eyes closed," she advised. There was a pitcher of hot water set by the tub, to be used for rinsing. Mirielle poured part of the water over Gavin's head, sending a fresh cascade of soap suds down his face. Enormously satisfied by his continued grumbling about the soap, which according to him was in his eyes again, she began to scrub his shoulders, arms, and chest.

"I'll have no skin left when you are done," he complained.

"Why, my lord, I thought you would be glad to be rid of all the dirt and dust of that long journey from the Holy Land," she said. "If you will sit forward, I will wash your back next."

"What, and leave it as raw as if I had been flogged?" he exclaimed. "Have done, Mirielle. God's teeth, woman, if you scrub my belly any lower, I'll be completely unmanned!"

" 'Twould serve you right if you were."

Her rage at him partially assuaged by his discomfort and by her vigorous activity with soap and cloth, Mirielle sat back on her heels, her fingertips still on the edge of the tub. Gavin's blue eyes—admittedly somewhat reddened by the harsh soap she had used on him—met hers. His lashes were much too long for a man, and they were spiky from his dousing with water and suds. He looked like a chastened young boy, much like Robin after he had been scrubbed and scolded. A bit more of Mirielle's anger drained away.

"Circumstances forced me to lie to you," Gavin said. "I did not expect to find a woman like you at Wroxley when I first came here. I thought keeping the truth from you would protect you." He took one of her hands and began to kiss it, until Mirielle pulled it away. But still she knelt beside the tub, near enough to him to lean forward and kiss his lips if she wanted. Her own lips parted softly at the thought, until she thrust it away with a resurgence of anger. Gavin's words were sweet, but he had lied before; therefore, he could lie again. He might be lying now.

179

"My dear lady," he whispered, "will you trust me once more, just for a while longer?"

"I cannot. It hurts too much to discover that you have been lying to me. I could not bear it a second time. From now on, if you expect me to believe what you say, you will have to offer proof."

With no warning he stood, water sluicing off his muscular form and splashing onto the floor. Mirielle looked up at him. His masculinity was so formidable that she began to tremble. A part of her wanted him to pick her up and and carry her to the huge bed that dominated the room, to lie there with her, kissing her and slowly undressing her, making her his. Rocked by her own lascivious thoughts yet still distrustful of his motives, she turned her eyes away from him. When she looked back he had a linen towel wrapped around his waist. It covered him to the knees, but it could not smother the flame of her longing for him. Again their eyes met, and Mirielle knew that Gavin was fully aware of her tangled emotions.

"My lord." Brice was knocking at the door. "May I speak with you?"

All the lingering boyishness vanished from Gavin's face. He was the tough warrior and lord of the castle once more, a man who hid his true feelings behind a mask of practiced dissimulation. With absolute lack of concern for his unclothed state, Gavin strode in towel and his bare feet to the door and flung it open.

"Come in, Sir Brice."

"Thank you, my lord. Oh, there you are, Mirielle. One of the maidservants was looking for you." Brice accepted his ward's unchaperoned presence in the baron's bedchamber with perfect calmness.

"Lady Mirielle has been extending the castle's hospitality to me," said Gavin. "For which I do thank you, my lady. Seldom have I been so well-scrubbed, not even in a bathhouse I once patronized in Constantinople."

"I shall take that as a great compliment, my lord." Mirielle waved a hand toward the center of the room. "I will send servants to remove the water and tub."

She did not ask his permission to leave. She simply went.

Chapter Twelve

"My lord," said Brice, "I hope now that you are at home again, you will retain me as your seneschal."

"Do you, indeed?" Gavin folded his arms across his bare chest and tilted his head to one side as if he were observing a newly discovered insect. "Why should I do that, Sir Brice?"

"As you will find when you examine your ledgers, I have been an excellent steward of your interests. The lands around Wroxley are greatly improved since I came here." Brice went on to describe all the changes for the better which he had effected. Gavin was silent, listening, giving no indication of what he was thinking.

"I will consider the matter," Gavin said when Brice finally ran out of words. "For the present, you may continue to act as seneschal while I make myself familiar with my barony. If I am pleased with what you have done, and if you and I get along well together, then perhaps I will keep you here permanently."

"Thank you, my lord."

Gavin saw the flare of hope in Brice's eyes. Was the man an utter fool, to think someone would not tell the lord of the castle about his affair with Alda? Or that Gavin would not then feel compelled to take some action against him? Brice must know it would happen soon. Gavin gave him grudging respect for his courage in staying on at Wroxley, when staying might mean his death. Or was there some other reason for Brice's self-serving appearance in the lord's chamber?

"You may leave me now," Gavin said.

He did not want to kill Brice, but it was better if Brice did not know that. For Mirielle's sake, Gavin would avoid shedding her cousin's blood. If he could; if Alda and Brice together did not force him into a confrontation he did not want.

Mirielle. The mere thought of her set his blood aflame. She was an impediment to his plans, to all he was pledged to achieve, and his growing desire for her led him to acts of astonishing stupidity.

What had he been thinking of, to remove his clothes before Mirielle and demand that she bathe him? He had never in the past shown an inclination toward the kind of self-inflicted torments of which anchorites and flagellants and other religious fanatics were so fond. Yet in the last hour he had voluntarily subjected himself to the most exquisite torture. Wanting Mirielle, he had insisted that she repeatedly touch his unclothed body. His lips lifted in genuine humor at the memory of how rough she

183

had been. But he had seen in her eyes that, though she no longer trusted him, she wanted him as much as he wanted her.

The need to lift her in his arms, to take her to his bed and make long, slow love to her until their hearts merged in a glorious fulfillment that would wipe out all deception—that need had almost overpowered him. He might have given in to it if Brice had not come knocking at the door of the lord's chamber to promote his own interests.

And so, Gavin thought, *the man who has cuckolded me has unknowingly prevented me from making his cousin my mistress. There's irony for you.*

Now I, who am half mad with longing for one woman, must pretend desire for another, whom I do not want. I must do it and make her believe it! But I am not sure I can do it. And what will happen if she decides to accept me back into her bed? Oh, Mirielle, sweet lady, my task would be so simple if it were not for you.

Alda's bedchamber was entirely too warm. To keep it that way six braziers glowed with red-hot charcoal. When Gavin let himself into the room a maidservant was tossing juniper branches onto the coals to scent the room.

Alda was still wearing her blue silk gown, but the maid had unpinned her hair from its tight braids and had brushed the golden tresses until they fell in a smooth slide over Alda's shoulders and down to her waist.

Gavin noted that Alda had nothing at all on under her dress. Thus, it was easy to appreciate her figure. Which, Gavin guessed, was the purpose of her habit

184

of wearing only the scantiest amount of clothing, a habit that would have shocked any honorable noblewoman.

For a woman who had borne two children and who was approaching her twenty-eighth birthday, Alda's figure remained remarkably youthful. Her breasts were small and high, and Gavin could see her nipples rubbing against the light silk whenever she took a breath. Her abdomen was flat beneath the blue folds of her skirt, and he remembered that her legs were long and graceful. Once he had taken great pleasure in caressing Alda's legs. Now, he saw the petulant line of her mouth and the frown on her brow that marred her otherwise perfect beauty.

She disgusted him. He wanted to leave her chamber and never set foot in it again. He wanted to send her far away from Wroxley. But first, he had to fulfill his commission from King Henry.

"What do you want?" Alda did not trouble herself to be polite to him, not even with the maidservant watching and listening.

"As I have this day reclaimed my castle," he said, "so I am here to reclaim my rights as your husband."

"I told you, no." Alda's mouth twisted in a decidedly unattractive way.

"You have no right to deny me." Gavin looked from his wife to her maidservant. "Leave us," he said.

"Stay here." Alda countermanded Gavin's order. Confused, the maidservant looked from husband to wife.

"Leave," Gavin said between gritted teeth, his eyes on Alda. The servant fled before the contest of wills could continue.

"It is clear to me," Gavin said when they were alone, "that you have done much as you please over the last eleven years."

"I have not! Your father allowed me no freedom at all."

"Then," said Gavin, considering with great care the meaning of each word he used, "you have enjoyed the freedom you want only since my father's death."

"I do not know what you mean by freedom. I am a near prisoner here, in this dreary place. The only pleasure I have is in my too-brief days at court each year."

"You will not be going to court this spring," Gavin informed her. "I have already paid the days I owe to King Henry for this year and he has agreed that I need not return until the spring of next year. Since I am not going to court, you will not go."

"You would take every pleasure away from me!" Alda cried. In sudden fury she shouted, "You despicable man! I hate you!"

"So you used to tell me when we were younger," Gavin said, "though I have never understood why you should dislike me so violently. I tried to be kind to you."

"Kind?" Alda snarled. "I do not want a man to be kind. I want passion. I crave excitement. You never gave me pleasure."

"Perhaps because you did not strike a note of passion in me," he said. "There is nothing unusual in that. Most noble marriages are founded on friendship between two families, or upon their mutual interest in land or a title. Love between the husband and wife requires time to grow. You were raised to duty, as I was, and duty claims our days. All the responsibilities of our noble estate give meaning to our lives. And there are many compensations. Tell me, Alda, where are the children?"

"What children?"

She was staring at him as if he were a madman and Gavin knew she did not understand, or chose to reject, everything he had just said to her. In truth, he was not sure he believed his own stern words. Not after holding and kissing Mirielle.

"*Our* children," he said to Alda. "Yours and mine. Where is Warrick?"

"Your son," Alda responded in a voice full of malice, "is a page at Cliffvale Castle, in Lancashire."

"I know where it is," Gavin said.

"From the reports I have had of him," Alda went on, "Warrick is not well-behaved. In that, he is much like his father."

"What of the other child?" Gavin asked, discounting her last remarks as intended to provoke him. He would not allow Alda to make him angry. "When we parted eleven years ago, you were with child for the second time. Or so you claimed when you refused to lie with me on my final night at home."

"You mean, on the night before you left me!" she cried.

Gavin did not tell her what he was thinking, that months before his leaving it had been clear to him and should have been clear to her that they would never deal well together. The young man he had once been could not bear Alda's shrieking rages or her insulting complaints about his masculinity. Having provided his father with the healthy future heir Lord Udo wanted and with Alda carrying a second child, the younger Gavin had believed that the kindest thing he could do would be to take the cross and leave England. If he were killed on crusade, Alda would be free to marry someone more pleasing to her. In the meantime, his father would take care of Alda and her children, and Udo was strong enough to keep Alda under control.

The older, wiser Gavin knew he had run away from an unhappy marriage. In his youth he had been a coward in the face of Alda's ever-increasing fury, and all the honors and wealth he had won for his valor fighting in the Holy Land meant nothing in the face of that cowardice. Gavin was convinced that everything that had gone wrong at Wroxley was his fault, because he had not been there to prevent it. Now, all he could do was try to put things right.

"Was it a son or daughter you bore?" he asked his wife. "Alda, did the babe live?"

"It lived." Alda glared at him. "It was a girl. Udo had chosen names for his expected grandson or granddaughter. He insisted if the child were a girl it should be named Matilda, for your mother."

"I am glad." Gavin smiled at her. "She must have been a joy to you. Alda, I thank you for my daughter. Where is little Matilda now? I would like to meet her."

"I refused to name her as Udo wished," Alda said. "Your father was away from home when she was born and I had her privately baptized before he could return to prevent me from doing as I wished. Her name is Emma."

"I see. There must have been a quarrel about that, when he learned what you had done."

"The child scarcely mattered." Alda lifted her chin

as if she were still defying her father-in-law. "It was my first victory over Udo. That was all I cared about. Later, there were . . . other victories."

"I am sorry if you got along with my father no better than you did with me," Gavin said. "You have not told me where Emma is. I want to see my daughter."

"You will have a long journey for that." Alda's smile was drenched in wicked glee.

"Why? Did she die in childhood?" Young children often died. Gavin knew a moment of grief for the child he had never seen, until Alda spoke again. Then Gavin thought he had never before seen or heard such malice in any human.

"Emma is very much alive. She is ten years old now and also fostering at Cliffvale Castle with Warrick. For reasons I cannot comprehend, she is on excellent terms with her half-brother."

"Half-brother?" Gavin repeated, trying to make sense out of Alda's words.

"Welcome home, Gavin." Triumph filled Alda's voice; malice still curled her lips. "I have dreamed of this moment for years. You can thank my parents for their vigilance in the months just before our marriage. Because of the close watch they kept on me, Warrick is most assuredly your son. However, your control over me was somewhat lax, especially when we were at court. As a result, Emma is not your daughter."

Gavin could not speak for a long time. He just stared at her.

"I could divorce you for adultery," he finally said. "The Church would allow it."

"I should much prefer that you rid yourself of me

on the grounds that I was not a virgin when we wed," she told him.

"I did wonder," he said. "But you pretended so well and at the time, I was still enchanted by your beauty. False loveliness, as I now know."

"Do it, Gavin. Have the marriage declared invalid from the first," she dared him, mocking him with her laughter. "Make bastards of both children. Then that stupid brat, Warrick, will not inherit anything of yours or of Udo's."

"I can understand a girl's distaste for a husband who was chosen to suit her parents rather than herself, but how can a mother dislike her own children?" When Alda only laughed again and did not answer the question, Gavin asked another. "Who is Emma's father?"

"I will never tell you, no matter what you do to me." Alda was still smiling, still laughing at him. "Come now, kind-hearted Gavin, will you destroy a little girl's life by publicly proclaiming her mother an adulteress? And just think of the effect on Warrick, who dotes on his sister. No, I see in your face that you will not set me aside. I thought not. The shame would be too great for you to endure."

"Do not forget," Gavin said in a quiet tone designed to hide all he was feeling, "that I have spent a decade in the Holy Land, where the Saracens are famous for their subtle, prolonged, and incredibly painful tortures. You do not know me at all, Alda."

He saw fear touch her lovely face, before she recovered her self-possession enough to laugh at him again. She took a deep breath, thrusting her breasts against the silk of her dress, letting him see her hard little nipples.

"Tell me, Gavin," she purred, "do you still wish to claim a husband's rights over me?"

"I would as soon make love to a moldering corpse," he said, and left her.

In her workroom Mirielle brewed a kettle of hot water with dried mint and lavender flowers. When the infusion was ready she drank a cup of it, wishing it were instead some of Hugh's stimulating yet soothing *tcha*, for she had much work to do. She needed to replenish her supply of the medicines she had taken to the village. She planned to try a stronger version of the preparation she was using to treat Donada's illness. Alda wanted more rosewater and a fresh jar of the lotion she used on her hands to keep them smooth and white. Mirielle told herself to keep busy, so she would have no time to think.

But she found she could not work. She sat on the bench, elbows on the table, head in her hands, while unwanted thoughts crowded into her mind. She had risen that morning still sad over Giles's departure, but unashamed to admit to herself that she cared for him. Long ago, that morning—had it been years since then or only a single day?—when she had still been ignorant of the truth, she had believed she would always care for Giles . . . who was not Giles . . . who was another man entirely. Now she knew how foolish she had been to love so easily and to trust a man she did not know.

In Mirielle's imagination a chasm had opened between herself and the man she wanted, a gulf contrived of false hopes and dreams, of lies told and truths unspoken. It was wrong of her to think of Lord Gavin. He was married. At this very moment he was abed with his wife. Alda's maidservant had come giggling into the great hall to spread the tale of Gavin's sudden appearance in Alda's bedchamber and his brusque command to the maid to leave them alone. Judging from his temper, the maid predicted, the baron would take his wife by force if she resisted him. The hall was abuzz with gossip, for everyone knew about Alda and Brice, and Brice had not appeared for the evening meal.

Assured by Donada that Brice had merely gone to the mews to see his falcon and that he did not want to be disturbed, Mirielle had fled to her own place of refuge.

"May I join you?" Hugh had materialized in the doorway while Mirielle was deep in thought.

"If Lord Gavin orders Brice and me out of Wroxley," Mirielle said, "this may soon become your workroom."

"I do not think that will happen." Hugh sat down beside her. At once Minn left her warm spot by the furnace to curve around Hugh's legs. He reached down to scratch behind the cat's ears.

"You are wearing your own face, Master Hugh." Mirielle asked. "Am I to take that as a good omen, or a bad one?"

"Take it as a sign that I will be honest with you."

"I wish you had been honest the last time you were in this room." Her voice was sharp with the anger and hurt she felt. She would have risen to put distance between herself and Hugh, but he placed one hand on her arm and Mirielle discovered she was unable to move.

"At the time, I could not tell you more than I did. For people like you and me, there are certain tests that must be faced, and passed or failed, and during those tests no other person can do anything to help. All I could do was teach you what I believed you ought to know and then leave it to you to rescue Gavin. You passed that particular test splendidly. You learned valuable lessons from it, as you were meant to do.

"Once again, I must ask for your help," Hugh continued. "As I told you at our last meeting, there is a dark magic at work here at Wroxley, a force determined to forestall Gavin's efforts to take and hold his rightful inheritance. I was warned of this force—never mind how or by whom—and so I advised Gavin to come here first in disguise."

"A powerful mage would be aware that you were here." Mirielle put a touch of sarcasm into her voice to let Hugh know she would not be easily won over this second time.

"There are curious gaps in the fabric of this force," Hugh said. "I do not understand why it is so. Perhaps, when we know more, when we have identified the source of it, those same gaps will provide us with a means to overcome the evil."

"Evil," Mirielle repeated, feeling as if a chill wind had touched her.

"I have no doubt that the dark strength we face is evil," Hugh said. "Everyone in this castle is affected by it. No one is immune, not you or your cousin, not Alda, not that good woman Donada or her son. Will you help?"

"When last you were here, you lied to me," Mirielle said stubbornly. "Why should I believe you now?"

"I have never lied to you," Hugh said.

"Indeed, he has not." Gavin walked into the workroom.

At once Mirielle was freed from the force that kept her beside Hugh on the bench. With painful awareness that Gavin had just come from Alda's bed, Mirielle rose to face him. He did not look like a man who had taken pleasure with his wife. Gavin's face was haggard, his movements were stiff and controlled, and his eyes burned with a bitter light that frightened Mirielle.

"I am the one who deceived you," Gavin said to her. "My excuse must be that I did so on the king's authority. Here is the proof you demanded of me. This is the king's writ. I want you to read it." He handed Mirielle a roll of parchment.

"This grants you Wroxley in fief for the duration of your life." Mirielle scanned the words written by the royal clerks.

"Read further," said Hugh.

"King Henry orders you to use whatever means are required to uproot and cast out any usurpers, criminals, traitors—or wizards. The king further grants you the right to punish any and all malefactors whenever and in whatever way you deem proper." Mirielle looked from the parchment to Gavin. "This is an enlargement on the rights held by most nobles."

"What is in that document was written there for my protection, so no one can question what I choose to do here," Gavin said. "This is a war to the death, in which, as Hugh as just told you, we need your help."

She stared at him, unable to answer at first because she was fighting her own war, with herself.

Her mind told her to be cautious in all her dealings with this man. Her heart urged her to do everything he asked of her.

"Mirielle," Gavin went on, "I want the writ put in a safe location, where even magic cannot touch it. Do you know of such a place?"

"Yes," she said, relenting a little because he trusted her enough to depend on her in this important matter. "Beneath the altar in the chapel is an empty space where, I have been told, jewels and plate and other treasures can be hidden in time of war."

"I remember it." Gavin nodded. "A chapel is not a place where an evil mage is likely to go."

"It would be safer still if you were to have a cross set on the altar," Mirielle suggested.

"Where is the gold cross my father had made for the chapel?" Gavin asked. "Where are the candlesticks, the chalice and paten, and the other vessels?"

"I do not know," Mirielle said. "I have never seen any of those furnishings. It is my understanding that the last priest at Wroxley left shortly after Lord Udo's funeral. When I came here, the chapel was empty, as it is now."

"Didn't you question that?" Gavin frowned at her. "In my childhood, there was always a priest in residence, who said Mass every day."

"I did ask Alda about it once. She acted as if she was not interested in the subject. I must tell you, my lord, that I am not deeply attached to the *official* Church. The nature of my work makes me cautious around priests who may be intolerant of my personal beliefs."

"I observe a similar caution," Hugh remarked.

Mirielle expected some comment from Gavin on what she had revealed. Instead, he changed the subject to speak about Brice.

"I have told your cousin he may remain here temporarily, until I have made a decision about a permanent seneschal," Gavin said. "I hope you will remain, too, Mirielle."

"From what you and Master Hugh have told me, I think I must stay. I believe my skills will be needed." She answered him with reluctance, her emotions still at war with reason and the memory of his deceit. She turned her attention to Hugh. It would be easier to forgive him than Gavin, for Hugh was not the man to whom she had given her heart. "Well, Master Hugh, it would appear that you and I will have an opportunity to learn from each other after all. I will tell no one your true identity." Mirielle looked down at the royal document in her hands and then at Gavin again. She forced herself to speak through trembling lips.

"Brice wants to continue as seneschal, and later to move on to some more important post. He is ambitious for land and a title and he wants to amass a good dowry for me. He is too concerned with earthly renown, but I do not believe he is an evil man. Gavin, I feel compelled to remind you of what you know already, what you learned on your secret visit here, and what others also know. Brice and Alda are lovers. I know you cannot let that pass, not when they have been indiscreet to the point of folly. What will you do to my cousin?"

"If Brice proves, as I suspect he will, to be a victim of the dark force that Hugh has detected, then your cousin will need to be rescued, rather than challenged," Gavin answered.

"What about Alda?" Mirielle had to ask. She saw the bitter rage in Gavin, before he turned away to face the still-empty shelves where jars of healing herbs had once been stored. That rage shocked her and left her unable to say anything more, for it suggested to her that Gavin cared for Alda and was hurt by his wife's adultery. His next words only confused her.

"Alda needs nothing that I can give her," Gavin said.

An hour later, Gavin and Hugh stood together in the bare little chapel. The single oil lamp they had brought with them burned on the altar. By its feeble light Gavin deposited the document from King Henry, along with a few other objects, into the safe hiding place Mirielle had suggested. With the stone over the opening beneath the altar replaced, no one who did not know of the secret space could have guessed it existed.

"Will you really let Sir Brice live?" Hugh asked.

"You heard what I told Mirielle," Gavin said. "If Brice has been caught in a mage's web against his will, then we will help him, and if he survives the coming contest, I will do no harm to him. But if he proves to be allied with the dark magic—and he may well be, since he craves wealth and power—then let us hope we can entrap him along with the dark mage you have sensed. Thus, we will prove to Mirielle how false her dear cousin is and, in that case, when we destroy the mage, we will destroy Brice with him."

"What of Mirielle, then?" Hugh cast a sharp eye on his friend. "She may not forgive you for Brice's downfall."

"Mirielle." Gavin sighed. "From her reactions today, I doubt if she and I can ever be friends after the way I deceived her on our first visit to Wroxley."

"You want more than friendship from her," Hugh said. "Admit it. Be honest with yourself."

"Mirielle touches my heart as Alda, with her famous and strangely unchanging beauty, never did. Mirielle is good. There is a purity at her heart that evil will never touch." Gavin's voice lowered and he spoke with profound sorrow.

"Whether Mirielle can forgive me for past and present deceits or not, no love can pass between us, for I am a married man. No matter what Alda has done, if I would be worthy of Mirielle, I cannot break the vows I took on my wedding day."

"Good, you are here." Alda brushed past Brice at the doorway to his room.

"Where else would I be at this hour?" Brice rubbed his sleep-heavy eyes. "Have you lost your wits completely, to come to my room so late at night? You belong with your husband."

"I will never again lie with Gavin of Wroxley. He will get no more children from my body." Alda whirled to face Brice, her loose hair floating outward like a fine golden veil.

"It is your duty to give him children." Brice's eyes were on her hair. He knew just how those silken strands would feel, entwined in his fingers.

"I have always preferred passion to duty." Alda's declaration was quite unnecessary, since Brice was kept continually aware of her passion, as well as her lack of interest in duty.

"Nonetheless," Brice insisted, "you must do as your husband commands."

"Never! I have ways of avoiding those events which I do not want to happen. And of bending men to my will."

"I do not think you will be able to cajole Gavin," Brice said.

"Cajole him?" Alda repeated with a throaty chuckle. "Mere cajolery is not what I have in mind. I would ensorcel Gavin, snare him with unbreakable cords, bewitch him into total immobility to keep him out of my bed—and torture him when he cannot protect himself. It would serve him well, after the way he insulted me."

"What are you saying?" Brice had thrown on a loose robe when he had risen from his bed to answer Alda's furious rapping at his door. Now he drew the robe close about himself, as if a sudden chill was touching him.

"Do you know what he told me?" Alda demanded.

"How should I know?" Brice asked. "Do you imagine I kept my ear pressed to your door to hear your moans of delight? Or his?"

"He said he would rather bed a moldering corpse than me. The insult! The rudeness! After the care I take of myself, the things I do—and have done—to keep my beauty intact. Gavin will pay in blood for those words. I'll see to it."

"So you did not leave his hot embrace to come to me," Brice said.

"Did you imagine I had?"

"I think you might find it exciting. I assure you, I would not."

Alda paid no attention to what Brice was saying. She was busy pulling her gown over her head. Brice heard the sound of ripping stitches, and for a moment he envisioned Donada carefully sewing the gown. He put that image away. This was not the time or place to be thinking about Donada.

"Does this look like a corpse to you?" Letting her gown fall to the floor Alda stood before Brice in all her naked glory. She took Brice's hands and pressed one to each of her breasts. "Is this flesh warm and living? Can you feel my heart beating? You know how hot I am inside, there where you want to be." Alda's hands slid beneath his robe, stroking, teasing, and Brice began to harden.

"In the name of heaven, Alda!" Brice meant to push her away from him. Instead, he found himself pulling her closer. "You should not be here. What if someone discovers us? It will mean my life—and yours, too."

"Are you expecting someone else?" Alda's hands clutched at a sensitive spot, holding him as if she would pinch. "Another woman, perhaps? Have you been false to me, Brice?"

"You know better than that."

"Do I?" Her fingers tightened until they began to hurt. Brice growled. Alda laughed and turned the threatening touch into an erotic gesture. "Imagine what I would do to you if I should discover that you have given this to another woman. And what I would do to the woman. You belong to me, Brice. Especially this most useful part of you."

Brice was by now so stiff with desire that he

thought he would burst. His body was blazing hot wherever Alda touched him. The threat of pain only excited him further.

Alda slipped out of his reach to kneel on his bed, luring him with a smile. When Brice tried to join her there she placed both of her hands on his chest, holding him away.

"Tell me I am beautiful," she ordered.

"You are the most beautiful woman I have ever seen."

"Say you worship me."

"You know I do."

"Beg me to give you the pleasure only I can give."

"Alda, please!" Brice bit back a groan. He knew he was going to die if Alda did not open her thighs at once and give him what he craved.

"Again," she commanded. "I want you to plead with me."

"Alda, I beg you! I cannot contain myself any longer."

"You will wait until I tell you otherwise." She was merciless. "Ask me again."

"Please. Please." Against his own will Brice was on his knees on the floor beside the bed, his clasped hands held up toward his beautiful tormentor. Through the mist of lust that surrounded him, he could see that his pleas were exciting Alda. Her bosom was heaving, her nipples were dark red and hard. With her eyes on his and a sly smile on her red lips, she slid one hand down between her thighs.

"No," Brice gasped. "Let me do that. Alda, I implore you."

"Well, then, you great, stupid beast." Alda lay back

on the bed. "Come and take your pleasure. And I will take what I need from you."

There was a part of Brice that despised Alda and hated grovelling to her. There was a part of him that felt sullied every time he left her body. But he could not resist her. No matter how many times or how recently they had coupled, she could always rouse him anew. Gratefully, Brice sank into her heat. Following the orders she gave him in a gasping, husky voice, he treated her as roughly as she demanded for as long as she required. At the end she granted him the release he sought, the long, hot spiral of delight that took him out of himself and let him forget both the caution he knew he ought to exercise and his shame at what he was doing. In the end, there was only the moist place between Alda's quivering thighs, and his own desire, and a deep, aching weariness when the act was finished.

Chapter Thirteen

Shortly before noon of the next day, as preparations for the welcoming feast that Mirielle had organized for Gavin and his men were being completed, Captain Oliver appeared in the great hall, bringing with him five people. Two of them were men-at-arms, and those Captain Oliver sent off to join the men of Wroxley for the feast, promising warm places to sleep before the visitors began their return journey on the morrow.

Left with a middle-aged priest and two children in his charge, Captain Oliver approached the high table, where Mirielle and Hugh were awaiting the arrival of the lord and lady of the castle.

"My lady Mirielle," Captain Oliver said, "this good priest is Father John. He has escorted Lord Gavin's children home from Cliffvale Castle. I thought it best to bring Warrick and Emma directly to you."

Mirielle advanced to the edge of the dais. The priest's tall and ascetically thin frame suggested a disdain for the mortal pleasures of food and drink. His disapproving scowl and the sour line of his mouth as he regarded Mirielle hinted at a further strictness of spirit that did much to explain the attitudes of the children with him.

The girl, who was about eleven years of age, looked frightened. The boy was a sulky thirteen-year-old. In her own youth Mirielle had on occasion clashed with priests who disapproved of certain aspects of her work, so she recognized in the children before her two who had doubtless been browbeaten all the way from Cliffvale to Wroxley.

"Welcome home," she said to them. "We were not expecting you, but you come at an opportune time. Your father has also returned home after long years of crusading. I know he will be happy to see you."

"Not when he hears what I have to tell him," said the priest, turning what was apparently a perpetual frown from Mirielle to the children and then back to Mirielle again. "These two deserve no welcome but, rather, a severe punishment."

As Mirielle sought a response that would reassure the children while not offending Father John, she was rescued by Hugh.

"Good Father," said Hugh to the priest, "I am certain you must want to refresh yourself before joining us for the feast we plan."

"I do not require any luxury," the priest said in a lofty tone. "My life is dedicated to holy simplicity."

"A noble point of view," Hugh responded, "speaking in the holiest sense of that word, of course. It was my thought that if you were seated at the high table, any conversation you wish to hold with Lord Gavin and his lady would be more easily accomplished."

"I see." Father John looked from his own dusty hands to the spotless white linen covering the high table. "Perhaps I ought to wash."

"I will be happy to escort you to a place where you can do so." With an elegant motion of one hand, Hugh indicated the way the priest should go.

"He's clever," said young Warrick, gazing after the departing men. "I wish I could talk that filthy priest into doing what I want so easily."

"Perhaps Hugh will teach you," said Captain Oliver, who had a distinct twinkle in his eyes. "Warrick, if your father agrees, I will be happy to see you in the practice yard tomorrow, with the other fellows of your age. Your servant, my lady." Captain Oliver bowed to Mirielle and left the little group by the dais.

"I am not going to take up weapons." Warrick thrust out his jaw in a fair approximation of a determined man.

"Warrick, you must," said his sister. "You know you must. It is a nobleman's duty."

"I don't care!" What else young Warrick might have said on the subject was interrupted by Donada.

"Warrick?" Donada's wan face was lit by a wide smile. "Is it really you?"

"Donada!" All the sulkiness vanished from Warrick's expression. He turned to Donada as if to embrace her. Just in time he recalled his manners and stood very straight. Then he bowed. "It is good to see you again, dear lady. I trust you are in excellent health."

"Well enough, I thank you, sir." Donada looked at Mirielle. "If you like, I will see to Warrick's needs. Robin is washing his face and hands. Warrick could join him. I see saddlebags in the entry, which will probably contain a change of tunic for the feast."

"Robin is still here?" Now Warrick's face was filled with boyish eagerness.

"He will be glad to see you again." Donada then explained to Mirielle, "When they were little, Warrick and my son were inseparable. They spent a lot of time in the seneschal's quarters with me and my late husband."

"Captain Oliver told me that Sir Paul died soon after my grandfather," Warrick said. "I am sorry. He was much like a father to me."

"He thought of you as another son, in the absence of your own father," Donada said. "Come, I'll show you to Robin."

They went out of the great hall together, which left Mirielle alone with Emma. The girl still looked frightened. Mirielle began to wonder why the children had been sent home so unexpectedly.

"Your father will be very happy to have you with him," Mirielle said, by way of beginning a conversation that she hoped would elicit some information.

"I do not think that will be so when he learns why we have come," Emma replied.

"I have always found," Mirielle said, "that when I am concerned about a meeting, it helps my spirits if I look as neat and tidy as possible. We won't have time before the meal begins for you to bathe and change your clothes, but if you wash your hands and face and brush your hair, I think you will be quite presentable."

"My mother will not think so." Emma allowed herself to be guided out of the great hall to a pantry off the screens passage. At Mirielle's order, hot water and a towel were brought and while Emma washed, Mirielle arranged for bedchambers to be made ready for the children and for Father John. Uncertain what Gavin or Alda would want done, she simply assigned a guest room to each of the newcomers.

"We should hurry," Mirielle said to Emma, who was now brushing her long, black hair with considerable vigor. "Your parents will be coming into the hall soon. Your father is a punctual man."

"What is he like?" Emma's eyes were dark brown, with hints of purple in the irises, and at the moment they were wide with hope. "I have never met him. I was born after he went away."

"He is very tall and handsome." Mirielle searched for the right words to describe Gavin to his daughter. Not knowing what mischief the children had gotten into, she added, "He can be fierce at times, but he is fair and he has a kind heart."

"I hope so." Emma's brown eyes swam with tears. "My brother and I have both disobeyed the lady of Cliffvale. Father John says Warrick has been very wicked and ought to be made to perform a severe penance. I could not let my brother come home to face our mother alone for a misdeed that is in part my fault. I had to come with him. My lady of Cliffvale said I could not return to her if I left. I insisted, and refused to eat or stop crying until she released me."

"I think I understand." Mirielle bent down until her head was level with Emma's. She spoke as if she were telling a great secret. "My cousin is seneschal here, and even though he is older and my guardian, sometimes when he does something wrong I feel I have to protect him, because I love him so much. I think your father will appreciate your loyalty to your brother and so he will not punish you too harshly for what you have done."

"I hope you are right, Lady Mirielle." Emma slipped her small hand into Mirielle's and together they returned to the great hall.

They were just in time. Gavin and Alda walked into the hall in formal procession with Brice attending them, and Alda's maidservants and Gavin's squires behind them. Alda's fingertips barely touched Gavin's sleeve and every movement of her body spoke of her distaste for any contact with him. When they were seated in the two large chairs at the high table, Alda turned away from Gavin at once to speak to Brice, who sat at her other side. Gavin did not appear to notice.

With Emma's hand still firmly clasped in hers, Mirielle moved forward until she was standing directly in front of Gavin. She knew what she was about to do was improper, but from what the children had said and what she knew of Alda, Mirielle thought their best chance of a fair hearing lay in a public confrontation.

"My lord," Mirielle said to Gavin, "we have three unexpected guests to help us celebrate your homecoming. May I present to you your daughter Emma."

The girl made a pretty curtsy. She lifted her face

to regard Gavin with eager expectation written upon her delicate features. Then Alda spoke and at the sound of her mother's voice fear replaced the other emotions in Emma's eyes and on her face.

"Why are you here? I did not send for you." Alda's hissed question made Gavin look sharply at her. His own face was a mask of frozen composure. But he did not fail the child who stood trembling before the dais.

"Welcome home, Emma," he said.

"Thank you, my lord father." Emma's voice was a soft whisper and she glanced nervously toward Alda.

"It was my thought," Mirielle said to Gavin, "that Emma might join us at the high table. I am convinced her manners are acceptable. Perhaps you would allow her to sit beside you for this meal."

"A child at the high table?" Alda objected. "Certainly not. Put her at one of the lower tables."

"Would you deny your own daughter?" Gavin's voice carried a message that Mirielle could not decipher. "I cannot think why you would do so, Alda. Emma looks quite presentable to me." The look he gave Alda was filled with loathing. His wife stared back at him, her own features rigid with hatred.

That there was a battle raging between them Mirielle could see, but she did not know why it was happening. Was it something about Emma, or was the child merely a handy weapon? Mirielle prayed that Gavin would not stoop to use a child in such a shameful way.

"That girl has been sent home in disgrace for some misdeed!" Alda declared.

"She does not seem particularly wicked to me."

Gavin regarded Emma with a softer look than he had previously sent her way. "Lady Mirielle is right, Emma. You ought to sit at the high table."

At this point they were interrupted by the arrival of Hugh with Father John and Donada with Warrick and Robin, all of whom came into the great hall at the same time. Mirielle was pleased to see that Warrick was talking in an animated way with Robin. When he smiled, the boy was a younger version of his handsome father. But Warrick's good humor vanished when he noticed Father John and then the grownups at the high table.

"My lord." Father John hurried forward to address Gavin. "I come to you bringing with me these two wicked children, whom the lord and lady of Cliffvale have returned to Wroxley for parental punishment. I am ordered to recount their misdeeds to you and to advise you as to Lord Cliffvale's opinion on what that punishment should be."

"I knew it!" Alda was on her feet, pointing at the children. "You brats have disgraced me."

"No, we have not!" Emma cried. "Warrick is not wicked."

Mirielle observed with interest that Warrick and Robin had moved to stand on either side of Emma, as if to protect her. Warrick took Emma's hand. Mirielle also saw that Gavin was giving close attention to the children's actions.

"Before anyone can be punished," Gavin said, "I must hear what these two are accused of doing."

"In private, of course," Alda began. "I see no reason why all these common folk should be entertained—"

"Let them be entertained," Warrick cried. "Let it be a public trial."

"I will not have you treating your mother so rudely, Warrick," Gavin said, his heavier voice cutting across his son's impassioned words. "You were sent to Cliffvale as a page to learn manners and courtly bearing. Those same good manners now require an apology for interrupting your mother when she was speaking."

"My lady mother." At once, Warrick bowed to Alda. "I do most sincerely apologize for my rudeness."

"I do not forgive you," Alda said.

"That was well and promptly done, Warrick." Gavin nodded his approval at his son. "Now, Robin, I see no reason why you should stand here with those two accused miscreants." The words were spoken with a smile, to which Robin responded with passion.

"Warrick is my friend," he said.

"I will take note of the fact that you think Warrick is worthy of your loyalty. However, since you lads have not seen each other for some years, you cannot have anything of value to add to his tale."

"He told me what happened at Cliffvale while we were washing our hands," Robin said.

"What you heard was Warrick's version of events," Gavin said, "which I am certain he is perfectly able to recount to me in his own behalf. Donada, take your son to the table with you and keep him there."

"Yes, my lord." Donada put an arm around Robin's shoulders. The boy resisted the pressure she was exerting.

"Go on, Robin," Warrick said. "Don't get into trouble on my account. Thank you for trying to help."

"I'm your friend no matter what they do to you," Robin declared, finally allowing Donada to take him to their usual seats at one of the lower tables.

Once more Mirielle was aware of how carefully Gavin was attending to all that the children said or did.

"Father John," Gavin said to the priest, "what have you to tell me about these children?"

"The boy is by far the worse of the two," Father John began. "He finds excuses to avoid weapons practice. He has not made friends with the other pages. Warrick claims the other boys are stupid. He would spend all his days reading. Reading, my lord! Lord and Lady Cliffvale feel, and I entirely agree with them, that this is not a suitable activity for a youth who is in training to become a knight."

"I don't want to be a knight," Warrick declared in a loud voice, speaking as though he wanted everyone in the hall to hear him. "I want to be a scholar instead. I have already begun my studies and I will not stop, not even if you beat me or imprison me."

"Never!" Alda cried. "My son will not be a cleric! Nor will I allow him to join the priesthood."

"My lady," said Father John, "I fear the Church is closed to young Warrick if he persists in his present foolishness. Indeed, his very soul is in danger."

"Not from reading," Gavin said with a disparaging smile for Father John's concern. "I can read and I do assure you, father, my soul is not in any danger from it."

"You have not heard the whole of Warrick's offenses," Father John insisted. "The boy is determined to pursue the study of alchemy."

"Is he?" said Hugh, looking at Warrick with new interest.

"None of this is particularly disturbing," Gavin said. "I see no reason why the boy cannot combine his knightly training with the studies he wants to pursue."

"You still have not heard all, my lord," Father John said. "It was his latest escapade that resulted in his expulsion from Cliffvale. I am commanded to tell you that under no circumstances will Warrick or his sister be permitted to return." The priest ended his remarks with an expression of great satisfaction on his thin face, as if he felt that he had discharged a disagreeable duty to the best of his ability.

"What did you do, Warrick?" asked his father. When Warrick looked at his toes with a sullen air instead of answering, Gavin said, "It will be worse for you if you refuse to tell me and I am thus forced to inquire of Father John for the details."

"It wasn't his fault," Emma cried. "He was proving an experiment he had read about, that I said could not be done. Warrick was only trying to show me how to heat sulfur, which he combined—" She stopped, gulping back tears.

"Sir," said Warrick, straightening his shoulders as if he expected a blow to fall on them, "I set the still-room at Cliffvale on fire. All of Lady Cliffvale's dried herbs were burnt and the walls were blackened."

"Lad," murmured Hugh, who was standing behind the children, "you must learn to be more careful in your work."

"There was a great flash of fire," Warrick said,

speaking over his shoulder to Hugh, "and a revolting smell."

"I am sure there was," Hugh responded.

Mirielle could see that Gavin was more amused than annoyed by this story, but she knew he would not be indulgent toward his son. Whatever the boy's personal wishes might be, and however sympathetic Gavin was to them, Warrick was the heir to Wroxley and thus he was required to learn how to defend the castle and how to be ready to do his duty to King Henry when called upon. His other interests would have to take second place.

"Father John," Gavin said. "I thank you for your good care of these young ones. I would ask you to remain at Wroxley for a few days, if you can. We have had no resident priest for some time and I am certain my people would be grateful to make their confessions and take communion from you."

"Of course." Father John bowed. At Gavin's signal Hidern came forward to lead the priest to a seat at one end of the high table.

"Warrick," Gavin went on, "I leave you in Hugh's care for the present, while I consider what your punishment should be. Tomorrow morning, you will report to Hidern in the practice yard. He will begin to teach you the duties of a squire, since your days as a page have come to an end."

"Yes, my lord." Warrick did not look happy at his father's decision, but he made no protest.

"For this meal, you may join Robin and his mother," Gavin added.

"Thank you, Father." Warrick's face brightened at this order, which he promptly obeyed.

"Emma." Gavin motioned to her with one hand.

"Come here and sit between Lady Mirielle and me. I want to talk to you."

"Yes, my lord." Emma did as she was told, taking her place on the bench beside Gavin's chair. Her manners were excellent. She did not spill a drop of food, either on her clothes or the tablecloth, but Gavin could see how tense she was.

"What, exactly, was your part in Warrick's escapade?" Gavin asked her.

"I questioned what he told me about that experiment," Emma replied, adding, "I was right. It ended badly. Sometimes, what is written in a book is wrong."

"So I have occasionally found." Gavin tried to control the smile that tugged at his lips. The girl was so solemn. He suspected that she was still afraid, too. "Shall I assume from your remarks that you can read, Emma?"

"Warrick has been teaching me. Lady Cliffvale was glad of it, for I can write, too, so she set me to keep her stillroom ledger."

"Perhaps we can find a similar use for you here," Mirielle said. With a glance at Gavin she added, "It would be a good idea for Emma to learn the duties of a chatelaine."

"I have already begun," said Emma.

Gavin looked more closely at the girl. She was not blonde and beautiful like her mother. In fact, Emma's straight hair, which was left loose and flowing as was the custom for maidens, was so dark and shiny that it reminded him of Mirielle's hair.

And of Brice's. The thought was a thunderbolt cleaving through Gavin's mind. Was it possible? Leaning forward, he looked along the table toward

Brice, noting the similarities in the shape of the brow, the cheekbones, the jawline. Emma's bones were not yet set in their adult mold, and there was a soft, feminine sweetness about the child, but in Gavin's thoughts there could be no question.

Emma was Brice's child. Which meant that Alda and Brice had lain together while Gavin was still in England, years before Brice had come to Wroxley as seneschal. But Gavin had not been aware that in those days Alda and Brice had been anything more than distant relatives. The realization that they had been intimate a dozen years in the past opened new possibilities for Gavin to investigate.

Did Brice know he had a daughter? Judging from his behavior, he did not. It would be like Alda to keep the truth a secret, so she could use it at a time opportune for her, as she had done with Gavin on the previous evening. Her revelation about Emma had prevented Gavin from insisting that Alda allow him his conjugal rights. What Alda did not know was how glad Gavin had been to have an excuse to reject her.

And what of the girl? She appeared to be a sweet-natured child, with little of Alda in her character. The way in which Emma regarded Gavin with worshipful admiration brought out his protective, fatherly instincts. It was not Emma's fault that her mother was a cruel and selfish woman. The girl ought not to suffer for Alda's sins. Now, if Warrick had been a bastard, that would be a different matter. But anyone could see that Gavin and Warrick were father and son and thus there could be no question about inheritance.

"My lord father," Emma said, interrupting his

thoughts. "I am so happy to know you at last. For as long as I can remember, I have wanted to meet my father. I prayed for your safe return every day, and again each night before going to sleep. Now my prayers have been answered."

"Child." Gavin steeled himself to touch the girl who was not his. He put a gentle hand on Emma's soft little cheek. The look she gave him was one of pure adoration. Gavin's heart melted within him. He knew that Emma had spoken only the truth. She had longed for her absent father throughout her childhood and now that she had found him she was ready to love him with her whole heart. He could not break that innocent heart by rejecting her. He put his arm around her, drew her closer, and felt her cuddle against his side. His eyes began to smart. Over Emma's head he saw Mirielle smiling at him. Gavin swallowed hard against the lump in his throat.

"My dear daughter," he said. "I am glad you have come home. I plan to keep you with me for a long time."

When that long midday meal was over an important ceremony took place. One by one the men of Wroxley came forward to pledge themselves to the new baron. As was right and proper, Warrick was first. After a whispered word from Donada the boy approached the dais, where he knelt and put his hands between Gavin's and swore loyalty unto death. When Gavin lifted him and kissed him on either cheek it was more than a mere following of custom. Gavin embraced his son to the full approval of all those in the hall, except for Alda, who should have been glad to see her son so accepted. But Alda glared her dislike at both father and son.

Brice was next. He went to his knees before Gavin and spoke the words of the solemn oath calmly, in a firm voice. Watching her cousin, Mirielle hoped this oathtaking would signal the end of Brice's affair with Alda. Brice certainly appeared to be sincere. However, Alda's disdainful, faintly amused expression worried Mirielle. She was relieved when Brice stepped aside to allow Captain Oliver, as the next highest ranking man at Wroxley, to make his pledge. The other men followed in order of rank. Gavin was serious through all the oaths. Hugh nodded his approval and smiled at Mirielle when the ceremony was over. Alda looked as if she did not believe the words that anyone had spoken.

Chapter Fourteen

"I told the servants to prepare a room for you next to mine." Mirielle showed Emma into the guest chamber that, like her own room, was built into the fifteen-foot thickness of the wall of the tower keep.

"I am to have a room of my own? How luxurious. At Cliffvale, I slept with six other women." Emma looked with approval at the curtained bed, the table and stool, and the single, narrow window on which the shutter had been left open to admit light and fresh air.

The servant who had made up the bed with clean sheets and a quilt had also removed Emma's belongings from the saddlebag in which they were packed and had left them in a neat pile on top of the clothing chest. Mirielle noticed a hairbrush, a wooden comb, one extra dress, a second shift, a single pair of stockings. Otherwise, Emma possessed only the cloak in which she had come to Wroxley and the gown, shoes and undergarments she was wearing. All of the clothing was well worn and the dress Emma had on was too short for her.

"We will see Donada first thing in the morning," Mirielle said. "She will sew new clothes for you. I am sure she would appreciate your help if you are a good seamstress."

"I would like to make a new tunic for Warrick," Emma said. "His second one has a hole burnt in it."

"Warrick is fortunate that he was not badly hurt," Mirielle responded.

"He said I saved him when I threw a bucket of water over him." Emma changed the subject abruptly. "I remember Donada because she was always so pretty and so kind to Warrick and me. She looks old now."

"She has not been well."

"But you will cure her, I am sure. My father says you are a fine healer." Emma paused before continuing, as if she were deciding what to say and leaving out a fair part of her story as she told it. "I did not like Cliffvale. Neither did Warrick. Lord and Lady Cliffvale knew our mother did not care about us and that our father was far away, so they did not trouble themselves to treat us well."

"Surely you made friends among the other boys and girls who were fostering at Cliffvale," Mirielle said.

"Warrick is right about the boys. They are stupid, none of them can read and, what's worse, none of them care that they are unlettered. All they want to do is fight. There was only one other girl at Cliffvale, and she was as unhappy as I," Emma said. "Margaret wanted to come to Wroxley with me, but of course, Lady Cliffvale would not allow it. Lady Mirielle, may I visit your workroom?"

"If you promise not to set it on fire," Mirielle said, to tease the overly serious girl. But Emma did not smile.

"I would like to become your pupil, Lady Mirielle."

"Assisting me in my workroom will be part of your training, if your father agrees to my suggestion," Mirielle said.

"I want to learn everything you can teach me about the healing properties of herbs—and about your experiments with metals."

"Are you set upon the study of alchemy, like your brother?"

"It is in our blood," Emma said. "Because of our mother."

"I have never known Alda to display an interest in my work." Mirielle was surprised by the girl's assertion.

"Perhaps she has changed in my absence. Once, when I was small, I saw—" Emma stopped, as if she were confused. "I was very little then. It is possible that I misunderstood what I saw."

As his father had ordered, Warrick was sent to the practice yard the day after his arrival. There he was given a squire's short sword and his training in the use of it began at once.

On her way across the outer bailey to see Ewain, the blacksmith, Mirielle paused to watch the squires at work. Warrick was fending off a make-believe attack from Gavin's younger squire, Bevis, while Hidern, the older squire, watched and shouted occasional directions.

"Warrick does not look to me as if he has had much practice with a sword," Mirielle remarked to Hidern.

"I think it is more that he does not care," Hidern replied. He shook his head in undisguised irritation at Warrick's incompetence. Raising his voice, Hidern called, "Bevis, break off. Give the child a chance to catch his breath before the next round."

"I am not a child!" Warrick shouted at Hidern. When he saw Mirielle, his face flushed dark red, as if he were embarassed to be seen at less than his best by a lady.

"You will kill no enemies that way," Bevis jeered, walking away from Warrick to join his fellow squire.

"Warrick, think about what you are doing," Hidern added.

"And save your ill temper for another time," said Bevis.

"When your clever words will be more appropriate than a sword," Hidern said, finishing the thought.

"Must you taunt him?" Mirielle asked.

"The lad needs toughening," Bevis told her.

"Else he'll never make a good knight," Hidern said.

"It's not our fault he's a laggard," Bevis added.

"Or that he would rather be mixing herbs with you," said Hidern. "I mean no offense, my lady, but Warrick's training has been neglected—or perhaps he refused what was offered at Cliffvale Castle."

"And now he must make up for the time he has lost," Bevis concluded.

"I do understand," Mirielle said, "but you two are well advanced in your training. Perhaps Warrick would learn faster if he were paired with someone who is at his own level. Hidern, you and Bevis could watch and offer instruction when it's needed."

"No, my lady." Hidern was polite, but his refusal was firm. "This is men's work, and no concern of women."

"Which is just the problem," Bevis noted. "Warrick would rather do women's work."

"I would not!" Warrick yelled, having heard this last comment. "You are stupid, both of you. All you care about is weapons and armor, horses and warfare—"

"What else is there for a man?" asked Hidern. "Get back to work, lad. Lady Mirielle, you will have to excuse us."

Fearing that she might have made Warrick's situation worse by her well-meant interference, Mirielle continued on her way to Ewain's shop. When she got there she discovered that Gavin was with the blacksmith. Telling herself to act as if her heart was not pounding faster than usual, and to speak as if her throat was not suddenly dry or her tongue stumbling over the words, Mirielle greeted Gavin politely before addressing herself to her friend the blacksmith.

"Ewain, here is a fresh supply of burn ointment for you," she said, giving him the jar.

"I expect I'll have need of it." Ewain set the jar on a nearby shelf. "My lord Gavin plans to keep me busy, and glad I am of it, though I will want a new assistant or two to help with the work."

"Walk with me, Mirielle. I would have a word with

you." Gavin took her arm, drawing her with him out of the blacksmith's shop. They set off across the outer bailey toward the inner gatehouse.

"I want to talk to you, too," she said, deciding to make use of this opportunity. "It's about Warrick. I know it is not a woman's place to interfere in such matters, but it seems to me your squires are too harsh with him. They will only make him more sullen."

"I told Hidern to be hard," Gavin said. "Warrick's training has been sadly neglected. For that I blame Lord Cliffvale and his squires, but I intend to see the fault remedied as quickly as possible. Warrick has responsibilities to match his rank and he must learn to accept them."

"Perhaps he is ill-suited to be a knight. He seems to think so."

"You were correct, Mirielle, when you said it was not your place to interfere."

Mirielle should have been silenced by Gavin's cool words, but she had seen misery in Warrick's face and she had held another conversation with Emma that morning on the subject of the treatment the children had received while at Cliffvale Castle. Her heart went out to both Emma and Warrick. She was determined to do what she could to make their lives more pleasant now that they were at home.

"My lord, when I must administer a particularly bitter potion to someone who is ill, I add special sweet herbs and honey to mask the taste." Gavin said nothing to this. He just kept walking, so Mirielle continued. "If Warrick had a friend of his own age to practice with, someone who is even less used to weapons than he, then the practice might become a game and Warrick might take an interest in it, especially if he thought he could help his friend to learn."

"A friend," Gavin repeated. "I suppose you mean Robin?"

"Why not?" she asked. "His father was a knight, and a fine one, from all I have heard of him. Sir Paul's son ought to be a knight, too. It is shameful that Robin has been sent to the stables to work."

"Robin has found ways to deal with his exile in the stables. He is a clever boy."

"And an honest one," Mirielle said stoutly. "Robin is Warrick's best friend. Donada tells me they were inseparable before Warrick was sent to Cliffvale."

"I will think about your suggestion." Gavin's tone indicated that he was finished with the subject.

"I have another one to make," Mirielle persisted. "Send Warrick to Hugh for tutoring. Hugh will teach him how to contain his anger."

"I will talk to Hugh about Warrick." Gavin's sudden smile dazzled Mirielle. He paused by the inner gatehouse. "I suspect that Hugh will agree with all you have said. He will very likely have a full schedule of instruction in mind."

"Possibly." Mirielle answered his smile with her own. She had the feeling that Gavin wanted to touch her, perhaps to take her hand. Standing there in the busy outer bailey, with people moving in and out of the gatehouse, she felt as though they were in a private place, where no one could disturb them. Still smiling, they looked into each other's eyes and she knew they were in agreement about his son, and about Robin. She need not worry. Gavin would take care of both boys. Now, if he would give his permission for her to begin teaching Emma the skills required for herbal healing, Mirielle believed all three children would be set upon paths to lives far happier than their last few years had been.

As for her, much of her anger against Gavin had softened as she became aware of his concern for his children. A man who could be so thoughtful could not be a villain or a habitual liar. She now believed there must be good reasons for every falsehood he had uttered to her.

"Was there anything else?" Gavin asked.

"About your daughter." She stared at him in amazement as the warmth drained from his face and his eyes grew hard. Unable to stop herself, she put out a hand to him. "Gavin, what is wrong?"

"We cannot talk here."

"Then, come to the herb garden. It's much quieter there." Wondering at the sudden change in him, Mirielle led the way through the gatehouse and into the inner bailey.

In the sheltered garden the herbs Mirielle tended were leafing out in shades ranging from the yellow-green of angelica and celeriac, both of which were just pushing their thick stems up through the soil, to the brighter green of mint and the grayish tints of several varieties of thyme. A few of the plants were already in bloom and bees buzzed from flower to flower, winging their way to and from the small skep at one side of the garden. The wooden palisade around the garden kept out roaming animals or people and gave the illusion of privacy, though Mirielle was aware that conversations held in the garden could be overheard outside the wall, and that the windows on the upper levels of the tower keep provided a clear view of anyone in the garden. Still, in a crowded castle bailey, it was as close to privacy as one could get.

"Gavin, I note your disapproval. I do not want you to think I am trying to arrange the lives of your children with no consideration of what your desires for them may be," Mirielle said. "I only wanted to discuss with you Emma's request to become my pupil. She and Warrick do seem to have similar interests," she finished with a laugh, hoping to make him smile again.

Gavin did not smile. He stood looking down at a patch of gray-green thyme, poking at the plant with one toe, and the unhappy expression on his face reminded Mirielle of Warrick.

"I think Emma has been sadly neglected during her stay at Cliffvale," Mirielle went on. "And, to speak bluntly, my lord, her mother has made it obvious that she does not care what happens to the girl. But Emma has courage and she is a dear, loving child. I felt an immediate bond to her." Mirielle stopped, fearing she had said too much, particularly about Alda. Gavin regarded her in a bleak, sad way, and Mirielle realized that he was not annoyed by her impassioned words. Something else was bothering him.

"It does not surprise me that you should feel a closeness to Emma," he said in a low voice, "since she is your kin."

"No," she said, not understanding. "How could that be?"

"Use your wits, Mirielle. Brice is her father."

"Brice? Oh, no! Gavin, how can you be sure?"

"Alda herself took great pleasure in revealing that

Emma is not my child." Without warning Gavin's cautious reserve crumbled. Speaking as if he had to get the words out or choke on hateful facts, he told Mirielle about his bitter interview with Alda and his later recognition of Emma's parentage based on her resemblance to Brice. "I have not even told Hugh, and I did not mean to tell you, Mirielle, but the girl needs someone to care about her and you would seem to be the most likely person. If you are to be her teacher, you should know the truth."

"But, if what you believe is true, it would mean that Brice and Alda were lovers while you and Alda still—oh, Gavin." Amost at once, Mirielle had another related thought. "Do you believe that is why Alda asked for Brice to come here as seneschal? So they could renew their affair?"

"For that, and for other reasons."

"Yesterday, after you had deduced all of this, still you publicly acknowledged Emma as your daughter," Mirielle said. "Why?"

"Alda all but dared me to refuse the child. Never have I met a crueler mother," Gavin said. "When I saw the trusting look on Emma's sweet face, I could not break her heart by rejecting her."

"How good you are. How kind." She had been right to believe in him.

"Not entirely good," he objected. "There was another reason in my mind. Emma's beautiful black hair, those wide eyes of hers, though the color is different, even something in her voice, all endeared her to me because those attributes remind me of you. And that very reminding made me even more certain that she is your cousin's daughter."

"Oh, Gavin." She could think of nothing else to say.

"Given the angry way we parted eleven years ago, I expected nothing from Alda on my return," Gavin went on. "Still, seeing the malice in her that took such delight in telling me Emma is not my child, observing the way she treated both children yesterday—I tell you, Mirielle, I begin to understand why some men lock up their wives for years on end!"

"It hurts me to see you in such pain," she cried. Not caring if anyone looking down from the tower keep should see them, thinking only of him, she put her arms around his waist.

"The pain will pass, and soon," he said, holding her, his cheek on her smooth hair. "My pride is injured, not my heart. Any tenderness I felt toward Alda ended long ago."

Mirielle did not want to leave the sheltering warmth of Gavin's arms. Neither, apparently, did he want to end their embrace. They stood with Mirielle's head on his shoulder, while his arms slowly tightened around her and Mirielle gradually molded herself to his strong frame. She felt his lips on her brow and when she moved her head, he took her mouth in a kiss that startled her with its passion.

She could not deny him. She pressed herself against him, opening her mouth, offering the tenderness she sensed he needed of her.

For Gavin, Mirielle's generous affection was a rope thrown to a man drowning in a raging river of treachery and dark secrets. He was intensely aware of the delicious roundness of her breasts crushed against his chest and of the slender length of her that fit so perfectly into his arms. His body responded immediately to the warmth of her mouth beneath his. Her arms wound around him with surprising firmness. He had known since their first meeting that she was no weak, fragile female. His Mirielle possessed an inner strength of purpose that matched his own. She would never be deterred from doing what she believed was right.

She was not *his* Mirielle, he reminded himself with a feeling of despair. She could not be his so long as he was wed to Alda. The same strength of character that led her to insist that mistreated children should be dealt with fairly and that had made her angry at the lies he had told her on their first meeting would also prevent Mirielle from giving herself to a man who was bound to another woman.

He loved her for the very strength that would deny him what he wanted most from her. And he thought he might well die of the longing that surged through him each time he saw her, the longing that grew stronger every time he put his arms around her or kissed her.

He allowed himself one last kiss, while he savored the sensation of Mirielle embracing him, of her sweet mouth and her arms and her lithe young body. Slowly, he lifted his head. With his hands still on her shoulders, he stepped back a pace.

"We cannot continue in this way," he said. "We cannot meet like this again."

"I know. It is very wrong of me to permit it." Tears stood in her silver-gray eyes. "I only wanted to offer you the comfort I thought you needed. But comforting turned into something else. I am sorry if I have made your life more difficult."

"I do not regret kissing you, Mirielle, though the

memory of you in my arms may drive me mad with wanting you." Gavin paused, looking deep into her eyes while he willed himself to return to the realities of daily life.

"I give Emma into your care," he said. "Alda wants nothing to do with her daughter, and the child is legally mine, to keep with me or send away as I please. You will treat her kindly, I know. Teach her as you think best. Protect her from her uncaring mother. For Emma's sake, keep the secret of her birth. Love her." His voice cracked. "For my part, I will treat her as my own and try to give her the fatherly affection she wants and deserves."

"I will do all that you ask," Mirielle said. "I promise." She did not tell him that she believed he loved Emma already.

Alda was not in the best of humors the following day when she met Gavin in the entry hall just before the midday meal. With a coldly polite bow Gavin offered his arm. Usually, Alda placed her fingertips on his wrist, stuck her nose into the air, and without saying a word to him suffered Gavin to escort her into the hall for the main meal of the day. It was expected of the lord and lady of the castle that they would make a formal entrance. Before Gavin's return Alda had made a point of dressing in an elaborate style and entering the great hall on Brice's arm.

On this morning Brice was absent attending to some matter at the main gatehouse. Only a few squires were present in the entry, and all of them were hurrying into the hall to take their places for the meal.

"What are you doing among the squires, you wretched boy?" Alda cried, having caught sight of Robin, who was walking into the hall between Warrick and Hidern. "Sit with your mother, or else get out of the keep and go to the stables, where you belong."

"Robin belongs exactly where he is," Gavin said. "I have made him one of my squires." He braced himself for the confrontation he was sure would come.

"I will not have it," Alda declared. "Robin is an impudent churl. I will not allow him to associate with my son."

"You have nothing to say about it. The choosing of squires does not fall within your domain." Gavin kept his voice quiet. If Alda was going to provoke a loud and angry scene over the decisions he had made, he was not going to contribute to it. He waved the squires into the hall so that he and Alda were alone in the entry.

"Well, my lord," Alda said, "the disposition of female children does fall within my domain, and I must inform you that I am greatly displeased by the way you have given Emma into Mirielle's care."

"I was under the impression that you do not care what happens to the girl. That, in fact, you dislike her."

"Emma was one of my few mistakes." Alda sent a glance toward the great hall, where her daughter waited beside the high table with Mirielle and Hugh.

"I am encouraged to learn that you are capable of admitting to a fault." Gavin extended his arm again, and this time Alda put her fingertips on the cloth of his tunic just above his wrist. Her grimace suggested that she was avoiding contact with his skin.

"What I meant," Alda said in a low, vicious tone, "was that your late father, the great Lord Udo, was so eager for another grandson that as soon as he suspected I was with child for a second time, he set his servants to watch me closely and constantly until it was too late for me to rid myself of the creature without endangering my own life."

"Would you have done that?" Gavin watched her, as fascinated by her revelations as he would have been by the motions of a snake that was preparing to strike. There was still more venom in Alda, and he was sure it was about to surface.

"However," Alda went on, "I have not made that mistake again. Not since Emma's birth have I allowed a man's seed to root itself in my body."

"What you are telling me," Gavin said between gritted teeth, "is that you have had more than one lover."

"What if I have?" Alda tossed her head.

"If you will not think of my honor," Gavin said, "have you no regard for your own?"

Alda did not answer him. They were by now at the dais. Gavin dropped his arm and let Alda find her own seat. He could not bear to look at her, much less escort her to a chair. Gavin glanced from Warrick and Robin, who were talking together at the squires' table, to Donada, sitting pale and listless in her usual seat, to Emma beside him at the high table with her dark eyes on his face. Her happy response to his forced smile touched his aching heart. On Emma's other side, Mirielle looked at him with open affection.

"Good people," Gavin said, raising his voice. At

once, the talk in the hall stopped. Servants paused with platters and bowls in their hands to listen to what he would say. All heads swiveled toward the high table. "Father John tells me that the chapel is prepared. For the rest of this day and evening, he will hear confessions from those who wish to make them, and he will say Mass tomorrow morning and every other morning for the rest of his stay with us."

A murmur of approval went through the hall, though Gavin did notice a few scowls from some of the rougher men-at-arms, who presumably would have much to confess and heavy penances to fulfill before they were welcomed at the chapel altar. Satisfied with the reaction to his announcement, Gavin sat down in the lord's chair and motioned to the servants to resume passing the food.

"I will not attend." Alda's face was chalk white.

"Do you fear confession?" Gavin asked. "Or is it penance you would like to avoid?"

"The priest will leave in a few days and then all will be as it was before his coming." Alda sounded as if she was trying to convince herself. "You will not get another priest to come here soon, for Wroxley is too small to be a parish."

"We shall see about that." Steeling himself, Gavin leaned a little closer to his wife and gave her his command. "You will be in the chapel tomorrow morning, my lady, or by heaven, I will go to your bedchamber and drag you out of bed and take you to Mass in your shift. Or wearing nothing at all, if you prefer."

In fact, Alda did appear at the chapel door the next day, very late, just as an angry Gavin was about to go in search of her. She wore a brilliant red silk gown, a golden gauze veil topped by her wide gold circlet, and entirely too much jewelry.

"Did no one think to put a brazier in here?" she demanded. "This chapel is cold as the grave." She shivered repeatedly throughout the service and left the moment Father John was finished. She did not attend Mass again and she stayed well away from Father John until he departed Wroxley to return to Cliffvale Castle.

There followed several weeks of busy and harmonious activity. The weather grew warmer and there were even occasional bright days when it appeared as if the ever-present clouds might disappear. They never actually did. It was as though a battle was going on between sunlight and clouds. On most days the clouds won but, even so, any lightening of the perpetual gloom was welcome.

In the fields around the castle the plowing was well under way and some fields had already been planted. Warrick and Robin were settling into their duties as squires and Emma was proving to be an eager helper to Mirielle. Alda retreated more and more to her own room, appearing only at mealtimes, when she sat, icy and unapproachable, beside Gavin at the high table. She did not talk to her husband at all, and as far as Mirielle could tell, Alda had no meetings with Brice.

In the evenings after the day's labor was done, a little group gathered in Mirielle's workroom. There Hugh told Warrick and Emma tales of his travels from his distant home to England. The stories were entertaining, but the children were learning, too, for

Hugh took care to explain much of the knowledge he had gained along his way.

"Mirielle," Hugh said one night, "may I have a bowl of water? Emma has just asked how I reached England from Cathay without becoming lost during my long journey and I would like to demonstrate the method I used."

Mirielle filled a wide clay bowl with water and set it on the table. From his robe Hugh drew a piece of wood as long as his thumb and carved into the shape of a fish.

"Embedded in the fish's belly is a piece of lodestone," Hugh explained, setting the wooden object atop the water. He gave the fish a shove with one finger. It spun around once or twice, then stopped.

"Emma, make the fish spin again, as I just did," Hugh instructed.

When Emma obeyed, the fish stopped its motion when it was pointing in the same direction as before.

"Now it is your turn, Mirielle." Hugh indicated that she should spin the fish. Again it stopped in the same position. Warrick's attempt to alter the final position of the fish was also unsuccessful.

"It always points the same way." Emma clapped her hands in delight.

"Were you to take this bowl outside on a clear night," Hugh told the children, "you would see that the fish points toward the north star. Knowing the fish's position is unchanging, a traveler can always find the right direction."

"Even when it's cloudy, as it always is around Wroxley?" Warrick asked.

"Even then," Hugh assured him.

"This is a very useful magic," said Emma, who was almost breathless with excitement.

"No magic is involved," Hugh told her. "Only knowledge of the properties of a lodestone."

Under Hugh's supervision the children were allowed to try a few experiments. More often, they watched while Mirielle or Hugh worked and described what they were doing. Under this regime Warrick lost most of his former sulkiness and his resistance to his father's requirement that he learn to use weapons in preparation for eventual knighthood. Mirielle suspected that Hugh was providing additional training of some kind in the matter of weaponry, for Warrick began to display a quiet self-control similar to Hugh's own reliable calmness.

Emma, too, was blossoming under Mirielle's guidance. The girl was quick and intelligent and soon made herself a useful assistant to Mirielle.

On rare evenings Gavin joined the little group in Mirielle's workroom and when he did, he would add his own version of events in the Holy Land to Hugh's tales. Less often, Robin came to the workroom. Most evenings he spent with his mother, for the only worry to disturb the steady round of springtime activity was a growing concern over the state of Donada's health.

"My medicines do not help her at all," Mirielle said to Hugh. "Donada has grown weaker. She is terribly pale, her skin is dry and flaky, and sometimes she is confused. Today, she asked me why her husband, Paul, had not come to see her all day."

"Would she allow me to examine her?" Hugh asked.

"I think so. I know I would be grateful for any advice you can offer."

"I will go to her later."

The next day was Sunday. Since Father John had returned to Cliffvale there could be no Mass said, but early morning prayers were held in the chapel. As if in answer to those prayers the sun broke through the clouds about noontime. Thus, after the midday meal the unusual pleasure of a long, sunny afternoon of freedom stretched before the inhabitants of the castle, for on the Sabbath, only the most vital work was done.

Hugh took Warrick and Robin into Mirielle's workroom right after chapel, warning Mirielle and Emma to stay out because a surprise was in the making.

"It's to cheer Robin," Hugh confided. "I see how downcast he is of late and how often he stays by his mother's side. Mirielle, do you think you could convince Donada to venture as far as the fallow field on the western side of the castle?"

"I will try," Mirielle promised. "Perhaps it will do her good to leave the castle for a while."

"I am sure it will," Hugh said. "It will also give me a chance to look at her in bright light. I went to see her last evening, but there was only a single oil lamp in her room. I could not tell what is wrong with her."

It took a bit of coaxing from both Mirielle and Robin when the midday meal was over, but at last Donada agreed to join the party in the field outside the castle.

"Go on, Robin. Warrick is waiting for you. I will catch up later." Donada rose, waving the boy away. After he hurried from the great hall to meet his friends, Donada leaned heavily on the table where she had been sitting during the meal. "If I can walk that far," she added to Mirielle.

"You will not have to walk." Gavin joined them. "Hugh has told me about his surprise and I am eager to see it, too. I have ordered my most gentle horse brought to the keep steps. Donada, you will ride pillion behind me. All you will have to do is hold tight to my belt."

He swept Donada into his arms. With Mirielle close behind them Gavin carried the sick woman out of the hall and down the steps to the inner bailey. Gavin had also ordered a horse for Mirielle, and she took Emma up behind her. They rode through the inner and outer baileys to the main gatehouse, where a sour-faced Mauger was on duty.

"The others have gone through ahead of you," Mauger said to Gavin. He did not trouble himself to add the usual "my lord" to his announcement. Gavin did not appear to notice. As they clattered across the drawbridge, Mirielle looked back to see Mauger scowling after them.

The field where Hugh, Warrick, and Robin awaited them was covered with rough green growth. Mirielle and Emma chose the driest spot they could find, Gavin spread out a quilt, and they all helped Donada to sit on it.

"Mother, it's a wonderful surprise," Robin said, bouncing from foot to foot in excitement. "I know you will like it."

"I am sure I will, my dear." Donada looked a bit more healthy now that she was in the sunshine, with a soft breeze rippling the edges of her wimple. "What are those strange objects that Hugh and Warrick are holding? Is that what you did with the scraps of thin fabric you asked of me yesterday?"

"Hugh says they are called kites," Robin responded. "He promises we can make them fly."

"No, I do not think so," Donada said. "That would be magic."

"In my homeland, kites are often flown in the springtime," Hugh told her. "It is not magic that sends them into the air, but only the same wind that catches a sheet when you spread it out to dry and the breeze lifts it. The boys have twisted threads they unraveled from the edges of the cloth into string, to hold the kites so they won't blow away as sheets sometimes do."

Donada laughed at this explanation. She laughed again when Hugh and the two boys began to run across the field with kites in hand. Hugh's caught the breeze first, then Robin's and, lastly, Warrick's kite lifted into the air.

"I want a kite, too." Emma clapped her hands. "Will you show me how to make one?"

"Come here and hold mine for a while," Hugh invited.

Mirielle watched this scene with increasing pleasure. She noticed Donada's spirits lifting as if they were borne upward by one of the kites. After a while Mirielle became aware of Gavin standing close beside her.

"Thank you for the horses," she said. "I fear Donada could not have walked so far."

"She is very ill," he said in the same low voice Mirielle had used. "What is wrong with her?"

"I do not know. None of my medicines help her. I am hoping Hugh will give me good advice."

"If Hugh cannot," said Gavin, "then no one can."

His hand brushed along Mirielle's arm and downward to her wrist. One finger slid into her palm, to circle there for a moment before his hand fell away to his side.

No one who was not standing directly behind them could have seen it. The gesture sent a surge of warmth through Mirielle. She looked up, into his eyes. He made no other motion toward her and there was a foot of space between them, yet Mirielle felt as if Gavin were embracing her. The warm melting that began deep inside her each time he put his arms around her started now. His eyes held hers. His lips lifted in a half smile. Mirielle caught her breath.

"Father!" called Emma, who was flying Hugh's kite. "Come and try it. I have never had such fun!" Her happy laughter rang out.

"Go," Mirielle said when Gavin hesitated. "Let her show you how it's done."

"Lady Mirielle," Robin called to her. "My lady, would you—I mean, if you would like to try—I would be pleased to help you."

"Thank you, Robin." Mirielle did not care that the field was growing a bit muddy with so many people running about on it. Robin was smiling for the first time in days and this excursion was intended partly to cheer him.

After a quick word to Donada, Mirielle hurried to where Robin was standing and let him show her how to keep the kite aloft for half an hour or so. During that time there was much laughter among the kite flyers and their advisors, and many suggestions on what to do when a kite dipped too near the ground. Several villeins came along and stopped to watch, their mouths dropping open in amazement, while upon the castle ramparts the sentries called out jokes to Warrick and Robin.

A man on horseback rode out of the castle gate and into the field to join them. Recognizing the man, Mirielle sighed. Her relationship with Brice had become cooler and much more distant since she had learned that he was Emma's father. She was sorely disappointed in her cousin. To lie with a woman whose husband had been away from home for years was bad enough, though it might be understandable. To carry on an affair with a young woman, married only a year or two, who was, at least ostensibly, still sharing a bed with her husband, was a deed for which there was no excuse. What Brice and Alda had done was reprehensible. Mirielle was not sure which of the two she blamed more.

"Sir Brice," Emma greeted the seneschal, "would you like to try your hand?"

"I think not," Brice said. "I will keep Mistress Donada company." With a casual wave in Emma's direction, Brice dropped onto the quilt next to Donada.

Mirielle could see that he had no idea Emma was his child. Brice had said often enough that, while other men wanted sons, he wished to have a daughter one day. As kindly as Brice had treated Mirielle, he would have cared still more for his own child. Though Mirielle was deeply distressed by what her cousin had done with Alda, in some small part of her heart she pitied Brice for what he had lost because of the affair. Unless Alda chose to tell him,

Brice would very likely never know the truth about Emma.

But, for the moment, Brice was talking to Donada, making her laugh and look healthier than she had for weeks. For that, Mirielle was grateful to him.

Mirielle was to remember that happy afternoon later and to recall the laughter of children and grownups, the rare spring sunshine glinting on Robin's red-brown curly hair, the sparkling, breeze-rippled water in the castle moat, the scent of fresh, growing plants and, above all, the sense of carefree fun, as if those hours were a brief and lovely dream.

As the sun began to set behind a bank of clouds, its fading rays turning the walls of Wroxley Castle to a fiery shade of rose-gold, Gavin set Donada on his horse and Mirielle took Emma up behind her again. Brice joined them, leaving Hugh and the two boys to walk home with their somewhat bedraggled kites. Mirielle sent a last look toward the castle, thinking how beautiful it was in the late-day light.

There on the wall, standing in one of the crenels, was a slim figure wrapped in a flame-red cloak. A strand of golden hair blew out on a breath of air, to glitter briefly in a slanting ray of sunlight. The figure remained motionless, staring down at the little group of riders and pedestrians now making their way homeward.

Mirielle did not think anyone else had noticed and she did not call attention to the watcher on the wall. But she shuddered with an unnamable foreboding as she rode along the edge of the moat behind Gavin, and she marvelled at the waves of malice that emanated from Alda's still form.

Emma said something about the kites, and how clever Hugh was to be able to make make them from memory, and Mirielle pulled her attention from the castle wall to answer the girl. When she looked back, Alda was gone.

Chapter Fifteen

"Donada is being poisoned." Hugh took his accustomed place beside Mirielle on the bench in her workroom. Gavin, who had come in with Hugh, paced about the room. Mirielle turned from watching him to ask a question of her friend.

"Hugh, are you certain of this?" He sounded as if he entertained no doubts at all, but Mirielle was shaken by the implications of his blunt statement.

"I have seen similar symptoms in the past," Hugh said. "Indeed, I have known people to die most horribly of Donada's ailment."

"Who would do such a thing to her? Donada has no enemies."

"Has she not?" Gavin met Mirielle's eyes and held them. Mirielle thought of the day when she had seen Donada in Brice's arms in the mews.

"Alda?" Mirielle whispered, not wanting to say the

name aloud. "I cannot believe that Alda has the ability, much less the opportunity, to poison anyone. She would need a knowledge of herbs—" Mirielle halted, catching her breath as she recalled a recent conversation.

"What is it?" Gavin asked.

"Emma said something once about inheriting her interest in alchemy from her mother," Mirielle answered. "She'd seen Alda doing something but when I questioned what she said, Emma decided she must have been mistaken, because she was a very little girl at the time. And, knowing Alda as I do, I discounted the idea. Do you think Alda might know enough about herbs to have poisoned Donada?"

Hugh nodded. "It is possible. Most noblewomen have fairly extensive knowledge of the ordinary household and medical uses of herbs, even though they may not care to use that information. But, Mirielle, I am not talking about the misuse of common preparations made from monkshood or hemlock or hellebore. What is wrong with Donada is caused by the skillful administration of a metallic substance over a long period of time. Thus, the poisoning appears to be a disease and murder is never suspected."

"Murder?" Mirielle could feel the blood leaving her face. "We cannot allow it to happen. Master Hugh, tell me what the poison is and how we can counteract it to help Donada."

"The poison is made from realgar or from orpiment," Hugh said. "The ore is heated until the poison is sublimated. When it cools, it crystalizes. The crystals thus obtained are ground into a fine powder and introduced into food or drink. A large dose kills immediately, but the symptoms appear so suddenly and are so painful that it is obvious the person has been poisoned. Careful villains use the more subtle method that is being employed in Donada's case."

"If we discount Alda for the time being," Mirielle suggested, "there are only three people in this castle who have the knowledge required to make such a poison—you, myself, and, possibly, Ewain the blacksmith.

"I do not believe you would poison anyone, I know I would not, and I find it difficult to imagine Ewain doing such a thing. He would need an accomplice, for he is seldom near Donada. Ewain lives and works in the outer bailey, while Donada spends her days mostly in the tower keep."

"Whereas Alda is frequently with Donada," said Gavin. "Donada is constantly making new gowns for her."

"We cannot accuse a noblewoman of a terrible crime without adequate proof," Mirielle said.

"Have you ever kept realgar or orpiment in this room?" Gavin asked. "Or in your bedchamber, to keep it out of careless hands?"

"No," Mirielle answered. "Once, Ewain brought me antimony, and I tried to extract the mercury from it. I was not successful. Another time, he gave me some lead, which I attempted to change. But, as Ewain can tell you, all metals are expensive, and many ores are hard to come by. My alchemical efforts have continually faltered on that problem. If you are suggesting that Alda might have taken from this room the materials she needed to make a poison, it is impossible.

"Master Hugh," Mirielle went on, turning to him.

"We can discuss later who is to blame for what has happened to Donada. Our immediate concern must be how to help her."

"I know of only one antidote to the poison," Hugh said, "and it is not always effective."

"If it is the only possibility, then we must try it," Mirielle responded. "Make free use of this room to prepare the antidote. Any of my supplies that you might need are at your disposal and I will help you if you wish."

"Allow me to suggest," said Gavin, "that for her safety Donada be confined to her bedchamber and that she eat and drink only what the two of you prepare and carry to her with your own hands."

"Agreed." Hugh looked from Gavin to Mirielle. "I have a few supplies among my belongings. I will get them from my room and return shortly."

"If anyone can save your friend, it will be Hugh," Gavin said to Mirielle after Hugh had gone. "I have seen him work wonders on men near death from battle wounds."

"This is not exactly the same thing." Mirielle brushed at her eyes. "I am afraid for Donada."

Gavin caught one of her hands and lifted her fingers to his lips for a lingering kiss.

"Gavin." Her voice trembled. Her breath caught in her throat. She knew she ought to pull her hand out of his grasp, but she could not. Unable to stop herself, she touched his face with the hand he was not holding. Softly she traced along the line of his eyebrows, moved to his cheekbones, then down along his jaw. She ended the caress at his mouth, running her fingertips across the sensuous line of his lower lip. With a groan he turned his head away, but still he held her hand, his fingers now interlaced with hers.

"I would do more to show you how I feel," he said, "but we are pledged, you and I, to keep the marriage vows I once made to Alda. Mirielle, I promise you, I will find a pathway through the morass of deceit and evil that threatens this castle. And when we come out on the other side, there will be a future far different from the one we see now."

Then, at last, he did release the hand he had been holding all that time. He drew a deep breath as if to steady himself and when he spoke again, it was in his brisk, lord-of-the-castle voice.

"While you and Hugh do your best for Donada in this room," Gavin told her, "I will take steps to stop Alda from causing more trouble."

"Gavin, we cannot be absolutely certain that Alda is to blame," Mirielle insisted.

"I am certain," he said.

It took several hours for Hugh and Mirielle, working together, to complete preparation of the antidote to the poison Hugh believed was being fed to Donada. When it was ready, they took the medicine to Donada's room. Robin was there, hovering anxiously around his mother's bed.

"Lady Mirielle," Robin said as soon as he saw her, "my mother was so much better yesterday evening, after we all came in from flying our kites, but this afternoon, she fell ill again. I was just about to search for you, to ask you to come to her."

"We have some new medicine for her." Mirielle set the tray she was carrying down on the clothes chest. She had brought a stoppered bottle of the antidote, two clean cups, and a pitcher of fresh water that she had personally drawn from the castle well. While she mixed the antidote with water, Hugh explained the restrictions on food and drink which he wanted Donada to observe.

"Here you are." Mirielle brought the cup of medicine to Donada.

"I do not think I can swallow it," Donada rasped. "Since the midday meal, I have been so sick. I could not keep down the food I ate."

"You must take it." Hugh lifted Donada's head and motioned for Mirielle to hold the cup to her lips. "Sip by sip, it will make you better. Think of Robin. Think of all the pleasant things you plan to do this spring and summer. Donada, you must trust me when I say you will recover."

"I wish it were so." Donada sighed.

"It *will* be so." Hugh took the cup from Mirielle and held it to Donada's lips again. She took another sip.

Mirielle put an arm around Robin. She could feel him trembling. When she looked at Hugh, she could sense how worried he was.

Donada's appearance was enough to raise fear in the heart of anyone who beheld her. Her once thick and luxuriant hair, so like Robin's with its red-brown color and bouncy curls, lay thin and limp across her shoulders. Donada had been a comely, well-built woman; now she was pale and looked half starved. Her lips were drawn back in a grimace of pain and when Donada lifted a hand to her face, Mirielle saw that her nails had developed peculiar white streaks in them.

A voice in Mirielle's mind told her that, despite

her best efforts and Hugh's, Donada could not live much longer.

Well after midnight the special latch on the door to Mirielle's workroom unfastened. Without a sound the door swung open and a shadowy figure entered the unlit room. The figure stood for a moment as if making a decision. Contempt and cold rage flowed outward from that dark form.

As if a puny herbal medicine could stop me. What an innocent Mirielle is, she and that little man Hugh, who calls himself her friend. Their power combined will always be less than the darkness. And the darkness will win.

Nothing was taken from the workroom. Rather, something was left there. When the dark figure slipped out of the door and closed it again, when the special latch refastened itself at the silent command of that mysterious shadow, there remained inside Mirielle's workroom, on a shelf where jars of dried herbs usually sat, a plain, oblong wooden box.

"Robin is sick," Warrick told Mirielle. "He says it is the same illness his mother has. Robin says Mistress Donada began as he is doing."

"Hugh and I made some new medicine yesterday," Mirielle said. "I will take some to Robin. Perhaps it will prevent him from becoming as sick as his mother is."

"Lady Mirielle." Warrick hesitated, then spoke in a rush. "Will others catch this sickness, too? Because if so, I am the person most likely to develop it next, since I have been with Robin every day for weeks. Therefore, I ought to be the one to care for

Robin, to avoid making others sick. If Emma learns of his illness, she will insist on helping Robin. I want her to stay away from him. And you, too, my lady." Warrick's brow wrinkled. "I do not want either of you to become ill."

"That is very thoughtful of you," Mirielle said. "I promise you, the illness is not contagious. Where is Robin? I will go to him at once."

"He is in the garderobe." Warrick blushed a little. "He did not want me to tell anyone, but I think you need to know. Robin is suffering from stomach cramps and a dreadful bout of diarrhea."

"It is how his mother's illness began. Warrick, as soon as he can leave the garderobe, I want you to send Robin to his mother's room. Tell him not to eat or drink anything—not anything at all!—unless Hugh or I personally give it to him."

"Yes, my lady."

"Then you are to find your father. Take him aside and tell him in private what has happened. Tell no one else. If you should see Hugh, ask him to come to me."

To her despair, upon reaching Donada's room Mirielle found her friend even more sick than she had been on the previous day.

"I don't think your medicine is working." Donada could not speak above a whisper. She complained that her lips and throat felt as if they were burning, and she wept when Mirielle insisted she must swallow the medicine.

In the midst of Mirielle's attempts to help Donada, Robin appeared. After one look at the boy, Mirielle was convinced that he, too, was being poisoned. She put him on a trundle bed in his mother's room.

When Warrick arrived, eager to help his friend, Mirielle gave him strict instructions on how to deal with the sickness, and then she went in search of Hugh. She found him questioning Ewain the blacksmith.

"You must come at once," Mirielle said to Hugh. "Donada is worse, and now Robin is sick, too."

"Ah, that poor lady." Ewain shook his head. "When she was the seneschal's wife, she was always polite to me and my wife. That hasn't changed, though she has fallen in rank since Sir Paul died. I wish Mistress Donada well. Will you tell her so, Lady Mirielle?"

"Of course I will." Mirielle and Hugh left the blacksmith's shop, in their haste bumping against Mauger the watchman, who was just entering.

"Watch where you're going," said Mauger in his usual rude way.

"Now, there is a man I cannot like," murmured Hugh, turning around for a moment to look back at Mauger before Mirielle hurried him along toward the inner bailey and the keep.

They found Donada's condition unimproved since Mirielle had left her. During the remainder of that day and into the night Donada grew steadily weaker, until she could no longer swallow the medicine that Hugh and Mirielle offered, and from time to time her thoughts wandered.

When Robin dropped off into a restless sleep, Hugh took Warrick to the kitchen where, he told Mirielle, he would insist that the boy eat of food that Hugh knew was safe. Hugh's silent implication that Warrick was also in danger of being poisoned sent a chill through Mirielle.

"Mirielle," Donada whispered hoarsely, "this is no

common illness. All your herbs will not save me."

"We will try everything we can," Mirielle said.

"This is the way Lord Udo died." Donada rested a moment before speaking again. "And my dear Paul, too, because he knew how Udo was killed and who did it. Poor Brice, what will happen to him now?"

"Donada," Mirielle cried, "what are you saying?"

"I thought Brice was to blame," Donada whispered. "I tried to discover how he could have done it when he was not yet here at Wroxley."

"You believe that Lord Udo and your husband were both poisoned? And you thought my cousin Brice did it?" Mirielle's horrified whisper was no louder than Donada's painful rasp. "He would not murder anyone, not even to become seneschal of Wroxley!"

"I know that now," Donada said.

"Dear friend, I know you may not feel well enough to talk for very long." Mirielle spoke gently. "But this is important. If the person who poisoned Lord Udo and then your husband knows that you are aware of those wicked deeds, there would be good cause for the same person to try to kill you."

"Such a waste," Donada whispered, as if she had not heard what Mirielle had just said. "I never lay with Brice. I could not, when I thought he had killed Paul. I only wanted to learn if Brice was guilty-and then, later, how much he knew."

"Donada, do you know who has made you ill?"

"Not Brice," she said. "Poor, foolish Brice. I have grown fond of him, in spite of myself. But I never lay with him, so there was no need to punish—"

"Was it Alda who did this to you?" Mirielle fought her own impatient urge to shake the sick woman in an attempt to bring her wandering thoughts back to the important subject. Donada was so fragile, her hold on life so tenuous by now that she could barely endure the effort it took to speak a few words. "Donada, please tell me what you know about this. I am trying to help you. And help Robin."

"You will take care of him, won't you, Mirielle? He thinks you are a very great and wonderful lady. I know it was you who convinced Lord Gavin to raise my Robin from stableboy to his rightful place as a squire. Thank you for that."

"Donada, who is poisoning you?" Mirielle gripped Donada's hand, pressing it hard in the hope of drawing Donada's full attention to the question she had asked.

"The mage hides," Donada said. "And there is someone else—oh, Mirielle, the blackness! I cannot fight it."

Donada began to struggle then, and Mirielle, thinking she could not breathe well, lifted Donada until her head was resting on Mirielle's shoulder. She was still holding Donada that way when Hugh returned with Warrick.

"You sent a summons to me through Mauger!" Brice slammed shut the door of Alda's chamber. "You told a watchman, a common man-at-arms, to give *me* an order?"

"I need you, Brice."

As usual, the room was too hot and it smelled heavily of the rose-scented perfumes that Alda used so lavishly. Alda was wearing only a golden gauze veil, which she had draped over one shoulder in a manner that concealed nothing of her lovely body.

Her hair was loose, flowing down her back.

"Come to me." Alda held out her arms.

"Have you lost all your wits, woman?" Brice turned to leave. "You are married to my liege lord, who may walk in at any moment."

"Gavin will not come here. He does not want me. Gavin is unimportant. But you . . ." Alda's hands were on his back, sliding down his spine and along his flanks, her fingers conveying heat and the promise of intense pleasure to come. She spoke in a throaty purr. "Your passion strengthens me. It gives me power over you, Brice. And other powers, far greater, that you would not understand."

Brice stood transfixed by her caresses, completely unable to move. He wanted to leave Alda and he hated himself because he could not go. Donada, the woman he loved, lay close to death, and Brice suspected that Alda had something to do with Donada's illness. On receiving the summons that Mauger had so rudely delivered to him, Brice had decided to obey it and then to demand the truth of Alda. He would resort to hurting her if he must, but he would learn whether or not she was making Donada sick.

"Satisfy me, Brice." Alda's fingers worked their way between his legs. His flesh did not care what Alda had done, or might have done. His overheated, partially rigid manhood responded to the stimulation she was providing, and to the promise of the dark release he knew he would find in her.

"I despise you," he said to Alda.

"It does not matter." She stroked his growing hardness. "Give me this. It's all I need from you." She drew him toward the bed.

Brice pushed her down onto the coverlet. She

pulled him to her and Brice felt his body respond with a demand for immediate relief. Still, he hesitated a little longer. Every time he buried himself in Alda's flesh he betrayed his liege lord, betrayed gentle Donada, his cousin Mirielle's faith in him, and his own best interests. Furious with himself for his inability to break away from Alda, knowing he would find physical release but nothing else with her, Brice rammed himself into her squirming, wriggling body. Her cry of delighted triumph was like a serrated knife slashing across his mind and heart.

"Mother, don't leave me!" Robin held fast to Donada's hand.

"Mirielle will care for you now." Donada moved her head, which still rested on Mirielle's shoulder. "I wish Father John had stayed longer."

"I could ride to Bardney Abbey and fetch a priest," Warrick offered, "but it will take a few days."

"Thank you, Warrick, but I do not have the time to wait." Donada uttered a despairing sigh, and Mirielle thought she was gone. But she spoke again.

"If I cannot make my last confession, at least let me be buried with a priest to say prayers for my soul. Mirielle, don't let me be put into the ground until there is a priest here."

"I promise. I will see to it. Gavin will make no objection." There was no point in pretending that burial instructions were not necessary. All anyone could do for Donada now was to try to ease her mind, thus making her passage into the next life less painful.

"Thank you, Mirielle." Donada lifted a trembling

hand to touch her son's face. "Robin, my dear." Her hand dropped. Donada lay still. Hugh put his hand at her throat for a moment.

"She has left us," he said.

"Mother! No!" Robin burst into tears.

Gavin had come quietly into the room at the last, and now he bent to the bereaved boy.

"Robin," he began.

"I will stop crying in a moment," Robin said, gulping on a sob.

"Cry all you want. I wept, too, when my mother died." Gavin laid a hand on Robin's shoulder. "I only wanted to say that we will do as your mother asked. Donada's coffin will be placed in the crypt where my parents lie, and there she will stay until a priest can come to bury her properly."

"Thank you, my lord."

"And I do swear to you, Robin," Gavin went on, "that I will find out the villain who has killed your mother and made you sick, and when I do, that person will pay dearly for the crime."

Chapter Sixteen

"My friend," Hugh said to Gavin when the two of them stood outside the door of Donada's chamber, "will you allow me to arrange for the dispostion of that good lady's body?"

"Do you think you can learn something from her poor corpse?" asked Gavin. Seeing a certain closed look come into Hugh's eyes, Gavin went on, "Make any arrangements you think right, so long as you do not further distress young Robin or go against his wishes or Donada's. If anyone objects to what you do, send that person to me."

"Thank you for your trust," Hugh said. "And for not asking questions I would not be willing to answer until I am more certain of the facts surrounding these two illnesses. Mirielle and the other women are preparing Donada's body now. When they have finished, I will order her carried to the crypt, as you have told Robin will be done."

"You will want a coffin," Gavin said. "The carpenter usually has two or three ready in case of sudden need."

"No," Hugh responded instantly. "No coffin will be needed. Not yet. For the present, Donada is to be wrapped in her shroud, laid out on a bier, and covered with a plain linen sheet."

"I was right." Gavin looked hard at him. "You do have a plan. Do you think the killer will go to the crypt to see the results of this terrible deed?"

"That is always a possibility," Hugh replied, somewhat evasively.

"If only I had proof of what Alda has done," Gavin declared, "I would put her in chains in the dungeon where she once sent me. But, without proof, I cannot in good conscience imprison a noblewoman in that way. The most I can do is lock her into her room and set a guard at the door."

"If Alda truly is the source of the dark strength I sense in this castle, chains will not hold her," Hugh said, "nor locks and guards, either."

"While I can easily imagine Alda poisoning someone if she imagined she had a reason for the deed, I find it hard to believe that she is a sorceress," Gavin said. "I do not think she has the will to concentrate her thoughts for long periods, as you have told me you learned to do. And here's a question for you: If she is a sorceress, where did she learn her magical skills? Who was her teacher?"

"I have asked myself the same questions," Hugh replied. "I have no answers."

"Keep a close watch on Robin," Gavin ordered. "Do not let him become the next victim."

Leaving Hugh, Gavin made his way to Alda's room. He did not bother to knock. Availing himself of a husband's privilege, he walked right in. Alda was draping a golden gauze veil about her otherwise naked body. Her maidservant was making up the bed with fresh sheets.

"Out." Gavin looked at the maid and jerked his head in the direction of the door. With a sly smile the maid turned down the covers to make the bed ready for immediate use. Then she curtsied and left Gavin alone with his wife.

"Must you keep this room so infernally hot?" Gavin asked. "I am told you require vast quantities of charcoal."

"I am often cold." Alda did not look at him, instead occupying herself with the arrangement of the veil.

"If you wore the clothing that any decent woman wears, you would be warm without needing braziers." When Alda did not reply to this, Gavin said, "Donada has just died."

"Oh." Alda showed little interest in this information. "Well, she has not been much use to me of late, with her continual protestations that she was too sick to work on my new gowns."

"She *was* sick." Gavin frowned his disapproval at her, but Alda was still draping the folds of her veil and paying no attention to him. "Is that all you have to say about the death of a woman who spent a great deal of time with you and always gave you honest service?"

"I will have to find another seamstress at once."

Gavin flexed his fingers. He did not want to touch Alda. He thought his hands would be forever soiled if he did. But she seemed determined not to look at him, and he wanted to see her eyes when he made his accusation. Gritting his teeth, he grabbed his wife by the shoulders.

"Take your hands off me!" Alda's head came up as Gavin intended and her eyes blazed barely contained rage at him. "I told you I would never lie with you again."

"Nor would I defile myself by lying with you," Gavin shot back. "I only want to know the answer to one question. Did you poison Donada?"

"I?" Alda laughed at him. "Why should I want to rid myself of a perfectly good seamstress?"

"Perhaps you thought she was your lover's other mistress. If so, you were mistaken."

She did not rise to the challenge in his words by denying to her husband that she had a lover. Alda took a different direction, issuing her own challenge.

"If you want a poisoner," she said, "look to your precious Mirielle. She has the most amazing collection of harmful herbs in her workroom. Not long ago I tried to have them removed for the good of all who live at Wroxley, but I understand that she has been busy replenishing her supplies."

"Mirielle would never harm anyone," Gavin stated.

"Are you really so sure? Tell me, dear husband, has your mysterious friend determined what the poison was that killed Donada? If he has, I am willing to wager that same substance could be discovered in Mirielle's workroom, if someone were to look for it. But you will never find any poisons in my chamber, nor any proof of your false accusation against me. Now, let me go."

"There is a woman far better than you lying dead, and an innocent boy who is sick of the same poison that killed his mother. I am certain you are the cause of both calamities." Keeping a tight rein on his temper, refusing to give in to the violent urge that tempted him to strangle Alda, Gavin took his hands off her shoulders. He knew he could no longer allow her to roam freely about the castle. He spoke with controlled authority, laying down his newly made rules for her. "I will find the proof I need. Until I do, you are confined to this room. There will be two guards at your door at all times. Your personal maidservant will be assigned to other duties. I will choose a new maidservant for you, one who will report to me any attempt you make to leave your room or to send or receive a message."

With Donada's remains taken to the crypt under Hugh's supervision, Mirielle turned her full attention to Robin, who was complaining of pains in his abdomen and a terrible burning in his throat and mouth which was not alleviated by water or by the herbal infusions Mirielle offered. When Robin began to vomit, Mirielle's fears for him increased. She was certain his sorry condition was in part due to grief at the loss of his mother, but it was also true that his illness was progressing more rapidly than had Donada's.

"My lady, please do something for him." Warrick insisted on remaining with his friend. He looked frightened and he spoke in a whisper so Robin could not hear what he said. "I don't want Robin to die."

263

"Perhaps some of the special medicine that Hugh made will help. It was intended for a grownup, but I can dilute it with extra water." Mirielle looked at the tray on which she had carried the water pitcher, the cups, and the medicine to Donada's room. "Warrick, where is the medicine jar? I have been so busy tending to Robin that I did not notice it is gone."

"I think Hugh took it away with him," Warrick said. "Do you have more of it in your workroom? Or can you make another batch quickly? If there is anything I might do to help you, I will gladly do it, for Robin's sake."

"The best thing you can do is stay with Robin. Let no one but me or your father enter this room. I will find Hugh and ask him to make a preparation suitable for Robin."

Mirielle's search took her first to the crypt, where she hoped Hugh would still be. Donada's bier had been placed near Lord Udo's tomb. One of the crypt candelabra was set at her head and the other at her feet. The soft candlelight shone across the linen sheet that covered the dead woman to her chin. The same gentle glow lit Donada's waxlike features. Mirielle bowed her head, but only for a moment. Finding Hugh and doing what they could to save Robin was vitally important. Prayers for the dead would have to wait. Mirielle knew Donada would understand, for her son had been the dearest thing on earth to her.

As Mirielle moved toward the steps, she met Brice coming into the crypt. Tears streamed down his face. He stiffled a sob and bent to kiss Donada's cheek, which was only a little more pale than Brice's own. He straightened slowly, as if all of his joints ached.

"I blame myself," Brice said. "Gavin tells me that he suspects Alda is responsible for this death. If that is true, it may well have happened because Alda learned how deeply I cared for Donada."

"Brice, if you are truly sorry," Mirielle said, "then keep away from Alda. Your liaison with her cannot continue."

"I try to stay away, but she prevents me."

"She cannot prevent you if you are determined. Be a man, Brice! Do what you know is right." Mirielle trembled between tears and anger. "For more than a year now, you and Alda have been doing something very wrong. Whether you will acknowlege it or not, the evil generated by your actions has harmed everyone in this castle. Now you must end the affair, if Alda will not."

"She says I give her strength and power." Brice ran a hand through his dark hair. His ashen cheeks were still damp from the tears he had shed and he wore a haggard look, with purple shadows under his eyes. "In truth, I can believe Alda's claim, for when I leave her I feel drained, as if the heart has gone out of me along with my seed. Over and over again I promise myself I will not return to her, but when she summons me, I am compelled to obey. Once, when I did exert all my will and kept myself from her, she appeared in my bedchamber late at night and she humiliated me in a way that no man would be likely to forgive. That night, she was so voracious that I feared she would kill me.

"Forgive me, Mirielle," he said more calmly. "I should not speak this way to a maiden."

"Are you claiming that Alda has cast a spell over you that makes you unable to break free of her?" Mirielle asked.

"If I were to say so, it would be her denial against my word, and she could easily claim her beauty was the cause of my desire. What man, looking at Alda, would be surprised to know I cannot stop wanting her? But I am no longer blinded by lust, not after today's tragedy." Brice made as if to touch Donada's still form, then withdrew his hand.

"I have no right to lay a single finger of mine upon her," he said on a sigh. "My presence here mocks her goodness. I will leave." He paused with one hand at his head as if he were trying to gather his strength for the ascent to the upper level of the keep.

"Brice, are you ill?"

"Merely weary and overcome with sorrow for Donada's sake."

"I came to the crypt looking for Hugh," Mirielle said as they went up the steps together. "Have you seen him?"

"No." Brice responded absently. He appeared to be thinking of something other than Mirielle's question.

"If you should come upon him, will you ask him to join me in my workroom? Robin is sick and needs more medicine."

"Not Robin? He's a good lad, Mirielle. Take care of him. I know you will." They reached the top of the stairs. Leaving Mirielle's side Brice went to the door of the chapel. "This is the only place where I will find help. I will say a prayer for Robin. And for Donada's sweet soul." He went into the chapel, leaving Mirielle to continue by herself up the next flight of the spiral stairs.

Upon reaching the top of the steps, which ended in the entry hall, Mirielle discovered Hugh there with Gavin. Emma was with them and she was gazing up at Gavin in open adoration. As soon as Mirielle explained why she was searching for him, Hugh produced the missing stoppered jar from the scrip at his belt.

"I brought the medicine away with me," Hugh said. "There were serving women in and out of Donada's room, preparing her for burial, and I thought it best to keep this safe from any tampering."

"Will you come with me now and administer it to Robin? I fear greatly for him, and so does Warrick, who is sitting with Robin in my absence."

"I will go, too," Emma said. She put her hand in Mirielle's. "Robin is my friend. I want to be with him."

"Before you go, Mirielle, I would speak with you in private." Gavin's hand on Emma's back moved her gently away from Mirielle and toward Hugh. "Mirielle and I will join you shortly in Donada's room."

"Please don't be long," Emma begged. "I am sure Robin will be cheered by your presence, Father."

"Come to my workroom," Mirielle said to Gavin. "We can be private there."

Upon entering the workroom Gavin went at once to the furnace. Though the fire was banked, there was still residual heat radiating from it, and Minn lay sleeping in her usual corner next to it. Gavin held his hands over the furnace.

"I am cold," he said. "Perhaps it is because I have

267

just been to see Alda. Her lack of compassion for Donada's illness and death would chill any man who has a heart."

"You do not look well. Gavin, you are much too pale. I have never seen your hands shake before."

"With anger and not weakness, I assure you." Gavin clasped his hands behind his back where Mirielle could not see them. "Perhaps I have caught a chill. My throat and eyes are burning and my stomach is unsettled. Next my nose will begin to run," he ended on a laugh that Mirielle was certain was intended to make her smile in response.

She did not smile. She thought of Donada's symptoms, and of Robin's. She recalled Brice's pale face and the way he had moved in the crypt, as if he were a very old man.

"You are sick, too," she said. "So is Brice, I think. This is how Donada began."

"If that is so," Gavin replied, "then Robin and Brice and I ought to be well soon. I have ordered Alda confined to her chamber, so she can do no more harm."

"I am not sure physical confinement will stop her from causing trouble."

"Hugh suggested the same thing. Thus, I have made a decision about you and the children. I want to talk to you about it before I tell them. What is this?" Gavin broke off what he was saying when his eyes lit upon an oblong wooden box that sat on one of the shelves. "This was not here yesterday. I looked around the room, and particularly at those empty shelves. I remember thinking how much still needs to be replaced since your herbs and your equipment were ruined at Alda's command."

"I have never seen that box before," Mirielle said.

"No?" Gavin took the wooden object from the shelf and placed it on the table. "Will you open it, or shall I?"

Mirielle hesitated. She was filled with an unreasoning fear but she made herself reach out and remove the lid. The box contained a single small, gray rock with streaks of yellow and red in it.

Mirielle dropped the lid on the table and stepped away. Gavin caught her in his arms.

"Tell me what this is," he ordered, holding her close as if to protect her from danger.

"If you place that piece of ore over a very hot flame until it is sublimated," she said, her voice just above a whisper, "the vapor thus produced will solidify into crystals as it cools. Gavin, it is the poison Hugh described to us."

Gavin's arms tightened around her. His lips brushed her forehead as if to comfort her. Mirielle pulled away from him so she could look directly into his eyes.

"This is not my ore," she said. "Since the time when you and Hugh and I were here yesterday, someone has come into this room and left the box where you found it. How it was done, I do not know, because I always make certain to leave the door securely latched. Only Hugh has ever been able to enter here when that latch was set."

"The box may have been placed on that shelf to make us suspect Hugh, or to make Hugh and me suspect you," Gavin said.

"You may be right." Mirielle's heart lightened at his next words.

"I do not believe either of you has any evil intent."

"Thank you." But a new fear assaulted Mirielle. "If someone could enter here despite my best efforts, that same person might leave the door open upon leaving. Most of the castle folk are afraid to come into this room, but not so the children. Emma and Warrick come here freely each evening for their lessons, and sometimes Robin comes, too. Emma and Warrick in particular are extremely curious about the work I do and either of them might innocently take up and handle this dangerous substance."

"The children." As he listened to her, Gavin's face went even whiter than it had been. "This incident only confirms the wisdom of the decision I have made. Mirielle, I am going to lay a heavy responsibility on your shoulders. At this moment, you and Hugh and the men I brought here with me are the only people I can trust. Will you promise to do what I ask of you?"

"Of course, I promise." She put out her hands to him. At once he caught her in his arms. Then his mouth was on hers in a greedy, devouring kiss that Mirielle eagerly returned. In the days just past she had longed for the caresses and the tender intimacy they were forced to deny themselves. Certain as they now were of a growing danger, she did not think it was wrong for them to offer this much sustenance to each other. With lips and tongues and encircling arms they spoke of a tender emotion that threatened to overcome the limits they had placed upon it for honor's sake. Wanting each other, still they observed those limits.

As if he had received what he needed from her, Gavin softened the kiss from hungry passion to deep tenderness and then, finally, to the softest of caresses upon her lips. With a soft sigh Mirielle tucked her head into his shoulder. Gavin rested his cheek against her hair. They stood for a while with their arms still around each other, but not so tightly nor so desperately as before, and Mirielle was content to have their embrace end in this way.

"My dear heart," Gavin whispered, "above all else, I want you and the children to be safe. I know Hugh is right when he says the dark power in this place is steadily gaining strength. Donada's death proves the truth of that contention. I am not ashamed to tell you that Robin's illness frightens me. Only the darkest, most decadent evil would stoop low enough to attack an innocent child.

"Therefore, I have extracted your promise to obey me." Gavin shifted his hold on her so he could see Mirielle's face as he told her what he was going to require of her. "You are to tell no one of this plan. Tomorrow at first light, you and Hugh are to take those three children out of Wroxley. I will send my squire, Bevis, with you to help with the horses. I depend upon you and Hugh to use your powers to protect the children until you reach Bardney Abbey. There, in that holy place, all of you should be safe until I have vanquished the danger here at Wroxley."

"You cannot fight a dark mage by yourself," Mirielle cried. "Let me stay."

"I cannot do what I must if I am paralyzed by fear for you and the children," he retorted. "Do not quarrel with me over this, Mirielle. My mind is made up and I will not change it. And remember, you have promised to do as I ask."

"Then let Hugh stay with you. He would probably

be of more help than I could be to you," she admitted.

"I will have Captain Oliver, my second squire, Hidern, and my own men-at-arms to back me." Gavin would not be swayed from his plan, not even when Mirielle pointed out how useless men-at-arms would be against magic.

"Hugh and I are in agreement on this," Gavin said when she once more insisted that he could not face the unknown evil without powerful assistance. "He understands what we have come to Wroxley to accomplish. Hugh is going with you because he and I are agreed that Warrick must be kept safe. Whatever happens to me, my son must survive what is to come, for he is the next heir. Nor can I abandon Robin and Emma to an evil they are too young to withstand."

"You are right, my lord. Send Mirielle and the children away." So intent had Mirielle and Gavin been on their talk that they had not heard Brice come through the unlatched door and into the workroom. Mirielle's guardian said nothing about discovering his ward in the arms of a married man. Brice's face was ashen and his movements were stiff and slow.

"Brice, I can see that you are as sick as Robin is," Mirielle cried. "You should leave Wroxley with us. Gavin, order him to do so."

"My liege lord." Brushing aside Mirielle's concern, Brice addressed Gavin in a voice surprisingly forceful for a man as ill as he appeared to be. "Since Donada's death I have begun to realize that I have been ensnared by a power I do not understand—though, if the truth be told, I made little effort to resist what was happening. My worldly ambition led me to betray you in the most intimate and personal of ways. I believe I may be in part responsible for the harm that has been done to Donada and her son. Perhaps the illness that has come upon me today is my punishment for that betrayal. My lord, I ask only that you will allow me to fight by your side in the coming battle. You will find me as loyal now as I was false before." With a rough movement that looked to Mirielle as if it sorely jarred Brice's knees and back, he knelt before Gavin.

Gavin still had one arm around Mirielle. He looked down at Brice, who had bowed his head. Releasing his hold on Mirielle, Gavin put forth his right hand and lightly cuffed Brice on the shoulder.

"Arise, Sir Brice," Gavin said. "Be renewed in your knighthood and in my service by your confession and your promise of loyalty. Your faults and your wrong decisions are many and some of them are still unknown to you. However, believing that you are at heart an honest man and a truly repentant one, I trust you will not fail me again."

"I will not, my lord." Brice stood with some difficulty. "Though I have failed you many times, Mirielle has not. I thank you for your care of her, and I heartily approve of your decision to send her away from here."

"Brice." Mirielle would have gone to him, to try to offer some comfort for the grief and shame she knew he was experiencing. Gavin stopped her.

"No, Mirielle," Gavin said. "Go to Hugh. Tell him that you and I are in accord. He will understand what you mean. Do not mention our plan to anyone, nor to Hugh or me when we meet outside this room. Make whatever preparations for the journey you can without raising questions. Then follow Hugh's directions."

"Will you see us off tomorrow?" she asked.

"You are to leave as quietly as possible. This is our farewell." He took her right hand and, as if Brice were not there in the room, Gavin kissed her palm and folded her fingers over the spot where his lips had touched her skin. "Keep this, for my heart is in it. When we meet again after Wroxley is free of this malign influence, then I will ask you to return what I have just given you."

"Gavin." Tears stung her eyes. A sob she refused to utter stopped her voice. One of Gavin's fingers lay upon her lips, sealing any words she might have spoken. Putting his arm around her waist again, he guided her toward the door.

"Fare you well, my love," he whispered.

The few preparations Mirielle had cautiously made were almost complete. It was midnight and the children were all asleep. Hugh had taken Robin into his own room, saying he could better care for the boy there. Mirielle alone knew that Hugh's actual intent was to send Robin into a deep sleep, so the journey to Bardney Abbey would not cause irreparable harm to Robin's already damaged health. Hugh would bear Robin to the abbey in his own arms.

Mirielle had one last treasure to pack into the small bundle that contained both her own personal belongings and a few items for Emma's use. She took the crystal sphere out of her clothes chest, unwrapped it, and held it in the palm of her left hand. The light from the oil lamp flickered over the polished surface. Deep inside the sphere, where the tiny inclusion was, Mirielle could see a faint, silver sparkle when a beam of light broke on the irregularity.

The change came quickly, as if fog were spiraling outward from the sparkling light to fill the sphere. Within the blink of an eye the clear crystal turned milky white. As Mirielle gazed in rapt attention, flames and dark smoke began to swirl through the paleness. Mirielle's hand trembled. She could not look away, she could only stare at the images inside the sphere.

Slowly two figures emerged. One was clothed in shining red robes that matched the flames. The other shape was taller, broader, and garbed in black. Its outlines were shifting and blurred, as if it were part of the smoke. This second figure emitted waves of malevolent darkness, along with a cold that reached beyond the confines of the sphere to penetrate Mirielle's hand and travel up her arm to her heart. She could not see the face of either of the figures, but she thought the one in red had golden hair.

"Alda?" Mirielle whispered. "Oh, Alda, what have you done now? And what are you planning to do?"

Even as she spoke the two figures vanished behind a renewed burst of flame and smoke. As if the form shrouded in black had taken control of the vision, the sphere in Mirielle's palm began to change color, growing steadily darker. Here and there a few flashes of red glimmered and then the sphere went completely black. Mirielle continued to stare at the object in her palm, which now resembled a rounded chunk of charcoal. After a while the dull, frightening blackness disappeared and the sphere returned to its usual clear state. All Mirielle could see in it was a quick sparkle of silver light from far inside the crystal.

"Another mystery," Mirielle said to herself. "Who is that dark figure? Is it a demon from the Underworld? Or a person who resides here at Wroxley? Could it be a person living outside Wroxley, who has a mystical hold on Alda?"

Knowing she would find no answers in the now unresponsive crystal, Mirielle took up the silk and rewrapped the sphere. She tucked it into the bundle containing her personal possessions. She could not leave the sphere behind, and when she returned to Wroxley it would come with her.

"Even if it is the only thing I bring back," she whispered softly. "For I know what I have to do. If my life is lost, if the sphere is broken, so be it, but Gavin must be saved."

Chapter Seventeen

Bardney Abbey was noted for the hospitality dispensed by the Benedictine monks who lived there. The group from Wroxley Castle was made welcome by the guest master, who showed them to the well-appointed guest house and offered free use of the medicines made by the abbey's infirmarer.

"For that kindness, I thank you, brother," said Hugh, who was still carrying the sleeping Robin. "Your infirmarer may well have knowledge that I lack. Robin's case is a peculiar one, though I do assure you, we bring no contagion into your house."

It was quickly settled that Hugh and Robin should occupy one guest cell and Warrick and Bevis another, two doors away, with Mirielle and Emma in the middle cell.

"For safety's sake," Hugh explained, "though I cannot think there will be any danger to us in this place. Women and children may sleep here secure in the knowledge that they are protected by all that is good and decent."

There was a dining hall in the guest house, and there all of them save Robin partook of a generous evening meal of fish, bread and cheese, a hot vegetable stew, and well-spiced wine.

Mirielle was seated next to Hugh at one of the long tables. She could speak to him without fear of being overheard, for Bevis was entertaining Warrick, Emma, and two elderly female guests with tales of his travels in the Holy Land.

"Hugh, I can remain here only for this one night," Mirielle said. "I have fulfilled the promise I made to Gavin, to bring the children to this abbey. Now I must return to Wroxley."

"I see." A slight smile played along Hugh's lips.

Mirielle had expected him to make some objection or insist that she stay at Bardney, but he did not. He merely looked at her as if he had been expecting her to say something very like the speech she was making, and he let her talk until she was finished. Hugh's ability to be silent and listen well was one of his most attractive qualities. At that moment, when she was about to suggest something that she knew Gavin would oppose, Mirielle appreciated Hugh's discretion.

"I cannot leave Gavin to face that evil alone," Mirielle went on. "Brice is too weak in both body and spirit to be of much help to him, and Captain Oliver, for all his honest heart and good intentions, will be no match for the dark strength you and I have sensed at Wroxley. Gavin will need someone by his side who is acquainted with magic."

Mirielle paused for breath and looked at Hugh, a little surprised that he still did not protest her plan. She was even more surprised when he did not insist that he must be the one to go and that she should stay behind to nurse Robin and watch over the other children. That was what most men she knew would have done. But Hugh was not like most men. He was a mage and he continued to regard her with that same smile, as if he understood exactly what was in her heart, as if he knew what the outcome of her return to Wroxley would be.

"Say something," she begged, looking into his luminous eyes.

"You do realize that you will be endangering your life, all of your magical abilities, and perhaps your very soul?" he asked.

"Gavin cannot face that dark strength alone," she said. "I will do all I can—give all I have—to help him. The cost to me scarcely matters, for without Gavin . . ." She left the thought unfinished.

"Take Bevis with you," Hugh advised. "While he may not be of great help to you or Gavin after you have reached Wroxley, you will need him on the journey. A woman cannot safely travel without an escort. Nor is there any reason why Bevis should sit cooling his heels here at Bardney when these good monks will gladly perform any service for us that he might do."

"Thank you, Hugh." Mirielle touched his hand. "Thank you for not arguing with me."

"It is always useless to quarrel with destiny," he said.

"I know I need not ask you to guard the children well."

"If they are not safe at holy Bardney," Hugh said, "then they are not safe anywhere on earth, or even in heaven."

"At first, I thought Gavin was the mage, because he was so cold to me," Alda said. "I believed he might have learned the ancient secrets while he was in the Holy Land. It seemed possible. He is remarkably changed from the overly emotional boy who wed me all those years ago. But now I know the mage was Hugh. I feel a wonderful change since he has gone. I am growing stronger. And so are you," she added to her dark-clothed Companion.

"At least," the Companion responded, "you did not give way to madness this time, as you did during Hugh's first visit. You made too many mistakes then, Alda. You have made errors this time, too. For them, you deserve to be punished."

Alda looked more excited than frightened at the threat of punishment. She quivered expectantly as her dark Companion drew nearer.

"I have committed no errors," she said. "Donada earned her death by dallying with Brice when she knew he belonged to me. Killing her was no error on my part, but well-planned revenge. However, *you* have made a few mistakes. Shall I list them?"

"By causing Donada's death you have lost Brice to us, as I warned would happen," Alda's Companion reminded her.

"Brice is a weakling." Alda's voice was scornful.

"He was useful."

The Companion took another step toward her and Alda began to speak quickly, nervously.

"Even so, we will win. We two, together. And

when Wroxley Castle is ours, we will have the stronghold we need, the perfect base from which to extend our power, set directly over the intersection of the magical lines." Alda shivered. "It is always so cold when you are near."

"Is it?" The Companion took one more step and Alda began to shake violently in response to the cold that was enveloping her. The Companion's physical reaction to the beautiful, golden-haired woman was of a kind usually associated with warmth, but when he parted his garments to expose himself Alda only shook harder.

"I see," she said through chattering teeth, "that you are ready to punish me. What will it be this time? Will you . . . ?" With a trembling hand she made a suggestive movement.

"Oh, yes," said the Companion. "Always. And on this occasion, more than that. Much more."

Mirielle and Bevis rode hard from Bardney Abbey but they did not reach Wroxley until just after sunset. As they neared the castle the clouds closed in and it began to rain. They found the drawbridge up and Mauger the watchman on duty.

"Let us in," Mirielle cried, when he challenged them. "Mauger, you know we are friends."

"On Lord Gavin's order, the castle is barred to all comers," Mauger responded. "Lord Gavin says we do not know who can be trusted."

"This is ridiculous," Bevis muttered. Raising his voice he called, "Mauger, send a messenger to tell Lord Gavin who is at the gate and let him decide if we should enter or not. Do it now, man. He will be furious if he discovers you have kept Lady Mirielle waiting in the rain like this."

"I care naught for Lady Mirielle," Mauger retorted. "She can wait all night and drown in the rain if she's fool enough. She was sent away with those three brats. She should know by now that she's not wanted here, and she ought to have the good sense to stay away."

"Mauger, I order you to let down the drawbridge at once!" Mirielle commanded.

"Not I, lady. And not anyone under my orders, either." With that, Mauger turned his back on them.

Mirielle could see a few men-at-arms on the battlements, several of whom peered down with open curiosity at Bevis and herself. She looked from man to man, hoping to discover someone she knew who might be willing to take to Gavin the message that Mauger refused to send.

"Sitting here on our horses is a useless waste of time," Bevis said. "Mauger won't let us in and from what I know of him, when he is relieved he will be sure to tell the new watchman not to let us in, either. I wonder if I could scale the wall on the north side where the stone is rough? Or shoot an arrow into the inner bailey with a note for Gavin attached to it?"

"Perhaps there is an easier means of entry," Mirielle said, her eyes still on the figures upon the battlements. "Bevis, do not shout or make any sign that Mauger might notice, but tell me if that is your fellow squire, Hidern, standing on the wall to the right of the watchtower."

"Where?" Bevis squinted, looking along the wall as if he were trying to discern a way into the castle.

"By all the saints, yes! There he is, standing right by a torch so we can see him. Look, he's waving to us."

"Not waving," Mirielle corrected. "Signalling."

"He's telling us to go away. How dare he insult us like that?" Bevis cried. "Does he think we are cowards?"

"I think he imagines that we will use our wits," said Mirielle. "Come on, Bevis, we are going to follow Hidern's suggestion and leave."

"We just got here," the squire objected. "Mauger has issued a challenge and I, for one, will not cry off. We will wait where we are until Hidern can inform Lord Gavin of our presence. Then I would like to meet that scoundrel, Mauger, in man-to-man combat for the way he has treated us."

"For heaven's sake, Bevis," Mirielle said in exasperation. "Have you learned nothing from all your years with Gavin? Stop behaving like a typical, thick-headed squire and think what Gavin would do in this situation. Mauger has told us to go, and we are going to let him believe that we have given up. We are going to turn our horses and ride back down the castle road until he cannot see us any longer. Then we are going to circle around through the forest to the side of the wall nearest to the keep."

"Why?" asked Bevis. "We can't get in that way, either."

"If I understood Hidern's signals correctly," Mirielle said as patiently as she could, "he is planning to let us in by the small postern door."

"Of course he is!" Forgetting his annoyance with his fellow squire, Bevis grinned and spurred his horse. "I knew we could depend on Hidern."

Shaking her head at Bevis's sudden change in

mood, Mirielle followed him. They rode until they were well out of sight of the castle walls before they turned into the forest, where they and their mounts were immediately concealed by the trees and the undergrowth of Wroxley Forest. They watered the horses at a stream and fed them before tying them to a tree so they could not wander away until they were retrieved. Then it was time to begin the walk toward the postern gate. By now it was completely dark and raining so hard that it was unlikely they would be noticed as long as they were careful not to make a lot of noise or otherwise draw attention to themselves.

Their way led them across the fallow field to the west of the castle where Hugh and the children had flown kites on a sunny Sunday afternoon. The field was muddy, which made the walk difficult.

"This is too unpleasant and dangerous for a lady," Bevis grumbled. "You ought to let me go in alone. I will find Gavin and talk to him. Then he will order the main gate opened for you and greet you himself so Mauger cannot stop you from entering."

"I am going in through the postern door with you," Mirielle said.

"But we will have to cross the moat," Bevis warned. "The water is deep and not clean. Some of the garderobes empty into it."

"You may stay on this side if you wish," Mirielle informed him, "but I intend to swim the moat."

"You will drown," Bevis protested. "Your skirts will drag you down."

"You have a point. That is a problem." Mirielle considered for a moment. "The gown will be rendered useless in any case, so I will sacrifice it." She was wearing a belt with a small purse attached to it. This she unfastened while she removed her dress and her shoes and stockings. Then she refastened the belt at her waist. She would not discard it, for the purse contained the crystal sphere.

"My lady." Bevis could not see her clearly in the dark, but all the same she knew by his voice that he was shocked at her actions and at finding himself with an undressed woman. "You cannot carry your clothes across the moat. They will still weigh you down when they get wet."

"They are already wet from the rain," Mirielle said. "When we reach the middle of the moat, I will let them go. Find a few rocks that I can tie into the bundle. There ought to be some along the edge of the moat." While Bevis searched, Mirielle wound her long braids up onto the top of her head, where she secured them by tying them as if they were lengths of rope.

Bevis found the stones she wanted and Mirielle used her stockings and the sleeves of her gown to tie rocks, shoes and dress together into a damp, untidy package. She did not care about neatness. She only wanted the clothes to sink to the bottom of the moat so no one would notice them. Meanwhile, Bevis decided he would be able to swim more easily without his boots, and these he reluctantly removed.

"We could just leave our clothes in the field and get them later," Bevis said.

"We don't know what we will find once we are inside the castle," Mirielle pointed out. "It would be best not to leave any sign that we have been here. Do not think for a moment that Mauger has not noted what we were wearing. I have a feeling that we would be wise not to alert him that we have found a way into the castle."

"I suppose you are right. Well, I am ready." Carrying his boots, Bevis stepped toward the moat.

"Remember, we must be very quiet," Mirielle cautioned. "No splashing, and no crying out if the water is cold."

"I know, my lady. If I start to drown, I will not scream for help."

"I know you don't like this."

"I hate it," he told her. "That water is foul. We'll die of drinking it, if we don't drown first."

"Bevis, I promise you, if you swallow a single drop, as soon as we get inside I will take you to my workroom and give you medicine to prevent any illness."

"Your medicine didn't help Mistress Donada," Bevis objected in a fierce whisper.

"Mistress Donada was poisoned," Mirielle pointed out.

"So will we be, if we drink any of that water. I have seen sieges where the castle defenders flung all manner of ordure into a moat to prevent attackers from swimming it, and anyone who ventured into that befouled water died soon after of a horrible sickness."

"Your liege lord is inside," Mirielle reminded him. "He needs our help."

"I am not afraid for myself," Bevis muttered. "It's you I am trying to discourage, my lady, because if anything were to happen to you while you are in my care, Gavin would have me drawn and quartered."

"Then, let us get inside the castle before anything can happen," Mirielle urged. "Or before Hidern is discovered and we are prevented from using that postern door."

Hoping to forestall any further discussion with the overly pessimistic squire, Mirielle stepped into the inky water of the moat. She knew, for Brice had told her once, that the ground appeared to slope off gradually into the moat, but about a yard out from the edge the bottom dropped precipitously to a full twelve feet. She whispered a warning to Bevis and when she felt the ground sliding from beneath her feet, Mirielle dropped the weighted bundle of clothing and began to swim. She was careful to keep her head out of the water and she hoped Bevis was doing the same.

They came to the castle side of the moat and Mirielle hauled herself out onto the narrow band of wet grass that grew at the base of the wall. Bevis scrambled out next to her, breathing hard. By the faint light cast by the torches high on the battlements Mirielle was relieved to see that they had left the water almost exactly in front of the postern door. The door swung open with a swishing sound and a figure issued forth.

"Hidern?" Bevis hissed. "Is that you?"

"Lucky for you that it is. I have been waiting for you. Lady Mirielle, you should not be here."

"That is what Mauger told us," Mirielle said. "I cannot abide that man."

"Neither can I," Hidern told her. "My lady, I knew you would both be drenched, so I brought two cloaks along to cover you and Bevis. We really ought to get inside before someone sees us and reports to Mauger that you have circumvented his orders. I hear that he does not like to be crossed."

They went into the passage that led through the thickness of the castle wall. Hidern relocked the postern door. Before he could lead them out the other side, Mirielle stopped the two squires.

"Bevis, did you swallow any moat water?" she asked.

"No, my lady. I do not think I will need the medicine you offered."

"Then go to the bathhouse and be sure to scrub yourself well. Discard the clothing you are wearing now. Stay out of sight of Mauger or his men. Let Hidern hide you, and wait until he brings you a message from Gavin."

"My lady, what do you plan to do?" asked Hidern, adding in a wondering voice, "It is strange. I seldom go up on the wall, but tonight I felt compelled to do so. I am glad I did. I was greatly surprised to see you and Bevis at the gate. I trust you have a good reason for returning after Gavin ordered you to leave."

"I expect that there will be trouble before long, and that Gavin will need my assistance," Mirielle said. "I cannot tell you the whole of it, but I do think you ought to pass the word quietly to Gavin's men who came here with you. They will be loyal to him. Tell those men to be prepared to do battle at any time, and to know, if they have not already discovered it, that there are two factions among the men-at-arms. One is led by Captain Oliver. I believe for the most part they are honest men who will prove themselves loyal to my cousin, Brice, which means they will fight for Gavin. The others are Alda's people, who came with her from her childhood home and who regard Mauger as their leader."

"Master Hugh warned us of that division before

we came here." By the light of the oil lamp he carried, Hidern looked hard at her. "My lady, you have not said what you will do. Shall I send a maidservant to attend you?"

"I want no servants involved in this. First, I will have a bath and fresh clothing," she said. "Then, as quickly as I can I'll find Gavin. I won't require your escort any longer, Bevis. Tend to your own needs and get some rest. I thank you for what you have done for me this day."

"My lady." Bevis went down on one knee and took Mirielle's muddy hand in his own. "Never have I met a braver lady. I am always happy to provide any service for you. Only ask, and I will obey."

Mirielle waited inside the inner bailey until Hidern had secured the postern door. Since the key he used belonged to Gavin, Mirielle took it from the squire, saying she would return it.

"He does not know I have it," Hidern said.

"Don't worry. You won't be reprimanded for what you have done for me and Bevis."

"Gavin should be in the lord's chamber," Hidern informed her.

After the two squires moved off in the direction of the bathhouse, which was frequented mostly by the men-at-arms and the women they kept and which was thus unappealing to Mirielle, she hastened to the kitchen, where she knew she could find hot water and soap. It was so late that few people were about. Using the method Hugh had taught her to disguise herself from sight, Mirielle was able to snatch a bucket of water, a dish of soap, and a towel, and carry them to a small, deserted pantry without being noticed. There, with the door shut, she made a quick job of scrubbing away the muck from the moat. It felt wonderful to be clean, even if the soap was harsh and the towel inadequate. After dumping the bucket of dirty water into the kitchen drain, which emptied into the moat, she returned the bucket and towel to their places. Satisfied that no one would guess she had been in the kitchen, Mirielle wrapped herself again in the cloak Hidern had provided and hurried to her room to dress.

Gavin and Brice were sitting together in the lord's chamber, talking in low voices when Mirielle walked in without knocking.

"What the devil?" Gavin leapt to his feet, one hand on the pommel of his sword. He relaxed when he saw who had intruded into his private quarters.

"Cousin, you ought to be miles away from here." Brice rose more slowly, levering himself upward with his hands on the chair arms.

"I believe this is yours, my lord." Walking across the room to Gavin, Mirielle laid the postern door key into his hand.

"How did you get here?" Brice demanded.

"I took off my gown and swam the moat." While Brice sputtered his outrage at this statement, Mirielle returned her attention to Gavin. "Bevis came with me, but you ought not to scold him. Hugh ordered him to acCompany me, and Bevis knew if he did not, I would ride from Bardney alone. I believe he felt it was his duty to protect me on the way."

"What of Hugh?" Gavin asked. "I have told your cousin of our true purpose in coming to Wroxley and my original disguise. You may speak freely in front of him."

Mirrelle glanced quickly from one man to the other, and then continued.

"Hugh made no effort to stop me," she said. "He spoke of destiny."

"Destiny," Gavin repeated softly. "I wanted you safely away from this place, but by heaven, Mirielle, I am glad to see you!"

She thought that, if Brice had not been in the room, Gavin would have taken her into his arms. Instead, he looked at her as if he would devour her with his eyes. She saw how pale he was. He had aged in just two days. There were new lines around his eyes and threads of gray in his hair. The changes would have been attractive to her if they had been caused by the normal passage of time, but Mirielle knew they were unnatural and so they frightened her.

"Well," Brice said into the long silence, "now that you are here, Mirielle, you are to go to your room and stay there. Gavin and I have serious work to do this night and you are to stay out of it."

"If you mean to face down Alda," Mirielle replied, still looking into Gavin's eyes, "then it is essential that I be with you. You will need my aid. Hugh agrees."

"Go to your room," Brice repeated in a severe tone.

"She stays." Gavin's voice was soft. "We cannot defeat Alda without her."

"My lord, she is *my* ward," Brice objected.

"She is my very heart." Gavin's voice did not change.

Brice stared at him and then nodded abruptly. In that moment Mirielle realized how weakened her cousin was. There had been a time, and not so long ago, either, when Brice would not have backed down so easily.

"It is difficult to accept," Brice said, as if he were continuing the conversation he and Gavin were having before Mirielle had appeared, "that Alda, who seldom leaves her chamber except to parade into the great hall to show off her beauty and her fashionable clothes, this woman who has always been indifferent to Wroxley and its people, should cause so much distress. To watch her or listen to her, one would think castle and people alike were beneath her notice. You will not know this, Mirielle, but since you left, four of Gavin's knights have fallen ill with the same sickness that killed Donada and that now afflicts Gavin, young Robin, and me. Gavin says Alda is to blame for all of it."

"That is what Hugh and I think, too," Mirielle revealed. "Alda is involved with the poisoner's art, and with dark magic."

"I find your conclusions all too easy to believe." Brice took a long, shaky breath before continuing. "Alda told me once that she draws strength from me each time we lie together. At the time, I believed she meant that I gave her the courage to go on with her life, which she claimed was sadly empty. After listening to the two of you, I think my affair with Alda is the reason why I am so weak and drained. She sapped my strength and my manhood from me until I became too exhausted to resist her. But even at the beginning, I was morally weak." Brice turned away, stifling a sob.

Mirielle would have gone to him, but Gavin prevented her.

"He is consumed with guilt," Gavin said in a low voice. "He cannot fully believe that I have forgiven him for taking to bed a woman whom I willingly deserted years ago. Brice insists that he must expiate his sins against me by standing at my side when I announce Alda's punishment to her."

"Brice is right. You should not have to do it alone. Alda is sure to fight back." Mirielle slipped her hand into his and Gavin pressed it. "I will be there, too."

Chapter Eighteen

*"Ley Lines . . . a 'fairy chain' stretched across
the land . . . lines of magnetic energy which are
believed to lie beneath the surface of the earth.
Where the lines intersect the energy coursing
through them is especially strong."*
> —Alfred Watkins, et al.
> *Mystic Places*

Alda's chamber door was latched from the inside.

"I'll break it down," Brice offered. He moved back
a few paces in preparation for a lunge at the door.

"Save your strength," Mirielle put a restraining
hand on his arm. "You will need it to face Alda.
Brice, she may try to seduce you again."

"She won't succeed," Brice promised.

"Can you open the door?" Gavin asked Mirielle.

"I think so."

"Mirielle?" Brice looked confused. "How are you going to do it?"

"By magic." Mirielle could not help smiling at the expression on her cousin's face. Brice had no idea how far her work had taken her. He thought she was only able to make herbal medicines or packets of bath herbs and scented soaps. She was amused when he and Gavin obeyed without question the order she gave next. "Stand back, both of you, and keep perfectly silent until I tell you it is safe to enter."

She had learned more from Hugh than she realized. His lessons, taught to her during pleasant evenings in her workroom, came to her without any effort. In her mind's eye Mirielle could see the latch on the other side of the door. Directing all of her thoughts to the bolt, she envisioned it moving back slowly, without a sound, until the door was unfastened. She waited, listening, but heard nothing from within, no cry of alarm to indicate that Alda was aware of the use of an unusual skill. Mirielle put out her hand to push the door open.

"This isn't right." Brice spoke before Mirielle's fingers could make contact with the wood. "Alda is the one who is in the wrong here. Are we to sneak into her room like thieves at midnight? We ought to burst in on her with our swords drawn and give her a good fright. Then she might do what we want."

"Brice, do be quiet!" Mirielle whispered.

"If you do not follow Mirielle's instructions," came Gavin's low murmur, "I will have you confined to your room. This is no task for blundering warriors."

295

Brice muttered something beneath his breath, then fell silent.

"Stay behind me," Mirielle whispered. She put out her hand a second time and pushed on the door of Alda's room. It swung inward and hot, perfumed air wafted outward. Mirielle advanced to the threshold.

The room was well lit with expensive wax candles and all the braziers were burning charcoal. Alda was not there. She was beyond, in the *other* room, the square chamber that extended from the outer wall of the tower, where no room ought to be. Mirielle understood at once that what she was seeing was a magical illusion created by Alda for her personal use.

Black draperies cloaked the walls of that unreal room. A fire burned in a round pit set into the exact center of the floor. At the far side of the room stood a polished black stone altar. Clad in a flame-red gown with her hair caught high in a golden net, Alda stood facing the altar. She was oblivious to the three intruders who clustered at the entrance to her bedchamber. Engrossed in some mysterious rite, Alda lifted a glittering black goblet in both hands and spoke words incomprehensible to the unseen listeners.

Mirielle was aware of the movement at her back when Brice crossed himself. She heard Gavin's indrawn breath.

"It is not real," she whispered to them. "Believe with all your hearts and minds that it is not there and it will vanish. See in your minds the solid stone of the castle wall, see this room as it actually is, without Alda's enchantment on it."

Mirielle sent all her strength of will toward the

wall she knew existed in the place where Alda's secret chamber appeared to be. She sensed Gavin's brave will joining hers, then Brice's weaker but still determined will. The black draperies on the walls of the unreal room rippled and wavered as if a wind were blowing across them. The room began to fade and blur.

The goblet Alda was holding slipped from her fingers to crash onto the black altar. Alda went rigid, then whirled to face the three who had moved to stand just within the entrance to her bedchamber. With a wild shriek she rushed out of the unreal room and into the bedchamber. Just as she set her feet onto the floor of the bedchamber, the unreal room disappeared with a loud popping noise. In its place the wall of the tower keep appeared as it ought to be, solid gray stone with a bright tapestry hanging on it.

"How dare you enter my chamber uninvited?" Alda's head was thrown back and her eyes blazed with an unearthly red-gold light. Her whole being vibrated and the folds of her red skirts shimmered and moved about her like tongues of leaping flame.

"Sorceress!" Brice took a menacing step toward her. "Murderer!"

"You cannot accuse me. You know not who or what I am!" Alda spoke with slow intensity. "Feel my power *now!*" When she turned her eyes full on Brice he gasped and clutched at his stomach, then went down, doubling over in agony.

"Let him go," Mirielle said.

"When I am ready, I will." Alda watched Brice writhing on the floor before her, his face gray with pain.

"I loved you once," Brice cried. "Alda, have pity."

"You ask for pity, you weakling? And you prattle about love?" Alda's laugh was cruel. She lifted a foot as if she would kick Brice, but she apparently thought better of it. Instead, she spoke to him as if he were a half-wit. "Ever since I was a child, my only interest in you has been your weak will where I am concerned. I could always make you do whatever I wanted. Even now, knowing as you do that I used your passion for me to increase my own power, still, at this moment I could lure you to bed and you would go with me most willingly."

"No," Brice cried. "You killed Donada and made her son sick. I will never lie with you again."

"If you do not," Alda told him, "it will be only because I have no further use for you."

"Stop this at once!" Mirielle cried. "Leave my cousin alone."

Alda lifted her eyes from Brice's crumpled form to meet Mirielle's fierce look. Mirielle sensed the woman's building strength and knew Alda was about to inflict pain on Gavin and herself in addition to Brice. Quickly, before Alda could make a move, Mirielle stepped forward. Again using Hugh's teachings, she conjured a protection to keep Alda at bay. At Mirielle's silent command a thin veil rose between the two women, a netlike creation of Mirielle's mind that crackled and shook and spat sizzling sparks of energy. On Mirielle's side of it Brice lay groaning.

"She can't hurt you anymore, Brice," Mirielle said. "For the moment, I have her confined. I am sorry it took me so long to establish the net. Gavin, tell Alda what you mean to do with her. But hurry, please. I cannot contain her for more than a few minutes. She is too powerful."

"Alda," Gavin said, "I have applied to the Church for a Bill of Divorcement from you. It will not be difficult to obtain, since Brice freely admits to adultery with you."

"What is that to me?" Alda sneered.

"Despite the crimes of which I believe you guilty, still you are the mother of my son," Gavin went on. "Therefore, instead of killing you or imprisoning you as most men would do, I am willing to let you go into a strict convent for the rest of your life."

"Gavin, you don't understand," Mirielle broke in. "Alda would sooner die than be confined in a place where the very holiness of the ground would prevent her from exercising her power."

"Now, there you are right," Alda said. "I have not done all that I have done in order to be sent away like a rejected wife. Nor will I ever relinquish my power."

"If you will not submit to my authority, then I fear I will have to kill you," Gavin said.

"That you cannot do." Alda told him. "I am far too powerful for you to injure me in any way. And much too powerful for you to compel."

"Gavin," Mirielle whispered urgently, "I cannot hold the net around her much longer and when it fails, she will surely take some desperate action, for she must know you cannot let her remain free. You and Brice should leave the room now, before she tries to kill both of you."

"She will not let you live, either, and I will not desert you," Gavin said. Raising his voice, he spoke again to his fuming wife, who looked as if she might try to break through the confining net. "I have two last questions for you, Alda. How did my father die? How did his seneschal, Paul, die?"

Alda laughed at him. Mirielle struggled against the strength the woman was exerting in her effort to break free of the net that held her.

"Alda, I command you to answer my questions," Gavin said.

"On whose authority?" Alda asked. "Your strength is fast waning from illness. Brice is all but dead. Your friend Hugh has deserted you."

"I am here." Mirielle put all of her remaining will, all of her courage and her love for Gavin and for her cousin Brice into the net around Alda, tightening it. When Alda looked at her, startled by the increased pressure, Mirielle said, "Tell Gavin what he wants to know."

Alda did not respond at once. Believing she was about to launch an attack to gain her freedom, Mirielle recalled Hugh's most secret lessons and summoned up her final reserves to resist the attack and to add more pressure to the net. It was enough. Alda was compelled to speak.

"I killed Udo," Alda said. "When Sir Paul the seneschal was foolish enough to accuse me of the deed and threatened to see me punished for it, I killed him, too."

"Why?" Gavin demanded. "What reason could you have for causing so much pain and death, for harming people who meant you no ill?"

"I wanted this castle," Alda told him. "I will have it for my own before I am done. It is why I agreed to marry you. I could have stopped the arrangements my father made—even at that young age I was powerful enough—but Wroxley is in a perfect location."

"The lines," Gavin said. "Hugh has told me of them."

"He would know." Alda nodded as if she and Gavin were carrying on an ordinary conversation. "Wroxley sits on an intersection of the magical lines, you see. The mystical energy of the earth itself is strongest here, in this spot. Once I control Wroxley, once the castle is mine and not yours, my power can only grow."

"Power to do what?" Gavin asked.

"Isn't it clear?" Brice spoke, startling all of them. Pale and shaking, he dragged himself to his feet. "Alda has fed on my desire for her and, I suspect, on other men, too, draining all of us of our will and courage. But while a man's vital energy is limited, the energy of the earth is not. If Alda can gain control of Wroxley, she can feed indefinitely on the power of those magical lines, whatever they are. Alda is mad for power. She wants it for its own sake."

In turning her attention to Brice for an instant, Mirielle had allowed her firm upholding of the protective net around Alda to waver. It was a time no longer than the blink of an eye and a less determined sorceress might not have understood how to take advantage of it. Alda was no ordinary sorceress. She broke through the net with a fury that blazed red-hot in Mirielle's mind and that momentarily blinded her. Stunned by Alda's power, Mirielle would have fallen to the floor if Gavin had not caught her.

Alda did not stay to complete her victory over Mirielle. Instead, she raced out of the bedchamber and into the corridor beyond. Brice went after her.

"Follow them." Mirielle fought to regain her strength. "Brice does not know how to deal with her. She will kill him."

"I will not leave you alone. Alda may think I would, and she may have some scheme in mind to harm you when I am gone, as vengeance for the way you held her captive."

"Then we go together, for I know she will hurt Brice if we do not stop her." Holding tight to Gavin's hand, Mirielle hastened after Alda and Brice.

"This way," Gavin said, pulling her along the corridor. "I can hear heavy boots on the stairs."

The footsteps were heading upwards. Mirielle did not see Alda, but she caught a glimpse of Brice's dark blue tunic and his sturdy legs in brown hose and she assumed her cousin was chasing Alda. Mirielle gathered her skirts into her free hand so she would not trip and went up the spiral stairs with Gavin. Strangely, they met no one, though at that predawn hour when the watch was changed there should have been at least one or two men-at-arms coming down the steps or going up to the battlements.

"Alda, stop!" Brice shouted from above them. "Be reasonable. There is no place for you to go. Gavin will treat you fairly."

There was a derisive laugh from Alda, and then a howl of pain from Brice. Gavin released Mirielle's hand to hurry up the steps. Mirielle, having caught her breath and regained her emotional composure, was close on Gavin's heels. They found Brice on his knees at the top of the stairs.

"Leave me," Brice said, gasping. "Catch her before

she does something terrible that will destroy all of us. She's out on the battlements."

Gavin stepped over Brice and continued through the door. Alda had chosen the stairs to the highest watchtower in the keep and now she stood beside one of the crenels, a gap in the stone wall that topped the tower. Above her, on its pole, Gavin's blue-and-green pennant snapped bravely against a gray, windswept dawn. There were no men-at-arms here, either, though there should have been two on duty.

"It is time to surrender," Gavin said. "Give yourself up, Alda. I promise, your punishment will not be unjust."

"There will be no punishment," Alda shouted at him. "You cannot touch me. My power is greater than Mirielle's, or even than Hugh's. There is nothing any of you can do to me."

"But there is, and it is the thing you fear most." Supporting Brice, who insisted on staying with her, Mirielle moved out onto the battlements. Leaving her cousin to lean weakly against the stonework, Mirielle advanced to stand beside Gavin. "Gavin and Hugh and I together can strip you of your power. Hugh and I can hold you in a net far stronger than the one I have just used against you and, while we do, Gavin can send you to a convent as he has threatened. There, on holy ground, you will be unable to work your evil magic. There a simple stone cell and an ordinary lock on the door will suffice to hold you."

"Never!" Alda moved toward Mirielle. Her brilliantly colored gown swished over the stone paving like a snake hissing before it strikes. Alda's golden brown eyes burned hot gold and then changed to a flaming red that was painful to look upon. Alda's hair had come unbound in her flight up the stairs. The golden locks crackled and snapped with the energy of her magic. She pointed a long, slender finger at Mirielle. "You cannot stop me. I have had enough of your pious interference. You are neither sorceress nor ordinary person, but a creature caught between the two. Since I cannot use you, it is time for you to die."

Now it was Mirielle's turn to be caught in a net. The one she had called upon to hold Alda had been restrictive but not painful. Alda's conjuring produced a net that prevented Mirielle from breathing, that gripped her ever tighter, threatening to break all of Mirielle's bones and to squeeze the life out of her.

"No! Leave Mirielle alone!" Brice launched himself off the stonework and onto Alda, forcing her to loosen her hold on Mirielle in order to keep Brice from knocking her down.

But Brice would not stop. He swung a clenched fist at Alda, striking her on the shoulder. Alda spun around, screeching. Brice hit her again. To get away from him Alda scrambled up onto the broad stone at the base of one of the crenels. Grasping the stones at either side, she hung there, the red glow in her eyes searing all three of her opponents.

"You have no power over me," Alda screamed at them. "Weaklings! Villeins!"

"Alda," Brice panted, "in the name of God, come down from there. Repent, and you can gain absolution for your sins."

"I don't need absolution! I am part of a greater power."

"The power of darkness," Brice insisted. "Alda, if you will not give up for your soul's sake, then do so in the name of the love I once bore you, when you were an innocent girl."

"I was never innocent," she snarled at him, "and you were a fool to love me, for your love gave me power over you. Love is a mistake I have never made, nor ever will."

"Alda." Putting out his hands, Brice took a step toward her. "Please. Give up your magical power. I promise, if you do, you will find peace and you can live a contented life."

Alda did not bother to respond to this plea. She took her left hand off the stone at the side of the crenel and pointed a finger at Brice. With a strangled cry and his hands at his throat, he went to his knees. Alda threw back her head in the gesture so characteristic of her, and laughed at her writhing victim.

From behind Gavin and Mirielle there came a sound like a rushing wind. The sky over the tower darkened as if a heavy thunder cloud hovered above it. Alda's laughter died away. She stared at something over Gavin's shoulder and a look of fear crossed her face.

"No!" Alda shouted. She moved the hand she was pointing at Brice, holding it palm up, as if to ward off the rushing noise. "*I* am more powerful. *I*, not you!"

The sudden movement made Alda lose her balance. Teetering at the edge of the crenel, she caught at the stonework with both hands, but she had moved too far out. Her foot slipped on the smooth surface of the stone. She hung at the very edge of the crenel while the wind howled and the sky grew ever darker. Her red skirts billowed out around her and for an instant Alda looked as if she were standing on empty air. Then she disappeared over the edge.

Her long, drawn-out howl of rage and terror temporarily paralyzed the wits and chilled the blood of all who heard her.

The roaring wind stilled. There followed a moment of complete silence, before calls and shouted questions came from far below. Then a yell of fear, and more silence.

Up on the watchtower, Brice lay on the stone paving, trembling and panting for breath. Mirielle discovered she could move and breathe again, and Gavin took her into his arms.

"My love," he murmured. "Are you all right?"

"I think so." Mirielle took a long, deep breath, filling her lungs with air that was remarkably fresh and clean. She watched the rising sun break through a cloud, sending a single ray of soft light onto Gavin's triumphant blue-and-green banner with the scallop shell.

"Is she gone?" Brice levered himself up onto his elbows. "Is she really dead?"

"She must be," Gavin said. "No one, not even a powerful sorceress, could survive such a fall."

"Don't be too sure." Brice dragged himself toward the crenel. Leaning over the stone at its base, he looked down. "Something is wrong. Alda must have fallen onto the ground just at the edge of the moat. I can see a red dress and people are standing around, but—what is it? They are moving back from her. What has happened? Gavin, one of us should go down there."

Brice turned from the crenel to find Mirielle and Gavin with their arms around each other.

"I see," he said slowly, with the air of a man who is just beginning to waken from a terrible dream and observe the world around him with unclouded eyes. "Mirielle, I do not completely understand how you were able to hold Alda immobilized, but it is clear to me that the effort has exhausted you and that you have need of Gavin's support. I will go down to the moat and give the necessary orders about Alda's body. I am the seneschal. It is my duty." Brice appeared to be pulling himself together even as he spoke. He tested the movement of each hand and foot and of his legs and arms.

"Amazing," he said. "I am stronger already."

After Brice left them, Mirielle and Gavin lingered awhile longer on the watchtower. He stood with his arms around her and her head on his shoulder until Mirielle was completely recovered. Finally, Gavin stirred.

"My wife is dead," he said. "I should grieve for her lost soul, but all I can feel is relief that she will trouble us no more."

"Alda chose to lose her soul," Mirielle told him. "If she had accepted the punishment you wanted to lay upon her, she might have redeemed herself in time. The decision was hers and hers alone. Considering the deaths she caused, you were more than fair with her."

"Still, I wish there had been some other way to stop her," he said.

Mirielle saw the regret on his face and knew it was not only for the woman who should have been his loving wife, but also for those whom Alda had killed or made dangerously sick. Thanks to Alda, Gavin himself was not in the best of health, though Mirielle did not think he would admit to weakness.

"Come to your room," she coaxed. "Brice will find you there and present his report to you."

When they reached the lord's chamber Gavin refused to lie down on the bed as Mirielle advised. She was able to convince him to sit in a chair by the fire and she poured a cup of wine for him. He took it and set it on the table next to the chair. Then he pulled Mirielle onto his lap. She did not protest.

"I have been afraid many times in my life," Gavin said, holding her close, "but never so terrified as when I thought Alda was going to kill you. I knew you could not breathe, I saw you struggling for air, and I could do nothing to help you." His arms tightened around her. "In that horrible moment I knew how impossible my life would be without you."

Bending her back across his arm, he pressed his mouth to hers. Mirielle's fingers crept into his hair, feeling the smooth, silky texture of it. She was conscious of the hard-muscled thighs on which she sat and as Gavin's kiss deepened, she became aware of a different hardness that rose suddenly and insistently. Nor could she deny to herself her own warm reaction to his masculine arousal. When his hand moved downward from her shoulder to her breast, Mirielle pressed herself against his palm. Gavin's mouth slid from her lips to her cheek and ear, then to her throat. The hand on her breast moved farther, to Mirielle's thigh and then on to the hem of her dress. The delicate stroking of his fingertips on her calf made her moan deep in her throat.

"How soft you are." His fingers reached above her stocking to stroke the sensitive skin of her upper thigh.

Mirielle moved and twisted against his hand, wanting still more. She understood where this would end. She began to tremble, not from fear, but from the depth and extent of her emotions. In her heart she was already Gavin's, but she longed for him to take physical possession of her. She knew what they would do together, and she wanted it with every quivering inch of her body.

Her thighs opened without any thought on her part. He touched her in the place where she ached to feel him. His hand was not tentative but firm, clamping upon her in a way that jolted her to a new level of sensitivity. She buried her head against his shoulder, shuddering with suddenly awakened desire.

"Shall I stop?" he asked.

"No. Gavin, I want—I want—oh!" She tightened her arms around his neck as he slid one of his fingers into her while another stroked and circled, pressing gently yet firmly against her aching flesh. Mirielle felt as if the place between her thighs was on fire.

"I know what you want," he whispered. "It's what I want, too. I think the time has come for us to move to the bed."

"Don't take your hand away. I'll die if you do." Mirielle found she could not be embarassed by the desire she could no longer hide. What they were doing was all new and strange to her, but she felt as if she and Gavin were embarking on a wonderful journey together. With him, there was no cause for fear.

"You will lack my touch for only a short time, my dearest," he murmured. "Then we will be as close as two souls can be."

All the same, she whimpered at the loss of that sweet pressure when he released her and set her on her feet. At once he stood, too, and lifted her into his arms, pausing to kiss her once more before carrying her toward the bed. He had taken only two steps when someone knocked at the door.

"My lord," Brice called, "may I speak to you?"

"I forgot about your cousin," Gavin whispered. "I will have to see him."

Mirielle was on her feet again and Gavin steadied her for a moment, looking at her as if to question whether she was ready to face her cousin. Not until she smoothed back her hair and straightened her skirts and nodded her readiness did he stride to the door to fling it open.

Brice stumbled into the room. He barely glanced at Mirielle and made no comment on the fact that his ward had been alone with Gavin in his bedchamber for some time. Brice had information to impart and he gave all of his attention to Gavin.

"My lord," Brice cried, "I have come to make my report to you. Lady Alda . . . Lady . . . oh, God!" He covered his face with his hands.

"Here." Jerked out of her romantic trance by Brice's entrance and his dreadful appearance, Mirielle picked up the cup of wine, which Gavin had not touched. "I think you need this. Brice, you are shaking. Sit down."

"I feel as though I am burning up with fever."

Slumping into the chair Gavin had vacated, Brice drained the cup of wine and held it out for Mirielle to refill it.

"I think I understand your distress, Brice." Gavin sat opposite him. "I have seen the bodies of a few men, and women, too, who had fallen from great heights. It is a terrible sight, and most particularly when it is someone you know. Knowing that you loved Alda once, I should not have sent you to make the arrangements for her. I should have gone myself."

"You don't understand. It isn't that I loved Alda, though I did once." With his eyes shadowed and dark, he looked from Gavin to Mirielle. "There is no way to say it gently, so I will use plain words. I found Alda lying on her back directly below the crenel through which she fell. By her gown and her jewels and her size I knew her. Her golden hair was spread out around her head, but when I touched it, the hair came off in my hand." Brice rubbed his hands together, as if to wipe away the memory of Alda's beautiful tresses lying in his fingers.

"You heard the shouting of the men-at-arms and the workmen who were at that side of the castle," Brice continued. "They saw Alda fall and heard her last scream and ran to her. And then they all stood back in horror until I arrived, for no one dared to touch her. My lord, I have no doubt the body was Alda's, but she was so changed—so fearfully changed.

"It was the face of an old, old woman," Brice whispered. "All the dreadful things Alda had done in her life were written there, in the lines of her face, for all the world to see. There was no beauty left in that hideous visage.

"Mirielle." Brice raised his eyes to hers. "Could a person so vile, who is a sorceress, make herself appear to be a great beauty, even while she rots from within because of wickedness? Was Alda's enticing, unchanging loveliness no more than an illusion conjured by a sorceress? Each time I made love to her was I embracing a dreadful hag?"

"It is possible." Mirielle knelt beside her cousin and laid a hand on his knee as she used to do before they had come to Wroxley, while they were still as close in heart as brother and sister. "A woman who could conjure up a room that did not exist would certainly have the power to make everyone who beheld her imagine she was a rare beauty. But over time our actions and our characters mold the faces we were given at birth until in old age our true selves are revealed. Alda was a murderess. She plotted and schemed constantly to gather ever more power to herself. My old nurse, Cerra, used to say that the gift of magic, which is an inborn quality, should be used for the good of others and the welfare of the earth, rather than for personal gain. We know how Alda violated that rule. It is only reasonable to think that all the evil deeds she committed marked her face until in the end, her original beauty was gone and all she had to show to us was her misused magic. Then, when she died her magic died with her and her true face was revealed."

"She hated this room," Brice said, looking around. "She refused to come in here."

"No doubt because this is where she fed the final doses of poison to my father," Gavin put in. "She would not sleep in the bed where he died by her hand."

"I am responsible for a large part of what has happened in these last weeks," Brice said. "Were it not for me, Donada would still be alive."

"I am at fault, too," Gavin told him. "I originally planned to move against Alda as soon as I was sure she was involved in wrongdoing, but each time I resolved to begin, something prevented me from acting."

"Your will to action was restricted by the enchantment Alda had placed on Wroxley and on everyone who lived here, or who came here," Mirielle said. "Gavin, Brice, you must not blame yourselves so severely. Now that Alda is gone, the spell is broken. Soon we will all return to our usual selves."

"Let us hope so," Gavin muttered.

"Perhaps that same enchantment explains why you have not moved against me, my lord," Brice said. "It is your right to punish me for lying with your wife."

"I believe you are at heart a good man," Gavin responded, "though perhaps overly ambitious. Your care of Mirielle must count to your credit. She would not love you if you were completely unworthy."

"It is hard now to remember how certain I was that I could one day supplant you and hold Wroxley in my own name. Alda convinced me of it." Brice rubbed at his forehead as if that disloyal thought pained him.

"Given all that has happened, I believe I would be wise to allow you time in which to prove youself as seneschal before making any decision about whether you ought to be punished or not," Gavin said.

"Thank you, my lord." Brice said his thanks as if his life depended on his words. Then he returned to the original subject that had brought him to the lord's chamber. "I have ordered the carpenter to put Alda's body into a plain coffin and to nail the lid down tight. I did not think you would want to see her as she is now. I wish I had not seen her body. The sight will haunt me to the end of my life."

"You did well, Brice." Gavin's hand rested on his seneschal's shoulder. "She cannot lie in hallowed ground, so I will have her buried in the fallow field, out by the edge of the forest. We will do it now, today, before the midday meal. The sooner we put this unhappy time in the life of Wroxley behind us, the better it will be for all of its inhabitants."

On the highest watchtower a dark presence brooded unnoticed by the men-at-arms on duty there. Slowly the cloaked figure moved to the crenel from which Alda had fallen. Through the opening in the stone it was possible to see the place on the far side of a currently fallow field where a deep hole had been dug and into which a plain wooden coffin was being lowered. Only the servants who had done the digging and who were now holding the lowering ropes, two noblemen, and a lone woman were present at the makeshift funeral.

"Foolish Alda," the dark presence murmured. "I warned you that if you did not exercise your power with greater subtlety the day would come when I would have to destroy you. You did not heed my warning and now you have lost everything. But I—"

Here the figure paused for a moment, leaning forward to look over the edge to the spot where Alda's broken body had lain. "I shall not make the same mistakes. There will be a way for me to seize what you let slip between your fingers. I have long been patient; I am used to waiting. Just a little while more . . . a death or two . . . or three . . ."

Chapter Nineteen

"*Sorcerers could . . . stir up strife among
friendly folk, provoke epidemics, and raise
storms.*"

—Grillot de Givry
Witchcraft, Magic, and Alchemy

Alda's death produced some interesting repercussions. Out at the main gate a group of men-at-arms who counted themselves loyal to the late Lady of Wroxley got into an argument with a dozen or so men-at-arms who held a different loyalty. The result was a brief but bitter swordfight that ended only after intervention by Gavin's squires, Hidern and Bevis. Hearing the clash of weapons, the two squires sent a messenger to Gavin. Becoming impatient while waiting for the lord of the castle to appear, they gathered some of their fellow squires and a few pages about them and waded into the fray. One man-at-arms died with Alda's name on his lips, other combatants sustained various cuts and bruises, and half a dozen brave young men ended the morning with aching heads.

When Gavin and Captain Oliver arrived on the scene, Hidern and Bevis were holding the worst malefactors in a corner of the gatehouse. Thinking an immediate reward for loyalty would serve as a good example to all who had been involved in the fight, Gavin knighted his two squires on the spot, along with four other youths who had proven themselves worthy of the honor. Those who had begun the quarrel were also used to set an example. They were confined to the dungeon until Gavin had decided what to do with them.

Despite the resulting high spirits of the new young knights, who eagerly recounted the story of their prowess in battle to the prettiest of the serving girls, the midday meal was, from Mirielle's point of view, a somber feast. Neither the behavior of those at the lower tables nor the conversation among the men sitting at the dais with her gave her cause to think all problems were ended with Alda's death. Looking around the great hall she saw reason to fear that more violence was possible.

Those men-at-arms who remained loyal to Alda and who had escaped blame for the battle at the gatehouse grumbled and frowned and kept themselves apart from the other, more cheerful men. Mauger, who had not been present during the battle, came late to the meal. He ate little, drank much, and listened with a sour face to the men who complained that their mistress had not received a proper burial.

"I see the potential for further trouble there," Captain Oliver said to Gavin, voicing Mirielle's own concern.

"Watch them well," Gavin responded. "I want no one sent to the dungeon unjustly, but neither do I intend to allow another fight to occur. If you detect any hint of a quarrel brewing, lock up Mauger and his friends."

"We might do well to turn those men out of Wroxley," Brice suggested.

"In which case they will probably take to the woods and become outlaws," Gavin said. "Better to keep them here for now, so we have some control over them and they are not turned loose to rob and rape and murder as they please."

Listening to this discussion, Mirielle lost her appetite and could only sip a little wine. Aside from her worry over the immediate future she was intensely aware of Gavin sitting next to her. While he appeared to be listening carefully to Brice and Captain Oliver, Gavin frequently turned to her and his heated looks plainly said that he wanted to carry her off to his chamber to complete the romantic interlude that Brice had interrupted.

The memory of Gavin's hands upon her stirred a warmth deep in Mirielle's being. She was finding it almost impossible to control her feelings for him. She wanted to sit on his lap again and feel the strength of his muscular thighs—and that other part of him that had reacted so swiftly and boldly to her presence. She was not ashamed to admit to herself that she ached for the firm pressure of his hand and his body against the exquisitely sensitive place between her thighs. With his hot kisses and even hotter caresses Gavin had created this desire in her and only Gavin could assuage it.

She longed to touch him, though she knew it would be most unseemly to do so when everyone in the hall could see them. She warned herself to stop thinking about such intimacies. She could tell by the heat sweeping over her that the color was rising in her face and she feared that anyone looking at her would know what was on her mind.

To distract herself she surveyed the empty places usually occupied by Hugh, Emma, Warrick, and Robin, seats she hoped would soon be filled again. But there were two places that would never be taken, those once filled by the women who had died. She found it very hard to feel pity for Alda, but for Donada, Mirielle sincerely grieved. In the face of Alda's unpredictable tantrums Donada had been a gentle and steady friend and Mirielle would miss her. It occurred to Mirielle that there was one last duty required by that friendship.

"Gavin," she said, during a lull in the men's discussion, "we still have not buried poor Donada. When you send to Bardney Abbey to tell Hugh it is safe to bring the children home, will you also ask for a priest to come with them?"

"I plan to do so. If Robin has recovered as we hope, he will be well enough to attend his mother's funeral. Let us pray the holy service will give the boy a measure of peace after his ordeal."

"He will miss his mother sorely," Mirielle said. "They were always close."

"I will see that Robin is kept too busy to grieve for

long," Gavin promised. "I will need new squires now that Hidern and Bevis have been promoted to knighthood. Warrick and Robin seem to be ideal candidates."

Anyone watching them would have seen Gavin smile politely at Mirielle as he spoke to her. Only she saw the look in his eyes that nearly reduced her to quivering jelly like the one made from calves' feet that was presently being served. Gavin did not touch her. He did not have to. All he had to do was glance at her and her heart began to pound. She almost cried out in disappointment when he took his eyes from her to look toward the lower tables.

"Hidern, Bevis," Gavin called.

"Aye, my lord." The newly made knights were on their feet at once, hastening to stand before the high table so they could hear their liege lord's bidding.

"Tomorrow morning you are to depart for Bardney Abbey," Gavin said. "I will give you letters to carry to Hugh and to the abbot. Choose half a dozen men-at-arms to act as escorts when you bring the children home."

"Yes, my lord." The two spoke in unison and Mirielle could see they were hard put to keep their faces serious at their assignment, which indicated how honored they were to be chosen for such an important mission.

"Your children will be safe in our care," Hidern said.

"We will guard them with our very lives," Bevis added.

"And die rather than let them be harmed," Hidern finished.

"We will keep Master Hugh safe, too," Bevis put

in, unwilling to allow his best friend to have the last word.

"I am sure you will." Gavin sent them back to their table with an expression on his face that suggested he, too, was hiding elation. The eyes he turned on Mirielle were dancing with a humor that did not completely hide either desire or longing.

"I did not sleep last night," he said. "Nor, I am sure, did you or Brice. I think that once the meal is ended we would all do well to retire for a rest."

"Brice does look as though he would be the better for a nap," Mirielle murmured.

"So would I. So, I am sure, would you."

Mirielle knew what he was asking. She thought she would faint from the intensity of his gaze. Her cheeks burned. Her lips were dry, and she ran her tongue across them. It was difficult for her to breathe. She saw that Brice had risen from his seat and was standing behind Gavin's chair, waiting to make one last comment to him before leaving the dais. Mirielle was afraid her cousin would understand the meaning behind anything she might say to Gavin.

"Perhaps, my lord," she faltered, "a pitcher of wine with some sleeping herbs in it would help you to a sounder rest. I would be happy to prepare it for you."

"An excellent idea," he agreed solemnly. "But I beg you, do not make the infusion of herbs too strong. I do not want to sleep away the entire day."

"I understand, my lord. I will see that you have your wine with no delay. And what of you, Brice?" Mirielle asked, hoping to dispel any curiosity on his part. "Shall I prepare wine for you, also?"

"I thank you, but no," Brice said. "I have a final dose left of the medicine you gave me, and I think I will take it. 'Tis strange, Mirielle, but for the first hour after Alda's death I felt greatly improved in health, as if the sickness was leaving me, yet now I am weak again and sorry I ate so much."

"It may take several days before you are completely recovered," Mirielle told him. "Rest and eat lightly, and if you need more medicine, I will make it for you."

It was almost an hour later when Mirielle, carrying a pitcher of wine, knocked on Gavin's bedchamber door. He opened it at once, as if he had been impatiently awaiting her arrival. She thought he looked a bit pale but, recalling his comment about not having slept at all during the previous night, she put his lack of color down to a need for rest.

Or perhaps, while she was burning with desire for him, he was pale with wanting her. She set the pitcher of wine on the table near his big wooden chair and then faced him with fast-beating heart and shallow breath.

"I agreed to your suggestion that you come to me," he said, "because we are less likely to be disturbed here than in your chamber, if I were to visit you there."

"What would you have done if I had sent a serving woman with the wine?" she asked.

"I would have taken the wine and sent the serving woman away, however pretty she might be," he answered. "I want no one but you. I hope—I believe—that you want me as much. I have no marriage vows to keep us apart any longer. But I know you are a maiden, Mirielle, and if you do not wish to give me—if you would prefer—God's holy teeth!" he swore. "What is wrong with me? I have never in my life sounded so weak in the presence of a woman."

"You do not sound weak to me," she said. "You sound like a man who will not force a maiden against her will."

"I have never done so."

"Have there been many women?" she asked. "Many maidens?"

"More than a few. I am no monk," he responded. "But never have I made any woman, maiden or not, do aught with me than what she wanted. Nor will I force you now, though I do believe I will die a slow and terrible death if you should say no to me."

"I see." His evident confusion and his reluctance to do anything to which she did not agree were having a curious effect on Mirielle. She had come to his room beseiged by a mixture of emotions. Her longing for him had grown since their first meeting, when she had sensed that he was the one man who could give her not only passion, but a steady affection to last for all of their lives. She yearned to throw herself into his arms and beg him to make her his without further delay.

Yet there remained with her a slight fear of the unknown. Once she had given herself to Gavin there could be no turning back. She would belong to him forever. And she knew in her heart that, fear or not, she had made her final decision in the moment when she had picked up the wine pitcher and taken the first step toward his bedchamber. Thus she stood before him in virginal apprehension, confused, filled with love, hoping to be all he could want or expect without knowing precisely what his expectations of her might be.

"I would not want you to die, my lord."

"Would you not?" The look in his eyes deepened, holding her as if his arms were already embracing her.

"Especially since your death from unsatisfied desire would mean my own immediate demise of the same illness."

"We will talk no more of illness and death. There has lately been too much of both. We will speak instead of happiness and of the sweetness that cannot be taken from a woman, but must be given freely." He held out his hands to her. "Will you give me that sweetness, Mirielle? I warn you, if you put your hands in mine, I will never let you go."

"Yes, my lord." She laid her hands in his. He raised them to his lips to kiss her fingers and her palms before, with a glad cry, he wrapped his arms around her waist and, laughing, lifted her off her feet to swing her around.

Still holding her, he began to kiss her. He had not said he loved her, though she thought he did. He had not mentioned marriage. She did not care. She loved him with her whole heart and she had recently learned how perilous life could be. She would give to him all she had to give of love and passion, of her chatelaine's skills for his home and her true affection for his children, and she would take from him the joy of his desire for her. It would be enough. They stood heart to heart, thigh to thigh, with Mirielle on tiptoe and her arms around his neck. His mouth was warm and sure on hers, his tongue seeking out her own tongue, thrusting against it, urging

her without words to reciprocate his every movement. His hands caressing her back sent little shiv-
ers of delight along her spine.

They undressed each other with such haste that
Mirielle did not pause to reflect on what they were
doing until she wore only her shift and Gavin was
completely naked.

"Oh." She stared, swallowing hard. "Oh, my."

"There is nothing to fear." He took her hand and
placed it on himself.

"It isn't fear. It's awe." She rubbed him gently,
feeling his heat and an eager, leaping motion at the
touch of her fingers.

The blood surged to her cheeks. Her ears rang.
She was trembling so hard that she thought she
would faint. Gavin lifted her and laid her on his bed.
She put her hands on his shoulders, holding him
away when he would have kissed her again.

"Trust me," he said.

"I do. I will." But she thought her heart would
burst from an innocent apprehension that what they
were about to do would take her instantly from
maidenhood to maturity and the possibility of
motherhood. Why had she not considered that aspect of what they were doing before coming to his
room? Until this moment, all she had been able to
think about was Gavin and how much she wanted
him. Now she thought about having his child.
Gavin's baby. She met his serious eyes and smiled
at the thought of holding his son or daughter in her
arms.

Gavin lay down beside her. Balancing on one elbow, he caught her chin, holding her face steady
while he gazed at her. Slowly he lowered his head,

his lips moving toward hers. Mirielle caught her breath, waiting. This kiss was sweet, his tongue only teasing at the margin of her lips. She became aware of his fingers leaving her chin to glide along her throat to her breast, which fit into the palm of his large hand as if the two were made to be together.

His gentleness perplexed her. She knew Gavin could be forceful. He had kissed her hard on several occasions, and he used a calm and quiet manner in his daily life as lord of the castle to disguise both his physical strength and his steely determination to have things done his way. She was distracted from these thoughts when his fingers began to play with her nipple, setting off a simultaneous twinge far inside her body at his insistent, teasing touch.

Gavin's mouth was still on hers and now he deepened the kiss, pressing Mirielle back into the pillow. His fingers never stopped their insidious movements on her breast. Her nipple grew hard and erect. She could feel it tightening and, worse, her other breast was crushed against his chest, her sensitive skin rubbing against the hair on his chest until she wanted to scream.

Gasping for breath, Mirielle twisted her head away from Gavin's mouth. He did not complain. Still holding her down with the hand that was tormenting her breast, he began to nibble at her chin. Then his mouth moved on to her throat, her shoulders, and, finally, her aching breasts, where he continued to nibble and lick and kiss. Mirielle was by this time frustrated by a growing sensation of hollowness deep in her belly, an emptiness that cried out to be filled. Gavin's mouth fastened over her taut nipple. She did scream then and began thrashing her legs.

Gavin threw one of his legs over hers, his hard thigh holding her where he wanted her. With this change in position Mirielle was once more aware of his arousal. He was breathing hard and she could tell that he was every bit as agitated as she was.

At last he left her breast alone, but only to continue his explorations with his hands and with the licking and kissing that was driving her wild. He caressed her abdomen and her hips and thighs with devastating skill, moving ever closer to the place between her thighs that was burning for his touch.

"Gavin, please," she cried. "Stop tormenting me."

"I am tormenting myself far more than you," he rasped.

She moved restlessly, seeking she knew not what, opening her legs in the hope that he would caress her where she wanted, but feeling too shy to ask. Gavin moved, too, placing one knee between her thighs. She felt his hand on her and his fingers began to slide into her hotness. This was what she ached for, what she had imagined would alleviate her distress, though now she found to her bewilderment that his actions were only making her unsettled condition worse.

"Warm and moist and sweet," he murmured. "Are you ready for me so soon, then?"

"Soon?" she gasped. "You started this before midday, my lord. I have been waiting, thinking of what you did then and wanting you to—oh!" She bit off a cry, for his circling finger had reached a spot so sensitive that speech had just become impossible. All of her consciousness was centered on his finger

Flora Speer

and the seductive motions it was making.

"Have you been waiting for this?" he teased. "I have thought of little else, either. I believe the time has come to end our waiting."

Waves of heat and pleasure swept over Mirielle, stemming from the place where Gavin's finger was. Overcome by what was happening to her, she closed her eyes and thus did not see exactly what he was doing, when she felt his huge manhood begin to enter her.

"Gavin!" Her hands clutched at his shoulders as she tried to drag him upward so she could kiss him.

He did not answer her. He moved his hands to hold her buttocks and slowly he stroked into her. She felt a sharp pain that was gone before she knew it. Even as she caught her breath he was deep inside her and the aching, gnawing hollow place was filled.

She opened her eyes, meaning to tell him what a relief it was and to thank him for stopping that most uncomfortable ache, but she saw his tense face and again she could not speak. She did not know what would happen next, but she did comprehend that he was holding himself under tight control. Perhaps he feared he would hurt her, for he was an enormous man. Filled with love and tenderness, Mirielle drew him down to her and kissed his mouth. He groaned as if he was in pain.

Having adjusted to his hardness inside her, Mirielle experimented by moving her hips. The motion produced a remarkably pleasant sensation. Mirielle moved again. Gavin groaned once more and gritted his teeth.

"Tell me what to do," she cried. "How to—to help you. If you are in pain, then cease what you are doing for my benefit, for I fear—I fear I cannot—oh, dear!" In fact, her hips were moving of their own volition and the motion was creating more and more heat. Mirielle was certain she was about to burst into flame.

"Pain?" Gavin loosed a choked laugh. "The sweetest pain I have ever known. Ah, Mirielle, forgive me. I cannot stop. Nor can I wait any longer."

She thought he was withdrawing from her. She wanted to prevent him from leaving her, but if he was in pain she knew she must let him go. Still, she could not stop her soft cry of loss, nor could she keep her hips from lifting as he pulled away. Her distress turned to joy when he surged back into her with a fierce pressure. He left again and came back a second time. Mirielle began to understand. She let her body do what came naturally, meeting his every thrust, letting him fill her over and over again until she could bear no more, until Gavin possessed her as completely as she possessed him and she felt herself opening to accept his hot seed. In that moment Mirielle knew the true meaning of magic.

She wakened in late afternoon to deepening gloom and heavy rain. Gavin was not in the bed with her. Mirielle rolled over, stretching out a searching arm. The sheets were cold, which meant he had been gone for some time. Thinking he might be in his chair drinking the wine she had brought, she sat up to look for him, but he was not in the room. With her senses more deeply attuned to him than ever after their lovemaking, she knew something was wrong.

She dressed in haste, smoothed back her disheveled hair without taking time to look for a comb, and went in search of her love.

She found him leaving the garderobe. Brice was with him and both men were obviously sick. To Mirielle's eyes they looked much like Donada shortly before she died.

Mirielle wasted no time. Heavy footsteps sounded on the staircase. She hurried to intercept the man-at-arms who was climbing to his watch on the battlements. Fortunately, she recognized him as one of Captain Oliver's friends, so she was reasonably sure he could be trusted.

"See Sir Brice to his room. Make certain he gets into bed at once and stay with him until I get there," Mirielle ordered. "I will explain to Captain Oliver why you are late for your watch. Now, my lord Gavin, let me help you to your bed."

"I wakened intending to make love to you again," Gavin said, as she saw him into bed and pulled the covers over his shivering form, "but as soon as I lifted my head from the pillow the sickness overtook me. Why, Mirielle? With Alda dead, Brice and I should be recovering. Instead, I think I am like to die, and Brice says he feels the same."

"You are not going to die. I will not lose either of you." She spoke with such firmness that Gavin smiled before he doubled up in pain.

"I have been sick before, once with a terrible fever that lasted for days, but this is far worse. My mouth burns," he choked. "My belly aches. But I do not think I have a fever. I am so cold."

"I know." She placed a hand on his clammy forehead. "Gavin, promise you will stay in bed until I can prepare medicine for you and Brice."

"I cannot. There is too much to do." He pushed himself up on one arm, hung there shaking for a time, then collapsed back onto the bed. "It seems I will have to obey your orders, at least for a while."

"A wise decision, my lord." Not wanting to reveal how worried she was, she adopted a crisp tone and a bustling manner. "It will not be for long."

He caught the hand that pulled the covers up to his shoulders again and held it tightly so she could not leave him.

"You look like a woman who has recently made love," he whispered.

"So I have," she said, smiling to cheer him, "and I plan to do so again as soon as possible." She bent to kiss him, only to discover that his cheek and lips were as cold as Donada's face the last time she had seen her alive. With fear clutching at her heart Mirielle headed for the door, eager to get to her workroom and begin preparing the medicine that might do no more good for Gavin and Brice than it had done for Donada. But it was the only medicine available, her sole hope for her lover and her cousin.

"Mirielle." Gavin's weak voice stopped her with her hand on the latch. "You must send a message to Hugh. Tell him not to bring the children home yet. With Brice and me both sick, it is still too dangerous here." He broke off with a smothered moan.

"I will tell Captain Oliver to send his best rider on the fastest horse in the stables to intercept Hidern and Bevis," she promised. "Have no fear for the children, nor for the castle, either. Captain Oliver and I will see to whatever needs to be done."

* * *

At Bardney Abbey, Hugh had already made his decision about the children.

"Reverend Father," he said to the abbot, "I am convinced that a new danger has arisen at Wroxley Castle. I must leave the children in your care and go to Wroxley to help my friends."

"The children are, of course, welcome here," the abbot responded.

"If anyone should come to take them back to Wroxley during my absence," Hugh went on, "you must refuse to let them leave. Release them to me alone. Only thus can I be sure of their safety."

"As you wish," said the abbot, sending a keen look in Hugh's direction. He was a learned man himself and, perhaps because of his learning, he was more tolerant of foreign knowledge and unconventional views than were most clergymen. Ever since Hugh's arrival at Bardney, the two of them had enjoyed a challenging, ongoing conversation that spanned many subjects. Now the abbot nodded his understanding of the need to protect the children, for Hugh had told him some of what had recently happened at Wroxley and part, though not all, of the reasons why he and Gavin had been sent to the castle by King Henry.

"The time has come," the abbot went on, "as you said it would, when the evil that holds Wroxley in its grip must be undone. Rest assured that I will see to the welfare of those innocent young ones whom you have entrusted to me. Know also that my constant prayers will go with you."

"Reverend Father," said Hugh, "your prayers may prove to be more valuable than the strength of all the king's men-at-arms would be."

Chapter Twenty

> *"The tools of the smith share a . . . sacred
> quality. The hammer, the bellows, and the anvil
> are . . . miraculous objects."*
> —Mircea Eliade
> *The Forge and the Crucible*

Alone in her own room, Mirielle lit an oil lamp before she took the crystal sphere from her clothing chest and unwrapped it. Holding the cool, polished orb in the palm of her left hand, she gazed into it.

At first she could not properly control her thoughts, for there was much to distract her. Outside her window the rain fell and early morning clouds roiled, dark and ominous. Through the preceeding evening and the long night that followed she had fed medicine to Gavin and Brice, to no avail.

Both men were still sick. To make matters worse, Captain Oliver and several more of Gavin's knights had also fallen ill, along with a few of the castle servants.

Nor was Mirielle unaffected by the mysterious sickness sweeping through the castle. She was decidedly weaker than usual, and was finding it difficult to concentrate on her daily chores. Fearing that she might be about to fall victim to the illness, she had chosen two healthy-looking squires who she believed were honest and had sent one of them to stay with Gavin. The other she had ordered to watch over Brice.

"I know this is not the duty you would wish for," she told them.

"Not so, my lady," said Philip, the squire assigned to Gavin. "If my lord were wounded in battle, it would fall to me to nurse him. I cannot see that an illness is much different. We are glad to do this service for a good master. My lady, you do not look well to me. Rest in your own bed this night. I will send for you if there is any change in Lord Gavin's condition."

Mirielle had followed the squire's advice, though she had not slept well at all. Constant fear for Gavin ate at her, along with guilt over her inability to do anything to help either him or Brice.

"Show me what to do," she whispered to the crystal sphere she held. "Give me a sign. If I do not take action soon, two men I love will die, and many other good people besides. There must be a way to prevent such a tragedy. It may be that the medicine I have prepared is wrong. If that is so, then show me how to correct my mistake."

A tiny spark of light flickered near the inclusion at the heart of the crystal. So quickly did the light come and go that someone looking less intently than Mirielle would have missed it. She focused all of her thoughts on the spot. Soon another spark appeared, flashing for scarcely an instant. Mirielle continued to gaze into the sphere.

Slowly a darkness came over the clear crystal. Within the sphere a black fog rolled and billowed, much like the clouds above the castle. A lightning-like bolt shot across the sphere and where it ended, bright red flames appeared. Through the fog and the fire Mirielle could see the battlements of a great castle. Another jagged flash of lightning revealed men fighting atop these battlements. As Mirielle stared into the clouded crystal the castle walls crumbled until the once-great edifice was but a ruin. Behind the fallen walls stood a gigantic, unearthly figure cloaked in black, a nebulous form that lifted its arms to the dark sky and threw back its head as if it were laughing wildly in unholy glee, rejoicing at the fire and destruction it had wrought.

A final blast of lightning turned the sphere a brilliant, hot white that hurt Mirielle's eyes and burned her hand so that she almost dropped the orb. Then the crystal went perfectly clear again.

Mirielle sank down on her bed, staring at the still-warm globe in her hand. The sign she had asked for had been given to her, though not in the way she expected. She knew she must make what she could from what she had seen in the sphere. And she also knew there was only one person in the castle to whom she could reveal her vision.

Rewrapping the sphere, she placed it back in her

clothing chest and shut the lid with a sense of finality. She went to the window to look out upon the storm-tossed sky and the shadowed castle walls. She stayed there for a long time, thinking.

"Gavin, are you asleep? Can you hear me?" Mirielle perched on the side of his bed. She had sent the squire Philip, away, telling him to get some food before returning. She wanted no one else to hear what she was about to say to Gavin.

"Mirielle." The hand holding hers was entirely too cold, but Gavin did look a bit more alert than the last time she had seen him, and she thought his voice was firmer. "I can hear well enough."

"It has occurred to me that I may have been trying to help you in the wrong way," she said. "It is possible that you are not sick of the poison Alda used. Your illness may be an enchantment made to seem like the poison that killed Donada and made Robin so ill. If I am right, then mere medicine will not cure you or Brice, or any of the other people who are presently sick. Rather than treating the symptoms, we must find the cause. Then we must destroy it," she ended on a whisper.

"I thought Alda was the cause," Gavin said.

"So did I. So did Hugh. But what if this apparent poisoning is intended to throw us off the scent of the real villain? Gavin, this morning I recalled something Donada said to me before she died. You will remember she became involved with Brice because she was trying to discover who had killed her husband and your father."

"I remember," Gavin said. "It's why Alda poisoned her."

"Donada believed Alda's reason was jealousy over Brice," Mirielle said with some impatience. "Why Donada was killed isn't the point, Gavin. Among the last words she said to me were, 'The mage hides. And there is someone else.'"

"'Someone else,'" Gavin repeated.

"The fact that you and Brice, as well as more than a dozen other people, are sick of the same disease that killed Donada is proof that the evil was not banished when Alda died," Mirielle said. "I think there is a second mage at Wroxley, who continues to hold the castle in his grip while he remains hidden. It is this mage who is making you sick, and until we rid ourselves of him my medicines will not help you or anyone else."

"Who is it?" Gavin shoved himself up against the pillows. His full interest caught by what Mirielle was saying, he looked decidedly more healthy than when she had first sat down on his bed. "Do you suspect anyone?"

"No. This is a master mage, Gavin. He even controls the weather around Wroxley, so I do not doubt he is able to conceal himself beyond our finding. But we *must* discover who he is. Our lives depend on it."

"You think he controls the weather?" Gavin looked as if he could not believe this assertion.

"Haven't you wondered why it rains all the time?" she asked. "I did, when I first came here, but everyone I asked said that the weather has always been cold and dreary. Which, I suppose, means that the mage has been here for a long time."

"You aren't right about the rain," Gavin objected. "We have enjoyed a few sunny days this spring."

"Yes, when Warrick and Emma first arrived so unexpectedly," Mirielle said. "Our last sunny day was the Sunday when we left the castle and went into the field to fly the kites Hugh and the children had made. That was shortly before Donada died. Since that day, we have endured constant fog and rain and a series of dreadful storms. Now that I think of it, perhaps Hugh had something to do with the clear weather on that one day. Or, perhaps the evil mage was as surprised as we were at the unexpected appearance of two innocent children, and of a priest who, for a short time, provided the pastoral care we have lacked since Alda sent the last priest away after your father's funeral. It is possible that the priest and the children together unknowingly interfered with the mage's control of the weather, at least for a time."

"There is good reasoning in what you say. I believe every word," Gavin's hand tightened on hers. "We must discover who this master mage is and then find a way to stop him, before he destroys us. But how can we uncover his identity?"

"I have been thinking about that. Alda spoke of the magical lines that would increase her power once she held the castle in her own name," Mirielle said. "And Brice accused her of feeding on his strength to make her power greater. Suppose this mage requires a similar kind of nourishment?"

"Now, there's an idea," Gavin muttered. "Look for a man who uses women as ruthlessly as Alda used men."

"Perhaps." Mirielle considered this notion, then shook her head. "I don't think so. This mage is far stronger than Alda ever was. It is even possible that Alda may have been under his control."

"What makes you say that?" Gavin demanded.

"Because I don't think Alda fell from that crenel. I think she was pushed, or forced, over the edge. In that last moment she screamed at someone—or something—behind us. She pointed and cried out that hers was the greater power."

"I thought she was screaming at you," Gavin said.

"So did I, at first. But no longer, not after thinking about everything that happened from the time we first confronted Alda and found her at the altar in that unreal room.

"There is something else, Gavin. It has to do with my magic. I worry that if I tell you about it you will refuse to believe me."

"Have you forgotten that I have spent several years with Hugh? I may not have the inborn ability to work magic, but I have learned from him. Like Hugh, you have never told me an untruth. I will believe you, Mirielle."

She did not doubt his words. He had never questioned her abilities. She knew she had Hugh to thank for Gavin's openmindedness where another man might have accused her of heresy or witchcraft. In Hugh's absence, Gavin was the only person she could trust. In the midst of danger and deception and dark magic, they had only each other for strength.

"On the day of my tenth birthday my nurse Cerra gave me a crystal sphere," she began. She told him all of it, from her first vision before her parents and Cerra died to the image she had seen in the crystal just an hour before, when she had watched while the walls of Wroxley fell into rubble and flame at the climax of a terrible battle, and she recounted how she had seen a dark shape laughing in triumph over the wreck of the castle.

"We must prevent this dreadful end," she finished. "I place my power at your disposal, Gavin. I am willing to do whatever needs to be done to free Wroxley and its people and to make you and Brice well again."

"How are we to accomplish this when we don't know who it is we are fighting?" he asked.

"It is possible that Ewain the blacksmith could help us."

"Ewain?" Gavin shook his head. "He's a good man and I think an honest one, but what can a blacksmith do against a powerful mage?"

"Ewain works with metals," she said. "He has a strong affinity with the ores he uses and thus with the earth itself. When I first began to experiment in alchemy, Ewain surprised me by how much he knew that I did not. He may know about those lines that made Alda so interested in this castle. I am going to talk to him."

"Not without me, you aren't." Tossing back the covers, Gavin swung his feet to the floor.

"You are too ill to be out of bed," Mirielle protested. Hearing the squire come into the room she looked to him to back her. "Philip, this madman thinks he can leave his bed. Please tell him otherwise."

"If he thinks he can, then he will," said the squire. "What are your orders, my lord?"

"You have both lost your wits!" Mirielle cried.

When Gavin stood up she turned her back on him because he was naked and she did not want to embarass the squire with evidence of her familiarity with his master's body. She fought the strong urge to go into Gavin's arms. She wanted to make love with him again. Telling herself that passion must wait until a safer time, she spoke over her shoulder.

"This is irresponsible of you, my lord. We need you healthy and you will not recover if you do not stay in bed. Leave this matter to me. I will talk to Ewain."

"Better to die armed and fighting," Gavin said, pulling on his shirt and hose as he spoke, "than to give in to weakness and die in bed. Philip, bring me my chainmail. I have a feeling I am going to need it."

"No!" Mireille yelled at the squire.

"My lady, I would remind you that I give the orders here," Gavin told her. "Philip, when you have finished arming me you are to go to Sir Brice's room and ask him to join his cousin and me in the outer bailey. If he is well enough," Gavin added, with a stern look at Mirielle, who whirled on him in anger at these instructions.

She was surprised to discover how quickly he had dressed. Philip held the chainmail tunic while Gavin thrust his arms into it. Mirielle could see there was no stopping Gavin. He was going to do what he thought was right. But perhaps she could still protect her cousin.

"Tell Sir Brice he is to stay in bed," Mirielle said to the squire.

"Inform him that we have been coddled enough," Gavin interrupted, his face and tousled hair emerging through the neck of the tunic. "Tell Sir Brice it is time for true men to be on their feet, fighting for their lives and their loved ones. Say he can redeem any blot that he imagines still stains his honor by fighting at my side."

"Aye, my lord. I will tell him." Having adjusted Gavin's chainmail so it hung evenly from his wide shoulders, Philip handed him his sword and belt. At Gavin's nod, the squire escaped the room in rather unseemly haste.

"You have frightened off the lad," Gavin complained, fastening his sword belt.

"Would that I could frighten you back into bed," Mirielle snapped at him.

"I thought you would understand that no knight worthy of his title would let a woman fight his battles for him while he lounges in bed."

"I do understand." Tears sparkled on her eyelashes. She took a deep breath to calm herself before she continued. "It is my fear for you speaking. I know we are bound to fight to the last breath."

"If we do not," he said, "this mage will destroy us and use the power in those magical lines you talk about to control Wroxley so firmly that he can never be driven out. I know this as surely as if Hugh was speaking in my ear. Then what will happen to the people who live here? What will become of you and me?"

"I am afraid you will be killed." The words were torn from her heart. They voiced her deepest, most horrifying fear. If it were necessary in a good cause, she could give up her magic, her alchemical experiments, even her simplest herbal nostrums. She could give up her own life. But she could not give up Gavin.

He caught her arms, drawing her near and, despite his pale and gaunt face, there was in him a flash of the Gavin she had seen on that very first day, when Mauger had refused to allow two unknown pilgrims into the castle.

"Whatever happens to us, we cannot let the evil mage win," Gavin said.

"No." She put her hands on his shoulders, feeling the cool chainmail links and, beneath the armor, the muscled strength of him. "I am not afraid for myself, only for you. Gavin—" She stopped, wondering if this was the right time to tell him what she had not said while they lay together, or if the speaking of that truth might weaken him by making him overly cautious for her sake.

"I love you." He said it for her. "And if you love me, there is no magic on earth that can prevail against us. Your love will give me all the strength and courage I need."

"You are everything to me. You owned my heart long before I gave my body to you," she told him. He pulled her closer still, and she did not care that she was pressed against metal when she would have preferred his warm skin. His lips were warm. His tongue was hot. The arms clasping her seemed as strong as ever.

"Put down those bellows," Ewain said to his apprentice. "Get some water from the well and cool yourself for a few minutes. Take your time about it, and when you come back bring a bucket of water for me." Ewain waited until the boy was gone before he looked at Gavin.

"Yes, my lord, I do know of those lines." Seen in the glow from his forge, Ewain's broad face revealed his puzzlement. "Your friend Hugh asked me about them, too."

"Tell us about them," Gavin commanded.

"They are ancient. The lines were here before men came to this part of England."

"*What* are they?" Gavin asked.

"It's hard to explain." Ewain scratched his head, thinking. "You see, my lord, there is an energy that courses through the earth, and those lines are the paths the energy takes. 'Tis said the energy is greatest in the places where the lines cross."

"And Wroxley is such a place," Mirielle stated, recalling what Alda had said about the power that lay deep inside the earth.

"Aye, my lady, it is," Ewain agreed with her. "The man who was smith before me told me when I started as his apprentice that the energy of those lines gave added strength to the metals he forged. Since I have been the castle smith, I have only rarely had any problem with metals.

"It's odd," Ewain went on, "that the times when I have trouble are the times of death. When Lord Udo died, I could make no usable object for two days beforehand and for a week afterward. The same thing happened when Sir Paul the seneschal died. That was a bad time for me, with the seneschal's death coming so close on Lord Udo's. For almost a month my forge did not heat well and everything I made cracked or was so poorly shaped it had to be destroyed. 'Twas a long time to go without even a decent horseshoe for all my work."

"What of the weeks since I have returned?" Gavin asked. "Have there been any interruptions since then?"

"I could not work well during Mistress Donada's last days," Ewain said. "But,'tis strange, my lord, that Lady Alda's death has had no bad effect. In fact, my work goes better now than it has for years."

"Which is just what we would expect," Gavin said to Mirielle.

"My lord, may I speak plainly?"

"Of course, Ewain. Anything you can tell us may prove useful."

"From the questions you have put to me I think you know that all has not been well at Wroxley for some time. I date my own sense of uneasiness from the time of your father's death. After Lord Udo was no more, Lady Alda was in charge and, if you will forgive me for saying so, my lord, your late wife was not a good woman. I know she hated me, though why I never could discover."

"It was because of the lines, Ewain." Mirielle spoke because Gavin was frowning at the blacksmith's words and she did not want Ewain to think he was in any way at fault for his master's ill humor. "Alda had discovered how to use the power of the lines. She probably resented the legitimate strength that you are able to draw from them."

"She was a sorceress?" Ewain nodded. "I can believe it. There were rumors that she used magic to keep herself so beautiful through the years. But, Lady Mirielle, if that's so and Lady Alda is dead, then Wroxley ought to be released from her spells."

"It isn't," Gavin said. "Not yet. But it soon will be, I promise you."

"You are saying there is someone else." Ewain spoke slowly, looking from Gavin to Mirielle. "Do you think I am the second mage? Is that why you asked those questions?"

"Not at all," Mirielle said at once. "I know you too well ever to think ill of you, Ewain. You are a good and true man. We have questioned you because Lord Gavin and I wondered if you might know something that would help us discover who the second mage is."

"Perhaps I should not say this." Ewain hesitated. "It's not my way to accuse anyone without cause, but I have always wondered about Mauger's unflinching loyalty to Lady Alda. For a man of his rough character, his devotion seemed peculiar to me. Of course, it was Lady Alda who insisted that he be made watchman a few years ago, so his loyalty might have been gratitude on Mauger's part."

"Mauger." Gavin spoke the name slowly, mulling over a thought he was as yet unwilling to speak.

"Mauger knew Lady Alda all of her life," Ewain said. "He might know something about her, and about this unknown mage, that could be useful to you, my lord."

"Mauger first came to Wroxley with Alda, when I brought her here as my bride." Still Gavin spoke slowly. "We will most certainly ask a few questions of that watchman and insist on honest answers from him. I have no doubt that what he says will prove interesting." Taking Mirielle by the elbow, Gavin stepped to the door of Ewain's workshop.

"My lord!" Ewain's voice rose in fear. "Look!"

They did not need to look. From the silence and the sudden darkness in the workshop it was easy to tell why Ewain was afraid. A moment ago the forge had been roaring with flames, for Ewain's apprentice had applied the bellows just as Gavin and Mirielle appeared. But now that same red-hot forge was cold and dark. The oil lamps that Ewain kept hanging from the rafters to provide the light he needed for his work had also gone out. A cold wind gusted through the smith's workshop.

"Stay inside," Gavin ordered Mirielle. "You, too, Ewain."

Mirielle did not obey him. She followed Gavin out of the workshop with Ewain right behind her. Minn had come to the blacksmith's with Mirielle and now she insinuated her furry body between Mirielle and Ewain as if seeking protection

The outer bailey was deep in gloom. Heavy gray clouds loomed just above the battlements and the wind was rising. The bailey, usually a bustling place, was deserted. Instinctively, Mirielle knew that the inner bailey was also empty. Wherever the inhabitants of Wroxley were in that dark hour, they were not out of doors. She could only hope they were safe.

Those thoughts vanished when Ewain cried out and pointed to the battlements. There, near the left tower of the main gate, a lone figure stood looking down at them. There were no men-at-arms to be seen, just that one man in a black cloak that billowed outward in the wind.

"Mauger," Gavin shouted. "Come down from there. I want to talk to you."

Mirielle could see Mauger throw back his head and laugh, though no sound carried to her ears. Mauger's laughter was borne away on the wind. An eerie sense of recognition engulfed Mirielle. She had observed this scene before. Watching Mauger, she comprehended the secret meaning of her vision.

"Gavin," she cried. "He is the second mage. I am certain of it. This is the scene I watched in the crystal sphere and Mauger is the man I saw, who caused the downfall of Wroxley."

"I cannot allow that to happen." Gavin gave no sign of surprise at Mirielle's words, a fact that made her think he had worked out in his own mind who the mage must be. "If Mauger will not obey me and come down, then I will go to him. Stay here, Mirielle." Unsheathing his sword Gavin started for the gatehouse and the nearest steps that led to the battlements.

"Wait!" Mirielle went after him, with Minn at her heels. "You cannot overcome a mage with a sword. Gavin!"

It seemed to Mirielle that time was unravelling. She was racing up the stairs to the battlements, the same spiral stairs down which she had hurried on a foggy day in March, to meet Gavin and her destiny. Minn had been with her then. On that day, too, Mauger had been on the battlements. Now she was running back up the stairs, again hastening to Gavin and to whatever fate awaited them when they reached Mauger. From the image she had seen that morning in the crystal sphere, it would not be a happy destiny.

Unless she used her magical skills to change fate.

She was out of breath when she reached the top of the stairs and stepped from the gatehouse tower onto the battlements, but her breathlessness was not the result of fear. With firm and steady steps she moved to where Gavin stood, just a few feet away from Mauger. Minn was with her, a small gray shadow at her side.

"I told you to stay below," Gavin said to her.

"You should know by now, my lord, that I do not often follow the orders of men," she told him. "You need me here. Defeating Mauger will require more than a sword. You will want magic."

"Your magic is not strong enough to destroy me." Mauger laughed at her. Never had the watchman seemed so large and burly to Mirielle. Or so wicked.

"Alda's faithful henchman," Gavin said, not hiding his contempt.

"Not her henchman. Her master. Her first lover." Mauger threw the words at Gavin with a sneer. "She did not go to your marriage bed a virgin. I had her first."

"I know," Gavin said.

"Furthermore, she consoled herself with Brice before and after you were wed. The female brat that Alda bore is of his getting, not yours."

"I know that, too." Gavin's voice remained calm.

Mauger looked surprised at Gavin's lack of anger. Mirielle thought he was trying to goad Gavin into attacking with his sword. She decided the time had come to distract Mauger from Gavin.

"We know about the lines," she said to Mauger. "And we know that Alda planned to use the power in the lines to hold the castle for herself. What we do not know and are curious about is your part in this scheme, Mauger."

"Mine was the greater part." Mauger appeared to grow in size as he spoke and Mirielle was reminded again of the scene in her crystal.

"Who are you, Mauger?" Mirielle cried. "Why are you here? What do you want of us?"

"I am *Chaos*." Mauger's voice boomed forth, resonating with an unnatural quality. "I come to destroy the peace of the earth. Unlike Alda, I do not need the lines to increase my power. Torture, murder, destruction, disease, and rape are my delight."

"Evil incarnate," Gavin muttered. "This is the devil's own spawn."

"I heard that." Mauger lifted one finger and Gavin went down, writhing in pain.

Minn hissed, her back arching, her fur standing on end. From her throat issued a low, eerie sound of warning.

Seeing the man she loved caught by Mauger's magic, Mirielle did not waste her vital energy in words. Instead, she prompty constructed a net around Mauger as she had done around Alda.

Again Mauger lifted a finger, pointing at Mirielle. With a loud sizzling noise the net vanished. Try as she might, Mirielle could not restore it. Beside her, Minn yowled.

Mauger's finger moved. Pain lanced through Mirielle, taking her breath away. She was on her knees, but she was not finished. She began to gather her strength and to concentrate it.

"What a pity," Mauger said to her. "What a bore. I hoped that when our final meeting occurred, you would prove to be a greater and far more interesting challenge. You have been wasting your days with herbal preparations, Mirielle, when you should have been studying a deeper, darker magic. A stronger magic, like mine.

"Now, behold the power that might have been

yours if you were not so timid about risking your soul," Mauger went on. "Watch what I can do."

Mirielle saw Mauger lift his head and sensed that he was going to raise not just a single finger but his whole hand. He was going to turn the full force of his dark power against Gavin. Mirielle knew it. Mauger would not kill her first, he would kill Gavin, so he could watch and draw strength from her grief. He would take great pleasure in seeing her weep. What he might do to her before he killed her she did not want to think. But it would not matter to her, not if Gavin were dead.

Knowing she had only an instant in which to react, Mirielle threw at Mauger all the power at her command. She imagined an arrow winging its way straight to his black heart. She heard the invisible arrow whistle through the air and sensed the feathers on its shaft quivering with the swift movement, though she saw them only in her mind. She heard the sound as the arrow struck Mauger in the chest.

He reeled backward, staggering. With a roar of rage he straightened, lifted both arms, and moved toward Mirielle. With a glow of white-hot, righteous anger, she resisted his advance. They struggled there on the battlements in a state of precarious balance, with Mirielle still on her knees, fighting with every skill she possessed, every bit of strength in her body and soul, every drop of love in her heart. Mauger hovered above her, arms raised like the wings of some huge bird of prey about to swoop down on its victim.

A tiny corner of her mind that was not occupied in fighting Mauger was reaching out to Gavin. Mirielle was aware of her love struggling to his feet, sword still in his hand. Gavin swung the sword at Mauger, connecting with the mage's undefended left side. A black, viscous substance welled and bubbled around the spot where Gavin's sword had bitten into Mauger's flesh.

Mauger howled with rage and pain. Lightning flashed along the blade of Gavin's sword. The blade disappeared, leaving Gavin holding only the empty hilt. He threw it at Mauger.

Reaching out one hand, Mauger grabbed Gavin by the wrist.

"No!" Mirielle was on her feet. Step by slow, difficult step she approached Mauger, fighting the invisible protective shield he was using to keep her away. "Let Gavin go! Release him!"

Mauger only laughed. Gavin continued to wrestle against the mage's greater strength, but he could not free his arm.

Mirielle realized with an icy sensation at her heart that the only way to save Gavin was to kill Mauger. This was not the use to which she wanted to put her magic. She had never hurt another person. The skills she had learned from Hugh were intended to be used for good and her plan had been to bind Mauger, to keep him powerless until he could be brought to justice. But, it took her less than a single heartbeat to make her decision. If she did not stop Mauger at once, Gavin would surely die and Mauger would go on to destroy the castle. Besting Mauger would take all the magic Mirielle knew and she was not sure she could do it, but she was going to try. She kept moving toward Mauger, pacing steadily forward, focusing all of her waning strength on him and on the shield that prevented her from getting too close. Minn, hissing and spitting, went forward with her.

Mauger stepped back one pace.

Elated, Mirielle took another step toward him. And another.

Mauger dropped Gavin's arm.

Mirielle kept walking toward Mauger, knowing he was now free to turn all of his force on her. But she was glad of this, for Mauger could not harm Gavin while he was concentrating on trying to hurt Mirielle. And he was hurting her. Mirielle's chest ached with the effort to draw breath. Her arms and legs felt as if they were weighted with lead. Minn crawled along, her body stretched flat upon the walkway, struggling to stay with Mirielle.

Suddenly a small, round object flew past Mirielle's ear, aimed at Mauger. It landed just in front of the mage and on impact with the stonework the object exploded with a flash of light, a loud noise, and a scattering of a black, powdery substance. The stench of rotten eggs reached Mirielle's nose. She became aware that more people were arriving on the battlements. Someone moved to stand beside her, staff in hand, joining magic to magic.

Hugh! She could not speak his name aloud. It was all she could do to hold Mauger in one place. But now Hugh was helping and he was stronger than she, his energies fresh and unsapped by the contest Mirielle was fighting.

"Brice opened the wicket gate for us," Hugh said, "and Ewain led us to you. I see we were just in time."

We? As if she had asked aloud the question that was in her mind, a youthful voice responded.

"It's Warrick, Lady Mirielle. With you and my father in danger, I could not let Hugh come alone. It is time for me to begin to use the lessons Hugh has taught me. I am only sorry the powder he showed me how to make did not have a greater effect on Mauger."

Though she could not turn to look at them, Mirielle was aware that Brice and Ewain had come onto the battlements with Hugh and Warrick, to stand a little behind the three who possessed magical abilities. And now, with Hugh's help and backed by Warrick's newfound abilities, Mirielle rewove the net around Mauger, confining him. The dark mage shrieked his fury, then went perfectly still.

"When he falls silent, take care," Hugh cautioned, raising his staff to ward off the expected impact of Mauger's dark magic. "He is not finished with us yet."

The attack came in Mirielle's mind. She thought her head would split open from the ice-cold blade that slashed across her thoughts, breaking her concentration on the net. She heard Hugh and Warrick cry out in pain, heard Gavin's shout, and someone else—was it Ewain or her cousin Brice?—yelled a curse on Mauger in a hoarse voice.

The net was gone. Mauger had vanished. In his place was a large black raven with flaming wings and fire pouring from its beak. Mirielle could feel the heat but she could do nothing to protect herself or Gavin, for the icy knife was still in her mind, driving the very life from her.

The fiery wings flapped, lifting the bird above the battlements. Minn howled in agony. The bird's head moved, its eyes focusing on the cat.

"Damn you, Mauger, you won't get away! Not after all the trouble you've caused." With sword in hand Brice darted forward to slash at the hovering bird. His blade connected with a wing. For the second time lightning flashed and a sword blade disappeared in the glare. Brice fell, screaming at the pain in his badly burned hand.

Mirielle remained immobilized. Hugh and Warrick also stood unmoving, all of them held where they were by Mauger's dark strength.

It was Ewain who rushed past Mirielle and her fallen comrades—Ewain, the one person unaffected by Mauger's magic, who threw the only weapon he had, his blacksmith's hammer, at the fiery raven. The hammer flew through the air and hit the bird square in the chest. The instant the hammer touched the raven, both bird and hammer exploded into fire in midair.

A rain of dark ashes fell upon the battlement walkway. The charred remnants of the blacksmith's hammer clattered down on top of the ashes.

The knife was gone from Mirielle's mind. Too weak to stand, she slumped onto the stones. Gavin, apparently also unable to stand as well, crawled to her and put his arms around her. Nearby, Warrick stretched upon the stones, taking in gulps of air. Brice moaned softly, clutching his injured hand to his chest. Minn lay on her side, panting, her green eyes wide open.

"Mauger is gone," said Hugh. He and Ewain were the only ones left on their feet, and Hugh was leaning heavily on his staff and on Ewain's brawny arm. "Well done, my friends, all of you. That dark mage will trouble us no more."

Those were the last words Mirielle heard before she fell against Gavin's chest in a deep swoon.

Chapter Twenty-one

"Hope is the first and last breath of life."
—Sören Kierkegaard

Mirielle awakened slowly to brilliant sunlight streaming through windows with the shutters thrown back. A breath of warm air touched her cheek. She lay quietly, letting the mist of sleep dissipate from her mind and trying to recall what had made her feel so light-hearted and peaceful.

"Meow?" Minn jumped onto her chest, purring. After a moment spent rubbing her face against her mistress's shoulder the cat jumped off Mirielle and stalked across the bed.

That bed was much too wide and its curtains were green, not blue, as they ought to be. Furthermore, Mirielle realized, there was someone in bed with her, someone who made a sleepy noise and reached out a well-muscled arm to brush aside Minn's overly inquisitive nose.

"Gavin?" Mirielle sat up, making Minn pause in her curious inspection of the man to regard her mistress with wide green eyes. "This is the lord's chamber. Minn, what are you doing here?"

"She would not leave you," Gavin said, yawning. "When she began to howl outside the door and leap upon the wood and scratch it with her claws, Hugh suggested that I allow her to spend the night. She has been sleeping on the floor beside you ever since."

"Indeed, my lord? And why, may I ask you, am I in your bedchamber where, I assume, you also have been sleeping beside me all night?"

"I carried you here," he said.

"You could have taken me to my own room."

"I did not want to be separated from you, and your chamber is much too small for two. This room is far more comfortable."

"You do realize that by your act you have ruined my reputation?"

"I know a simple remedy for that problem." He caught her hand, carrying it to his lips.

"As my guardian, Brice will feel honor-bound to challenge you," she noted before he could explain what his remedy was.

"Brice is not likely to hold a sword again for a long time, if ever," Gavin told her. "Not after the injury he suffered for lifting his blade against Mauger. Hugh has done the best he can to repair those terrible burns and he says the hand will heal in time, but whether Brice's fingers will recover the strength to grip a sword is questionable. At the moment, your cousin's right hand and wrist are so thickly bound in strips of clean linen that he cannot use the hand at all. So I believe my life is safe enough. I would say that, deed for deed, Brice and I are even," Gavin finished with a look that made Mirielle blush.

"The battle." Memory flooded back. "It was Mauger all the time. Oh, Gavin, is he really gone?"

"You and Hugh vanquished him."

"And Warrick. Your son did his part. Not to mention Ewain's final, mighty blow. It took all of us—including Minn—to destroy that wicked mage." Without warning Mirielle began to shake. Before her eyes the scene on the battlements replayed itself and she saw again the dark clouds, with Mauger's darker, menacing figure against the sky, certain of his superior power. She could feel once more the pain Mauger had inflicted on her mind and body during their battle, and the strength slowly leaking out of her as she tried to contain the evil mage.

Then Gavin's arms were around her, pulling her down to lie against his hard body.

"It's over," he said, pushing her loose hair off her face. "Everyone who was sick has recovered. With Mauger's death the weather has cleared and, whether it be the power of bright sunshine or the breaking of Mauger's enchantment I do not know, but tempers are more pleasant and all hearts more cheerful than they have been since I returned home. I saw these changes happening even as I carried you from the battlements to this room after you fainted."

"You are well again? Truly?" She touched him to be sure. "My lord, you are unclothed."

"So are you." He let his hand rest on her bare shoulder.

"This is most unseemly," she said, but she made no attempt to move away from him.

"I agree. It is highly improper behavior for a nobly born lady." Amusement gleamed in his eyes. "Reprehensible, in fact. Shocking. And absolutely delightful."

"All of that and more," she said, unable to hold back the smile that would tell him she did not mind at all waking to discover herself in his bed.

Gavin lowered his mouth toward hers. Mirielle's fingers moved over the hair on his chest; then her hand curled around the nape of his neck to pull him closer. His lips brushed across hers.

"Meow!" Minn leapt onto Gavin's shoulder, her sharp claws digging into his skin.

"Stop that!" Gavin grabbed the cat by the scruff of the neck.

"Don't hurt her!" Mirielle cried.

"I will not," he promised. "But neither will I allow this animal to interfere when I want to make love with you." Shifting his hold on the cat to a gentler grip, Gavin rose from the bed to put Minn out of the room.

"I have not said that I want to make love with you, my lord," Mirielle informed him.

"I will do my best to convert you to my way of thinking," he responded, grinning. In the next instant his expression changed to one of fury. "God's teeth! That cat is more slippery than a snake!"

He had not closed the door quickly enough. Minn, taking advantage of the fact that Gavin had turned his attention from her to Mirielle, had rushed between Gavin's legs and back into the room. With an arrogant flick of her tail the cat jumped onto the bed, where she took up a position at Mirielle's side.

"Out!" Gavin reached for the cat. With claws unsheathed, Minn slashed at his hand, then disappeared under the bed.

"She is trying to protect me." Mirielle fought back laughter.

When Gavin went to his knees to search beneath the bed, Mirielle hung her head over the edge of the mattress to see what he was doing to her beloved pet. She was not unduly worried, for she knew Gavin liked cats and she had often seen him stop to pet Minn.

"Do be careful, my lord, or she will scratch you again. If you will step into the corridor for a moment or two," Mirielle suggested, "I am sure I can coax Minn to come out from under the bed. You have frightened her; she will not obey you."

"I have never known a cat to obey anyone," Gavin declared, adding in a fierce voice, "I refuse to be driven out of my own bedchamber by that animal!"

"Oh, my lord, I can see that you are near to bursting with indignation!" Mirielle could not stop laughing. It was so wonderful to feel carefree, wonderful to be with Gavin and know they were safe at last.

"You can see that, can you?" Gavin clamped an arm around her waist and pulled her off the bed and down to the floor.

Mirielle squealed in surprise, a sound promptly smothered when Gavin's mouth crushed hers. She did not mind a bit. She grabbed at his shoulders, holding him tight, giving herself up to a kiss that drugged and stimulated her at the same time. His hands caressed her breasts in the most delightful way and when he abandoned her lips to trail a line of hot kisses along her chin and down her throat to end at one nipple, she groaned in pleasure.

Gavin's body was firm against hers, his manhood against her thigh offering solid proof that they had indeed survived the terrible battle. Gavin's hand stroked down between her thighs and Mirielle sighed, rejoicing in life and love. Loving Gavin, she touched him freely, inciting him to more fervent demonstrations of his rapidly rising passion.

There was in Mirielle's deepest core a growing emptiness that cried out to be filled. She let the emptiness build, not fearing it, knowing that within a few moments Gavin would fill it as they joined together to make each other complete. He shifted position and Mirielle caught her breath. The dearest, sweetest invasion life had to offer was about to occur.

"My lord?" After a single knock on the door, a serving woman opened it and stuck her head around the edge. "It is almost time for the midday meal. I am sent to ask if you will be there, or if we should begin without you and Lady Mirielle."

"Close that door!" Gavin roared.

At the sound of his furious voice, Minn forsook her safe position under the bed and dashed through the door. The serving woman gasped, though whether from the cat's action or from the sight of the lord of Wroxley Castle quite naked on his bedchamber floor, his limbs entangled with those of a woman who was also naked, Mirielle could not tell.

"I said, shut it!"

"Yes, my lord." The door shut.

Gavin returned his attention to Mirielle's breasts. The interruption had cooled her growing abandon a bit, but not his. He promptly set about reclaiming her full attention.

"My lord," she whispered, "there is a perfectly good bed above us."

"And a perfectly good floor beneath us," he responded.

"There are splinters," she whispered.

"Let no one ever say I was unchivalrous." Gavin rolled over, adjusting their positions so his back was on the floor and Mirielle was straddling him. Her unbound hair swung around them like a curtain.

"God's teeth, but you are beautiful." His large hands caressed her shoulders with reverent tenderness before moving to her breasts again. A short time later, when Mirielle began to sigh and move restlessly, Gavin's hands moved down to her slender waist and onward to her gently swelling hips. He grabbed her hips with both hands, lifting her, moving beneath her until he was poised, hot and hard, at the entrance to her body.

"Gavin, what are you—oh! Ohhh." Mirielle closed her eyes, overcome by this new sensation, for Gavin had set her down so that he surged into her, filling her completely in one swift, sure movement. Her head swam and she thought she would faint. She might have fallen had he not held her upright while he lifted his own hips, thrusting hard into her.

Mirielle did not know what to do at first. She had never imagined a woman could ride a man in this way, but Gavin was with her, helping her, showing her the way, his hands never ceasing in their intimate caresses until he strained upward one last time, shuddering and crying out. Mirielle's cry echoed his.

She collapsed, gasping, onto his chest, her heart pounding with the beauty and the power of their love. Her long hair swirled over them, covering them with silken strands into which Gavin wove his fingers.

"My love," he said. "My dear and only love. Never leave me."

"I could not," she murmured. "I would die without you."

"Live with me instead." He was about to say more, but for a second time they were interrupted by a sharp rap on the door. This time the person knocking did not open the door, but neither did he stop knocking.

"My lord." Captain Oliver's voice came through the thick wood. "I am sorry to disturb you, but I must speak to you on a matter of great importance."

"I'm busy." To illustrate the fact to Mirielle, if not to his captain of the guard, Gavin began to nibble on Mirielle's earlobe. "I may not come out until to-morrow."

Mirielle could hear Captain Oliver chuckling, a sound quickly suppressed. There was another tap on the door.

"My lord, I do apologize for my insistance, but Hugh has sent me to you with a message."

"Is a weary baron to have no rest?" Gavin grumbled. In a louder voice, he added, "Hold on a moment, Oliver."

With remarkable ease considering how sick he had been only the day before, Gavin picked Mirielle up and tucked her into bed, pulling the covers up to her chin.

"This will hardly disguise what we have been doing," she remarked.

"I have no wish for disguise, but neither do I want any other man looking at you." His eyes were warm when they rested on her face. "Let me discover what our good captain of the guard wants of me and then I will join you there in bed."

Gavin snatched up his tunic, pulled it over his head, and went barefoot and barelegged to open the door.

"You had better have a good reason for this interruption," he said to Captain Oliver.

"Good day to you, my lord. My lady." The captain of the guard favored both Gavin and Mirielle with a broad smile, which widened still more when he saw the way Gavin was dressed.

"Well?" Fists planted on his hips, Gavin regarded the intruder. Captain Oliver only grinned the more. Gavin prodded in a lordly tone, "What is Hugh's so-important message?"

"My lord, I am to tell you that your presence is required below, in the crypt."

"The crypt?" Mirielle echoed.

"At once, if you please, my lady."

"Tell Hugh," said Gavin, "that, if he wants to see me, he may do so in the great hall *when* I decide I am ready to appear there."

"No, wait." Mirielle swung her legs to the floor. Seeing Captain Oliver's eyes widen at the sight of her bare feet and ankles, she immediately pulled her legs back beneath the covers. She could have sworn the captain had just winked at her. It was most unlike him. Captain Oliver was usually a serious man.

Yet he was still smiling, in spite of the harsh tone Gavin had used with him.

"Tell Hugh that we will join him as soon as we are properly dressed," Mirielle said. To avert the irritation she saw growing on Gavin's face, she said to him, "My lord, Hugh knows we were both near to death after yesterday's battle. If he disturbs our rest, we can be sure it is for an important reason. You may stay here if you like, but I intend to see what Hugh is doing in the crypt.

"You are right, of course," Gavin said. "He would not send an urgent message for a trivial reason. We will continue our conversation later, Mirielle."

At this, Captain Oliver cleared his throat rather loudly and assumed a more serious expression.

"If you will excuse me, my lord," Captain Oliver said, "I must also deliver the message to Sir Brice."

"Do you suppose that Hugh has made some new discovery about Alda or Mauger?" Gavin asked of Mirielle as soon as Captain Oliver had closed the bedroom door behind himself.

"The best way to answer that question is to go to Hugh." Now Mirielle did leave the bed. She found a clean shift and stockings and a fresh gown of green wool folded on top of Gavin's clothes chest, proof that when he had brought her to his room he had considered practical needs as well as romantic desires. By the time she was dressed and had fastened her shoes and tied her hair back with a ribbon, Gavin was also ready. Together they hastened below to the entry hall and then down the curving staircase, past the chapel and into the crypt.

The low-ceilinged vault was blazing with light. All the candles in both candelabra were lit and there were extra torches burning in wall sconces to chase away the last of the shadows that usually lurked in that chamber of tombs. As the captain of the guard had promised, Hugh was there, with Captain Oliver himself and—

Mirielle stopped, both hands at her mouth, gaping at an unbelievable sight. Hugh was busy, so at his slightly distracted nod, Captain Oliver began the explanation.

"After what happened yesterday, I thought it well to inspect the entire castle," Captain Oliver said. "First, I personally checked the security of the walls and of the inner and outer baileys. Finding nothing amiss, I proceeded to the top of the tower keep and worked my way down, level by level, until at the very last I came here to the crypt, where I found Mistress Donada still lying on her bier, still unburied for lack of a priest. I thought it odd that after so many days there was no stink. The crypt is cold, but not cold enough to stop the stench of death," Captain Oliver noted in his blunt soldier's way.

"When I moved to the bier to look more closely at Mistress Donada and to say a prayer for her, I saw that her eyes were open, though I distinctly remembered that they were closed when last I looked upon her face shortly after we put her on that bier. Then, as I watched in amazement, she took a breath. That was when I searched out Master Hugh and brought him here."

"Donada?" Mirielle moved forward. The shroud around Donada had been loosened and the linen sheet covering her had been pushed back. Hugh was feeding her sips from a cup. Mirielle recognized the scent of his hot brewed *tcha*. "Donada, you are alive!"

"It's a miracle." Captain Oliver crossed himself.

"No miracle that Alda's poison did not kill her," Hugh said. "The miracle, if there is one, lies in the fact that we did not bury her. It was Donada's own insistence on having a priest at her funeral that saved her life."

"And, probably, your medicine that kept Alda's poison from working," Mirielle said, watching Donada take another sip from the cup Hugh was holding. Donada seemed to be barely alive. She had not spoken, but she was obeying Hugh's gentle urging that she drink the *tcha* he offered.

"I do not think Alda meant for Donada to die of the poison." Hugh spoke softly, his eyes on Donada's waxen face as if he were gauging her recovery. "I believe Alda planned for Donada to waken *after* she was buried. What better revenge on the woman Alda saw as a rival, than for Donada to regain consciousness, only to find she was buried alive, with no hope of rescue?"

"That woman was a demon straight from Hell." Captain Oliver crossed himself again. "I thank God and all His saints for protecting Mistress Donada."

"Now that she is waking, we are the ones who must protect her," Hugh said. "I want Donada carried to her room and put to bed. We will need braziers to warm the room, heated stones to lay at her feet, and a constant supply of boiling water, so I can continue to feed her cups of hot *tcha*. It may take days for her to recover fully, and in the meantime we would be wise not to press her to speak or to move from her room."

"I will give orders at once to have her old bed-chamber prepared and her belongings returned to it." Mirielle took the still-icy hand that lay atop the linen sheet. "Donada, do not try to speak to me. I only want you to know that Robin is safe at Bardney Abbey and we believe he is recovering from his illness. You will see him soon, I am sure. We are all so glad to have you back! I am going now to see to your room." Mirielle pressed a kiss on Donada's cold cheek and turned to leave the crypt. As she did, Brice arrived, looking as if he had dressed in great haste.

"What has happened?" Brice cried. "Why did you summon—dear God in heaven! My love! My dearest Donada!" He ran down the last few steps, heading for the bier where Donada lay.

"Stop right there." Gavin caught Brice's arm, pulling him to a halt. "It would be dangerous to upset her, so do not talk to her. She is to be put to bed and there is every expectation that she will recover in time."

"Thank heaven! Oh, Donada!" Brice looked as if he would burst into tears. "Everything she has suffered was for my sake. What can I do to help her?"

"Just leave her in peace until she wants to see you," Hugh said.

"I shall be the one to carry her to her room," Brice insisted.

"Sir Brice, you are injured and still weak after your confrontation with Mauger," Captain Oliver pointed out with a glance at Brice's heavily bandaged right hand. "I discovered Mistress Donada alive; therefore, I should be the one to carry her."

"So you shall," Hugh said, "and you may do it

now. Take her gently, please, and give her into Mirielle's care until I follow in a moment. I believe Lord Gavin has something to say to me."

They rewrapped Donada in the sheet and Captain Oliver took her into his arms to carry her up the stairs. He was preceded by Mirielle. Gavin heard her call out to a serving woman when she reached the upper level, giving orders for all the supplies Hugh had requested. Brice brought up the end of the procession, alternately shaking his head in disbelief and reciting prayers of thanksgiving for Donada's return to life.

"It's too bad he didn't say his prayers more often while Alda was alive," Gavin said, looking after him until Brice disappeared around the curve of the steps. Face pale, Gavin turned back to his friend to ask the questions that threatened to destroy his hard-earned peace. "Hugh, what of my father? What of Donada's husband? Donada insisted that she suffered from the same sickness that killed both men. I cannot bear to think that Alda fed to them the same poison she used on Donada. To think of anyone, buried and later waking to that indescribable horror—oh, God!"

"Alda wanted revenge on Donada, because she believed Donada had stolen Brice," Hugh said in a measured, reasonable tone. "But in the case of your father and Sir Paul, Alda simply wanted them dead, so she would have a free hand here at Wroxley. There was no reason for her to indulge in additional cruelty."

"She might, if she hated them enough. Alda took great pleasure in being cruel." Gavin walked to his father's tomb and laid a hand on it. "We will never know the truth of this, will we?"

"What we do know is that Lord Udo and Sir Paul were buried properly, in their own faith, with a priest in attendance and many prayers for their souls. If they did suffer beyond our comprehension, surely that horror must be counted in their favor wherever their spirits now reside. I am as certain of that," Hugh went on, "as I am that Alda and Mauger are dealing at this moment with an implacable heavenly justice. Deeds as wicked as theirs, which upset and interfere with the balanced course of Nature, are always severely punished in the end."

"If there is such justice, then Alda and Mauger are burning in Hell." Gavin's face was grim.

"The priests of your faith would say so. For myself, I believe those two villains will pay for what they have done, over and over again, until the very end of time."

"Father." Gavin's hand moved gently on the polished marble beneath which Udo's remains lay.

"Whatever else is true," Hugh said, "he and Sir Paul are at peace now. Do not drive yourself mad with terrible conjecture. You have your life to live well, duties and responsibilities to fulfill as baron of Wroxley, a son to raise. Here you have friends, loyalty that you have earned, love honest and deep."

"I know you are right." Gavin took his hand from his father's tomb to lay it on Hugh's shoulder. "I have fulfilled my promise to him. His murderers have been brought before the only judge strong enough to condemn them. Now, as you say, it is time for me to think of the inheritance he left to me—and of the honest love that found me when I least expected it."

Chapter Twenty-two

*"To the medieval mind, justice was the highest
earthly good."*

—Sir Arthur Bryant
The Age of Chivalry

With Hugh as her physician, Donada's progress toward restored health was assured. While she was convalescing, Gavin worked to put his barony to rights after the long enchantment. Warm, bright weather helped, as did the good will of the residents of Wroxley Castle and the villeins who laboured in the surrounding fields. At Gavin's order Brice continued as seneschal, working side by side with Gavin and by his own declaration doing his best to atone for his past errors.

Believing it was time for Warrick to begin learning what his future duties would be, Gavin made an effort to keep his son closely involved in what he was doing. Thus, Warrick was with him when Gavin visited the blacksmith's workshop.

"This is a joyful time," Ewain greeted them. "The whole castle has heard Mistress Donada's wonderful story. My wife wept for half an hour when she learned of it."

"Ewain, we have much to thank you for," Gavin said. "It was you who finally brought Mauger down."

"Master Ewain," Warrick put in, "how did you know your hammer would destroy that evil mage?"

"A smith's hammer daily beats upon metal that comes from this good earth on which we stand, and works that metal into useful tools," Ewain answered. "Furthermore, my forge stands on the exact spot where the lines of energy within the earth intersect. It stands to reason that some of that energy must enter my hammer as I use it."

"I have often heard that a smith's hammer is a magical instrument," Gavin said.

"Aye, my lord, so it is." Ewain nodded. "What's more, I *threw* the hammer at Mauger. It left my hand. When it hit Mauger, there was no physical connection to me. That is why he could not hurt me in the same way he hurt you and Sir Brice, whose swords were clasped in your hands when they connected with Mauger's body. I do not have to remind you of what Mauger did through that connection, how he destroyed your blades and how he laid you low and burned Sir Brice's hand."

"Ewain, have you another hammer?" Gavin asked.

"I have several, though the one I lost to Mauger

was my favorite. Still, I cannot regret its loss, since it happened for a good cause." Ewain's bright eyes sparkled. "Have you a task for one of those other hammers and for me, my lord?"

"I want you to make a new suit of chain mail," Gavin said. "My son here will need armor soon and I would have you forge those links, Ewain. You will work into the metal a portion of your own honest strength, so that Warrick will be well protected when he wears that mail."

"I can think of no task I would rather undertake." Ewain's broad face flushed with pleasure. "As you know, my lord, it takes many months to make a full suit of chainmail. But your son is still young and he's still growing. I will make the suit large enough to fit him when the day of his knighting arrives."

"Thank you." Gavin's hand rested for a moment on Ewain's brawny shoulder. "My good friend, you and your family will never want for anything so long as I or my son are alive."

"We will always remember what you did for us, Ewain," Warrick added to his father's words.

Gavin could see that although Warrick controlled his feelings well, he was disturbed by this conversation. His observation was confirmed once they were outside the smith's workshop and headed across the sun-filled outer bailey toward the inner gatehouse. Warrick fairly burst into impassioned speech.

"Father, I have told you again and again that I do not want to be a knight. How can you expect it of me after what my mother did? Let Ewain make that suit of mail. It's a fitting task for him, a fair reward for his bravery that will not insult his pride with open charity. I know you will pay him well for the work he will do. But when he is finished, let someone else wear that chainmail."

"I see no connection between your mother's wicked deeds and your future career," Gavin said.

"Do you not?" Warrick stopped walking, forcing Gavin to halt, too, and to turn to him. Warrick's youthful face was distorted by a deep frown. Gavin had the feeling the boy was trying not to cry.

"There is no reason for you to bear your mother's crimes on your shoulders," Gavin said. "I do not blame you for them, nor does anyone else at Wroxley."

"Because I am her son, her magic is inborn in me," Warrick said in a curiously mature, artificially steady voice. "I have known this since I was a little boy. I also know that as I reach manhood the magic will become stronger. If I do not learn how to control it before then, the magic will control me."

"Could that be what happened to Alda?" Gavin asked.

"I think so," Warrick told him. "I think Mauger may have promised to teach her what she needed to know in order to hold her power in check and then, under the guise of instruction, he corrupted her."

"She must have been willing to be corrupted or Mauger could not have succeeded," Gavin said. "Like so much else to do with those two, we will never know the truth of it."

"Whatever the truth of my mother's life," Warrick responded, "she was evil. I must rise above that wicked taint in my blood so I can use my magical abilities for good, as Mirielle and Master Hugh do.

374

I cannot become a knight and dedicate my life to battle and bloodshed. It would be the worst thing for me. Father, I do not want to inherit Wroxley. I would be a danger to the castle and, because of those lines Ewain spoke of, Wroxley would be a danger—and a constant temptation—to me as it was to my mother. It is in me to destroy all that you and Master Hugh and Lady Mirielle have achieved here." Warrick's voice broke and he stopped.

"You fought on our side," Gavin reminded him.

"This time, I did," Warrick said. "A future battle might have a different result. Never do I want to fight against you, but that possibility does exist.

"There is more, Father, and I may as well tell you now. Emma has the inborn magic, too. Together, uncontrolled, she and I could wreck a terrible destruction that would make what Mauger and my mother did seem like a child's game."

"Emma." Gavin took a deep breath, thinking of the child who was not his.

"That is why I must leave Wroxley at once," Warrick went on, interrupting Gavin's unhappy thoughts.

"But we have only just met. I want to know you as intimately as my father knew me. My son should not be a stranger to me." Gavin laid an arm across Warrick's stiff shoulders. "Will you take a bit of fatherly advice?"

"I will consider it, sir." Warrick's demeanor was so grave that Gavin could not help smiling, though his heart was aching in sympathy with the boy's pain.

"Stay here with us for a while. I can think of no better teacher for your purposes than Hugh, and I am sure Mirielle will be happy to help you in any way she can. If, at the end of a year you still want to leave, then I will not prevent you."

"A whole year?" In Warrick's voice was all the impatience of youth.

"I know it seems like a long time," Gavin said. "But, remember, Hugh is here. You will be learning from him every day."

"That's true." Warrick was silent for a moment. Then, "I will stay. I would like to know you, too, Father. Master Hugh says you are a remarkable man."

"I must remember to thank Hugh for those words," Gavin murmured.

On the fourth day after her miraculous awakening, Donada asked Mirielle to bring Brice to her room. He appeared wearing his best tunic, his cheeks a little flushed from excitement. His right hand was still bandaged, as it would be for some time to come.

"Mirielle," Donada said, "I want you to stay and hear my words, too."

"As you wish." Mirielle sat on the edge of Donada's bed. "Do not tire yourself, my dear. Hugh warns that it will take a while yet for you to regain your strength."

"I will do as Master Hugh orders," Donada said, "for I believe he saved my life."

"Donada," Brice broke in, "I see some color in your cheeks and your voice is as strong as ever. You will be well soon, my dearest."

"Sir Brice," Donada said, looking into his eyes, "I am sorry."

"For what?" he cried. "My dear, sweet lady, you have done nothing to injure me."

"I think perhaps I have." Donada gave him a sad little smile. "I led you to believe I care for you."

"As I care for you," Brice declared, reaching for her hand. Donada moved her hand, not letting him take it, and Brice looked puzzled and a bit wary.

"It was a trick, Sir Brice," Donada said. "The only way I could think of to discover who had killed my beloved Paul was to gain your confidence so you would reveal your thoughts to me. I simply could not believe that Paul's illness and death were natural. For a time I thought you had plotted his death so that you could become seneschal in his place."

"My appointment as seneschal was entirely Alda's idea," Brice told her, "though, I admit, I jumped at the opportunity as soon as she suggested it."

"I know that now," Donada said. "I should have seen it then, except that I was not thinking clearly."

"None of us were," Mirielle said. "Mauger's gloomy enchantment held us all, and in your case, Donada, your feelings were complicated by grief for your husband."

"Sir Brice," Donada said, "I am sorry if I hurt you, but I do not love you. It was all pretense."

"I see." Brice's face was frozen into a semblance of calm.

"I am also sorry that I ever believed you capable of murder. I hope you can forgive me."

"I forgive you." Brice's voice was cold. "Have you anything else to say to me?"

"No, Sir Brice."

"Then I will leave you to your recovery. I trust it

will be a speedy one." With an abrupt little bow, Brice made his exit.

"My lord, I am determined to leave Wroxley." An hour after his interview with Donada, Brice confronted Gavin in the privacy of the lord's chamber.

"You are the second person today to tell me so." Gavin regarded his seneschal with raised eyebrows. "May I ask why you want to go from here?"

"There are two reasons," Brice said. "First and most important, when I became Alda's lover I betrayed the trust and the duty I owed to you as your seneschal. While you say you do not blame me for that liaison, I blame myself and thus I find it difficult to remain in a place where I have done so much wrong. My second reason for wanting to leave is that the woman I love does not love me."

"Ah." Gavin looked at him for a long moment, measuring the quality of the man and wishing they could have met under different circumstances. Brice was at heart a decent person, as his loving treatment of Mirielle and his present remorse proved. Were it not for Alda, the two men might have become close friends. Gavin felt a sense of loss for the comradeship that would never be, but he understood Brice's scruples.

"To begin with your second reason," Gavin said to Brice, "it is a burden many men must bear. I bore it once myself, when the wife my father chose for me would not love me. For your first reason, considering how beautiful Alda was and the fact that you first loved her when you were only a lad, I do not see how you could have resisted her blandishments. No man with the wits to understand what has happened lately at this castle could hold you fully responsible for your affair with Alda. I know I do not."

"You are more generous than I deserve," Brice murmured.

"You may not think so when you learn what I have been doing in this room with your cousin."

"I do not care if you choose to punish me for what I have done, my lord." Brice's face went hard and he took a menacing step forward. "But, I warn you, if you hurt Mirielle in any way—"

"Call it quits between us, Brice." Gavin held up his hands in a gesture of peace and spoke in a wry tone. "You risked your life against Mauger for Mirielle's sake. I will never forget that. Lest you still think you ought to challenge me to protect her honor, it's only fair to tell you that I intend to marry Mirielle, if she will have me."

"I think she will, my lord." Brice relaxed his fierce stance. "I may sometimes act the fool, but I am not completely blind. I can see she loves you, and I think you will care for her and make her happy. It's all I have ever wanted for Mirielle."

Brice seemed about to say something more, perhaps to open discussion of a marriage settlement or to mention Mirielle's lack of a dowry, but Gavin had more important matters in mind and he spoke before Brice could.

"There is something you should know, Brice. It is a piece of information that Alda told to me and that Mauger later confirmed. Though neither of them was notable for honesty, I think in this case they told the truth."

"What is it, my lord?"

Seeing that Brice appeared to be bracing himself for a coming blow, Gavin dealt it as gently as he could, though there was no real way to soften the news he had to impart. Gavin knew it was going to hit Brice hard.

"Emma is not my daughter," Gavin told him. "She is yours."

"What?" Brice stumbled back a pace and sat down hard in Gavin's big chair. "Emma? That beautiful little girl? Emma is *mine?* Oh, dear God in heaven!" Brice buried his face in his hands. "Alda never told me and I never guessed."

"I rather think she kept the truth about Emma's birth as a secret weapon, so she could use it against you if the need arose," Gavin said. "She used the fact against me, instead."

"I have a daughter—that sweet child—if only I had known!" Brice cried.

"Brice, listen to me." Not standing on lordly ceremony, Gavin disregarded the fact that Brice was in his chair and took the smaller seat for himself, facing his seneschal. "You have several decisions to make. Knowing what I have just told you, will you change your mind and stay at Wroxley?"

"This news does not alter anything I have done. How can I stay, after my complicity in Alda's schemes?" Brice groaned, clutching his bandaged hand. "I no longer care whether I am seneschal here or not. All my ambition is gone."

"Perhaps it was Alda's ambition you felt, and not yours," Gavin suggested.

"That may be." Brice heaved a great sigh. "What am I to do? Until a moment ago, all I wanted was to leave Wroxley behind and travel far away in hope of easing my guilty conscience. Now, I have a child to worry about. How can I drag Emma along with me?"

"There is no need to do so. Emma can remain here, with Mirielle and me. We, along with you and Hugh, are the only ones who know the truth of Emma's parentage. None of us will tell her if you do not want Emma to know."

"You are willing to let her go on believing that you are her father?" Brice gaped at him, uncertain he could depend on this generosity. "She does love you, my lord. It's there in her every word and gesture toward you."

"The choice is yours, Brice," Gavin said in a quiet voice. "Tell her the truth or not, as you wish. Whatever you decide, Emma is welcome to stay here, under Mirielle's tutelage, and I will provide a dowry for her, since I know you cannot."

"My lord, you make me ashamed of all I have done."

"That was not my intent, and it's not for you I make the offer," Gavin said. "It's for Emma's sake. I have grown fond of her and I know Mirielle loves her. So you need not base your decision on what is best for Emma. She will always be well cared for, whatever you decide."

"How can I not think of what is best for Emma? I'm her father." Brice brushed at his eyes, wiping away unshed tears. "I always wanted a daughter. It's one of the reasons why I love Mirielle so dearly. Now I find I have a daughter, but the best thing for her is to let her go on believing another man is her sire. I know it is the right thing to do, but it breaks my heart.

"I will leave Wroxley," Brice said, "and I give my daughter into your care, allowing you to decide when—or—if—she should know the truth."

"That decision took courage," Gavin said, reaching forward to clasp his hand, thus sealing their agreement. "Now, here's another choice for you. Donada is well enough that Hugh feels it is safe to absent himself from Wroxley for a few days. He is leaving tomorrow for Bardney Abbey to bring Emma and Robin home again. If you wish, you may go with him. Hugh says the abbot of Bardney is an admirable man. You might find it helpful to make your confession to him and accept whatever penance he lays on you."

"I have heard it said that the Saracens have devised the most subtle and painful tortures known to man," Brice said. "Did you learn from them during your time in the Holy Land, my lord? I am to go to Bardney, there to see my own child and never tell her she is mine? A fine, subtle punishment, and exquisitely painful."

"I will not force you to it," Gavin responded. "If you prefer, you may take the road that leads in the opposite direction from Bardney and never see Emma again."

"That's what I meant by subtle," Brice muttered. "You have left the choice to me. Well, I will accept the punishment. It is just, after all. I will go to Bardney and see Emma and not say a word of this truth that would hurt her innocent heart. I will confess all to the abbot there and then perform whatever penance he requires of me. But I will not stay at Bardney. The place is too near to Wroxley and I might weaken later and decide that I want to see my girl and hear her call me Father. I think it would be best for me to leave England. A long pilgrimage would seem to be in order. Perhaps, remembering the claim by which you first gained entrance to this castle, I will make my way to Santiago de Compostela."

●

Later that same day, Gavin received other guests in his private chamber. Mirielle, Hugh, and Warrick came to see him to discuss how much Emma and Robin ought to be told about the recent events at Wroxley.

"It is my idea," Mirielle said, "that we should explain how Alda was held under an evil spell by a wicked mage and that she did not mean any of the bad things she did. I think it is best to soften the truth for the children, especially if Robin has not recovered from his illness. There will be ample time later for the entire story. For the present, Donada's amazing resurrection will be enough for them to accept."

"Agreed." Gavin readily gave his approval to what Mirielle wanted. "There is no point in upsetting them, or in making Emma feel guilty for anything her mother has done," Gavin finished with a long look at Warrick, remembering the guilt that consumed his son.

"Father," Warrick said, "I am going to Bardney with Hugh and Sir Brice."

"Only if you give me your word of honor that you will return when Hugh does," Gavin warned in a stern voice.

"There is no need for threats," said Hugh. "Warrick will not go on pilgrimage with Brice. We have reached an agreement about his future plans."

"Without consulting me?" Gavin frowned.

"Since you have been very busy today, they talked to me," Mirielle said with a smile that soothed Gavin's irritation as nothing else could have done. "Hugh and I are going to continue our lessons with Warrick and Emma. In return, Warrick has promised to apply himself to his duties as a squire for at least the next year, and possibly for two years' time."

"In that case," Gavin told his son, "you ought to take yourself off to bed. You will spend a long day in the saddle tomorrow." Gavin knew his voice was gruff. He thought by the look on his son's face that Warrick understood why.

"Since I still have preparations to make, I will also say good evening," Hugh said with his usual discretion as he followed Warrick to the door.

"Well, now." Gavin eyed Mirielle. "Will you desert me, too?"

"Only if you wish to be alone with your thoughts, my lord," she answered demurely.

"I would rather be alone with you." He opened his arms and Mirielle went into them, nestling close to his heart. "How did you convince Warrick to do what I want him to do? For that matter, how did you know what I want him to do?"

"By magic, my lord," she whispered, lifting her lips to his.

"There is a matter still to be settled," Gavin said. "One final detail."

The castle was quiet, most of its inhabitants asleep, for it was well past midnight. In the big bed in the lord's chamber Gavin raised himself to look into Mirielle's eyes. They were pure silver in the moonlight.

"What matter is that?" she asked, stretching in lazy contentment.

"Will you marry me?"

"Marry?" She stared at him. "Gavin, I have no dowry, nothing to bring to you."

"You have proven your honesty, your courage, and your steadfast devotion to me and to my children," he said. "You risked your life for me. What greater dowry could any man require?"

"Besides," he added, looking deep into her eyes, "I love you with all of my heart."

"Oh, Gavin." Mirielle had to blink back sudden tears. "How could any woman refuse such a declaration? Yes, my dearest love." There was more she would have said, but Gavin's mouth was on hers, warm and sweet with the promise of love to last for the rest of their lives. Knowing she would have years in which to say all that was in her heart, Mirielle wrapped her arms around him and drew him close, while the moonlight washed over their entwined bodies in a silvery benediction.

Chapter Twenty-three

"Tell Warrick and Robin they may move my clothing chest to the lord's chamber in just a little while," Mirielle said. "For now, I would like to be alone."

"I understand, my lady." The serving woman accepted Mirielle's dismissal with a smile. "Every bride has private thoughts on her wedding day. But as an old married woman, I advise you not to be late for the ceremony. Lord Gavin is the most eager bridegroom I have ever seen."

"That is because I have refused him so much as a kiss for the last two weeks," Mirielle replied with a chuckle.

After the serving woman responded to her remark with a hearty laugh and slipped out the door, Mirielle looked around the room where she had slept for the last year and a half, since first coming to Wroxley as a poverty-stricken orphan. It was hard for her to realize that before the day ended, she would be a baroness and the Lady of Wroxley.

Being careful not to soil her pale blue silk gown, Mirielle knelt to open her clothes chest and take out the crystal sphere. Unwrapping it and placing it in her left palm, she held it up so the sunlight streaming through the window shone full upon it.

"The only blight on my happiness today," she whispered, "is Brice's absence. Though I understand why he had to leave, I miss him every day. What will become of him?"

Staring at the tiny imperfection in the globe, Mirielle centered all of her thoughts on her cousin. It took only an instant for a spark to flare in the depths of the crystal. The sphere filled with light and gradually a scene took shape. Mirielle saw a blazing sun shining down on rocks and desert sand. A towering castle built of pale stone loomed in the background. A man stood before the castle, clad in chainmail, his surcoat bearing a crusader's cross. In his left hand the man held a sword. Though he was helmed, and thus she could not see his features clearly, Mirielle recognized Brice. She knew his right hand was weakened and would remain so for the rest of his life; even so, that hand was strong enough to hold the staff from which flew a white banner bearing a red cross. His entire being radiated calm confidence and courage.

"Oh, Brice." Tears trickled down Mirielle's cheeks. "I prayed you would find peace. I see that, in time, you will. I know you are an honest knight and always will be." She gazed until the scene in the globe faded and the crystal was clear again.

"Now," Mirielle whispered, "just once more before I meet Gavin at the chapel door, let me see if what I have come to believe in these last few days is true for if it is, it will be the very best wedding gift I can give to my husband."

Again the crystal brightened and when the new scene formed it was a familiar one. Mirielle saw herself standing in the lord's chamber. In her arms a swaddled bundle lay and, at her side, Gavin gazed in wonder at the child she held. Gavin's arm was around her waist and their heads were close together.

Mirielle could not see the child's face distinctly, nor could she tell whether it was a son or a daughter. That did not matter. Gavin would love their child for the same reason she did: It had been made from their love for each other.

The crystal cleared. With a soft smile on her lips, Mirielle watched the luminous object in her palm for a while longer.

"I will ask no more for this day," she said at last, "though I have a feeling I will use you often in the years to come."

A moment later Mirielle opened her chamber door to Warrick's firm knock. With him were Robin and Donada, both restored to glowing health, and Emma, who could barely contain her excitement. Also at the door was Captain Oliver, who was to act in Brice's place as Mirielle's guardian and was to hand her into Gavin's keeping.

"I am ready," Mirielle told them.

"First, we have to move the chest," said Warrick. He and Robin, one at each end, picked up the wooden chest that held all of Mirielle's worldly goods. Mirielle knew she would soon have many more belongings—new gowns and jewels awaited her in the lord's chamber—but the dearest treasures of her life were even now crowding into her room to escort her to her wedding, or were awaiting her below at the chapel door.

"I promise, we will not begin without you," Mirielle said to her son-to-be. Then, with Emma and Donada leading the way and Captain Oliver's firm hand at her elbow, Mirielle started down the stairs to meet her love. And a small gray cat emerged from beneath Mirielle's bed to scamper after her.

Epilogue

Two years later

"Now, don't cry, Mother. You promised you wouldn't," Robin said. "I will return someday and until then you will have your new baby to worry about."

"I will love the new baby when it comes, but you are my first child." A tearful Donada embraced her son.

"Take care of her, sir." Robin put out his hand to the man who kept an arm around his mother's shoulders.

"I will protect her with my very life." Sir Oliver, promoted from captain of the guard to seneschal of Wroxley, shook hands with the lad who had been his stepson for six months.

A short distance away, also in the outer bailey between the stables and the blacksmith's workshop, Mirielle, Gavin, and Emma were saying their farewells to Warrick.

"I do understand how important leaving is to you, Warrick, and I am glad you and Robin will travel eastward with Hugh," Gavin said. "All the same, Wroxley will be empty without you."

"And without Robin," murmured Emma.

"You and Mirielle now have another son to raise," Warrick reminded his father. "My lord, if King Henry agrees, as I am sure he will since you are among his most loyal barons, let my younger brother, Giles, inherit Wroxley when the time comes. For myself, I will earn my lands and title after I have learned to master this power inside me."

"Warrick, I will hold in trust for you the land your mother brought to me as her dowry," Gavin promised. "She never lived there, so the place has no taint of evil magic to it. When you return, it will be yours."

"Oh, Warrick!" Emma threw herself into her brother's arms. "How I wish I could go with you. What shall I do without you and Robin?"

"We will all meet again, Emma." Robin joined them, having finished his farewells to his mother and stepfather. "I do promise you, the three of us will be together once more before you know it.

"My dear lady." Robin made an admirably executed bow to Mirielle. "I do not know how to thank you for all your kindnesses to me and to my mother."

"Come now, Robin, there is no need for such formality among old friends. I have much to thank you for, too. I will miss you almost as much as Emma will." She did not have to bend over to kiss his cheek.

Robin had grown in the last two years. But his awe of her had not changed. He blushed bright red at the touch of Mirielle's lips, and blushed again when Emma timidly rose on tiptoe to kiss his other cheek.

After Warrick and Robin had mounted their horses there was a brief period of silence in the outer bailey while they all waited for Hugh, who was in the blacksmith's shop saying good-bye to Ewain. Hugh emerged from the shop to shake hands one last time with Gavin.

Mirielle would not be satisfied with a handclasp. She put her arms around Hugh's neck and kissed him.

"Ah, now," said Gavin with a choked laugh, "perhaps it's a good thing you are leaving, old friend. I might grow jealous of my wife's affection for you."

"No need for that. Mirielle's heart belongs to you and no one else," Hugh said. "Don't weep, Mirielle. Haven't I taught you that life follows a strange and wonderful plan? Who knows when we will meet again? Now, as for you, Emma, stop those tears."

From the folds of his robe Hugh pulled a packet of cord-tied silk and put it into the hands of the sobbing girl.

"Don't open it until I am gone," he said, his hand under her chin turning her face up toward his. "Study hard, Emma. Learn all you can from Mirielle, for she knows as much as I could teach her."

Mounting his horse, Hugh followed his young companions toward the castle gate. As Warrick and Robin each gave a last wave to their families and rode across the drawbridge, Hugh turned in his saddle to look upon the group assembled in the outer bailey. Ewain stood to one side, wearing his leather apron, hammer in hand, his face ruddy from the heat of his forge. On the other side, Sir Oliver kept a supportive arm around Donada's waist. In the middle stood Gavin, with Mirielle's head on his shoulder and Emma leaning back against him as he held the girl close. In one hand Emma clutched the packet Hugh had given her and with the other she waved to him. Mirielle lifted her head to smile at her teacher and friend.

"Yes," Hugh said to himself. "A job well done. Now, there is only one task remaining."

With his left hand Hugh made a sign, conjuring happiness and long life for all of them. Seeing it, Mirielle returned the gesture.

Then Hugh made another magical sign and he and the two boys with him disappeared from sight.

Circles In Time by Tess Mallory. Investigative reporter Kendra O'Brien knows it's a dream, so when wildly handsome Navarre de Galliard charges up in chain mail, she does what any modern career girl would do. She caresses his cuirass. But to Navarre, Kendra seems a sorceress. How else can her sultry glances make the knight feel like a blushing page, as her eyes speak volumes to his spellbound heart? And worse, the enchanting woman is the prophesied salvation of his enemy, King Richard–a man he is sworn to destroy. But as the tables turn, his love for the mysterious miss deepens, and Navarre realizes that Kendra isn't Richard's salvation, but his own.

——52201-2 $5.50 US/$6.50 CAN

A Time to Love Again by Flora Speer. When India Baldwin goes to work one Saturday, she has no idea she'll end up transported back to the time of Charlemagne. There is no way a modern-day woman can adjust to life in such a barbaric age, but India quickly finds herself merrily munching on boar, quaffing ale, and yearning for the nights when the virile Theuderic of Metz's masterful touch leaves her wondering if she ever wants to return to her own time.

——52196-2 $5.50 US/$6.50 CAN

Dorchester Publishing Co., Inc.
65 Commerce Road
Stamford, CT 06902

Please add $1.75 for shipping and handling for the first book and $.50 for each book thereafter. NY, NYC, PA and CT residents, please add appropriate sales tax. No cash, stamps, or C.O.D.s. All orders shipped within 6 weeks via postal service book rate. Canadian orders require $2.00 extra postage and must be paid in U.S. dollars through a U.S. banking facility.

Name _____
Address_____
City_____ State _____ Zip_____
I have enclosed $ _____ in payment for the checked book(s).
Payment <u>must</u> accompany all orders. ☐ Please send a free catalog.

FLORA SPEER
Rose Red
A Faerie Tale Romance

Once upon a time...they lived happily ever after.

"I HAVE TWO DAUGHTERS, ONE A FLOWER AS PURE AND WHITE AS THE NEW-FALLEN SNOW AND THE OTHER A ROSE AS RED AND SWEET AS THE FIRES OF PASSION."

Bianca and Rosalinda are the only treasures left to their mother after her husband, the Duke of Monteferro, is murdered. Fleeing a remote villa in the shadows of the Alps of Northern Italy, she raises her daughters in hiding and swears revenge on the enemy who has brought her low.

The years pass until one stormy night a stranger appears from out of the swirling snow, half-frozen and wild, wrapped only in a bearskin. To gentle Bianca he appears a gallant suitor. To their mother he is the son of an assassin. But to Rosalinda he is the one man who can light the fires of passion and make them burn as sweet and red as her namesake.

_52139-3 $5.99 US/$6.99 CAN

FOR LOVE AND HONOR

FLORA SPEER

Bestselling Author Of *Love Just In Time*

Falsely accused of murder, Sir Alain vows to move heaven and earth to clear his name and claim the sweet rose named Joanna. But in a world of deception and intrigue, the virile knight faces enemies who will do anything to thwart his quest of the heart.

From the sceptered isle of England to the sun-drenched shores of Sicily, the star-crossed lovers will weather a winter of discontent. And before they can share a glorious summer of passion, they will have to risk their reputations, their happiness, and their lives for love and honor.

__3816-1 $4.99 US/$5.99 CAN

Lady Lure — Flora Speer

"Flora Speer opens up new vistas for the romance reader!"

—*Romantic Times*

A valiant admiral felled by stellar pirates, Halvo Gibal fears he is doomed to a bleak future. Then an enchanting vision of shimmering red hair and stunning green eyes takes him captive, and he burns to taste the wildfire smoldering beneath her cool charm.

But feisty and defiant Perri will not be an easy conquest. Hers is a mission of the heart: She must deliver Halvo to his enemies or her betrothed will be put to death. Blinded by duty, Perri is ready to betray her prisoner—until he steals a kiss that awakens her desire and plunges them into a web of treachery that will test the very limits of their love.

_52072-9 $5.99 US/$7.99 CAN

TIMESWEPT

Christmas Carol
FLORA SPEER

Bestselling Author of *A Love Beyond Time*

Bah! Humbug! That is what Carol Simmons says to the holidays, mistletoe, and the ghost in her room. But the mysterious specter has come to save the heartless spinster from a loveless life. Soon Carol is traveling through the ages to three different London Yuletides—and into the arms of a trio of dashing suitors. From Christmas past to Christmas future, the passionate caresses of the one man meant for her teach Carol that the season is about a lot more than Christmas presents.

_51986-0 $4.99 US/$5.99 CAN